Sam Bossino was born ...., two cats and his expanding waistline. He has spent much of his life exploring the concept of enthusiasm and has reached the conclusion that it's all a bit too much like hard work.

Nigel Terry was born in 1969 and lives with his wife, two children and a fully expanded waistline. He has an insatiable appetite for success not mirrored by his best friend.

Back To Nature is the culmination of a lifelong friendship and the answer to the question: 'do you reckon there's a book in that?'

Back to Nature

Sam Bossino & Nigel Terry

Back to Nature
Sam Bossino & Nigel Terry

First Published in the UK in December 2010 by Hirst Publishing

Hirst Publishing, Suite 285 Andover House, George Yard, Andover, Hants, SP10 1PB

ISBN 978-1-907959-10-3

Cover Design by Robert Hammond

Printed and bound by Good News Digital Books

Paper stock used is natural, recyclable and made from wood grown in sustainable forests. The manufacturing processes conform to environmental regulations.

www.hirstbooks.com

This book is dedicated to our long suffering and ever supportive families – we told you we'd get there in the end! - and to our dear friend Andy: you know what you did. While the events in this book are entirely fictitious, the spirit of friendship in which it was written is most definitely real.

EVERYTHING I LEARNED ABOUT LIFE...

"I've had an epiphany!" Neil said enthusiastically, by way of a greeting.

"Don't use words you can't spell." Neil looked at me and smiled sarcastically. He was wearing his shorts and AC/DC concert T-shirt, and I suspected he hadn't moved far from his sofa all evening. Neil was a solid, round, hairy man who wore a full beard that may well have started at his navel, and the overall impression given when in the comfort of his lounge was that of an out-of-work roadie, or perhaps one that just hadn't yet found the right band.

I chucked my keys on the table by the door and walked through to the living room. The large television dominating the room was muted over credits rolling up the screen. Neil sat impatiently, waiting for me to drop down onto the opposing sofa, to get comfortable in the arse-space I'd spent many years moulding to perfection. "Go on then, enlighten me."

"Two words," he said, "The answer to everything."

"Blow job?" I ventured. "'I don't want one, if you're offering." Neil looked at me again and I began to wonder how many exasperated expressions I could raise out of him in one conversation. It was a game I played sometimes, to pass the time. We spent enough of it together that I had it to waste and Neil was used to it, expected it even. To be honest, it was an integral part of our relationship.

"You're miserable, right?" he continued. He had a point to make, I could tell.

"Only on days with a 'y' in them," I replied. His eyebrows furrowed. I could set a new record tonight.

"But I'm right though aren't I? You are miserable? Well, me too. Bored anyway. And Adam."

"Miserable or bored?" I was losing track of the conversation, losing the will to live if I'm honest. I couldn't blame the latter entirely on Neil, but he certainly wasn't helping.

"Both! That's my point! We're all stuck. Trapped, miserable – in a rut. Three blokes – going nowhere." I looked around the place and couldn't fault him, so far. The television went black and then started flashing up copyright laws for countries I hadn't even heard of.

"And you have the solution?" I asked sceptically.

"Yep," he said smugly. He looked like the guy who'd figured out the Colonel's Secret Recipe. "Like I said, an epiphany. Well, a damn good idea anyway. No, scratch that, a fabulous idea. Do you want a beer?" I nodded. He was going to make me wait. I got comfortable while he walked to the kitchen. He brought back two Buds, passed one to me and sat back down.

"Cheers," I said, taking a swig. Sometimes there just wasn't enough beer. "So are you going to tell me then, or what?"

"Wait, Adam will be here soon. It involves all of us. So perfect though, trust me." I started to worry that he wasn't going to be able to keep all this in. He was almost bouncing on the sofa. I changed the subject, unable to muster the same enthusiasm, for now anyway. He looked like he was going to wet himself. I pointed towards the box.

"So what you been watching?" Neil stared at the television as if it was going to spoil his big revelation, he fumbled for the remote and switched it off.

"Wait," he said again. I took another swig of my beer.

A long night. They always were.

Adam arrived, an hour and a half later. I'd bargained enough to get the television switched back on but it was still on mute, as if the sound would burst the bubble of anticipation Neil had been so desperate to create. I was making up words to the songs on the music channels. Neil was biting his nails. He was obviously planning on checking the box for every single cliché of eagerness invented.

"Alright guys?" Adam said, as he joined us in the living room. He was wearing jeans and a polo shirt, and for some reason it occurred to me that I had never seen him wearing anything else.

Adam was the oldest of us, the voice of reason, the thought we had the second before doing something stupid. He was a little over six feet tall, stocky, and - in complete contrast to his two closest friends - he worked out a little. He wore his long, angular face clean-shaven, but only - I always suspected - because he was waiting for the right time to try 'Just For Men.' He was Neil's wife's best friend's boyfriend - practically family as far as we were concerned - and he fit right in; we knew it the first time we met him. He'd stayed up with us after our respective other halves had gone to bed - an initiation, so to speak, a night with two practising insomniacs. He'd done well. He was in. "So what's this about, then?"

"Did you bring your stuff?" Neil asked Adam. I sat back in my chair, perplexed. Adam lived an hour away. It was a Friday night. Something was going on.

"Yes," he replied, his eyes curious. Adam had learnt not to ask too many questions; we were open to flights of fancy and it was obviously part of our charm, but I was usually in the loop. "So what *is* this about?"

"You're miserable, right?" Neil asked him. I sighed, got up and got us all some beers. A long night indeed. I walked back in to the living room and handed them around to distracted words of thanks. Back together again, the three of us. Just like old times. I sat back down and waited, waited for the idea that would rescue us all. Adam had agreed to Neil's statement in an awkward fashion.

9

Admitting he was miserable to Neil meant admitting it to Neil's wife - his girlfriend's best friend. There was a decision there, but he was among family. We had no secrets from each other. We were unique in that way. "I know what we need to do."

"So you keep saying." Adam and I responded together. I had to admit I was intrigued. Neil had a look about him that I hadn't seen in awhile. It was a look that I missed - that I needed. Maybe he did have the answer.

"Ferris Bueller," Neil said. It was a statement. He looked at us, searching for our understanding, any hint of realisation with no explanation offered, like Adam and I were stupid to be taking this long to join his party. "Ferris Bueller!"

"Yeah…"

"The movie?" Neil prompted.

"Yeah…" I looked at Adam, just to make sure I wasn't the last one to get this.

"Well, it's obvious," Neil said. I could see he was getting disheartened. "The guy was a genius. I just finished watching the movie and it came to me. It's the answer to all our problems. You're both miserable -"

"We've covered this." I interrupted.

"Bored," Neil continued, "We've all lost something. Adam, you've been saying for ages that you need to get away, that life's been getting on top of you. Your missus wants kids, you've bought a house together, what are you now? Thirty-six?"

"Thirty-five, and are you trying to cheer me up? Cos it's not working!" Neil ignored him while he gained momentum.

"And Steve… Steve." He looked at me. This was going to hurt. "You've just been dumped. Well, I say 'just', I mean it's been six months -"

"Four and a half actually," I corrected, for whose benefit I would never know.

10

"Whatever, it's been awhile. But not that you'd fucking know it! You're a slave to your mobile phone. A goddamned workaholic at twenty-seven years old. It's pathetic." I dropped my head down, shook it. I wanted to argue but I couldn't put my case together. Once again, Neil had a point.

"And you?" I asked weakly. Why should we be the only people feeling like shit?

"Don't even get me started. Thirty-one, married, two kids and a mortgage, crappy job, no money. I'm bored. Abso-fucking-lutely bored stupid." I looked at Adam. I felt like we had a winner.

"So Ferris Bueller has the answer?" Adam said. "So what's your point? A day off? A drive in a Ferrari? Help us out just a little."

"It's right there." Neil was waving his arms. It was like watching Flipper trying to explain something. I lit a cigarette, threw one at Neil and pretended not to see Adam looking disapprovingly at me.

"I thought you quit?" he said.

"I have, I quit twenty times a day." Adam looked back at Neil - he was turning purple.

"At the beginning and the end. He says it twice. 'Life moves pretty fast, if you don't stop to look around once in awhile, you might miss it!' He was talking to us. Well to me anyway, but you know what I mean. So it hits me." He lit his cigarette and let the words sink in.

"You want to go to the city?" I said, confused. I needed more beer, a lot more beer - or a translator. Hell, new friends would have done.

"We should take a road trip!" Neil said triumphantly, "It's perfect. The three of us, on the road, away from it all, no women, no worries, no work." He was looking at me again. "It's perfect."

11

"A road trip? This is Andover, not Arizona Neil. Where do you want to go? Tesco?" I wanted to feel his excitement but the cynicism just wouldn't budge.

"We leave tomorrow. Scotland beckons baby!"

"Scotland?" I looked at him incredulously. It was something I'd never tried before. I wanted to check my mobile but daren't. I wanted to go back to the moment I walked in to Neil's house and start this whole evening again. "Tomorrow?"

"You've got something better to do? A date or something?"

"Low blow." But Neil pressed on

"But I can't just go to Scotland." The voice of reason had stepped in. I was saved.

"Yes actually you can. Jane's going down to yours, in fact she's probably just arrived. She's spending the week with Fiona and she's taking the kids. It'll be practice for when you have your own." Neil laughed. I could tell he wanted to shake his belly as if this moment alone would justify its existence. To him this was hilarious. Adam just looked petrified.

"But -" I had nothing

"The whole week?" That made two of us.

"The whole week. The three of us, camping in the highlands of Scotland. Perfect."

"But I have to work?" I ventured. I knew I was lying. I had the week off.

"You fucking liar, you've got the week off!" Bugger.

"But I haven't." Adam said. A reprieve.

"Actually you have. Fiona's sorting it on Monday with your boss, I called her. It's your birthday present. Apparently she feels the same as you." Adam looked betrayed. He looked back at me and then across at Neil.

"You sneaky bastard." We said together. It felt like the only thing we could say. He had an answer for everything. Ferris Bueller was going to pay.

"But I had plans this week!" I felt like a kid being told he was going to stay at his auntie's during the holidays.

"Shut up, Steve. You planned to be miserable. To spend the week wallowing around in your flat listening to sad pussy music being a tart. She's gone, my life's over. Blah blah blah."

"It was still a plan," I said defensively. I hated that he knew me so well.

"We're going to Scotland. We're going to camp under the stars, eat well and drink until we fall over. The boys, on the road. Good music, good company, good times."

"You're making me sick. I feel like I'm watching an American beer advert."

"Sounds more like 'Brokeback Mountain' to me," Adam said, finishing his drink. I laughed, and it felt like a strange sensation since the last couple of months.

"Shut the fuck up and start getting into this, would you?"

"But you said we were only going for the weekend?" Adam pointed out, a look of genuine panic on his face. "I haven't brought enough pants."

"Well how many pairs did you bring?"

"Only six." We both stared at him.

"For the weekend? What the hell were you planning? Do you know what? Don't answer that." Neil got up and paced around his living room. We weren't getting out of this, that much was clear. Neil had sorted everything. For all we knew he had booked the car and packed it, too. But we weren't going to make this easy for him. Why should we? We had been ambushed. We were being kidnapped. And I hated to admit it, but I was starting to look forward to it. "Look, pants aside, it's all taken care of. I'm picking the car up in two hours. We leave first thing in the morning."

"But you just finished watching the damn movie when I got here! What are you, the Yellow Pages?" Neil pulled a face at me. We were kids again.

"I paused it. Like I said, the guy says it twice and I've seen it like fifty times anyway. So... tell me it's not perfect." Adam and I looked at each other. We were beaten. We sat back in our seats and let the realisation wash over us like the sea crashing over a dam. Our defences had been breached. Events had been set into motion. We were going to enjoy ourselves and we had no choice about it.

"It's perfect," we admitted. And it was. Everything we didn't know we needed.

"Exactly. Perfect. I had an epiphany." Smug bastard.

We spent the next hour talking about the trip. It was open past tomorrow, no plans. Just Scotland and four hundred miles to it. Adam got his bag out of his car, meticulously packed for no known destination. I still had to go back to the flat and get mine done. There would be time for that later though. Neil's enthusiasm was infectious and pretty soon we were all jumping about the living room, laughing and arguing about what CD's we should pack. Three men, different ages, vastly different musical tastes - it was going to get ugly.

"No, no, no," I said, "We need to be fair." Neil was looking shocked.

"Fair? Fair? Are you fucking kidding me? Boyzone is not fucking fair! I don't even own any bloody Boyzone CD's!" Adam was looking hurt but Neil was not giving an inch. "I am not spending a week in a car listening to Femboy and the Bum Bandits! It's not happening!"

"Okay but we need to let him choose something. *That's* only fair."

"He obviously has no taste, I don't even want to think about it. I reserve the right to veto." I felt like the United Nations.

"Okay, but he gets to choose without interruption. Adam, knock yourself out." I pointed to the shelves holding a lifetime's worth of memories or a substantial overdraft, depending on your point of view. I took Neil out to the kitchen to put the kettle on. We needed coffee and Adam needed to be alone with his choices.

"You're a stubborn bastard you know?" I said, sorting out the cups.

"It was fucking Boyzone," he said again shaking his head. Neil looked as if he were trying to work out how he'd let a Boyzone fan into his circle of friends and was coming up empty.

"I was talking about the trip. We could have been busy." Neil huffed, as if the concept was simply inconceivable. I filled the cups up - two black one white with sugar - then stood back in the kitchen and let him answer.

"Yeah well, sometimes you just need to be told. If I'd have *asked* you two then you would have had excuses coming out of your arses. You need to get away, I need to get away, Adam needs it too. You're a mess." I laughed, he really knew me to well.

"But you didn't really do all this tonight did you?" He paused before answering.

"Honestly? I've been toying with it for a couple of weeks - the movie was really just a catalyst. Jane just looked at me earlier on, I dunno, I was daydreaming I think, and she just said, 'right – we're off, do it now.' She knew you had the time off - that was the real key, the now or never thing I think - and she'd obviously mentioned the idea to Fiona, and she was up for it. Before I knew it Jane had shoved Ben and Tom in the motor and kissed me goodbye. I don't want to say she was keen or anything but she stunned even me. I think she wanted to do it before I talked myself out of it. Then I started watching the movie again and was like 'fuck yeah!' A couple of phone calls later and here we are."

"Weeks?" I said. Surprised, amazed or simply just confused, I really couldn't tell. To be fair, I think I was wondering more where the time had gone.

15

"Steve, we haven't seen you in ages. Not really, not like the old days. A few visits here and there but not the quality time we're used to. We've been friends for thirteen years, you're my little brother, and I'm doing what big brothers do – looking out for you."

I didn't know what to say, I felt guilty. Guilty that I'd let our friendship slip, let time pass without taking more care of it. Time had a habit of doing that, pushing on like an unstoppable force, it reminded me of my mother in that way. I patted Neil on the back, my oldest closest friend - my brother. I smiled at him and gestured to the door. We took the drinks through to Adam and went to review his choices.

Adam was sat on the floor surrounded by CD's, a small pile to the left of him, a huge scattering of abandoned choices to the right. I sat back on the sofa, comforted by the familiar. I felt like I was home from home. Neil bent down and picked up Adams chosen few and went back to his own sofa. I looked around the living room while Neil began his analysis.

The walls were covered in pictures, a lifetime frozen in an instant, captured, framed and lovingly displayed for all to see. Jane laughing with Ben and Tom, a cheerful family with handsome kids that were clearly a happy mistake of nature given Neil's input. I saw myself in several of them, caught in various states of enjoyment and a couple of embarrassing moments I had pleaded for them not to keep. It occurred to me that most of the best moments in my life had been spent with Neil. He was right, I did need this trip.

"So what's on the play-list?" I asked, trying to drag my mind out of the wistful melancholy that had sneaked up on me. Neil looked up at me, pulling his own thoughts back to the moment.

"Not bad so far, a varied enough selection, some eighties, some nineties. Safe choices." Neil was bopping his head from side to side, he looked like a teacher grading a promising but reserved student. Any minute now I thought he was going to say 'but I was hoping for so much more...where's the flair?'

"How can you be so critical? They're your bloody CD's! That you bought!" I stated. Adam continued fingering through the shelves, like the prize find was there for the taking, the choice that would earn him the respect and appreciation that until now he hadn't realised he was lacking. I could feel him begging for a clue.

"Throw him a bone, Steve."

"Don't look at me mate, I say go with what he's got." We went with what he had. We would add our own input later. I looked at my watch, another half an hour had slipped by in the sip of a drink. I shot a glance towards Neil and gestured towards the front door. "You'd better go and get the car and I need to go and pack." Neil checked his watch and agreed. We left Adam still picking through racks, ever the perfectionist.

As we reached the door, I grabbed my keys and followed Neil out of the house. The August sun was starting to look lazy, like the effort of pleasing everyone had become monotonous. It sagged and looked down at the horizon longingly. It would be dark in a couple of hours and twilight would hit just after nine.

We got in my car and both reached for the air-conditioning devices some people foolishly called windows, rolled them down and took up our positions. Cigarettes lit, arms propped on the door, radio on. I started up the old Ford. I think it had been an Escort in a past life, now it was just a memory of one. It had spirit though, a grim determination to trek on until the wheels fell off or the engine dropped out or I earned enough money to replace it. I liked that. It was inspiring, in a tragic sort of way.

We pulled out of the estate and headed into town. Neil gave me the address of the rental company and I nosed the car round the ring road and pulled off at the nearest turning to the industrial estate. We passed new buildings, empty buildings, buildings being renovated, rumours of progress and exciting new ventures nestled amongst the remnants of failed ones. The town itself never changed, but the wardrobe did.

We found the rental company hidden beneath a nondescript sign that promised nothing in the way of customer re-assurance. It may as well have been called Rent-A-Heap. I pulled around to the parking bays, reversed in and took a glance around. Mine was the only car on the estate, I couldn't even tell where the staff were parked. Neil looked at me, threw on a 'don't panic – it'll be fine' smile and got out of the car, leaned back in the window and said he'd meet me back at his place in an hour. He tapped the roof and strolled casually over to the reception. I didn't wait for him to go in. I headed out of the industrial estate expecting to see tumbleweeds roll on past me. Friday night in Andover - it left something to be desired.

I was back at my flat in ten minutes. It felt empty. Not an easy task to pull off for a one bedroom apartment, it was the sort of place that felt crowded when the phone rang. I didn't want to hang around too long - Kelly's things were still there bagged up in a cupboard. I'd hidden them after the row, which was as close to closure as I was likely to get but it got me through. That and staying out of the flat as often as I could. I'm childish, but at least I'm big enough to admit it.

I packed quickly and just remembered the sleeping bag stuffed in the top of the wardrobe, probably still damp from the last time I'd been brave enough to sleep in it. I pulled it down and had to fight back the gag reflex from the smell that it dropped on me. I wondered briefly how I'd managed to live in the flat for so many years without the neighbours complaining about it. A part of me was relieved that I'd discovered the source of the stench, having spent many a recent night trying to imagine the state of the decaying creature that could have been the only cause of such foulness. I made a mental note to apologise to Neil and Adam in advance then pondered whether a Pine Fresh car tree was up to the challenge.

I chucked my packed bag, ridge-tent and toxic sleep sack by the door, switched off all of the lights and used the bathroom before heading out. As I washed my hands I caught a glance of myself in the mirror and barely recognised the man staring back at me. He looked vaguely familiar but that was as much as I could say. I wouldn't commit myself to being able to spot him in a line-up. Tall and thin with short blond hair I had skin still recovering from a vicious childhood spent figuring out that the Braille on my face spelt acne. There was stubble on my face that did nothing more for my image than serve as a cruel reminder of the beard I would never seem to be able to grow and the bags I carried under my eyes could have easily replaced those by the door.

I slapped myself, I was going to enjoy myself, and I would start by getting out of the flat.

I picked up my bags, ran out the front door and managed to get all of halfway down the hallway before I had to turn around and check that I had locked the door. It wasn't obsessive compulsive disorder, it was worse than that, it was hereditary with no known cure. I shot back through the corridor, down the stairwell and out to my car. I'm not normally that energetic, I just didn't want to risk being trapped in a lift.

The ten-minute drive back to Neil's house dissolved in a swirl of thought. The dominant one being to wonder why every journey I took around Andover was ten minutes long. It had to be a scientific marvel, a rip in the space-time continuum, worm holes invisible to the naked eye. There was no explanation for it other than the mundane and I wasn't ready to admit that my habitat was that claustrophobic. Denial was an important factor in my life.

I pulled up outside the familiar three-bedroom terrace but saw no sign of life. I checked my watch and realised I was a couple of minutes early. Time enough to rescue Adam from the living room. I entered the house and found him in much the same state we'd left him in. I knew Neil had a lot of CD's but I doubt whether he'd taken as long choosing which ones to buy as Adam was spending picking his selection.

"Step away from the music Adam, we've only got a week." He turned from his trance and smiled at me, like a prisoner in solitude finally being released.

"Alright Steve, got some more for the pile," he replied, pointing down to a stack that was starting to resemble an exhibit in the Tate Modern. There was something detached about his voice, like he'd spent so long thinking about the answer that he'd forgotten the original question. The enthusiasm for the trip had apparently walked out of the house when Neil and I left earlier.

"You okay? About all this?" I probed, hoping he wouldn't start discussing his selection. He picked up the thread and thought about it for a moment. There was a response coming, another considered reply to a question that had left my lips as a basic reflex. I didn't want to start analysing things, wanted less for Adam to. This was supposed to be a week off, a week away from problems, from women, work and worries. But it could only start if we were all on the same foot. "Adam?"

"Hmm? Yeah, I'm okay, I guess. Feel sort of like we've been-."

"Ambushed?" I ventured.

"Well yeah. Sort of. I'm not meaning to sound ungrateful. And I am really looking forward to it," his eyebrows portrayed a 'but' coming, "But it's just out of the blue."

"Is that so bad? Really?" I sat down on my side of the sofa, lit a cigarette and realised that in its self was insensitive.

"I mean when was the last time we all got together? Five months ago? Six even? I reckon we've earned a bit of 'us' time." My argument sounded thinner than I was.

"But I had stuff to do, at work next week." I cut him off.

"Jesus Adam, you sound worse than me. Forget about it. It's been taken care of. I stay at work because I'm sad and not so recently lonely. Neil's right, as much as it pains me to say it. And he's sorted all of this out for us, to get us away from everything. Sounds pretty perfect to me."

"And I agree, but what happens while we're away?"

"I don't follow you?" I looked at him. I was heading down a route with no exit. At the end of my journey was a week away in Scotland with my two best friends. Adam had apparently taken a detour. Then I passed a signpost. "Hang on a minute, you're not worried about Fiona are you? She's crazy about you."

"Depends on what you mean by worried?"

"Well, you know, *worried* worried, about her playing away or something. You know Jane's going to be with her all week? Jane and the kids. Both of them. The small people that hang around here sometimes, make a lot of noise. Those ones." I wished Neil would turn up. To say I was evidently piss-poor at this sort of conversation would be the understatement of the year. My confidence in giving advice about relationships was at an all time low, I felt like reminding Adam of my recent personal success in the field but it was hard to say it without sounding bitter.

"Yeah I know, and no I'm not worried about her playing away. I'm worried about her enjoying herself too much." I didn't follow.

"I don't follow? You think she won't want you to come back or something?" Adam looked at me as if I had started speaking French.

"No," he replied, leaving the word 'dumbass' hanging unspoken but ever present. "What I mean is I think a week with Jane and the kids is going to make her impatient as

21

hell. And for that little by-product I'll be eternally grateful to Neil. She's already ticking Steve, it's so bloody loud most nights it keeps me awake."

"But I thought you were desperate for marriage and kids? The whole nuclear family?" Adam was clearly trying to make a point but all I kept coming up with was a circle.

"I am. But when we're both ready." He said. There was something on his mind and I felt like the guy who tugs at a tear in the wallpaper only to have to whole wall collapse on his head. "I mean we've only just bought the house. I was hoping to let the paint dry before we started decorating again you know?"

"Fair point." I said as I patted him on the shoulder. It was a tired cliché, the 'there are no words, friend' act that men have tried and tested and come to rely on. I realised now it was for moments like this. I genuinely couldn't think of anything else to say. The more I thought about it the more I started to think he had a point, but agreeing with him was absolutely the last thing I wanted to do. This week was about getting his mind off of all this stuff. It was as much for him as it was for me. It was the one solid fact emerging from the whole evening. The other fact was that Neil had set himself an impossible task, this wasn't a holiday it was a support group outing and as such, I needed him there. No support group was complete without its leader.

I looked around the living room, I'd broken eye contact with Adam and now I needed something engrossing to do, something that would plausibly allow me to concentrate on anything other than the end of a conversation I didn't know how to have. I thought about making a coffee; I contemplated alphabetising Neil's CD collection; I considered re-decorating the whole damn room. The silence wasn't just oppressive it was forming its own government and starting a fascist regime. Sooner or later I was going to crack.

And then it happened.

The sound, a trumpet of rebellion from the street. A heavenly noise of hope, liberation and more importantly distraction. It was a car horn beeping. I looked back at Adam and gestured over to the front door. We shared a smile of relief, Adam for the end of a train of thought that was leading him to misery, me for simply being rescued from drowning.

We filed over towards the door, opened it and strolled out to the road. The air was still thick with the late summer heat but it was refreshing to be outside. We could hear a car turning in the garage bays at the end of the close but the vision still escaped us. To say anticipation was building would be to exaggerate the truly unspectacular. We were waiting for a friend, in a car. We didn't know what car of course, but to grasp on to *that* as a cause of joviality was to kid ourselves our friend was going to arrive in a stretch-Hummer. The headlights edged out passed the wall of the end garage and my eyebrows clenched. Adam was smiling and joking but the words were bouncing off of me. The focus of my attention was the man I used to call a friend. The man currently sitting behind the wheel of a vehicle that I feared he had exchanged good money for. When I became aware of the absence of noise from Adam beside me it was obvious that he had seen it too. This was not a joke.

Neil pulled up to the curb and opened the window. He grinned at us both. Not a smile, not the start of a laugh but a genuinely huge Cheshire cat grin. He was going to say something, somebody had to and Adam and I had been left momentarily speechless.

"Well? What do you think?" Neil looked around at the interior nodding all the while. I wanted to hit him. Nobody could be that excited by an old blue Vauxhall Zafira. It was just wrong. "Is this the bollocks or what?"

"Stop nodding Neil. Stop nodding and tell us what you've done."

"It's blue." said Adam. I turned to him. I felt there was more to be said. "It's... blue." he said again, pointing at the car. His arm dropped back down to his side. To be exact, it was a sky blue insurance write-off that I wouldn't trust to get us to the end of the road let alone to Scotland. I walked around the vehicle slowly. I had to. If I'd rushed it I would have experienced some sort of sensory shut-down.

I checked off the basics. It had four wheels. I couldn't be certain that they were round, but they were there. Tick. It had doors, four of them, and only three of them were scratched. Tick. There were windows filling the spaces where they should. Tick. It was in the very basest sense, a car. Tick.

"It's blue," said Adam for the third time. We were going to have to clear this up.

"Yes," I said, "it's blue. I wasn't aware they made them in this particular colour either, Adam."

"They don't, officially," Neil replied, "This is custom." He almost nodded again. "It's quality."

"Custom? Who the fuck customises a Zafira?" Adam again. Finally on the same page.

"Come on! It's our ride. It's the Blues Mobile!"

"Tell me that's not why you chose it?" I enquired fiercely. Neil looked guilty.

"No," he said defensively, "It was the cheapest thing they had."

"So you did pay for it then? They weren't like giving it away with a litre of oil at the garage or something?"

"We're going to look like the fucking Smurfs, Neil." Adam said, "You've hired a Smurf-mobile is what you've done."

"You two are fucking unbelievable. It's got loads of room, a CD player, air-con, an air bag, alloy wheels. And. It. Was. Cheap. Job done." Neil got out and lit a cigarette. He stood next to us to admire his achievement. We all took a moment. We were bonding in that way that occurs when

24

people share a tragedy together. More words would have spoilt the moment. Like it or not, this was our ride. Eventually we would have to concede.

CONFESSIONS OF AN ACTION MAN

It took us a while to get back into the house. The car had placed us in a trance, the blue seemed to have a calming hypnotic effect that had deflated any feelings of anger or animosity we had at first felt rising at the sight of it. Adam and I shuffled back in like chastised penguins, the Emperor had spoken and we had been corrected. We all sat back down in the living room and reassessed the situation. Our bags sat in the middle of the room, packed to the best of our knowledge. Which was slight. We had a mini-van, or at least a vehicle that one day aspired to being classed as such, we all had time booked off of work, and through a long-endured process of elimination, we had a soundtrack for the trip. All things considered, it was a positive start. I almost admitted as such.

"There's just one other thing," added Neil. "The pièce-de-resistance. You're gonna shit."

"Talking of shitting. Anyone packed any bog-roll yet?" This was Adam, ever logical. Thank Christ for logical.

I clicked my tongue and pointed at him. "Good plan Batman, I'll grab some." I went upstairs and raided the airing cupboard for supplies. Neil had disappeared into the kitchen and was no doubt going to return with three air rifles, a can opener and a rule about only eating what we could kill. I thought about hiding in the cupboard.

"Steve, while you're up there grab the Vaseline and Preparation H, it's in the bathroom cabinet." I got but a step from the bathroom before freezing, the words floating magically across my eyes as if uttered by Harry Potter himself. The image was terrifying, worse than cheap German porn. Three men in the wilderness desperate for female interaction suddenly find themselves drunk and in

26

need of some special attention. I wasn't ready to add that temptation. We were all close, but not 'prison' close.

"What the hell are you thinking about?" I bellowed, trying to add an octave of manliness to my response.

"My haemorrhoids you sick bastard. Steve, you've got to lay off the porn, mate. Really." I grabbed the offending products if for no other reason than to avoid the possibility of acquiring that label just yet. Porn King was a torch I wasn't ready to carry and it was stuck well and truly in Neil's hand. Yes, I was a supporter. Yes, I was dedicated. Yes, okay, I was becoming obsessed. I may have stood close enough to the flame to get a tan, but I definitely wasn't going to be the one holding it.

I ran back down to the living room and threw the medicines in Neil's bag. I stood the multi-pack of toilet rolls on the edge of the unit and wondered whether nine would be enough to see us through. To Monday. I had spent a lot of time with my best friends and if I knew nothing else, I knew they were full of shit.

Neil came through the house from the kitchen carrying what could only be described as Tupperware. Because that's what it was. I didn't immediately recognise it, having never before seen him use it. This was a first, but not necessarily one for the scrapbook. He stood before us again in what was becoming an almost familiar pose, certainly familiar enough for one evening, and I looked over at Adam to see if he had any idea at all as to our next task but he shot me a look of relative despair. Whether he knew or not, the outlook seemed bleak. Neil took the tub in one hand and slowly popped the lid off. He looked down into what I feared was Pandora's box, then he stepped over to Adam and offered him a peek. Adam almost retched. "Get that the fuck out of my face, now."

"What? They're maggots," said Neil, "Chilled." He shook the box a little for effect.

27

"Don't tell me to chill you fucking lunatic." Adam was turning green.

"I said chilled, not chill, you spanner. They've been in the fridge, to preserve the freshness." I stood to peer in the box out of morbid curiosity. I'd never seen maggots before. They looked like special-fried rice.

"Preserve the freshness? They're still a-fucking-live, how much fresher can they be?" I couldn't help myself. It just came out.

"Don't you start, you big tart. They're maggots, and they're coming with us." He put the lid back on and tapped the top of the box. "Boys, we're doing some fishing."

"Fishing? You're having a giraffe. What the hell do we know about fishing?" Again, I looked at Adam and hoped I wasn't the only one lacking such vital manly skills. Adam was just hoping he would get through the rest of the night without seeing his lunch again.

"Well, nothing. Yet. But that's the point isn't it? New experiences, new adventures. It's all good."

"New experiences?" Adam interrupted. "I've been sick before, thanks. It's not been a new experience for some years now."

"Adam's right, Neil. What are you talking about? We've never even mentioned fishing before. Where's this coming from?"

"I just thought it would be something different. And we're doing it, alright? This is not a debate, this is part of the healing process, for all of us. We're doing it. I can picture it so clearly I've almost got wet feet." Adam shook his head. We had both begun to realise that our opinion, while negative, would count for nothing. He looked over at me and smiled.

"It could have been worse mate. It could have been bungee jumping." Neil's eyes widened and I'm certain he would have said something if not for us throwing seat cushions at his head.

We loaded the car. Three holdalls, three sleeping bags, three tents, three pillows, a stack of disposable barbecues, an inflatable mattress, three newly acquired yet clearly fourth hand fishing rods, the maggots, of course, and a nine-pack of toilet rolls. The remaining essentials we would carry with us. I wanted a GPS tracking system and route to be logged with mountain rescue but was informed by Neil that there was simply no time or room for such luxuries as a preservation instinct.

He closed the door of the boot and we all heard the vehicle groan under the strain. I wanted a moment alone with the car, a chance for a pre-match pep talk and some encouraging words of support and understanding. I wanted it to know that we would all be going through this together and while if at times it might seem like it was doing all of the work, we would all be suffering equally. I wasn't sure how to break the news that Neil would be driving the first leg of the journey, and I planned to deny with evident plausibility that Adam even had a driving licence. I'd been a car with Adam many times before and somehow there were no words to describe the experience, even to a vehicle that looked as abused as ours did. I settled for patting the top of the car, then caught myself checking to make sure the gentle impact hadn't caused anything to drop off it.

Back in the house we made noises to the effect of suggesting we get some shut-eye. We planned to grab a few hours of quality sleep, a final night in a proper bed with springs and a duvet and no small animals trying to nest in our ears. The time had spun round to a quarter past eleven and I hoped that our time away wouldn't pass as quickly as the evening had seemed to.

We climbed the staircase content in the knowledge we had done all we could do to prepare for the trip. The Smurf-mobile was full of petrol, Neil and I had accumulated enough cigarettes to warrant adding a trailer to the car and Adam had tidied up the living room. It doesn't sound like much, but to Adam tidying was not so much a courteous mark of respect for hospitality as an affliction. Left to his own devices, Adam had once been caught vacuuming his garden. When the doctors had pulled him screaming from his mother the general thought was that he had only been so upset because he had spent the last nine months getting the place inside 'just right'. Neil and I would try not to draw attention to his ways, as habits went it was preferable to our. And who ever complained about someone tidying up?

We retired to our respective rooms, Neil to his own bed and Adam and I to the bunk beds in the kids' room. We got undressed, hurried through the usual 'skinny bastard – hairy-back Mary' banter that masks the heterosexual male's embarrassment at being confined almost naked in a small space with another man, then we said goodnight.

As I climbed up the ladder and wedged myself in the crack between the bed and the ceiling I made a mental note never to suggest potholing as a potential hobby. It was only upon lying on the mattresses that we realised Neil had been referring more to his own comfort than ours at the earlier suggestion of a good nights sleep. We both stood over six feet tall, incidentally a good foot more than either of the beds accommodated for. I opted for lying diagonally, knees bent and pressed against the rails, toes poking out from the end of the bed. Adam I could only imagine had done the same judging by the noises emanating from beneath me.

"Leave it alone Adam. It's only the first night."

"What the fuck ever, Steve. It's not my fault I need the extra room, knobless."

"Hey, I've had no complaints." A weak response, but I was tired and uncomfortable and yet in no way ready to fall asleep.

"Yeah well Mistress Palm is very forgiving." I laughed, rolled over and smacked my nose on the wall. "What was that?"

"By dose." I rubbed my nose and checked for blood very melodramatically.

"Your what?"

"My nose, you deaf bastard. I just walloped my head into the wall. Jesus, I'd have more room sleeping in the car. Are you comfortable?"

"Oh yeah. I've got an Action Man exploring my crevice and my feet are wedged between two very cold bars at the end of the bed. I'm peachy." I carefully slid my head to the edge of the bed and looked down at him. He was either telling the truth about the Action Man or he had the wedgie from hell. From this angle there was no way to tell and I had no intention of dropping down for a closer look.

"Hasn't Neil got like a super-king size bed?"

"You mean the one we all put together that weekend? The huge one with its own postcode? Yeah he has, why?"

"Cos I've got no intention of sleeping on this bloody thing all night, that's why." I brought the rest of my body to the edge of the bed while the Artex paintwork stabbed at me like a blind acupuncturist with a grudge. I dropped noisily to the floor and looked back at Adam, by now on first name terms with the toy soldier. "You coming?"

"Not yet, but the night is young."

"You're sick. You know that, don't you?"

"Must just be the company I keep." He got up and we went through to Neil's room.

If it was possible to describe someone as literally swimming in their bed, then that's what Neil was doing. He lay in the middle of the gargantuan mattress with ample room for Hugh Hefner's cast-offs to sleep comfortably in the same bed without feeling like their personal space was being compromised, and the bastard was already asleep. Not bad for an insomniac.

"Fuck it. I'm sleeping in there." I walked over to the bed, got in and started arranging the duvet so it tucked right down between me and Neil. He didn't even stir.

Adam had a look of doubt about him, as if the act would somehow tarnish him. Then he thought back to his experience with the Action Man and reasoned he'd been tarnished enough by now. He climbed in on the other side of the bed. Now I was comfortable. I shut my eyes and went back to the image of the Playboy bunnies.

It was impossible to tell how much time had passed. I don't remember falling asleep, but then who does? I do remember waking up though, the image is burned in to my retinas.

At some point in the night I had turned over, while at some other point I had dislodged the safety of the well-positioned duvet. At the point that, from this time on, will be referred to as the moment of horror, Adam appeared to have spooned and practically rolled on top of Neil.

My eyes had opened to reveal my face barely inches from my two closest friends getting more comfortable than I had ever hoped they would be.

I yelled. They woke up. They yelled. Adam launched himself in to the air pulling the duvet clean off the bed allowing us to see that yes indeed my leg had slipped beneath Neil's. We all yelled again. I scrambled from the bed and can only imagine what Neil must have been thinking. He had after all climbed in to bed alone and woken to find he was involved in a ménage-à-trois from hell. I felt for him, but only metaphorically.

When we had all calmed down, we reasoned it would be best to give up on the whole sleeping thing. Neil tried to venture forth with the statement that he had been enjoying one of the best rests of his life, but all that did was make Adam and I want a shower - in different houses. The bedside clock blipped digitally round to twelve thirty-three. We'd managed less than forty minutes and yet further hope of sleep was, for me at least, well out of reach. I went back to the kids' room and grabbed our clothes, got dressed and threw Adam's to him.

I went back downstairs and lit a cigarette while trying to rid my mind of the image of post-coital irony. It wasn't long before Neil and Adam joined me. I went through to the kitchen, put the kettle on and made the drinks. I took them back through to the living room to find Adam and Neil sitting in silence.

"Maybe we should just get on the road now?" I said, passing the drinks around. "Get some miles between us and the morning."

"It's one o'clock, Steve," said Adam, the new king of stating the obvious.

"Do you want to go back to bed?"

"Good point." He sipped his drink and looked at Neil for the first time since they had both sat down. "What do you reckon? Seeing as you were going to do the first leg and all."

"It's fine by me, I'm an insomniac remember?"

"Oh yeah. You looked wide awake upstairs when we came in to the room." I said, smiling.

"Fuck off."

"A sufferer of the truest kind," Adam agreed.

"Fuck off."

"Not so much Sleeping Beauty as Sleeping Butt-Ugly." He flipped the bird at me as an end to the topic and went back to his coffee.

"Okay so I grabbed forty winks, but that was all. First good sleep I've had in ages," he added.

"I thought we agreed not to talk about that again. Ever." Adam sipped his tea resolutely. I laughed and waited for a decision. Neil looked at his watch.

"Maybe it's not a bad idea. We've got around four hundred miles to cover before we cross the border and as yet still no place to sleep for the night or any idea as to

33

where we're actually going. Sooner we're on the road the better."

"Certainly sounds like it." Adam said.

So we had a plan. Load up the last of our gear, and head on out. Suddenly the excitement was back - the prospect of the open road. It was infectious. We each grabbed our final hand luggage, the CD's, cigarettes and jumpers that would see us through the journey, checked through the house and switched off the non-essentials. We all got to the door together and then Adam stopped us. "Final checklist, boys. Have we got everything?"

"Yes mum."

"I'm being serious. Last chance before we head out."

"If you tell us to use the toilet before we go then I'm leaving you here," said Neil, turning back to the door.

"That's not a bad idea," I said, suddenly feeling like I was seven again.

"I was talking about the stuff. Have we got everything?"

"If we haven't already got it then we don't need it," said Neil, growing impatient.

"Well that's fine advice. Remind me not to go parachute jumping with you any time soon." Neil ignored him and opened the door.

Adam and I went and used the facilities while Neil huffed out to the car. It was the middle of the night, the air was chill and fresh and more effective than caffeine. He got in the car and waited for us, drumming his fingers on the steering wheel. We came out a couple of minutes later. I let Adam close the front door, knowing he wouldn't trust anyone else to do it properly even though it wasn't his house. I called shotgun and jumped in the front seat. Adam climbed in behind us.

"Finally," Neil said after Adam had strapped himself in. "Can we please get on the road now? I could have gotten another half hour's kip in, waiting for you two girls."

"Yeah, yeah, whatever," we said together. I slapped my hands on my knees to indicate that we were all ready now.

"Anything else? Music?" Neil asked. "Maybe touch up your make-up before we set off?" I switched on the radio and tuned into a local station, tuned Neil out while I was doing it. There'd be another hour of this at least.

Neil jangled the car keys as if to point out a momentous occasion. It was, sort of. This was the beginning. The preamble was over. As soon as the car started, we'd be officially on our way. This was the start of our holiday. He put the key in the ignition, turned it and shuffled in his seat. Nothing happened. I wasn't expecting fireworks or a fanfare, I knew the queen wasn't going to smash a bottle of champagne on the bonnet, but I had expected the engine to start at least.

I laughed, loudly. I was trying to be supportive but had clearly lost track. The next door neighbours' bathroom light came on. I'd manage to wake them up. It wasn't my fault of course - the noise travelled that much further without the distracting sound of an engine to muffle it. Neil did not look pleased. I couldn't blame him. The Smurf-mobile had stolen his thunder, albeit very quietly. I was starting to like this car more and more.

"Has it got any pet -"

"Shut up, Adam."

"Right." Neil took out the keys and had a look at them, just to make sure he hadn't tried to jam the shed key into the ignition by mistake. The key appeared to be correct, but I couldn't tell if that was a good thing or not. He flicked through the bunch, found another Vauxhall key further around the loop.

"Okay, okay. It's all good. Nobody panic."

I turned in my seat to look at Adam in the back. He'd been about to switch on the interior light before thinking better of it. Apparently his was the voice he heard a second before doing something stupid too. I laughed again and

35

bounced in the seat. With the second key in hand, Neil tried again and this time the engine sprang in to life. "Ha," he said triumphantly, "That was the boot key. I remember the fella said something about separate keys when I picked the motor up. Should have listened a bit closer I guess." He slipped the car into first gear and pulled out of the parking space.

Now we were on our way.

Saturday

THREE SHEETS TO THE WIND: MASTURBATION AND THE HIDDEN ART OF MALE BONDING

It felt good to be moving. Neil was taking it easy but with over four hundred miles to cover, none of us were complaining about the progress we were making. That's the beautiful thing about driving in the middle of the night, very few people have the same ridiculous idea. The roads were largely empty aside from the usual procession of articulated lorries toiling away with the variety of products that people just expected to find on the shelves of their local supermarket. The occasional glimpse of the drivers gave us more than enough cause not to want to stop too often at unmarked lay-by's or for that matter well-marked 'rest-spots' that may as well have been sign posted with 'murderers welcome'. We just pushed on, slowly racking up the miles, each of us appreciating the moment for what it was. Boredom.

The world takes on an altogether different appearance in the small hours of the morning. The first and by far most laborious leg of our journey was to navigate through the back roads to something that resembled a northbound motorway. But at two in the morning back roads aren't just back roads, they're poorly lit, badly maintained treacherous paths to the essence of your desire to undertake the journey you have partaken of. The absence of vehicles or, indeed, any signs of life is a huge indication that there is a very sound reason why people don't generally drive about at that hour. When you do pass something resembling civilisation you are abruptly confronted with life's hidden populous, the zombie-esque beings that shuffle towards light like forgotten extras from a George A Romero movie. I turned away from the window and fought the urge to click on the central locking and caught a look at Adam trying to read a map in the dark.

None of us had spoken once the vehicle had started moving, we had all been waiting for the captain to turn off the 'seatbelt' lights and allow us to get past the initial shock of inertia that was more commonly referred to as Neil's driving. I lit the first cigarette of many and handed one across to Neil then waited for the utterance of complaint from Adam. He didn't say a word. "That's odd," I said to Neil as I buzzed down the window two inches.

"Suits me. I wasn't sure how to break the news that I wasn't going to make it to Scotland without a fag." I laughed and turned back to Adam. He had the map held up to his face at eye level and was presumably plotting a course along the path of least resistance.

"So where we headed, bud?" I asked him, but the map didn't move. "Neil, we did remember to let Adam get in the car before we left, didn't we? Yo! Adam!" I reached back and flicked the map at the crease. Adam hit the roof.

"You cheeky bastard! You were asleep, weren't you?" said Neil.

"No, I was reading the map." Adam folded it closed and placed it on the seat beside him.

"You liar. You were out cold."

Adam was looking at me with his best poker face and mustering sincerity from the depths of his character, "Don't be daft," he eventually said.

"Adam, you were out mate. Trust me. I was talking to you for like five minutes." Neil chuckled and bit his lip.

"He's right mate. You were away with the fairies. Well and truly in the land of nod." Adam yawned widely but continued to deny all of it.

39

"Adam, I know you were asleep because I'm smoking a fag. In the car. Right now." Adam looked at us disapprovingly. I hated that look.

"So where are we then?" Adam asked trying to change the subject.

"Well you had the map mate, you tell us?"

"I was busy looking ahead. So are we on the motorway yet then or what?" Neil and I looked out of the windows at the passing countryside. It wasn't so much dark outside, more a vacuous blackness that seemed to suck in the scenery around us. Despite this, it was clear that we were not on the motorway yet. We looked back at Adam, tried to form the correct response that would cause the least offence. Neil took the lead.

"No, you clown, we've only been driving for an hour." I wasn't sure he'd achieved it.

Adam stretched and rubbed his arms against the night chill made worse by the front windows' being open. "Fair enough. So what'd I miss then?"

"Darkness, and lots of it." I turned the radio up. The unmistakable opening bars of Iggy Pop's 'Passenger' throbbed through the speakers. We all smiled and individually began to bob our heads, each taking a different section of the beat. It wasn't long before the feet tapping, steering wheel rapping map slapping crescendo came and we were all bellowing out the chorus at the tops of our voices. It just seemed appropriate somehow.

Hi, you're on the radio with Mick In The Morning, what's your problem?
It's Billy
Don't need to know your name friend, just your pain...
Well, it's a little, um, embarrassing. I don't know what it is exactly, you know, how to explain it like.
Just start at the beginning, we're here to help...
Well, you know, it's me coc-

Whoa, whoa, whoa Billy, you're live on the air right now. Choose your words, friend...

I thought this was bloody 'Sex Confidential'?

That's right Billy, it is, and our listeners would love to know what you're going through...

Listeners? Well that's not very bloody confidential is it?

Well Billy, this is a radio station, we have got some *listeners... hopefully. What's your pain friend?*

Can I say 'knob' then? [*Muffled laughter*]

Well Billy, you kind of just have...

How about 'tool'?

Another fine choice Billy, so what's the problem with your 'manhood'?

My 'manhood'? I've got a problem with me dick like! [*Uproarious laughter*] There's nothin' wrong with me manhood! Are you calling me a poof?

No Billy, lets calm down and start from the beginning, nobody's name-calling, we're all just here to help.

Well it's me fella like, it's gone a funny colour

Okay, go on...

Well that's it like, what the bloody hell else do you want to know?

Well, how about what were you doing when it changed colour?

Havin' a wan-. [*Click*]

We'll be right back after these messages...

"First time then?" Neil asked. 'Sex Confidential' had started something.

"With or without a woman?" Adam said.

"Without."

"Well now that's a funny story." I said, still aching from the confessions of Billy and his Willy. "I'm not proud of it. But I can see the humour in it. I'm big enough to share this story."

"That's not what I've heard." I shot Adam my own disapproving look then laughed and lit a cigarette. I was about to bare my soul and Billy was about to get a friend.

41

"I don't remember exactly when it started, but I had a crush on this girl with absolutely no idea why - but she was literally all I could think about for weeks on end-."

"On who?" Asked Neil, ever one for the details.

"Helen Slater, she played Supergirl in 'Supergirl – The Movie.' I remember seeing it on the TV and it was literally a defining moment in my childhood. I found a picture of her and cut it out of the TV Times and stashed it under my pillow but one day my mum found it and I remember just wanting to die."

"That's tragic Steve, really."

"Shut up Adam, I was young and she wore a tight outfit. I liked it, I just didn't know why. The thing was, after I lost the first photo I started develop a bit of a habit, I was gathering nuts for a winter I had no idea would arrive."

"Don't worry mate, I gathered my nuts a few times myself as a boy." Neil adjusted himself in his seat and went back to listening to the story while Adam just laughed like a drain.

"Anyway," I continued, "I had this box under my bed, god knows why. I'd started butchering magazines and my mums' catalogues, all the lingerie models and the likes. I remember I had a quest going for my first Page 3 cut out. God if I'd have found proper porn I think I would have passed out."

"Don't worry mate, we've all been there." Somehow I couldn't see Adam meaning that.

"Why do you think I had a paper round all those years?" But Neil was no effort at all.

"You see that's what I needed. That would have been like the having the keys to the sweet shop."

"How old were you?" Asked Adam.

"About ten."

"Ten? Are you kidding? Jeez when I was ten I was looking for comics not porn. You started early then?"

"I always told you he was proper wanker," added Neil.

"No! That's my point. I wasn't doing anything, I just had this box full of pictures that for some reason I liked to look at."

"Yeah but you must have noticed something happening, you know, downstairs."

"My mum didn't have a clue."

"No you putz, I meant in your pants!"

"Well yeah of course. But I was ten, so what the hell did it mean to me?" Neil couldn't stop himself from laughing by now. "I do remember liking the feeling though."

"No shit!" he said.

"Yeah alright, but I was without male guidance, remember? Not that I would have wanted to ask my dad about it or anything, I only saw him every couple of weeks. Somehow it never came up."

"Sounds like a first for you." I was leaving myself open for this.

"Yeah, yeah, whatever."

"Old Stonker Steve." Adam added patting me on the shoulder.

"Do you want me to finish this or not?"

"Sorry," they said together. "Go on."

"So, I'm there, I've got a box of the softest pictures in the world, a junior woody and a quickened pulse."

"So what happened?"

"Well, nothing. For two years."

"That's a shit story Steve. As they go, that's really piss poor." Neil could be so patient sometimes.

"I mean nothing happened because I wasn't doing anything. I didn't even know there was something I *could* do. I was ten when this fascination started and it was a long couple of years before I got that bit of information. For two years it was like owning a Playstation without a plug, all the gear with no idea what it could do. By now though I was literally sweating, you've got to understand I'd been titillating myself for years, it was intense. I think I might

43

have inadvertently discovered tantric sex. It was like I'd been cramming for an exam or something. And then one day it happened. Well, one night actually."

"What happened?"

"Wet dream," I said mournfully. The boys nodded. I let the words hang there, to feel the mutual sympathetic understanding. The bond of a shared truth, a nightmare long forgotten. "I thought I'd pissed myself. I was drenched. God it was awful. It was just everywhere. I practically ruined my Star Wars duvet. It was years before I could look at a Wookiee the same way."

"That's just wrong."

"Tell me about it." I sighed defensively.

"We've watched that film together before now Steve, god only knows what you were thinking about, I feel violated."

"Wet dreams eh?" pressed Adam, trying to pull us out of a hole, "They are the worst."

Neil silently pondered this new information then lit a cigarette.

"What a waste though!" he said eventually. We looked at him dubiously.

"How do you mean exactly?"

"I mean two years of planning, stockpiling 'material', the old visual aids which let's be honest were frankly adequate for your limited needs, and you blow your load in your sleep. That's so pathetic!"

"Hang on a sec you cruel bastard, it's not like I had a choice about it or anything."

"Well do you even remember the dream?" Adam said, trying to help.

"Was it about Supergirl?" Neil said in a mock voice.

"Fuck off."

"She-Ra? That bird from the Thundercats cartoon?" Neil started slapping the steering wheel as tears rolled down his face and I feared momentarily for our safety.

"Shut up."

44

"Which one?" asked Adam.

"I think you're missing the point," I said, apparently to myself.

"The one with the red hair of course."

"Cor yeah, she was fit."

"Boys. You digress - *way* off the mark. I was twelve years old and covered in the cream of creation. Do you honestly think I gave a damn about the dream I'd had?"

"I would have."

"Thanks Neil."

"I thought we were talking about spanking off anyway?" Adam had a knack. "Wet dreams don't count."

"I'm getting to that."

"Well if you could mate, we've only got four hundred miles so in your own time."

"So like I said, *that* happened later, but until then I'd found a release, of sorts. I started taking afternoon naps so often my mum thought I was narcoleptic. I was getting so good at it that I had to make a preparation kit for the eventuality."

"I'm afraid to ask?" Said Neil rubbing his forehead.

"Clean skiddies, tissues and a bag. Or spare pants, something to help me clean up and a place to hide the evidence."

"There's something wrong with you, Steve. You need help mate."

"Anyway," I pressed on, "The first time I remember being conscious doing it was in the bath. And why the hell did nobody ever mention the mess that that makes?"

"Like the safety glue they make you use at school." Neil and I both turned to look at Adam.

"What? I was a kid once too."

"Good analogy as it happens. Exactly like that. Trouble is though, I thought I'd broken it."

"Broken what? The bath?" said Adam, obviously having difficulty keeping up.

"No you fuck-munch, my todger."

"You had to ask?"

"I'd never done it before, I didn't know the science of it. I was kind of washing myself at the time and it sort of just, well, splodged out."

"STEVE!"

"Sorry but that's how it happened. I've got to say though, talk about a happy accident."

"So you still didn't use your box then?"

"Nope, I was boxless for a few years." Neil and Adam began laughing uncontrollably and we covered a good couple of miles before the conversation I wish I'd never started managed to carry on.

"So you didn't have a kit for that then?" Said Neil.

"Not a kit, no. But I did work out a system."

"Go on." They sighed nervously.

"Very economical, this should appeal to you actually Adam," I said, turning to check his level of interest. It was a hook, but one I knew would work. "Three sheets," I said triumphantly.

"Three sheets?" said Adam.

"Three sheets."

"I don't get it?" Said Neil, lighting two cigarettes and handing one over.

"Very simple. One to catch, one to clean, and one to carry the other two." I blew a smoke ring and rested my head triumphantly back against the rest.

"Of bog roll? How small is your dick exactly?" Said Adam sitting back in his seat. "On a scale of one to 'woman'."

"Not bog roll. King Size Kleenex. Manly tissues," I said feebly. Neil glanced back at Adam.

"Bog roll," they agreed. Bastards.

Neil looked over at me and smiled. It was a brotherly smile of understanding, one that admitted he knew what it meant to have shared that insight and though he could have probably gone his whole life without ever wanting to know

46

such information, it was part of what made our relationship special. "If it makes you feel any better," he said, "my Dad walked in on me banging one out over a catalogue once."

"You're kidding?" said Adam, and I wondered briefly what sort of stories he was hiding. I had a feeling I'd find out over the coming week.

"The look on his face was priceless," Neil continued, "Though mine couldn't have been much better." He laughed for a moment in reminiscence. "I've never moved so fast in my life, almost ripped it off trying to cover up. Still, it wasn't all bad, he came back in ten minutes later and gave me my first porn mag." I looked at him incredulously.

"You lucky fucker."

"Yep, proper chap my dad. Proper chap." I sat, stunned, recalling all of the paper cuts of my youth. "You see, that's your problem Steve, you never think outside the box."

"Luck literally just drops in your lap doesn't it?" I uttered, only half-joking.

"Not always mate, not always."

"Did he knock first?" Only Adam could have thought of it.

We drove on in silence after that, all lost in the past. But Neil was right. I did feel better. It was true that I most likely did need help, but at least I wasn't alone. I had a feeling that as long as I knew Adam and Neil, I never would be.

THINGS THAT GO BUMP IN THE NIGHT

Let me tell you something about fear, real, primeval, back to the wall facing a giant long-toothed beasty kind of fear. The sort of fear some people feel towards spiders. The sort of fear that allows others to watch the colour drain out of your face and makes your hair turn white in front of their eyes. Fear of an impending terror, like just before a rollercoaster pulls away and drags you up two hundred feet only to drop you speeding into a seemingly endless barrel of twists and turns and stomach-wrenching forces that let you taste what you've eaten for the second time that day. Just not that much fun. It's what I experienced sitting in the front seat with Adam at the wheel.

He'd taken over somewhere past Birmingham. Time had dissolved for me by that point, but the small electronic clock on the dashboard tried in vain to tell me it was just approaching five in the morning. If nothing else, we were making incredibly good time; I just hoped that those wouldn't be my last words.

I'd gone through the human state recognised as 'a bit sleepy,' beyond a condition of adrenaline induced alertness and now I was relying solely on a recently developed habit of just having my eyes open. I think I wanted to sleep, in fact I'm certain of it. I was daydreaming of being asleep. Just with my eyes open. I had to concentrate on blinking to stop my eyeballs drying up from the unnatural heat spewing forth from the vents in the car.

But with Adam driving, there was no way I could keep them closed. It was like my eyelids were elastic, snapping back open with the force of a whip cracking. I watched cars pass by as if they were parked along the middle lane.

Watched as the cat's eyes in the road ahead merged into one long beam of reflective light guiding us towards our final destination. These sights were just futile distractions though, for the focus of my attention was Adam. I had one single thought in my mind that played round and round like a record at a cheap disco; if he yawns, I'm going to stab him in the leg.

It wasn't that we were driving fast, fast I could handle. Fast implied an element of efficiency, of man and machine working in harmony to achieve an ultimate goal. It wasn't even that we were testing whether the reverse parking sensors on a BMW work when the cars are moving forwards, speeding silently up on them like a demonic chariot unleashed from hell trying to intimidate the paint work off of the rear bumpers. It was the silence. We had stopped talking, the radio had crossed so many local stations that the DJ's were getting travel sick and the only sound I could hear was that of my heart thumping in my ears.

Neil and I were concentrating hard on willing the vehicle not to take off, concentrating so hard we were starting to use the force. I wanted Adam to laugh uproariously like an evil genius whose plan was coming together. It would have comforted me somehow, allowed me to believe that my life was being risked in some higher purpose. And it would have proven to me that Adam was awake. Right now that was worth more to me than all of the coffee at Starbucks.

At the speed we were travelling we were due to arrive before we left home and that was the sort of science that messed with my head. We needed to stop, and to stop long enough for the rest of my body to catch up. I wrenched my head around to see Neil clinging frantically to the armrests, white knuckled and mumbling Hail-Marys. I tried to mouth the words 'service station,' as I feared that actual sound couldn't be contained in a car travelling at this velocity. I caught his eye and he managed to nod in wholehearted agreement.

A few seconds and too many miles later we came across Carlisle service station.

In the early hours of the morning most places take on a surreal quality. People move about like mist, animals stop to stare at you and remind you that in the grander scale of things, they were here first. Were it not for the articulated lorries, I would have believed them.

Neil and I were not discernible beings without coffee. We couldn't wait for the car to stop moving. It just didn't seem like a possibility worth even considering. These were not normal circumstances so the normal rules of logic did not apply. But you had to ask, in retrospect, how bad could things have been inside the car that jumping out of it whilst it was still moving seemed like the safer of the two options? So let me try and explain.

Adam is a man who likes to do things properly. A man who believes in the order of things, in civility, of everything having its place and there being a place for everything. It's a characteristic that ordinarily I admire, from a distance. But when this said sense of order means driving around a desolate car park, over spaces so close to the door of a building you could be forgiven for thinking it a 'drive-in', you had to wonder. Onwards he drove, round and round further still before aiming towards a cluster of vehicles evidently abandoned by disheartened joy riders. My belief is that Adam had felt a calling, but I just wasn't prepared to sit around long enough to find out. Neil followed suit, great minds thinking alike, and we could only assume that Adam would eventually catch up once he'd checked out the competition and measured the rims on a nearby Renault Espace.

We skipped towards the entrance of the haven thankful to be moving at a more respectable, sedate pace that I hoped would soon be adopted as the national speed limit in the not too distant future. We were in search of caffeine and someplace warm to consume it. And there were more basic needs to be attended to as well. We made a route towards the toilets and enjoyed each step that allowed us to unfold our aching limbs. We stretched, we yawned and finally, we spoke. "What the hell just happened?"

"Hey?" Neil stepped up to the urinal and shook his head to clear the fog.

"What just happened? Back then, in the car. Back then in the car. What happened to Adam?"

"I don't even want to talk about it. Can we move on?"

"Move on? I don't ever want to move again after that journey. That was one of the most terrifying experiences of my life. I'm pissing myself just thinking about it."

"Then open your fly," Neil said dryly. "What can I say, he wanted to take the next leg of the journey and I was too tired to argue."

"Did you get any sleep then? Cause I sure as hell didn't."

"Are you kidding, I may have had my eyes closed but only to pray."

"I mean the guy is just full of surprises. Narcoleptic one moment then wide-eyed and crazy the next. Unbelievable."

We finished up, washed our hands and walked out to the breakfast counter, Neil casually adjusted his jeans, tugging at them as if there simply wasn't room in his pants. I ordered two coffees and one to go for Adam, then strolled over to a sad looking corner that reluctantly explained that smoking would be tolerated, but only if you absolutely positively had to be so rude. We decided that we did.

As I sat down in the padded, worn, abused armchair I chuckled to myself at the thought of the proposed smoking ban I'd heard talk of starting in Scotland the following March. I couldn't see it catching on somehow, but then what the hell did I know? The world around me was changing in ways I had yet to even imagine – I couldn't even see what was going on in my own flat.

51

"Christ I'm tired," Neil said, easing himself into the armchair opposite and yet still looking uncomfortable, "I feel like I haven't slept in a week."

"Well of course not, you're a bloody insomniac."

"You know what I mean." Sadly, I did. I lit a cigarette and handed one over to Neil. "I mean like dog tired. I really need this break, I know I keep saying it but I don't think you both realise how much this means to me. It's not just about doing something positive for you two, that's a big part of it of course but I need it too. I'm really looking forward to just kicking back and being a bloke again. Having a laugh. Chilling out without having to worry about offending anyone. We should have done this a long time ago." I couldn't tell if I was just tired or if there actually was an underlying statement struggling to get free, but either way I was too exhausted to spot any flags being waved, or to wave any myself for that matter.

"Well it hasn't exactly been too relaxing so far, but I think I know what you're getting at." I was nodding while I thought about it again.

The realisation that this was all part of the trip was escaping me somewhat, but I hadn't slept in about twenty-four hours and that had to be a factor. We were in a limbo state, halfway from where we started to where we were going. Not unlike my own life in that respect, but more enjoyable so far. Aneurysm-inducing driving aside, it felt good to be with my friends, and this was certainly having the desired effect of taking my mind off of things. And by things I meant Kelly, and I hadn't thought about her in what seemed like days.

"So what really happened with you and Kelly then?" All good things, I thought.

I took a drag of my cigarette while I tried to formulate a response. The question had come out of the blue, but only to me. I had a feeling that this had been playing on Neil's mind for some time and evidently now was as good a time as any to release it in to the world. Personally I didn't think it was ready to fend for itself, but then what did I know?

Neil looked at me and I could tell that a response was required before we could move on to a more socially acceptable topic of conversation, but it was a response I didn't have, or one that I didn't know, or want to face, or whatever. It was a shitty time to ask, that was for sure, like offering a drink to an alcoholic on his third day on the wagon. The words swam around my head like sharks. "She was cheating on me," I said. There was no other way to put it. Time wasn't healing me, it was just giving me a sense of perspective about how fucked off it made me. The longer I felt wound up, the more obvious it became. And nobody ever says that to you, do they?

"How come you never said anything? To me I mean?"

"I wanted to. But then I wanted to disregard it too. Like it was a trivial fact that held no bearing on the eventual result. I'd spent the last year telling you about how crazy she was driving me, it somehow didn't seem fair to say anything more."

"You were trying to protect my opinion of her then?"

"No, that's not it. I think I was just trying to protect myself. It was just easier to think that we drifted apart, went our separate ways as friends and promised to write at Christmas. If I went the other way, I might be tempted to start asking why she did it. And who needs that?"

"Yes Steve. You're right. Denial is always the better option." He was smiling, so I didn't punch him

"Fuck off Neil, you wouldn't be human if you didn't ask yourself a few questions. It doesn't matter that I was miserable, that I was obviously making her feel the same way. Ultimately I drove her away. So what if I didn't like her that much towards the end. It's the principle that counts. She cheated on me ergo I'm a crappy boyfriend."

"That's bullshit and you know it."

"Do I?"

"Steve, you're still young. You didn't piss off out every night – more's the pity – you didn't drink or beat her or abuse her. You just, I dunno know, lost your way. But you were working, providing. Seems like you were doing your part, I think perhaps the term 'never satisfied' was invented for her." I laughed despite myself. "You were not, and are not, crap boyfriend material. In fact I seem to remember repeatedly getting drunk and telling *you* to cheat on *her*." This was true. "I tried to make you crap boyfriend material, but what can I say?"

"Whatever mate. It's all over now either way."

"But that's a good thing. Trust me."

"That may be, but right now it feels like I'm a twenty-seven year old workaholic with no money and no bird and no prospects. If it weren't for you and Adam I swear I'd have found a tall building by now."

"Or," he said, pausing to re-enforce his point, "it means you're young, free and single again. In a good way." He took a drink from his coffee and looked at me. "If I was a bird, I'd shag you."

"Always know when to stop Neil."

I glanced at my watch trying to grasp hold of time, but it felt like the tail end of a tethered rope that someone kept pulling just out of my reach. I was wondering where the hell Adam could have got to, whether we'd missed him walking past us during the impromptu counselling session that had just taken place. I thought about going back to the toilets to check the cubicles, but at five thirty in the morning you took your life in to your own hands doing that in Carlisle service station. I gestured to Neil that we should probably go looking for him so we got up and strolled towards the door.

"So are we going to try and get some sleep then or what?" I felt like the first person at the party to go home.

"Sure, I mean we can try, might be worth a shot before it gets too light."

We stepped through the doors and the fresh, crisp air hit us again in a way that invigorated more than coffee ever could. I scanned the car park through the grey morning mist that had descended from nowhere, trying to establish where it had been that we abandoned our friend. I saw no sign of chaos, no bodies lying strewn across the roads, in short no indication at all of where Adam had eventually settled.

"Can you see him anywhere?"

"Nope," said Neil, absently lighting a cigarette. "But he must be here somewhere. C'mon." He started off around the car park towards the most populated area. It must have been a difficult call to make.

"I kind of feel bad about leaving him like that. Do you think he got offended or something? Maybe fucked off without us?"

"Nah, he's our boy, he'll be here somewhere. He'll be asleep, but he'll be here." I looked around again and tried to muster the same optimism. "How hard could it be to spot a shagged out blue Zafira?"

"Where the fucking fuck is he?" I was bored. Tired, bored and getting cold. We had been walking for seven minutes but the length of time was not the issue. To me time was irrelevant. At that point, time could stroll off and go fuck itself. Time had got me longing for the Smurf-mobile, and for that I would never forgive it. I turned to see where Neil had got to and was immediately blinded by a tow-truck that had rolled out of an American horror movie. I raised my arm to shield my eyes and in the shadow found Neil doing the same. I jogged over to him and we watched the monstrosity growl by. It was a captivating sight that was not entirely without purpose. Once it had passed it illuminated the car park better than floodlights.

We followed the vision. It needed a soundtrack, 'The Ride of the Valkyres' maybe. I looked at Neil, he looked back at me. We shook our heads, smiled the 'takes all sorts' smile and followed in the wake of the truck. The coffee we'd bought for Adam was so cold now that the beans were reforming in the bottom of the cup, if we didn't find him soon we'd be tending a small plantation. I pointed over towards the last group of cars we hadn't yet checked and we cut across through the empty spaces. Neil just nodded in silent defeated agreement.

Up ahead of us were three cars parked in a row, a fairly commonplace occurrence in a car park, and alone they represented the fulfilment of the fundamental purpose of a car park, that being, to provide a relatively safe place to park your car. But they were not entirely alone. Aside from us slowly approaching there was another more ominous presence nearby. We just didn't know it yet.

The end car to the right looked familiar. In fairness, there could be only one. Only once in the entire history of automotive production could there have been such a car as ours. And it was neatly parked. It occurred to me that this was the key. Adam had started a line. It made so much sense that I couldn't believe it had taken us this long to figure it out. In the corner of the largely empty car park, someone had chosen the space in the far corner and in the spirit of solidarity, someone else had parked next to them. And then there was Adam, neatly parked, third in a newly formed row. Why he had taken the trouble to reverse in to the space is anybody's guess. But this was Adam, and it was why we loved him.

We approached the Zafira from the side trying to decipher the image before us. With the engine still running we could hear the heaters blasting even from a distance. The exhaust fumes swirled around the car and gave it an ethereal quality that implied it might simply float away in a strong breeze. We looked through the driver's side window to see Adam slumped forward, arms up around his head and hugging the steering wheel the way a bachelor hugs a toilet bowl after a stag night.

Through the patchy misted glass we could see something glinting through the window, something metallic poking out from Adam's armpit. It appeared from the narrowing distance to be two spears. And then they dropped down out of view. It was a detached headrest and it meant that Adam, the sneaky bastard, had been asleep. His movements were the slow sleepy disorientated gestures of a man remembering why he's feeling so bad, and if he didn't remember, I planned to remind him.

Adam had been awoken by a blinding light that swept across the bonnet of the car like a searchlight. Looking back, it's obvious now that that the offending vehicle had been travelling too fast to make the turn but at the time it seemed like a crawl. It arced round in the casual destructive way that a strimmer goes to grass and it connected with the front of the Zafira like an electromagnet. The tow-truck didn't even shudder as it ploughed in to the front bumper of our car, but from our position it seemed as if the entire back end of the Zafira was lifted from the ground on impact.

We saw Adam's head turn towards us, maybe away from the light in his eyes or maybe just in that instinctive way you move to protect your vulnerable parts from danger. Either way, it allowed us the perfect view of Adam punching himself in the face. The airbag exploded in a furious rush of post impact frenzy forcing his arm off the steering wheel and directly up towards his head. It was a cracking shot, and what it lacked in actual force it made up for in precision. The bag raged in a shocked sense of disbelief then deflated as quickly as it had appeared. What was left was a man bleeding from his nose, head lolled back over the front seat unsupported by a headrest that lay on his lap.

We didn't mean to laugh, really we didn't.

LIFE IN THE FAST LANE:
EMERGENCY ACCESS ONLY

I had assumed it was to be one of life's great-unanswered questions - how do you make a car like ours look worse than it already did? Apparently the answer was to apply a tow-truck liberally to the front end. Obvious. It's not a considered choice, more an impulse decision. Why have one complete bumper when you can have detachable pieces? Why go for one set of forward facing functional head light clusters when you can opt for the upgrade of an independent kaleidoscopic design? Really, when you look at it, there *is* no choice.

Imagine the government had impounded a car with the purpose of reverse-engineering it just to find out where the cup holder was. This was the position we were in. Customs and Excise would have made less mess looking for cocaine stashed under the bonnet. But that would have to wait, our first concern was Adam. We knew he was still alive because dead people couldn't have been as pissed off as he was. The language emanating from the car reminded me of a HBO special. I expected to see Adam leap out of the seat and pursue the offending vehicle Mel Gibson style down the road. This was not a happy man. I couldn't blame him. Most people only have to fear bad dreams when they're asleep – unless of course they're asleep in a car that Adam is driving – but Adam managed to manifest his nightmare into a fully fledged reality that the whole group could share. We were so grateful.

We rushed to the door and flung it open. The sight before us did nothing to improve our mood. Our friend was a state. Eyes wet, a trickle of blood dribbling down his lip, a hand pushed against his forehead in what we could only assume was humiliation and frustration. I searched for the words to ground us all.

"Shit." Neil patted me on the back and squeezed past me, crow-barring his shoulders around to square up to Adam and assess the damage from a less superficial point of view. Adam just sat there trying to let gravity stem the flow of blood. Neil raised his hand and cupped Adam's cheek.

"How you doing buddy?"

"Peachy. Just peachy. How bad is the motor?"

"Just a scratch mate, it's all good."

"Just a scra -" was all I managed before the elbow connected with my ribs. The forced smile from Neil told me to try a different approach, "Don't sweat it, this crate's got balls man, she'll ride again."

"Exactly. Now let's get you fixed up."

"What happened to the tow-truck?" Adam mumbled as Neil pushed the redundant airbag down between the foot well. The deployment had released a talc-like substance over the front dash that I knew would drive Adam crazy. If nothing else worked, we could cheer him up by letting him clean it.

"Honestly mate," I said, stepping back to give them some room to get out. "The damage is not that bad. We don't need a tow-truck." They both stopped to look at me as the words whistled past my eyes and back in to my brain. "Oh, *that* tow-truck. Well it kind of just reversed and fucked off somewhere. I don't even think the geezer noticed he hit you."

"I don't think I've ever felt more significant in my life." Adam said stepping out of the vehicle. Had it been able to, I think the Zafira would have shuddered in agreement. He patted himself down, touched his finger to his nose to check the bleeding then stretched and managed a yawn. Only Adam could still have felt sleepy at that point.

I lit a cigarette and almost thought about offering one to Adam but Neil got there first. He took it off me then walked around to the front of the car to assess the damage. I felt Neil had missed his calling as a mechanic. The cap seemed to fit better than the chassis of our car at least.

The situation was bleak. Bits of the car we had hired lay on the ground like confetti at a sadist's wedding. I couldn't identify where they had originally come from, my knowledge of cars being limited at best when they're all in one piece. As far as I could tell though, the damage was largely cosmetic. The bumper was cracked and the end that had taken the brunt of the impact was resting casually on the tarmac. Neil reassured me that this could be fixed with gaffer tape, then equally concerned me by informing us that he had some in his bag. I started to wonder what exactly he had planned for this trip.

There was a dent in the centre of the bonnet that made it look as if a pre-school kid had paper-machéd a rendition of the Grand Canyon on the front of our car. I poked it with my finger but I still can't tell you why. It just seemed like something you do. Neil was strafing around the vehicle gesturing in the affirmative. I was looking for something equally constructive to do. Adam meanwhile had wandered over to a nearby curb and was sat down watching us quizzically. I wouldn't have blamed him if he had wanted to turn back now. Then I considered whether Neil would stroll over and start assessing Adam in the same way that he was the car. Gaffer tape could work wonders for his looks.

The field repairs took us an hour. We bought more coffees, rolled around the concrete checking under the car, kicking tyres, rocking the suspension, testing the headlights and indicators. We taped the bumper back on to the front of the car, made sure the radio still worked, then looked for any signs of fluid dripping from areas that it shouldn't - all under Neil's guidance. He really came in to his own in these situations, which was fortunate as we frequently found ourselves in them.

Over the years we had been through countless cars, general household refurbishments, garden renovations and more. Of course these incidents never started out as moments of crisis, but when has blind optimism ever stopped that from happening? The one defining positive from them all was that we had each in our own way become battle-hardened. Together we could have resolved the situation in the Middle East, given the chance.

The moment of truth finally arrived. After debating whether or not we wanted to call the police, then whether or not we wanted to turn back and go home, we eventually arrived at the unanimous decision to press on. It would take more than a deranged tow-truck driver to get us down - Neil still needed the holiday, I just wanted to spend time with my mates, and Adam was convinced he could find the bastard that hit him. So there it was. We were on a mission, again. Back on the road, again. But the Zafira wouldn't start. Again.

"Question," I said as the traffic crawled along the motorway. I needed something to keep my mind buzzing as the traffic jam was draining my energy faster than it was the fuel. I could feel my will to live ebbing out of my fingers as I flicked the gearbox back and forth between first and second gears. "Shit, shitter or shittiest. Whose got the best 'worst break up story'?"

"Sorry Trisha, I don't think we've got time for this right now. Maybe after 'Ready, Steady, Wank' though yeah?" Neil was tired and famously sarcastic as such. He looked out the window and began to assess the company around us. There was enough to choose from. The road was packed. I projected ahead to the scene of what I hoped would be a worthwhile cause for this congestion. An alien spaceship crash-landed in the central reservation maybe, having taken out seven caravans on its way down. I smiled mischievously, I didn't do traffic jams well.

"I've got one," Adam said. It was the first time he'd spoken in an hour and both Neil and I had assumed he'd piggybacked the painkillers to the land of nod. We turned in our seats to look at him.

"Got one what?" Neil said.

"A shitty break-up story." he said. With the first hints of bruising starting to show, he looked like he really meant it.

"I expect you have mate, but do we really need to hear it? There are no women here you know? We don't need to get in touch with our feelings and start group hugging. There are no Brownie-points to earn you big tart."

"How bad? Shit, shitter or shittiest? There's a forfeit for the loser," I said, trying to overcome adversity. If I couldn't overcome the traffic jam, I was certainly going to get past this.

"Shittiest. For sure. Hands down. Legendary." I felt like pulling over to listen. "Flip back a few years, pre-Fi."

"The dark ages," Neil and I said together, laughing.

"Yeah, yeah, whatever. Anyway I was seeing this girl. Back when I was living down by the coast, in Weymouth. I met her in a bar, swear to god the only time it's ever happened to me. I'd been going to this place for a couple of weeks, trying on a new crowd sort of thing. I'd not long moved down there and was looking for a whole new start. Fresh faces, new experiences, the whole nine yards. I was buying in to it in a big way. The bar was called the 19th Hole, like in golf."

Adam sat forwards in the seat, stretching the seat belt to its furthest point. The gap between the vehicles around us allowed us to sit comfortably in the knowledge that the worst thing that could hit the car now would be a depressed horsefly. "So one night I'm sitting there, killing brain cells like a hobby. The landlord, I think his name was Dave or something, well he says I should maybe go talk to this girl

62

down the end of the bar. Real friendly he says, lovely girl. Apparently she made some comment about me a night or two before but to be honest with you I hadn't really noticed her."

"Amateur." This was Neil's input. I think just to prove he was paying attention, if only in the completely disinterested, slightly bored kind of way that people sometimes choose to do when they overhear a conversation on a train. "Only you could be in a bar full of people and not notice a woman in the corner. I bet you were trying to work out how long it would take to clean the place."

"Two and three quarter hours to do a proper job. And I never said she was stunning or anything. She was just there."

"So what *did* she look like?" I ventured. Details were important in a traffic jam. Details took me to the time and the place and captured the moment better than Kodak. Right now, details were very important.

"She was gorgeous. Show-stopping-jaw-on-the-floor-trouser-stretching stunning."

"Bollocks," Neil again, always a ray of sunshine. "That's horseshit. I'm vetoing this story on the basis that it's a complete fabrication. Not a chance in hell a good-looking bird would have been talking about you. It's just not possible. *Laughing* at you, now that I could believe. Pointing and staring, again very probable. But not talking about you, not in that way. That's beyond artistic licence. That's just, well."

"Bollocks," I concluded. Neil was right. It did sound implausible. This was Adam, god's gift to women he was not. God's gift to plastic surgery, maybe. "Anyway, I thought you said she wasn't stunning?"

"No, you just immediately assumed she *was* stunning. Now, I'm confirming it. But straight up, she was a looker. Honest." The sincerity in his voice was overwhelming, he looked like a kid who'd just told his parents that he'd found a puppy and wanted to keep it. "Which is why I laughed him off. That sort of thing just didn't happen to me. But then I started thinking, new pub, new possibilities. God I was naïve."

"How bad could it be? She wasn't on some sort of a bet or something? Practical joke from a cruel friend, some sort of charity act to cleanse a tainted soul? Am I getting warm?" Neil could be so harsh some times. Funny, but harsh.

"You know I wish you were right, any one of those would have been preferable. I could have lived with being the butt of a joke, I would have gladly gone out with her to help her win a bet, I'd have even tried to take her to heaven and back for a personal confession. But no such luck."

"Yeah, okay…" I was hanging, I could sense there was a plot twist to this story but it seemed it was as close as the end of the traffic jam.

"So you didn't shag her then?" Neil interrupted.

"Neil I think you maybe missing the point here." Then I had a thought, and looked back at Adam. "Adam, please tell me you do have a point."

"Doesn't count if he didn't shag her." Neil folded his arms and turned his head back to the window. I wished now that I'd picked up a Travel Scrabble back at the service station, something to keep the kids happy.

"Neil, shut up." Adam hadn't spoken in an hour, if Neil kept this up we might not hear another word from him until Tuesday.

"I'm just saying." He muttered under his breath.

"So anyway, I bought her a drink."

"Good start Casanova."

"She accepted it."

"Miraculous." I stared at Neil and he pretended to ignore me.

"Then we had another. Her name was Donna."

"How did I know?" snorted Neil, but Adam didn't hear - he had drifted back into the past for a moment, a wistful look of what appeared to be contentment floated across his face. Then it changed to one of bemusement then plummeted back to utter confusion. He reminded me of the way a baby looks when it's filling its nappy on the sly.

"She was nice. She was a paramedic, she had a great sense of humour. I remember she made me laugh so much that first night."

"God I'm trapped in a Barbara Cartland novel. Do you mind if I get out and walk for a bit?" Adam pressed on regardless. Neil lit a cigarette.

"We stayed until last orders. Shared an awkward 'maybe we could do this again sometime, do you want my number?' moment, a peck on the cheek then I went home."

"And knocked one out." I punched Neil in the leg, willing to risk the charge of 'reckless behaviour in a confined space'. "Still doesn't count."

"We met up a couple of nights later and went for a meal. She told me about her job, I lied about mine, trying to make it a little more glamorous sort of thing. She saved lives every day, and what was I doing? I repaired photocopiers. People were looking at us but I could tell my status was improving just by being seen with her. The thing was, we really got on. And it went on like this for a couple of weeks, dinners, drinks, a trip to the movies." I could hear Neil hitting his forehead against the window and couldn't help but be distracted. "I couldn't believe my luck."

"Sounds great Adam." I was trying to be encouraging.

"Yeah. It does. I mean it was. It was really great. I found myself thinking about her while I was at work, trying to think of funny things to say to her, places we could go. She made me want to try harder, at everything. I got a haircut, took a little more time shaving. Just little stuff really, but it made me think that I was falling for her. I guess I was. She really was gorgeous."

"So what happened?" I asked, feeling genuinely curious by this point and trying to do anything to take my mind off the fact that I couldn't feel my right leg anymore. The left was only hanging on because I'd taken to trying to press the clutch down using only one toe at a time. It's not an easy task at the best of times, with desert boots on its damn near impossible.

"Time was flying by, before we knew it we'd been seeing each other for nearly a month."

"Approximately the same amount of time we've been stuck in this traffic jam then?" Adam laughed but I don't think he got the joke.

"Then she said that she wanted to do something for me. A surprise, to celebrate our one month anniversary. I thought it sounded lovely."

"I'm sorry, did you actually just use the word 'lovely'? You thought it would be 'lovely'? God I think I'm going to be sick in a minute."

"Yes Neil," Adam said defiantly. "That's exactly what I said. And at the time it's what I thought. She asked me for my keys so I gave them to her without hesitation."

"She didn't rob you did she?" I asked.

"I wish," Neil and I looked at each other quizzically and waited for him to continue. "I figured she was just going to go around to mine and maybe cook us a romantic meal or something. We hadn't actually, well we hadn't properly, okay we hadn't done it yet. So I figured that was going to be the night." Adam rubbed his chin and I could see the contemplation going in to every word. "The day came around, I'd gone off to work as normal, bit of a spring in my step sort of thing, birds singing blah, blah, blah. The day passed as normal, we text, I told her how much I was looking forward to the evening and she just sort of said the same. I thought nothing of it.

"So I get home around seven, I have to knock on the door because she's got my keys, and I'm standing there on my

66

doorstep with a bunch of flowers and a box of chocolates and then the door opens. And it's not Donna. It's some bird I've never seen before." Neil and I looked back at Adam, eyebrows furrowing relentlessly. "I thought I'd got the wrong house, but she just smiles at me, this huge welcoming smile. Her whole face lights up and she's beckoning me in. Her name's Bev and she's kissing me on the cheek like a long lost friend. And I'm confused. I follow her through the house and there are people everywhere and I'm just looking at them and trying to work out what the fuck is going on. I've never seen any of these people before either. It's like the worst surprise party ever." I'm laughing by this point, I can see it all so clearly and knew it would be Adam's worst nightmare. Don't get me wrong, he's a sociable guy but he's also polite to a fault. The sort of person that would have sat in his own house all night talking to these people just so as not to appear rude.

"I'm looking around the place," he continued. "And I can't see Donna anywhere. She's not in the living room, she's not out in the kitchen, I don't know where the hell she is. So I ask 'Bev'," he said, spitting out her name. "And she says, with a smile, Donna's upstairs. Getting ready. Now I'm a little hacked off by this point. My house is full of strangers, it's our one-month anniversary, I'm horny and my girlfriend has decided to throw a party in my house. Full of people I don't know."

"You've mentioned that," said Neil, and for the first time with a modicum of interest.

"Well it fucking needed saying twice. I march upstairs, pushing passed these tossers on the way up and I want to find out what hell is going on. I storm up to the bedroom door, throw it open and there standing in front of me looking totally amazing, is Donna. In her uniform, looking fit. A few minor modifications I can only assume, or hope, have been added for my benefit. The top buttons are undone, I can see her bra and her cleavage and she's done her hair all nice and she looks awesome. And all of a sudden I'm not mad anymore, can't even remember why I would have been in the first place. She says to me 'happy anniversary baby', steps over to me and pops a couple more buttons on her uniform and I'm going wild. She kisses me, leads me over to the bed and sits down." Neil I can tell has skipped forwards a few steps because he's adjusting his position in the seat, I laugh and try and let Adam catch up.

"We start to fool around a little, she's really taking control, making it clear that this is *my* night. She wraps my tie around my head like a blindfold and then she's taking my clothes off, laughing and kissing me and doing all the usual shit that gets a man going, and then she's going down on me and I don't mind telling you it's fantastic. I'm in heaven, totally forgotten about the fact that my house is full of strangers. Her hands are all over me, it feels like she's got eight of them, I mean this girl had skills. I'm naked and blindfolded and my girlfriend has not only thrown me a party, but she's giving me about the best goddamn welcome home I've ever had. And, AND, she's got porn on the TV. Porn, and I hadn't even noticed."

"She must have been hot for that to happen." Suddenly Neil had engaged. Sometimes it was just about finding a way to connect to your audience.

Ahead of us the traffic had moved on about half a mile and a loud beep told me that perhaps I should go and join it. I found myself irritated by the fact I would have to start driving again.

"Anyway, this whole experience is ranking right up there with the all time best of my life, this is pure fantasy, it's so good in fact that I'm about to pop before we've even got properly started. And then there's a feeling that I can't explain. Not unpleasant as such, just one that takes me totally by surprise. And I don't know whether I like it. I mean I'm really sat on the fence on this one, it's got me thinking when I shouldn't be thinking anything. Got me

68

questioning when I should be just enjoying. But Donna's still down there and I'm asking myself 'do I say anything?' It's like, this is our first time, and she's already exceeded my expectations so god only knows what the actual sex will be like, do I really want to be the that guy?"

"What guy?" Neil said, turned fully in his chair and listening more intently than I have ever seen him listen to anything before in his life.

"*That* guy. The inexperienced guy. I'd been out of the saddle for a while and thought 'maybe I'm just behind on a few tricks. Maybe they do things differently in Weymouth.'"

"It's true, you never want to be that guy," I said. "And besides, he's right. Everyone knows that Weymouth is right up there with Amsterdam when it comes to people being sexually open-minded." The sarcasm hung in the air like smoke so I lit a cigarette to hide it. I looked back at Adam and shook my head. "You're such a plank sometimes, mate."

"Yeah, cheers. Your support is overwhelming," I stuck my fingers up and pulled a face. "So anyway, I'm torn right? What do I do? I really don't want to say anything so I slide my hand up the bed and slip off my tie from over my eyes. And it's horrifying." Adam put his hand over his mouth, I wanted to pull over to give this my full attention but we still had ground to cover and if anything at least this was keeping me awake. "I'm looking down the bed and there's Donna, bobbing up and down only now her uniform has been pulled right down to her knees."

"Got to be honest, can't see your problem so far bud, it's working for me." Neil wasn't lying, this was a subject he had deep-rooted opinions on. The man knew his shit.

"But that's not it. There's someone *else* looking at me, someone besides Donna, some fucking bloke dressed in a squaddy uniform and he's taking Donna, my girlfriend, from behind while she gobbles me off." Neil actually dropped his cigarette at this revelation, started fumbling frantically at his seat patting and grabbing in equal measure. He kept shaking his head as if the words wouldn't fit in his mind. The image was a difficult one to grasp, more than just a threesome, this was like stumbling in on amateur night - at your parents' house.

"So what did you do?" I asked, trying not to get slapped in the face by Neil's flailing hands. He could have a caught a fly in chopsticks with more grace and dexterity.

"I started to hyperventilate, like a full-blown panic attack right there on the bed, but Donna just thinks I'm enjoying it more. The fucking bloke gives me a thumbs-up for fucks sake. I start to thrash about on the bed and only then do I realise that the three of us are not alone and that Donna's got her finger up my arse. There's another couple up going at it up against the wall too - a bloke in a fireman's outfit and a bloody policewoman, and *she's* looking at me too. I swear to god I have never felt as naked and small as I did on that day."

"Whoa, whoa, whoa. She's got her finger up your arse?" I had to ask, I didn't want to, wished I hadn't but I just couldn't stop myself. Sexually I'm as experimental as the next man, and in my case the next man was Neil, so again, not so much the concept that was a problem – just the star of the show.

"You've never done that? You should try it, surprisingly different. Move on - I'm more in to the fact that he's been in an orgy." Ever reliable, Neil. At least he'd managed to pick up his cigarette.

"What do you mean 'move on'? This is Adam. You remember him don't you? Tall bloke, bit reserved, little obsessive, drives like he's got an ASBO?"

"Yeah, Adam, we always said he was anal."

"Ha ha!" We laughed together, it was hard not to. Besides it help me get past the fact that not for the first time in the weekend I felt that the prospect of falling peacefully asleep

70

was never going to be possible again. Nightmares of this would haunt me for years to come.

"So tell me," Neil said, composing himself. "What *is* it about you and Action man?"

"Oh you are so funny." Adam sat back in the seat and folded his arms. "Truly hilarious."

"So what happened next then?" I asked, I felt Adam had earned the right to finish his story. And so far at least, he was right, it was a shittier tale than I had in every sense of the word.

"I kicked her out." He said, and there was a hint of sadness in his voice. "I kicked all of them out. The little bastards were at it everywhere, it was like being surrounded by teenagers. Donna went mental, she said she'd never been so embarrassed in her life. *She'd* never been so embarrassed, get that? She said I showed her up in front of her friends. She even threw stuff at me as she was leaving. Told me I was a small-minded, pathetically frigid little man."

"That's just wrong. It's not like she'd told you about the whole swinging thing is it?" I said.

"Nope."

"Or the fancy dress," I added.

"Oh, it wasn't fancy dress, apparently there's a whole underground society of swinging uniform types." He said it so matter-of-factly that I was expecting him to provide me with the internet address. "More efficient I guess. I mean they've got their own outfits and everything." Good point, but one that only Adam could find.

"Personally I still can't see what your problem was." Adam stared at him from the back of the car, seeming to draw menacingly closer without moving an inch. "Sounds like a damn fine life-experience to me." Sadly part of me wanted to agree.

"Yeah well that's fine, except for the fact that I was falling for her and didn't relish the sight of seeing her with another bloke."

"I'm sorry mate. That must have been tough." I said, and I meant it. I was sensing that the atmosphere in the car had plummeted as much as the temperature outside. It wasn't the direction I was hoping to get the mood going in.

"Well, I'm sorry too," said Neil, and I foolishly thought that he was going to make amends. "Just not for the same reasons." He turned back around to look at Adam. "It doesn't count mate."

"What doesn't count?" I said, checking Adam's reaction in the rear-view mirror.

"The story," he exclaimed.

"What?" Adam yelled with sheer disbelief written all over his face. "How can you say that? After everything I've told you? The lies, the betrayal, the violence and violation? How much shittier could it get?"

"It doesn't count. You never shagged her. Doesn't count." I looked at Neil and we both started laughing. In the background I heard Adams hands drop to his knees in exasperation.

"Forfeit!" we called together in harmony.

"Wankers."

A SHOT IN THE DARK

In Scotland the weather is used as a defence mechanism designed to ward off unwanted attention, mainly from the English. It turns on you faster than a woman with PMT and the thought process that this action is designed to evoke is simple – bugger this for a laugh. But for those that know, for those that dare to push on past the initial crashing thunder that accompanies every mile covered, the rewards are limitless.

Scotland is a truly breathtaking country, full of quaint villages, vibrant cities and countryside so beautiful and humbling you could be forgiven for thinking you were standing in Gods garden. Of course, we didn't see any of this because we were enveloped in a fog so thick you could sweep it away from your face, and we had come to rest in a petrol station forecourt. We had driven four hundred miles to watch a Scotsman scratch his arse whilst eating a Ginsters. In the rain. You just couldn't put a price on moments like that.

The drizzle battled admirably to dampen our spirits but by this point nothing short of a natural disaster would turn us around and Adam wasn't due to get his hair cut for at least four weeks. Refuelled and momentarily refreshed, we stood in expectant anticipation. The terms of the forfeit had been agreed somewhere over the border - Hadrian's Wall having been cunningly side stepped with relative ease – and we had given Adam the money. He knew what he had to do. He had done this before, but probably not for about eighteen years.

"You're a couple of bastards, you really are."

"I think it's only fair, you agreed to the terms of the game, nobody forced you to play. Nobody forced you to bare your innermost embarrassment to us. Or to Donna for that matter." I couldn't resist that one.

"Sorry Adam, but Steve's right. Those are the rules. You owe it to the memory of Donna." Adam looked at us both, knowing that protest was pointless. You could tell he didn't really mind. The look on his face was nothing more than five o'clock shadow on a man that hadn't slept properly in thirty-one hours. Well, that was my interpretation and I was sticking to it. "Still, at least your nose has stopped bleeding."

Adam was shaking his head again. He turned back to look at the parked car, perhaps to check for tow-trucks, perhaps to judge whether he could make it back to the car and lock the doors before we could get there and stop him. You could see the decisions popping like bubbles around his head, the nervous sweat hidden by the rain did nothing to dispel the look of guilt he had plastered all over his face.

The beady-eyed old woman tending the cashier desk eyed him suspiciously through the glass and I feared that she might at any moment call the police to apprehend the least competent fuel thieves in Scotland. I nudged Adam towards the door and as he shuffled obediently forwards we fell into step behind him.

Inside the small but amply stocked shop there were all manor of impulse items on display, the forty-seven piece glove box sized ratchet set with tow rope, the wind-up shower radio with compass, the champagne decanters emblazoned with the logo of a petrochemical company for those particularly romantic occasions.

Neil and I browsed casually amongst the aisles while Adam dawdled alone in front of the magazines, his mental shopping list rolling reluctantly across his mind. We had given him a list of four items to procure with the fuel, three simple, safe and innocent purchases and one catalyst.

74

For men of a certain age there is a rite of passage that all will have experienced, and yet that will never be shared by future generations. Technology truly is the saviour of the meek and they will never know how lucky they are. If they ever did look up to wonder though, they could always ask Adam – or text him at least.

Adam was about to revisit his youth.

Sniggering in the back of the shop like truant schoolchildren we watched Adam as he approached the criminally alert old woman with his items. Of course, had she not been the very reason for our stop we wouldn't have given her a second look. She was perhaps ninety on a good day but despite her thick milk-bottle glasses she had followed him about the shop intently since he walked through the door.

The woman had a hard face and a very gentle shake about her movements that implied she might be unnaturally popular at the local rest home and she inspected Adam in a way that suggested she killed every third Englishman she served and the second had just left. He placed his items on the counter and hung his head low. The giggling was entirely ours.

"Pump number two," Adam said innocently, "please."

"Will you be buying this all together?" The woman bellowed in a startling fashion, gesturing at the items before her.

"Please." He whispered.

"Right, right. Okay, pump number two, that's forty-nine sixteen," she began. The cashier picked up the first item and began to zoom it to and from her field of vision. "One box o' Kleenex."

Adam nodded.

"Woss' this?" The woman exclaimed, waving a small pocket sized tube at Adams face.

"E45."

"E-what you say? I can't make it out."

75

"E45, its a..." Adam searched for a word he hoped to never find, "It's a lotion. Pocket sized."

"Pocket sized? We sell that do we?" She eyed him doubtfully as if he may yet have been trying to rob her.

"You do, yes." He sighed.

She scanned the item through the barcode reader and moved on.

"Fair enough, fair enough. One pocket sized tube o' lotion."

She picked up the third item and furrowed her brow quizzically, flipping it enthusiastically, "Shaven Ravers?" She announced to uproarious laughter. The magazine hid nothing with its plastic wrapper.

Adam nodded and raised his head in apologetic deference. The old woman lowered her glasses an inch and raised a somewhat suggestive eyebrow. To his credit Adam held her gaze. Right up until the moment she winked at him and smiled. I don't know what passes for a come-on in Scotland, but in Andover that'd get you married. She picked up the final item.

"And a Curly-Wurly," she said professionally. "Fifty-eight twelve." Adam began frantically counting out the change.

The journey had been long and arduous, but we had survived. Four hundred miles and we were still on speaking terms. No mean feat considering what we had been through. But our troubles had just begun, we needed food, it was undeniable. They just wouldn't deliver a korma to a field.

We stood outside the supermarket like mountaineers at base camp, arms on hips looking up at the task before us. We were men together, about to enter a shopping facility with a need for groceries and we were trying to mentally prepare. The physical and emotional endurance could well be enough to push us over the edge. Yes, we really were that pathetic, and to be fair, we had been pretty close to breaking point since leaving Carlisle.

"Right then gents," Adam said, "guess we'd better be going in then." I looked at Neil then we followed at a distance, I sensed with a mixed feeling of relief and dread that Adam might be at home here.

The supermarket looked like any other, although from the outside this one appeared to be pocket sized. They are all just a blueprint for hell on Earth, regardless. Dante would have been proud of the careful recreation of the inferno, his vision ad-infinitum. They are passionless places, staffed by Stepford rejects and the decision to make them available twenty-four hours a day was the final indication that Satan is not only alive but doing rather well for himself.

It's not that I'm an advocate of the 'local shop', I am as much a slave to convenience as the next man but every time I enter a supermarket I can't help from thinking that the idea was there but was lost in the overall execution. Sadly though, when one in every eight pounds spent in the UK is spent in one chain of supermarket it makes me realise I should list my business acumen alongside my skill at relationships. I decided to just suck it up.

Adam marched purposefully through the sliding doors, grabbed a basket and headed straight to the nearest employee. I wanted to stop him, realising that these people were suffering enough just having to repetitively stack consumables in a uniform without having to deal with Adam as well but he moved through the thin aisles like an Exocet missile. The employee offered Adam the same level of interest someone would normally reserve for noticing shit on a pavement. If you needed life assurance, a supermarket was not the place to go.

"Mate, do you sell lighter fluid?" The young man sighed in an accent of his own. Evidently customers were a regular disturbance to which courtesy was not the solution.

77

"What?" the man said, returning back to his green plastic stack of produce.

"Lighter fluid?" Adam asked again, politely.

The young man, whom if fortunate enough to be furnished with a name badge would have no doubt been called Colin, stopped again to look at Adam, wondering whether he was persistent enough to just be ignored, or perhaps punched, without getting fired. Could-be-Colin reasoned it was not worth the expenditure of effort either way. He beckoned for Adam to follow and lead us through the shop.

Could-be-Colin paced up the lane to the central aisle of the store moving purposefully through the herds of grazing cattle milling about his path. Adam meanwhile had become distracted by every single item that they passed. Sleep deprivation, it became apparent, was a dangerous thing with Adam.

To give credit where none is due, Could-be-Colin dutifully slowed at each of Adam's distractions and often turned to guide him back to the original destination. Neil and I felt like undercover shop security guards following them, hanging back in pursuit of a potential flasher. Neil and I would break off every now and then to fill the baskets we too had grabbed at the entrance but would always return just in time to see Adam make a turn. The shop felt endless.

When there was nowhere else to go Could-be-Colin gestured vaguely to the shelves around them and Neil grabbed what could only be described as a family-sized bottle of lighter fluid. Of course, it would be a family I held no desire to meet but given the size of the bottle it could be safely assumed that the alley would be far from dark. Adam smiled at our assistant gratefully.

"Now we just need bread," Adam said clapping his hands together gleefully. Could-be-Colin was closing his eyes for a moment longer than it takes to blink and I knew he was counting to five each time. "Just that Tesco value stuff will do buddy."

"We don't sell Tesco Value bread here." The assistant replied dejectedly.

"You don't sell it here?" Adam asked incredulously.

"No, Sir. We don't." One, two, three, four, five.

"Why not?"

"Because this is The Co-Op Sir. We sell our own bread here."

"Oh."

"Indeed."

With dignity, Adam smiled. "Fair play," He said before wandering off.

Who said sleep was essential?

Two hours can take you a fair distance in most places. But the belief that distances are a regulated commodity is a myth. For example, in the country a mile is an undefined distance between where you are and anywhere else you need to be. It's like that in Scotland, just worse. Of course it is largely dependent on your mode of transport. Two hours on Concorde would take you fairly close to a whole other continent, even on a horse two hours would probably take you a reasonable distance, whereas two hours travelling in something less powerful than a horse - like our car - will not. In Scotland, two hours from a foggy supermarket car park in Larkhall takes you from somewhere to nowhere. Specifically, to a place called Aberfeldy.

This was our first taste of Scotland. And apparently, it was closed. During our journey we had mustered up the idea that we would try and camp close to rivers or lochs. It was a good plan and it made sense, it was logical. It would be likely that we could find some flat ground and we'd have somewhere to wash in the morning. It was Adam's idea.

The map showed Aberfeldy as a lightly populated area that had laid foundations on either side of the water without burying it in commercialism.   To be fair, Scotland is a country two-thirds the size of England with a population the same as Greater London, commercialism is not their biggest problem. But for our first endeavour at camping in the wild, it seemed perfect. And by this point we were very, very tired.

We drove around criss-crossing back and forth over the river in search of somewhere that looked spacious enough to pitch up a tent. It doesn't sound difficult, but the Scots aren't too keen on living close to each other so every time we came across a suitable patch of land we would find a house buried at the end. The only thing we had to keep us smiling by this point was the fact that we had long passed the rain and found the last of the summer sun. Well, that and 'Shaven Ravers'.

Eventually we found the entrance to a large luscious empty field. And I was going to be sleeping there no matter what. The second idea that we had agreed on was that wherever possible, we would always ask permission from the owner to sleep on whatever land we came across.   Yes, that was Adam's idea too. Neil and I got out and looked around at our surroundings. We were pleased. Still tired, but pleased.

All we had to go on was a gravel track leading up a mountain opposite the entrance to the field. And judging by the gradient of the track and our luck to date, there could be no other alternative than to assume the owner lived at the top. We got back in the car, turned it around and eased it up the slope. Adam lay sleeping on the back seat. Two feet up the track and he was awake. The jumpers and coats subsided and a figure emerged in the rear-view mirror, yawning, scratching and looking beaten up and bewildered. I turned to see consciousness reluctantly crawl over Adam's face and tried to stop every loose item in the front of the car from dropping back through the seats and smacking him in the head. This wasn't a hill we were climbing, it was Ben Nevis' second cousin twice removed.

I leant forwards trying to add some weight as a counterbalance to the urge the car was having to simply roll arse-over-tit back down the hill. Whoever lived at the top of this hill must have either had very good friends or no friends at all. I prayed for the former.

The car levelled out and over the final rise we were able to see what looked to be a courtyard. We swung round on a fresh gravel driveway and disembarked. I sensed a decision was quietly being made amongst us, but with typical leadership tendencies Neil approached the front door first and we shuffled up behind him like the lagging Stooges. He tapped hard but with as much politeness as a person can imply when they've just turned up uninvited from over four hundred miles away.

We waited. Then waited some more until finally we heard the fast approaching scramble of a dog. The sound grew in intensity and with a very definite sense of malice. Adam and I took a step backwards, because that would help. I pictured a rare and unusual breed of highland dog standing eight feet tall with teeth to match charging the door with destruction on its mind. Evidently this was a misconception shared by the dog too.

As we stood nervously together hating the growing sound of an animal fast approaching we closed our eyes as if the option to simply return to the safety of our vehicle did not exist. And then the door shook with the impact of what could only be an animal connecting with an unmoveable object, head first. We jumped back and we shook a little, the door however did not. Dust sprinkled from the rafters of the porch above and then an old man opened the door laughing.

"Every day he does that," the man said pointing to his dog lying inert on the hallway floor. "Don't worry lads, we put a pillow on the back of the door after the fifth or sixth time. Doubt he ever had the sense he was born with anyway.

So," he said staring at us each in turn, "What are you selling?"

"Nothing, nothing at all Sir," Replied Neil laughing very much like a Bible salesman. "Actually we drove up here to ask whether you knew who owned the land down below," Neil pointed in the vague direction of the field and Adam and I stood back to allow for the unobstructed view of the man's driveway. "Specifically the field at the bottom opposite the entrance to the driveway."

"It's not for sale."

"Sorry?"

"The field. I said it's not for sale." Neil laughed again and we joined in trying to be supportive. We weren't very good at it as it turned out.

"No, no Sir, we don't wish to buy the field, we were merely wondering who if anyone owned it so that we might ask permission to stay in it for the night." Adam and I nodded, confirming any last lingering doubts that we were in fact morons.

"What would you be wanting to stay in the field for? There's nothing in it, in the way of amenities. We've got a B&B down the road there some."

"Well we've come up here to do some camping, and it seemed like an ideal place to, well, camp. It's right by a river and the ground is nice and flat. That's about all we're looking for in the way of amenities."

"Ah, I see. You're simple folk then are you?" Adam furrowed his brow and was about to step in to contest but I restrained him with a hand on the back of his shirt. "Fair enough. You can use the field. Just sitting there anyway. I won't ask for any money or anything given the lack of what normal folk would call amenities, but don't be leaving a mess down there, will you?"

"No Sir," Neil and I replied together.

"And stop calling me Sir, Stevens is the name."

"Yes Sir." Shit.

We turned back to the car, thanking the man again for his hospitality, and started the engine. As we turned in the driveway Mr Stevens came trotting out along side us. Neil buzzed the window down and leaned out. "Just one more thing lads, 'fore I forget. We'll be doing some shooting down in the field next along later on tonight. Don't be alarmed or anything. Just rabbits. Thought I better let you know." We nodded slowly and Neil buzzed the window back up again.

"Sorted then," he said, smiling, and drove on towards the summit.

"Oh yeah, marvellous. Just what we need when we haven't slept for thirty six hours," said Adam, arms folded defensively.

"Exactly, you really gonna care when you get your head down tonight? The main thing is we've got a place to bed down, food in and a little summer sunshine. Told you this would work out."

"You fucking, fucking liar!" Neil carefully eased his head to the opposite side in order to see Adam. Our movement was somewhat restricted by the under carriage of the Zafira.

"What?" Neil said, and I could feel he genuinely meant it.

"What do you mean fucking 'what'? This, Mr 'Told You This Would Work Out'! Getting shot at is not in my definition of things all working out!"

"You can be so sarcastic sometimes, you know that? It's not their fault, I mean they did tell us they'd be hunting tonight."

"Yes, yes they did. They said they'd be hunting *rabbits*, in the next fucking field over from this one!" A pellet whizzed past the car and embedded itself into a tree we had parked next to for extra cover from the wind. "You are absolutely right, it's not their fault. It's your fault you spanner."

"Boys, boys," I intervened, "We're all in this together. They can't keep at this for much longer - they've been at it

for an hour already. Let's just keep calm and wait it out."
We all looked forward and through the darkness could see
the beams from flashlights waving about in the field over
from ours.

"Why are they even shooting over here?" Adam asked,
"there's nothing *over* here."

I eased myself an inch past Neil to see the top of Adam's
head. "I don't think they're aiming for us Adam, I think it's
just random shots that are coming over."

"What are you, an American? There's a fucking hole in the
side of my tent. Random my arse, have they never seen a
rabbit? How big exactly do they think they are?"

"Adam, our tents are dark green. A similar colour in fact
to the field. And for that matter every other thing out here
tonight. Even the sodding car looks like part of the scenery.
It's black outside. No street lights, no local glow from a
nearby town, just darkness. Face it boys, we're in the
country." We looked back out from under the car as the
sounds of shotguns and rifles filled the silence like a
nightmare.

"And another thing," Adam continued. "Why are we
hiding *under* the car?"

"Do you want to stand up then Thumper?" I replied. Neil
turned to look at me and then a small puff of soil flew up
into our faces as a bullet thudded into the grass inches away
from us.

"You know sometimes he makes a good point," said Neil,
"Crawl backwards lads, we'll get in the other side." We
inched our way backwards, three grown men trying to
squeeze between the tyres like confused commandos. We
found ourselves hunched on our knees and pressed with our
backs up against the doors.

"Right then, who's got the keys?" said Neil.

"You have, surely?" Adam said.

"Why 'surely'?"

84

"Cos' you were driving the last." I said, "It's not that much of an assumption."

"Well I haven't got them. I gave them to you." It was a vague statement void of direction that Adam immediately took offence too.

"You fucking liar!" Adam said.

"Would you stop calling me a fucking liar. I don't have the keys!"

"So who's got them then?" Adam yelled.

"Is it even locked?" I ventured.

"Of course it's locked." Said Adam.

"Why?" Neil and I asked, "who's going to nick anything out here?"

"Is that really the issue here?" Adam said.

"Well if you know it's locked, then you must have locked it." Adam stood up to protest then patted his pockets and found the keys. "Ah."

"Ha!" We said both standing up. Adam pressed the central locking button and the indicator lights flashed as the car unlocked. We looked smug, which is difficult in the dark, and then a small window towards the back of the car exploded glass all over the ground. We dived to the floor.

"*That's* why we're not in the car." Said Neil.

Sunday

A VERY SCOTTISH COTTAGE

I wanted music. Something classical, something serene, something befitting to a beautiful Scottish morning first experienced through the slither of an opened zip on a tent. Neil however wanted toilet roll, and badly.

At first I was watching the shimmer of water cascading across a rocky riverbed, the crisp, bright morning sun blazing a trail across the surface. I was enjoying the moment, enjoying the clean air, feeling at one with nature. I was naked in my sleeping bag, arm outstretched through the door of the tent, gently playing with the grass running through my fingers. I could feel the last of the dew evaporating as I lay there - it was a perfect moment.

I felt happy, my day felt full of possibilities, in fact I was so content I was almost turning into somebody I would normally try to avoid meeting in a room. Nothing could ruin this moment of tranquil bliss, nothing except the sight of a half-naked man hopping through the grass in a pair of tidy-white underpants clutching his arse and sweating. Thank God for Neil.

"You alright mate?" I asked sleepily. I pulled on a pair of tracksuit bottoms, got out of the tent and stretched. The morning sun on my back felt incredible and I remembered for the briefest of seconds why I hated working in an office. I figured that at that precise moment Neil was remembering exactly why he *loved* working in an office. He stopped hopping and looked at me.

"I need a crap alright? I really, really need a crap."

"So go then, what's stopping you?"

"Adam is stopping me. He won't give me the car keys to get the bog roll. I think he's punishing me for last night but

I really don't think he's grasping the magnitude of the situation quite literally *at hand* here. Bob's coming and I think he's got a friend." I wanted to ask who 'Bob' was, but this really didn't seem like the time.

"So where's Adam then?"

"Where do you think? He's sat by the car, I think he's in a fucking trance or something."

"Why - Forget it, I'll sort it, go squat and I'll bring some over." Neil didn't need telling twice. Bob was obviously hosting a soiree. I strolled over towards the car and found Adam sat in apparent worship, from the side he bore a striking resemblance to Buddha. "Morning bud. Alright?"

"They shot the car."

"Yeah I remember. Funny huh?"

"They shot the car. Look." He pointed - I obliged. "There are tiny holes down the side of it. I can see in to the interior."

"Bummer. Mind if I smoke?" I asked, I didn't want to aggravate the situation. He waved his hand with disinterest and I lit up and dropped to the floor next to him. He needed support, I was awake enough to know that much. Seemed everyone needed *something* today. "Any other damage? All the tyres still intact?" I was only mildly interested to be honest, at eight a.m. on a Sunday morning it takes a lot to spark real enthusiasm.

"Look." He said again, pointing this time with both hands to emphasise his utter disbelief.

"Yes Adam. They shot the car. They shot your tent as well." It was true. They had.

"Bastards."

"Bastards," I agreed.

"Why isn't Neil here to see this?"

"He said he was here. He said you wouldn't give him any bog roll because you're punishing him. And he said 'Bob's coming'."

"Who's Bob?"

88

"No idea."

"Oh."

"Hmm. So can I have some then?"

"What?"

"Bog roll, reckon he'll be about done soon."

"Yeah it's in the boot. It was loose on top of the stuff."

"Well are you gonna unlock the car then?" I stood up and walked to the back of the vehicle. I patted the top of it. Everybody needed something today.

"It is unlocked. Who's gonna nick anything out here?" I laughed, grabbed the supplies and wandered back towards the camp. Somewhere, Bob had arrived.

"I never want to eat another sausage again," Neil said emerging from behind the tree.

"That's disgusting, Neil. Really, let me be first to say it." Neil looked at me sarcastically, "so you don't want breakfast then?"

"No. I'm good thanks. For the moment at least." He patted his stomach and walked over to Adams tent. He briefly inspected the damage before Adam joined him and then Adam began deconstructing it. It took seconds, which either meant he'd done this a few times before or that he had no idea what he was doing and it would never fit back in to the carrying bag. Time would tell. Neil and I were not fairing as well.

"All things considered. That was a pretty good night." Neil said, stepping over multiple folds of his tent. He moved about the ground, gathering in sheets and guide ropes from every corner. I was working on the poles of mine. I only stopped to consider the statement.

"We parked up, spent three hours sorting our tents out, flared up a barbecue and cooked a bag of forty sausages."

"Yeah. It was great wasn't it?"

"We hardly spoke." I said, forcing the poles into a bag at hand. "Then we all fell asleep. Within minutes of finishing the food."

"And then we got shot at." Adam yelled. I pointed a pole bag at him in agreement.

"And then we got shot at. Not exactly ticking all of the boxes for a great night Neil."

"But we camped. Out here. We ate in the open. We gazed at the stars."

"You went for a crap." I added.

"Exactly. Outside! Isn't it great?"

"Terrific mate. Blinding." Adam finished folding his tent up and slid it expertly into the carrier. He walked over to join us, a supervisory stance falling in as he stood to inspect our folding. He laughed, which about said everything and then walked off towards the car. "So what's the plan for the day then?" I asked, ignoring him.

"Dunno, what do you fancy Adam?" Said Neil, calling over towards the Zafira. A faceless voice bellowed back.

"Well, we've got the fishing gear in the car. Fancy that?"

"Umm…" That was all I had. Images were flooding into my brain so fast I was going to have to put my fingers into my ears.

"Sorted then." Neil said, there really wasn't any point in pursuing my immediate line of thought. "So, we get packed up here, hit the road and find a Little Chef and then, and then I say we do a spot of fishing." The floodgates broke.

"Excellent. We've had such a roaring success so far. Why not? I mean what could go wrong? Did you ever see Jaws?"

"Shut up."

"Deer Hunter?"

"Knob off."

"Deliverance?"

"Yeah what-the-fuck-ever Steve, it's fishing. Let's get this stuff in the car and get on the road. Where's Adam gone now?" I had no idea.

We lifted up the remaining gear and headed over to the boot of the car. The vehicle was shaking curiously and I feared for a moment that it was about to subside into the ground. Neil and I peered around each side of the Zafira and spontaneously dropped our bags. Adam was leaning over the bonnet wearing Marigolds and furiously scrubbing the windscreen. We walked towards him tentatively as if he were a wild and previously unseen animal foraging through our bins. Perhaps even with the same amount of fear one would expect at such an occasion too.

"Step away from the car Adam, put down the sponge, man." Adam looked up at us from his reverie. This was evidently normal behaviour. I wanted to put the moment into perspective for him, give it some relevance in everyday life. After all, we were in a field, somewhere across the border of Scotland. We had camped out, eaten meat with a side of more meat and cooked beans straight in the tin. We had slept in tents, shat in the woods and not washed our hands. We were being men. This was most definitely not normal behaviour. "They shot the car Adam, I don't think cleaning the windscreen is going to improve the overall status of the vehicle."

"But it was filthy."

"Who cares? I don't care. Neil, do you care?"

"Nope."

"See Adam, even Neil doesn't care. And he's driving. Just step away man, we're on holiday. No chicks remember?"

"Doesn't mean we have to live in filth."

"Yes it does. That's the point. We're doing things we don't get to do at home. This is why we came away. To be pigs. To eat meat with no veg and talk about porn, to drink beer straight out of the can and not worry about where we put it down and if it will leave a mark. We have to purge

91

ourselves, get it out of our system so that we can each live in normal society again for another year. This is cathartic. It's a healing process for repressed souls. We are men, we belch, we fart and then we laugh."

"Amen." Neil belched for effect. I could have hugged him.

"I was only cleaning the bugs off the windscreen."

"Well stop it. It's freaking me out. It's like camping with my mother."

"Now we're talking."

"Stop it Neil. You're a sick man and you need help. Now can we get going please? I badly need a coffee."

"Adam has to belch first. The man was caught wearing Marigolds in a field. Small animals are laughing at him. I'm not letting him in the car until he redeems himself."

"He's got a point Adam. I'm sorry – but you need to reclaim your manhood." I said.

"Jesus you make it sound like someone ran off with my cock."

"I think they probably have. Now belch so we can get in the car." He squeaked. Crickets stopped chirping in embarrassment. "That'll have to do."

"That was shite." Neil could be so succinct.

We drove in a northerly direction for another hour. We searched for a road that at least looked to aspire to the status of being a main road that might at some point give way to civilisation. I would have been happy just to find a burger van at that point but a plan was a plan. We had agreed on a Little Chef. Who was I to argue?

By eleven a.m. we saw it. A desolate place designed to attract nobody but those well and truly lost. The sign was like a beacon of hope. It really is difficult to describe how badly we needed caffeine. We pulled in to the car park and stretched again. We'd only been driving for two hours but evidently our bodies were still holding a grudge. I wasn't sure how to break the news to mine that there was another week of this still to come. I pressed on regardless.

Inside was the familiar photocopied layout of every Little Chef I'd ever been in, complete with a "Wait Here To Be Ignored" sign. The place was empty, but rules are rules. We waited patiently, tapped on the counter, did the British thing of coughing for attention but apparently you'd have to be Bronchial to get served in that place. Neil reached in to the lolly pot and out of nowhere a small plump woman appeared with a face on her that could fry an egg.

"Table for three?" she scowled. Neil looked around at us and counted but sarcasm hadn't reached the Highlands so the woman just snatched some menus and walked off towards the tables.

"Smoking if you've got 'em please." Neil said trying to keep up. The restaurant was tiny and the waitress could get lost in a long carpet but she had the take on us. She turned, grilled us all with another look and then bolted towards a window seat at the furthest point from the kitchen area. We followed dutifully and made a point to be extra nice from now on. Nobody likes hair in there brunch.

We sat around the table and each grabbed a menu. I managed to advance order a large pot of coffee before the waitress returned to the dimension she had appeared from. I started eyeing up the 'Olympic Breakfast', a working digestive system was for wimps. Neil lit two cigarettes, passed one over and Adam gazed out the window.

"Not hungry mate?" said Neil, "You should eat when you can. Our meals are somewhat limited of an evening. Adam, you listening?"

"I don't believe it!" Adam stated, "The cheeky bastard." Neil and I looked at each other, lost.

"What?" We said together.

"There, look." He was gesticulating wildly over the sauces. "It's that bloody tow-truck."

"Where? What 'bloody tow-truck'?" I said.

93

"What do you mean, 'what bloody tow-truck'? *The* bloody tow-truck. It's driving past, look!" We looked, saw nothing. This was a sensitive subject, we had to be sincere.

"So, breakfast then," said Neil.

Adam huffed, he was half-standing and leaning with his head against the glass. Neil and I looked over the menus again and left him there for a full half-minute.

"I'm having the omelette. Maybe some toast." So he was listening.

"Sorted, 'Olympic' Steve?"

"Oh yes." The waitress materialised with our coffee, finished pouring and had left before we'd even had a chance to form a smile. "She's... efficient."

"This is the life boys." Said Neil, tapping the table jovially. "Breakfast, coffee and an open road ahead."

"So no idea where we're going then?" said Adam, adding his milk and sugar.

"We're going fishing, like you suggested. Someplace quiet. Some place where we can pitch up a tent-."

"And not get shot at." I added for Adam's benefit.

"And not get shot at. Some place peaceful. I mean look at it," he pointed through the window, Adam and I tried to stare beyond the car park to the 'it' that Neil was referring to. "It's just amazing. I love it up here and we've barely scratched the surface. It's like being in a Western or something. I feel like I want to rustle cattle or something."

"Yeah I'm fairly certain that's illegal, but it would be worth it to see you do it in a Zafira." I said, immersing myself in the coffee.

"Or whittle." Neil continued, ignoring me completely. He was gazing. He could do that sometimes.

"Whittle?" Adam asked.

"Yeah, whittle." Neil did a little rattle of his head as he said it. It was a little disturbing. "You know, carve shit. Little horses and people and stuff. I want to create something."

"I'm sleeping in your tent tonight Adam. I'm just getting that in now okay? Safety in numbers." Adam laughed and looked back at Neil. He was smiling whimsically now. And the waitress had appeared again. I ordered the food and she was gone in a puff of smoke, but that was probably just from the cigarettes.

"So you want to carve little people and fish then? Don't tell me, we'll eat what we catch too?" Neil turned his head and his face illuminated. "That was a joke."

"Yeah I know." The light dimmed. Adam got up and went to wash his hands. You can take the man out of the town, but his mother goes everywhere. I sat back in the chair, felt the plastic burrow in to my skin, I yawned and then caught myself smiling. I was obviously relaxed and it felt good.

"Thank you for this." I said, patting Neil on the shoulder. "I mean it, it's really great."

"Thanks for coming. Wouldn't have been the same without you." Adam re-appeared and had acquired a waitress who more importantly had acquired our food. Silence fell over the table again, as much in anticipation of the feast as out of due respect for a quite terrifying woman who obviously didn't rely on tips to make ends meet.

"That toilet is huge." Said Adam with a mouth full of omelette.

"Are you sure it's just not relative to the size of you knob?" Neil said, staring worryingly at a sausage.

"Oh ha ha. I was just thinking that after the grub I might go for a wash. Got to wash where you can out here." Adam winked at Neil. "Seeing as I noticed nobody rushed down to the river this morning."

"Damn right I didn't." I said. "The sun might have been out but it would have been bloody freezing down there." I had been hoping that this wouldn't have been brought up just yet. I was still adjusting to life in the wild and I hadn't fully acclimatised to it yet. Cold water had never had a great

95

affect on me and I didn't have much to start with. I wasn't about to risk it on the first morning. "Anyway, you can talk."

"I know, that's my point. I'm not stupid either. I'll wait until I'm drunk or something."

"Oh yeah, that'll work," said Neil laughing. He chased his bean juice around the plate with a slice of white bread so thin it was transparent. "Don't think I'm jumping in to save your arse."

The thing was, we all did need a wash, it was undeniable. We were testing the outer limits of deodorant, beyond any normal lab experiment or endurance examination. We were quite literally field-testing it. It would have explained why our waitress didn't hang about too long. And why the enamel was peeling off the plates.

I know we were on holiday, but when you can't stand your own smell, you know there are issues to be dealt with. But we hadn't actually done anything to deserve it. Aside from the long-haul journey that while uncomfortable and physically draining was not strenuous in the usual sweaty sense, we hadn't really done anything at all. Yes we were unfit, yes it had taken a comical amount of time to erect three tents and a ready-made barbecue but that was no reason to explain our condition. We had created an altogether new aroma, a combined scent so pungent that woodland creatures were stepping forth with petitions for us to move on. Adam once again was right - we needed a wash. The problem was going to be how to go about it without creating an amateur gay-porn film.

"Brilliant." Neil said, stepping out of the massive cubicle. "God I love toilets."

"There's not a part of that statement I want you to take into more detail," said Adam who was washing his hands again. Evidently it was an integral part of his daily routine. I stood by the door surveying the situation. The amenities, while few, amply exceeded anything we had been privileged to so far on the trip. I thought back to the motorway service station showers fondly, wishing I had had the forethought to use them while available. The alternative was going to be complicated to say the least.

"What? It's the modern man's throne. His place to be at one with himself. A chance to think, a chance to read, you know I even rigged up the arrangement of my living room once so that I could still watch telly while on the pan."

"You're a great loss to interior design Neil," I said rubbing my chin. "So remind me again why we're all in the disabled toilets?"

"Actually that's my fault." Said Adam turning to dry his hands on the worlds' least absorbent paper towels. "I found it earlier. And there's a combination of factors involved."

"Of course there are." I said, patiently.

"The first is that by definition, everything is bigger."

"Surely by design too." Adam wasn't really listening.

"There's more floor space, bigger basins, more room in the toilet cubicle."

"All true," said Neil agreeably.

"And the other reason we're here," a pause for dramatic effect, "Is because the gents toilet is closed."

"Of course."

"Suck it up Steve." Neil jostled past me and admired himself in the mirror, the only feature that wasn't super-sized.

"Neil, never say that to me in a toilet again okay? My point was also to ask why we're all in the disabled toilets *together*? Isn't that a little strange?"

"What's the matter Steve, you shy?" I shot Adam a look, he still wasn't paying attention.

"Besides," said Neil, "it's cosy."

"No Neil, it's gay."

"Don't be so homophobic Steve, we're camping together, sharing the car, living in each other's pockets. It's a bonding

97

experience." Adam was really getting in to this trip now, and the change was both astonishing and, if this was an indication of the direction he was going, terrifying.

"No," I persisted, "it's cottaging."

"Only if you fancy me," said Neil. I laughed and walked in the toilet. I closed the door and got comfortable.

I wasn't really shy, I had once lost a game of strip poker playing against Neil and Jane and Adam and Fiona. My losing streak was legendary to the point that I was convinced the game was fixed. Nobody could be that unlucky in love *and* that bad at cards, but I was assured all was well. I was a little surprised at how stringently they all stuck to the rules, especially the extent to which I was made to strip, but it's astounding what a bottle of Vodka will make a man do.

Outside of the cubicle laughter was ensuing, laughter and the peculiar sound of a man struggling with the dynamics of a large wash basin against the inflexibility of his body, or at least his mind. I finished up and pulled off my shirt, opened the cubicle door and stepped through just as Neil straddled the washbasin and Adam flat palm slapped him across the back. He almost jumped through the window. I couldn't help but laugh. The sight of Neil eagle-squatting over the basin with his jeans around his ankles was enough on it's own, but with Adam's perfect handprint emblazoned across his back he was about the funniest sight I'd seen in a month.

"I thought these basins were supposed to be higher up, for people in wheel chairs and stuff," said Neil, hopping about either from the pain of the slap or the frustration of being made to feel inadequate by Armitage Shanks.

"No you berk they're lower so a wheel chair can get next to them. Now get out of the way so I can wash my hands."

"Don't you start, you're as bad as Adam. I'm practically starkers here mate."

"Well just shuffle out the way for a second or something." He shuffled and I stepped up.

"See it's alright for you, you lanky streak of piss. You can bend."

"I'm only washing my hands."

"Well hurry up." Adam pulled off his shirt and suddenly there was a pile of clothes on the floor. He stood there in his pants behind me. I stepped out of the way and stood in the corner. Despite the luxurious size of the room I suddenly found myself with nowhere to look. Adam brazenly washed himself clean, taking the trouble to fully lather up with a rather feminine smelling hand soap and then started washing from head to toe. I turned at completely the wrong moment.

"Jesus Adam, it's a quick wash mate not a bloody Roman bath." He turned his head to look at me sarcastically, "and don't bloody stop now either. Hurry up!" Neil pushed past him while Adam dripped all over the floor and he returned to the paper towel dispenser. There were three towels left.

"Don't get too wet boys, we've hit a shortage."

"Oh fan-bloody-tastic. It's a bit late now I'm soaked." Neil glistened with moisture.

"Well you're just have to improvise."

"Oh yeah, the world is just full of possibilities." He said, I looked around the room for him.

"Well there's a hand dryer?" I said, pointing, carefully.

Adam started patting himself down but seemed to just achieve the movement of water from one part of his body to another. He wasn't so much drying himself as channelling. Neil dropped down to his knees and hit the button. The hand dryer hummed into existence but the output was pathetic to say the least. He would have had a better chance of drying himself by standing next to an asthmatic pensioner.

I stood up to the now vacant basin and ran the water. It was cold, which is about the only thing nobody had mentioned so far throughout. I splashed some water over myself and dropped my jeans, started at the top with my

99

arms and armpits and worked down. I got to my mid-section and quickly whipped down my boxers in fear of an Adam-slap on my arse. I turned my head to check while straddling the sink.

"Well, this is the closest I've come to a blow-job for awhile," said Neil, angling his frame against the wall. Despite our situation, we had to laugh. And then we noticed the door had opened and our waitress was standing there, listening.

It was not a sight easy to describe. It was not a sight our waitress would likely forget, ever. It was soft gay porn with Ron Jeremy's three amigos. It was the biggest abuse of a Little Chef's facilities that had likely ever happened north of the border. Our waitress, whose name was Edna according to the name badge that stood proud on her chest and was the only thing I dared look at in this situation, just smiled at us.

"It's not what you think," said Adam, closest to the door.

"It bloody well is," said Neil still crouched under the hand dryer. "We're washing. What the hell do you want her to think?" Edna smiled some more. She was enjoying this. I wanted her to shout, to throw us out, to do anything other than smile. This story was going to be immortal amongst waitresses - Edna was going to be famous. I stepped in but unfortunately turned around to speak.

"Edna, is it? Edna, please excuse us-."

"Steve." I pressed on.

"We camped out last night, and well we really just needed to freshen up -"

"Steve."

"And I know that it's wrong to abuse the facilities like this but there was nobody else around in the restaurant so we thought now would be a good time because we wouldn't risk-."

"Steve!" Neil and Adam both yelled.

"What?"

"Your fella's out." Excellent, I was going to get done for indecent exposure now as well.

"Risk what?" Edna said. I could sense we were really building rapport.

"Exposing ourselves," I said, and then ran into the toilet cubicle.

"Get dressed, get up and get on out here boys would you?" Edna smiled again, and winked at Adam. We had a fan.

A few silent minutes later we joined her in the restaurant area. She shook her head still smiling. Clearly Edna had warmed to us, so much in fact that she had laid on some fresh coffee for us, and brought us each a lolly. It was a special moment.

We sat back down and asked her to join us, there was nobody else tending the waiting area and indeed no one else to tend, and she seemed grateful for the company. She asked us about our lives, the purpose of our trip and then our onward destination. We had to confess ignorance from that point on.

"So what you after then?" Edna said, sipping at a coffee we had brought for her.

"Well Adam here has suggested some fishing, but someplace quiet if possible."

"And you're not looking for camping sites and the like?"

"No, it's really not that kind of trip."

"Well that much was obvious in the toilets." Edna winked at me now. Suddenly I wanted to leave. "You want to go up the road some then. There's a spot, it's not easy to find, but it's still there. About an hour's drive away from here north. My husband and I found it one afternoon on a special trip of our own. Going back some years now of course." She sipped from her cup again and Neil and I lit a cigarette. Adam listened intently enough for all of us. "It's like an unused picnic area. Such a shame, it's a beautiful spot. Carry on out from here and the road will start to climb some. It'll get woody, and a bit twisty, the road will

101

bend round a loch. Just before the start of the loop that takes you full around the other side of it, there's a dirt track. It's not sign-posted, it's at a parallel to the road your on and it drops steeply down to the water side. But at the bottom, it's perfect for you. There's a large grass area, some tables and best of all, good cover from the road. Nobody goes there, nobody will see you."

"Sounds perfect. Any fish?" said Neil.

Edna laughed, "You'll have to tell me tomorrow," she said. "But there should be."

"One last thing. Any shops around here?" said Adam.

"Take a right at the crossroads and follow for half a mile. We've all got to eat you know." And with that, we paid and said our goodbyes.

We found the shop and stocked up again. Beer and whisky, enough meat for a week and some more adventurous tinned goods. Now it was time to fish.

MUCKING FAGGOTS

A sound roared through the mountains. It was not a natural sound, a sound that you would expect to hear had you been rambling in the woodlands. It aspired to be melodic, but failed. It dreamed of being harmonious, but was found wanting. It was, without a doubt, the worst rendition of Bohemian Rhapsody since Wayne and Garth stated they'd had an idea about a song.

It was fair to say we were in high spirits. We had eaten, washed and been outed in a Little Chef. We had shopped, re-stocked and obtained a destination. We had music, we had sunshine and we hadn't noticed the smell. This was what our holiday was about. The road wound gracefully through the hills of Scotland and for a moment we weren't driving a Zafira at all, we were in a convertible Mustang with the wind in our hair, living a dream of a different life.

The view was spectacular, the scenery truly humbling. We were peeling away the layers of a country largely uninhabited and feeling our way along towards happiness. We were children discovering a lost world, a secret garden to which only we had the key. This was fast becoming my favourite Sunday of all time.

The turning we were searching for was indeed well hidden. So well hidden that we drove past it completely. We blamed Adam for speeding, or for sleeping behind the wheel, but the truth was we were all having too much fun to be worrying about stopping. We attempted a three-point turn just short of a blind corner that in retrospect was the closest any of us had come to trying to commit suicide and then crawled back towards the dirt track. Thankfully, the roads were quiet. In fact they were so quiet I wondered whether the road we were on was actually closed. We hadn't seen another car since leaving the restaurant and even the shop that we had stopped at seemed to have dust on the parking spaces. But on the plus side that fact had no doubt saved our lives at the blind corner, and was now re-assuring us as we pulled over to the side and got out to inspect the turning.

We stood around the car and completed the obligatory stretches. The sun blazed across the blue sky and we shielded our eyes as we moved towards the trees. Adam was the first to step on to the track and we realised that his short detour had saved us the trouble of having to complete a terrifying hairpin turning on to a track that appeared to be slightly less than a car width across. We tested the ground and were relieved to see that it didn't subside beneath our feet. It held firm under our weight but it was difficult to be sure if the same could be said about the car. It looked untrustworthy, for soil. But the truth was, this was our spot. We had been told that glorious sights lay at the bottom, and there was no way we were going to be leaving the car by the side of the road all night.

We shrugged the now familiar "what the hell – it's a hire car" shrug and headed back. If we could survive Mr Stevens' driveway, we could survive this. It was an adventure, and adversity just added to the glory and satisfaction.

"Ready then?" said Adam who was clearly feeling concerned. He wanted reassurance, it was understandable - he knew what we were like. It had to be a joint effort or we'd just rib him about it for the rest of the holiday.

"Ready." We said together, offering none.

Adam indicated and the car moved forward an inch and then the windscreen was flooded with darkness and the Zafira shook violently. A deafening noise blasted through the open windows followed by a howling gust of wind that caused us all to flinch and cover our faces. A deep rumbling bass line trembled up through the vehicle and into our seats rattling us from the inside out. We reached out to hold on to the doors, eyes closed, teeth gritted, sphincters clenched. A horn blasted us and our eardrums cried out for mercy as the car continued to rock, and then just as quickly it was gone. We all turned in unison to see the tail end of a flatbed logging lorry snake round the corner and disappear off in to the woods.

"So, the roads not closed then." I said from the backseat, trying to regain hearing.

"It appears not," said Neil, "Now can we try looking before moving anywhere further? Please?" Adam still had his eyes shut. He nodded. We weren't re-assured, but I suppose we deserved that.

We edged over the road and angled the car down on to the dirt track, slowly letting the tyres test every inch of the way. We were proceeding with caution, despite being in the safest place that we had found in the last   half-hour. Neil and I were frankly just relieved to be off the road. At least here the tree trunks weren't moving at fifty miles an hour. The track dropped steeply downwards, well hidden as promised by trees on either side. We were suddenly in darkness again, crawling towards a slither of light that lay at a bend at the bottom. It practically glowed mythically and we all looked at each other as the anticipation built. I couldn't help but feel cynical for the briefest of moments, thinking that adversity was one thing to build a moment, but near death experiences would surely dwarf anything that could be found at the bottom of this hill. I said nothing and held my breath instead.

As the car approached the clearing, we started the turn and again had to shield our eyes from the light. We edged ever onwards and as the car levelled we turned again to park parallel to the track.   None of us had yet seen our destination but as the car pulled to a halt we all exhaled dramatically.

Some moments in life require accompaniment, moments where words alone will not suffice, where words would in fact spoil the essence of such a moment. A generation of people brought up on movies would expect a soundtrack to fade in at such a point, something to rouse a feeling of awe from those involved. They would expect it to be the sort of music that would spark warmth and feelings of camaraderie usually reserved for world-cup montages on Match of the Day or the 'this was the year that was' sections on the programs they show on New Year's Eve. But we didn't have a soundtrack, so we used beer instead. It was surprisingly effective as a substitute.

The sight before us was all that we had hoped for and more; we had landed on a peninsula of perfection. The grass was lush and green, fresh and untouched. To the right of us the land rose to a levelled area where a picnic bench sat ready and waiting for us. The ground ahead of us sloped gradually down to the water's edge, to the left of us it rose and levelled again to a cliff a foot above water. There was ample space for our tents, the car sat safely out of the way and we were protected from sight on all sides. Edna had done us proud.

We stood as if frozen in a postcard, gazing out over the calm still water, lost in our thoughts, lost in the tranquillity of the moment. The scale of the landscape before us was awe inspiring to a man that lived in the agoraphobic kingdom that was my one bedroom flat. I felt the walls of my misery crumbling away from me, corroding in the fresh clean air. I breathed in, deeply, dramatically. Inhaling through my nose, exhaling through my mouth. My chest expanded, the hair on my arms bristled as my senses awoke one by one. My ears picked up the sound of bird songs in the far distance. My eyes caught every reflective glimmer of sunshine that danced across the water as a gentle warm breeze caressed the surface. In through my nose, out through my mouth, in through my nose...

"Oh Jesus, what the fuck is that smell?"

"Sorry!"

"Adam!" Neil and I shouted together

"That could be the omelette." He said, thinking. Dare I say savouring. "It's quite unique actually isn't it?"

"I'm not even going to answer Adam, I can't risk keeping my mouth open any longer than I have to." Neil laughed at me as I genuinely gagged on a concoction scientists would be forced to class as suitable only for chemical warfare.

"Behave Steve, everyone enjoys their homebrew."

"Yeah well I think I'll stick to the imported stuff if you don't mind." I replied, heading back to the tents to get another round of Bud's. I heard them discussing the remnants like connoisseurs. I called back to confirm I was getting three beers and they answered in the affirmative. When I returned I was glad to find the conversation had moved on to more pleasant ground.

"We have struck gold here boys, we really have. Are we, or are we not, masters of all we survey? I mean look at this place. Green grass, a solid camp, beers and good company." Neil was pontificating.

"Gentleman, lets fish." Adam said. I looked at them both and realised I was witnessing the slow emancipation of man. "To the car." Adam ordered and turned and marched towards the Zafira. We followed, some more keen than others.

I'm not against fishing. I can see the merits of it on many levels. At the industrial and commercial level of course there are the many jobs and livelihoods supported by the trade. The villages and surrounding communities that thrive off of the business. The romanticism of those braving nature's fury to bring in the daily haul is not lost on me and more over is almost reminiscent of the days gone by when men would venture out in to the wilderness to provide for their families. The sea to me is the last great frontier of the unknown and terrifies me with its vast emptiness and casual

107

destructive whims, all of which I witness from the comfort of my sofa.

I'm not against fishing for those that wish to take a more dedicated stance and drag themselves out of bed at three a.m. to stand knee deep in the lakes and rivers for hours upon hours. And not catch anything. Their stoicism is testament to their passion for the sport. They own equipment and use words like 'spools' and 'floaters' without giggling. They have those trousers that look like incontinence pants for clowns and they wear them proudly and with purpose. They may well just be using fishing as a reason to sit somewhere peaceful and read a paper. I can see the attraction of that. Getting away from it all was the purpose of this trip. I am not against fishing.

"What the fuck do we know about fishing?" I'm really not.

"Honestly? Not a lot," said Neil, unperturbed. He was pulling out three sticks that had been passed off as rods. Or poles. Or whatever the hell they were supposed to be called. They looked broken and I was nowhere near them. I was maybe a little against fishing. "But that, that is the point." he said. He was starting to sound like Paul Daniels.

"Debbie, pass me the maggots." I'm kidding, he was talking to Adam.

Adam skipped around to the back seats and opened the door. I supped back my beer and watched dumbstruck. You just never knew who you shared a car with sometimes. I heard him make a noise, perhaps he was forcing doves into a box or sweet-talking a fluffy rabbit, I couldn't be sure from my angle of complete disinterest. "Neil," Adam called, "something's wrong."

I waited. Neil went around to join him. They were behind the car from my viewpoint but I wasn't about to get too involved. I was enjoying my role as the audience member waiting to be impressed while secretly hoping to get my money back for the ticket.

Neil flashed in front of my view through the windows and seemed to lean fully into the car and then further down behind the back of the driver's seat to the foot well. There was some commotion, Adam was leaning in over him and through what space I couldn't even begin to imagine. Something was apparently amiss. I heard voices, just out of earshot to be fully discernible and then both men jumped back dramatically.

"Problem?" I asked helpfully.

"That's just nasty." I heard Adam saying, "Really, really nasty." Neil was inching closer towards the car and I took the opportunity to stroll around the back of the car to join in, from a safe distance. My understanding of maggots is that they are not high on the list of mans natural predators. But small things in nature could often be misleading in that way and I wasn't about to take the chance of ending up in the 'humorous news' section of the Sun as the man that had lost his finger to a disgruntled grub. I peered. Neil and Adam inched forwards towards the door again.

"Oh shit, look, they're getting everywhere." Adam again, pointing frantically. It would seem he had taken the explanatory approach to resolving the crisis. Neil looked at him momentarily and for a second I feared he would roll up his sleeves and announce to the group that he 'was going in'. He just shook his head instead and approached the foot well again.

"Anyone care to share what the actual problem is?" I asked. Adam was standing uncomfortably, like he was itching. "What's the matter with you?" I tried again.

"The little bastards, they've mutated or something. It's, it's gross."

"Well how bad is it? Are we talking 'Tremors' mutated?"

"They're huge!" Adam replied, but I don't think he was conversing with me, it was more co-incidental interaction. I looked back towards the car for explanation just as Neil turned around, arms outstretched holding the infamous tupperware with his fingers covered in warty looking wriggling skin. I leapt back with a start and dropped my beer.

"Jesus!" I said, stumbling backwards. I practically fell on my arse. "What the hell is that?"

"I think they're awake. Warm and very, very much awake!" The maggots had smelled freedom and were organising an escape up Neil's arms. As he stood there we watched a steady flow of wiggling juice bubbles hurling themselves over the rim of the box and down to the grass below. The tupperware was occupied territory and these maggots wanted out.

"You are kidding me? I thought the cold just sort of made them last longer? I didn't realise they had been cryogenically frozen!" I said.

"You're talking to me like I knew this would happen."

"Well didn't you?"

"No! Why would I?"

"Because you bought them. Weren't they like this then too?"

"No!" Neil said defensively. "The bloke got them out of the fridge."

"Brilliant." I said, starting to feel a little itchy myself. I picked my beer bottle from the grass as I noticed a trail of concerted focus from the bugs towards the glass. I looked back up at Neil as a thought dawned on me. "They're still in the car aren't they?" I could see him trying to phrase his answer and I waited as he scrunched up his face in contemplation.

"They might be, a little. Yeah."

"Terrific."

"Maybe we could leave the door open and hope they sort of wiggle off?" Adam ventured. Even Neil looked at him sceptically at this suggestion.

"I don't think they're combat maggots, Adam." Neil said. He put the tub down on the ground and we took a step

110

towards it and re-considered. They certainly seemed active and mobile for a legless collection of grubs. Adam stepped out of the circle and was back almost instantly with three more beers, I hadn't even noticed him open the boot. He passed them around and we flipped the tops off and stood looking at the activity. "Still," Neil said taking a long neck of his drink. "They should make cracking bait!"

I had often wondered when witnessing stories of bizarre personal injury how the culprits had not seen the inevitable catastrophe staring them in the face in the moments before the incident. Looking back now I see how these things happen.

We sat legs dangling from the precipice to the left of our camp with beer and fishing rods abound. We had come to terms with the infestation of the Zafira and duly left the back doors open – ensuring we had turned the interior lights off to preserve the car battery. Adam had even pointed out to us the small hole of the shattered window for the more adventures maggots. We felt this was as much as could be done for now. Returning to the task at hand, we had handed out the rods and positioned ourselves at the water's edge and spent the next hour fiddling with wire and hooks. I had hoped for the ready-made starter kit induction to fishing, but Neil had apparently opted for the authentic experience. The task was made that much more complicated by the beer. Apparently it has an effect on co-ordination.

All that remained before cast-off was to load up the hooks with the bait. And all that took was for one of us to pick one up.

"Away you go then?" said Neil.

"Eh? How d'you reckon on that then? This was your idea sunshine, so after you," said Adam. Neil shook his head and then moved his hand towards the tub. He went in slowly with finger and thumb and plucked a juicy red one from the edge. He held it up wriggling and examined it, picked up his hook with the other hand and then went to work. He bowed his head in concentration and then swore loudly.

"Alright mate?" Adam said chuckling. Neil raised his finger lifting wire, hook and maggot in one motion.

"That's a little more bait than I think is required bud." I said laughing. I could see the hook protruding through the skin on the side of his finger, a little blood dribble forming at the edge. The maggot was impaled and squelching, it was just on the wrong side of the finger/hook kebab. He gave me a V sign and the motion tugged at the hook and the maggot dropped to his lap. "D'you want a plaster mate?"

"No, just get some more beers." He said patiently. I dutifully obliged as he wiped the blood on to his jeans and set about finding the maggot. Adam, who was feeling braver by this point, picked up a maggot and more carefully loaded his hook. I returned from the car laden with six bottles and asked him to do mine too. Neil looked at me scornfully but I just shrugged and handed out the drinks.

We cast our lines poorly. We were lucky not to lose an eye. It took four attempts. But I'm not against fishing so I didn't complain. Neil, who knew as much as the rest of us which combined was less than naff-all agreed that we should just sit back and let the lines lie where they lay. It was five o'clock and the sun was still shining on us as we sat down on the bank and waited for the magic to happen. We were quietly optimistic. Apparently beer does that too.

"Neil?" I said, forty minutes and two beers later.

"Yes Steve."

"Who's Bob?"

"Bob who?"

"Bob, Bob." I paused.

"Bob Bob?

"No not Bob Bob. Bob," I gesticulated. "Bob"

"Stop saying Bob before I hit you."

112

"Sorry Adam." I looked back at Neil. "Bob." I whispered. A maggot hit me on the side of the face. I guessed Adam had thrown it.

"I don't follow you." said Neil.

"Bob -" maggot "Stop throwing mucking faggots at me." I yelled turning back to Adam who was now creased up with laughter.

"Mucking faggots?" said Neil. "I don't follow you." I picked up a handful from the tub and threw them at him. They bounced off of him and he rolled backwards and tried to sweep them from his person laughing and swearing at me in equal measure.

I turned back to Adam. "You," I said pointing, "shut up. And you," I said swivelling back to Neil, "you know what I mean."

"I really don't." He said, still laughing.

"The bloke from this morning. The one you said was coming. Bob."

"Oh him. You know Bob." I looked at him blankly. "He's the curious turtle." He continued by way of an explanation.

I nodded, none the wiser. I thought about it for a moment, which seemed to take a little longer than normal. Apparently beer does that as well.

"Oh right." I said. "That Bob."

BOB THE CURIOUS TURTLE

Minutes had passed by in silence. I flicked the fishing rod every now and again with a view to stirring the fish in to action. Nothing happened. Nothing had happened since we set them up. The fish were revolting, and I hadn't even seen one yet. They didn't exist. We had been had. The fish were as elusive as Nessy.

"I don't get it." said Adam.

"Get what?" Neil replied, adjusting his fishing rod to yet another angle perfect for avoiding fish.

"Fishing?" I offered. "Cause that would make two of us." I poked the rod again just to watch the ripples.

"No, I don't get what we're talking about."

"What are we talking about?"

"All this 'Bob' stuff. I mean who is Bob?"

"Well," said Neil. "In the existential sense, we are *all* Bob." Neil nodded. Word-a-day toilet paper could still yet catch on.

"Oh ha, ha ha ha. Ha." Adam retorted dryly. "Fuck you very much." I looked over at Adam, our voice of reason was slurring. "How about just in the actual sense." Neil pondered the question and breathed deeply.

"Bob. Bob is," pause for dramatic effect, "a legend. An almost mythical being. He takes many forms. Some say he is a prophet for he speaks so often the truth. Some say he is a wise man for he knows our secrets, from our deepest recesses. You can not hide from Bob. You can not lie or deceive Bob. Bob *knows* things. Bob's the shit."

"He sounds amazing." And scarily, Adam seemed to mean this. I however remained both sceptical and somewhat inebriated, but I was having to work at it. "And he was here?"

"Oh he was here, he was most definitely here."

"You saw him, you actually saw him with your own eyes." I was confused. Sceptical, inebriated and now confused. It was turning out to be a busy afternoon.

"Couldn't miss him." Said Neil, savouring every minute of his awed-by-association moment.

"This morning?"

"Yep."

"Shit."

"Exactly."

"I missed him."

"By seconds."

"Shit."

"Indeed."

"Hang on." Something had just dropped into place. "Bob's the shit."

"Don't diss Bob Steve." Adam said, now defensive. "We should all be so lucky to see Bob."

"Really."

"Really, this could be it for us boys. This is our holiday story."

"I'm sorry?" I said frowning. "Our holiday story?" I was going for incredulous.

"Yeah, like a night on Absinthe, where we all see the green fairy. Only this is more spiritual, the three of us sharing some sort of life changing religious...thing." I had failed.

"Bob's the shit." I said. I couldn't have made it more of a statement if I had preceded it with the phrase 'Adam this is a statement:'

"That he is." said Neil nodding. I looked at him realising how much of a complete dick I had been, all the while Adam was demonstrating perfectly the simple ease in which a cult could be started.

"Steve, would you stop being so negative."

"Adam, would you stop drinking now please."

"Why? Does that help?"

"Help with what?"

"With being able to see him. Do I have to open myself up or something?"

"Oh yeah, got to be open." Neil answered knowingly. How he was keeping a straight face I did not know.

"What else do I have to do?" I gave up. I was in and now somehow against all the odds, Adam was out.

"Squatting helps." I said, can't beat 'em join 'em.

"And?"

"Well it's not an exact science Adam, there are no hard and fast rules to this. I guess you're just sort of born knowing how to do it."

"Unlike fishing," I added helpfully.

"You are so lucky."

"I know." said Neil. I passed around three more beers and cursed the lack of a camcorder. I was crying with silent laughter.

"Anything else."

"Got to be relaxed. You'll never see Bob if you're all wound up inside."

"Okay. Got it, got it. Relaxed, open and squatting."

"That ought to do it."

"And then I'll see Bob."

"Practically guaranteed."

"Bob's the shit." said Adam.

"Exactly." Neil and I said together.

Scottish folklore would never be the same.

Wondrous things have been known to happen when ideas are created and shared. Cures for disease, solutions to engineering problems, songs that survive the test of time. All of these things and more have at one point in time happened when people have sat around bouncing ideas off

116

of each other. I would like to be able to say that something similar happened to us that night, but I would be lying.

We had continued on with our jest, leading Adam down an obvious path until the light literally plopped out of the sky and splashed all over him. It was a glorious moment of realisation that had resulted in Adam spraying bottled beer all over us and throwing various blunt objects until we had at last stopped laughing.

Now though something had been born. A sheet had been grasped and we continued to tug until the whole roll had unravelled and we had covered every aspect of a truly churlish idea. We were not going to cure cancer, but we had sent boredom well into remission.

"So from the top then." I said

"Surely you mean from the bottom?" Adam had thrown himself into this now.

"Our protagonist, Bob."

"Proctologist would be better." said Neil. I gave him a look that said no matter how ridiculous this was, if we were going to do it then we would do it properly. He shook his head in mock apology and opened three more beers.

"Bob The Curious Turtle." It had a ring to it.

"It's got a ring to it." said Adam. Neil's eyes lit up and pleaded with me to let him just have this one.

"Leave it Neil. We're not going there."

"C'mon, you're killing me."

"This was supposed to be a children's story."

"Trust me, adults will have to read it too." He said.

"That's not the point. And don't sulk." He sulked. "Bob the Curious Turtle," I pressed on, "and Friends."

"So who've we got then?" Adam said swaying gently on the bank. We could have hooked a shark and been none the wiser at this point.

"Well there's Bob's best friend, Muffin Puffin."

"Good. Like it."

"Murtle Turtle, the love interest."

"Flaps the Seagull." added Adam.

"Right," I pointed, like a manager at a marketing meeting. "Yes, Flaps the Seagull. Then Fishy Fingers the Starfish, Squitty Squid and what was that other one?"

"I don't think we can use the other one Steve." Said Adam.

"Why?"

"Well, it's gross."

"From the man that gave us Fishy Fingers?"

"You've got to rephrase that." said Neil.

"What was it anyway?"

"You should know. This was your one."

"Humour me." I said.

"We have been all weekend."added Neil.

"Jammy Raggins the Sea Urchin." Adam said. I spat beer over the loch.

"Do we have the right to veto?" asked Neil.

"You want to veto Jammy Raggins." I was hurt. "On what grounds."

"Are we even having this conversation?" said Neil.

"He's an integral part of the story." I argued.

"What story?"

"We haven't covered that yet. But this is gold boys, trust me."

"No this is bollocks."

"They're so often confused." I reasoned.

"It crosses the line of good taste." Adam was making a point.

"We've never even seen that line." I retorted.

"He's right Adam, we couldn't find it if we had a map."

"You see," I pointed at Neil and then stopped to think about whether he was for or against me. "Neil's right."

"From the man that gave us iron-on wallpaper."

"Now *that* was a fucking great idea." Neil howled.

"Well done Adam-."

"Iron-on-fucking wallpaper.   Shove that one up your cyclone Dyson."

"I don't think you'd be troubling his market share somehow Neil." said Adam.

"C'mon, now just for a minute. Think about it. Wallpaper. That you iron on."   He did the motions against the gathering group of mosquitoes that had started to congregate around us.

"Iron-on wallpaper."   I agreed, because you had to. "The game's in the name."   Neil gesticulated triumphantly and slopped beer from his bottle over me.

"Fuckin' A."

"It's a winner."

THREE MEN AND A BUDDHA

In life we abide by certain rules, cause and effect, good and evil, right and wrong. Drink and you get drunk, break the law and you'll go to jail and so on. They exist in large part for our own safety, placed there by men in robes who in a moment of clarity saw imminent doom in the changing world around them and thought best to impart some useful best-practices on those too lazy to figure it out for themselves. These rules were often summarised and could be listed under headings like 'common-sense'. Which is a shame, because otherwise we would have been fine.

From the riverbank we staggered back towards the tents. It seemed to take us hours. Darkness had swarmed in faster than the mosquitoes yet at some point we had reasoned that night-vision was superfluous to beer-goggles. We had abandoned all pretence of fishing, and furthermore abandoned the fishing equipment, safe in the knowledge that it was unlikely to get yanked into the loch. We had also reasoned that seven hours of drinking somehow qualified us to build a fire. At the very least, it qualified us in the sense that we could think of no good reason why we shouldn't be entitled to build a fire. We had developed strong and vocal opinions on the matter.

If you have ever spotted warnings on household objects and wondered what sort of idiot they were for, what sort of complete moron would require such basic instruction and rudimentary interventions, then I offer you the following example. Three drunk men and a bottle of lighter fluid - it's not just a recipe for disaster, it's an entire cooking program.

I, it turned out, was somewhat of a pyromaniac. It was a side of me that I wasn't prepared for. A side I had until now not even realised existed. It didn't make me deep and it would be hard to bring up in comfortable conversation, but evidently it was there, burning brightly so to speak. It was in my mind a simple event that had sparked this discovery. We wanted a campfire, we had plenty of wood and we had lighter fluid. The world appeared to me to be in harmony. But what is not clear is my decision making process in determining just how much lighter fluid is required to get that homely boy-scout-marsh-mellow-roasting experience. I, it also turned out, have appalling judgement. Who knew?

Now I don't blame myself, that would be unfair to me. I blame my voice of reason, because he was pissed and clearly not paying attention. It was Adam's fault. But who really needs eyebrows anyway? The fire, I am fairly certain, was clearly visible from space. In fact, by classification I think what I had created was an inferno. And boy was I proud. I was in love with the fire. We danced together, we grew together, we shared warmth and happiness together. I nurtured it, fed it, adored it in every way. Neil and Adam were not so appreciative. I think the definition of their reaction would be 'scared'.

I sat down by the blaze, tanning. Neil and Adam wanted to stay at a safer distance, like in the next town, but I chastised them until they sat down next to me. This was the point of our holiday and we would enjoy it together. We had wanted a fire, and I had created one. To say anything else would be quibbling over technicalities. Yes, it may have been brighter than the midday sun had been. Okay, the rubber on the soles of my shoes was starting to grow 'tacky'. But it was a fire. Job done. I squirted the lighter fluid at the flame and watched a plume of fire streak towards the sky. I was fascinated. Neil shuffled backwards and tucked his legs in.

"You look like a Buddha sat like that." I said, poking the logs with a stick. "I should know. I used to have one."

121

"Have one what?" Said Adam, between a mouth-full of cheeseburger. He had whipped up supper while I had gone foraging for wood in the darkness. Disposable barbecues it transpired were more versatile than a microwave and cooked faster too. I was on my second cheeseburger and they were flying off at a rate that would put McDonalds to shame.

"A Buddha." I said.

"You've got a Buddha?" said Adam.

"*Had*, had a Buddha." Neil was silent. Nobody could enjoy cheeseburgers that much.

"What? I mean where? What are you on about you drunken fool?"

"I had a Buddha." It was a good burger. "Fat little fucker that used to sit in my garden."

"I thought that was you ex." And there he was.

"And?" said Adam, laughing.

"And what?"

"Well what happened? Did it like transcend to a higher plane or something?"

"No," I finished my cheeseburger and lit a cigarette from my stick. "It got nicked."

"Someone nicked your Buddha?"

"Is that a metaphor?" Neil added unhelpfully.

"Kidnapped." I corrected.

"What?" said Adam, then "fuck off." He returned to his barbecue. I could tell he was envious of my log-fire.

"Straight up. They pinched it."

"Doesn't say much for Karma does it?" Adam said.

"I dunno. Reckon they must have got a hernia shifting the bloody thing. It weighed a ton."

"And why kidnapped?"

"I got a ransom demand." Adam stopped cooking.

"You're kidding right?"

"Nope," I prodded my fire. "Proper job too. Newspaper cuttings, the works."

"And what were they asking for?"

"Fifty quid."

"And did you pay?"

"Would you?"

"Would I fuck!"

"Oh."

"You paid? You plank."

"Easy for you to say. I was being terrorised." I meant it too.

"What were they going to do? Post gravel through your door? Chip off an ear?"

"You weren't there."

"I worry about you sometimes Steve, really I do."

"I was attached. He brought me luck."

"In what way exactly?"

"He was a feature. I'd never had a garden feature before."

"So get a gnome!"

"It was a talking point. I thought it made me sort of mysterious."

"I'm starting to see why you're single again."

"Knob off."

"I'd sit in your garden for fifty-bloody-quid."

"It seemed like a reasonable exchange. Besides it wasn't mine to lose. It came with the flat, and it was symbolic of my inner peace."

"Symbollocks more like."

"I have a confession." Neil said quietly. I turned my head to look at him.

"Yeah?"

"Yeah."

"Well?"

"It was me. With the newspapers."

"You stole my Buddha?"

"Not exactly."

"And sent me ransom notes."

"Sort of."

"Every week for a month?"

"Pretty much."

"And the fifty quid?"

"Came in handy."

"You spunk-sack."

"That's a tad harsh. It's not like I shagged your bird or something."

"You might have been the only one not to," added Adam, who had until now been focused over the barbecue sensing obvious brotherly tensions growing. His input was inspired. "I did and now I wish I'd just nicked the Buddha." I punched him on the arm, it just had to be done.

"Seriously though," Neil continued, laughing. "I gave it back. No harm came to the stony dude."

"I should bloody well think so after I gave you fifty quid." There was something else though. Something slightly more tragic. "So where is it now then? In your shed?"

"Eh?"

"Well you nicked it again. A couple of weeks later after I got it back. What happened? Did you get tired of the newspaper cuttings?"

"Um, not me mate. I didn't nick it."

"Yeah, yeah whatever."

"Seriously mate, I didn't take it again. I haven't got it."

"Yeah okay, I believe you. Really I do."

"Steve, I haven't got it mate. Honestly. I took it once, for a giggle, made fifty quid and gave it back." He looked sincere.

"I have never seen you look more insincere in my life."

"Why would I nick it again? The little bastard weighed a ton!"

"Oh I don't know, maybe you were short of cash that week eh?" Neil was laughing but I wasn't letting up. Never mess with a man and his Karma. Some lines you just don't cross.

"Adam, help me out here would you. Tell him I haven't got it."

"He doesn't have it." Adam said flatly.

"Cheers mate," said Neil, nodding.

"And how can you be so sure?" I asked.

"Cos I took it after I finished shagging your bird."

Bastards.

The fire had eventually settled to a comfortable, calmer status and now crackled quietly in the background of our night throwing off warmth like a blanket. We lay on our backs staring at the night sky star gazing at the infinite emptiness above. The drink was still flowing freely and the mood was spinning in much the same way as the room would have been had we been in one. As it was, we just fell over further, more often. It was as good a reason as any to lay flat on the floor and move as little as possible.

"D'you know what the worst part about being single is?" I said to the sky, exhaling smoke and watching it dissipate

"Having to wank," pause, "yourself." replied Neil and I chuckled, but with a point to make.

"No, although yes, obviously, but no."

"Not knowing when the next pair of tits you'll see will be?" Adam enquired, waving his hands towards the darkness. He may or may not have been doing cupping-squeezing motions. "Or," I paused, waiting. "Bush." He finished after deliberation. I rolled my head to stare at him but he was oblivious and I couldn't possibly describe what hand motions he was doing now. "I could lend you Shaven Ravers," he offered, "but, well there's none in it. Bush that is." He giggled.

"Are you both trying to cheer me up here or what?"

"Well, yeah." They said genuinely.

"Well it's not working." I took a long drag from my cigarette and squinted my eyes, trying to make join-the-dot patterns in the stars.

"Has this question got anything to do with sex?" Neil enquired, as if a response in the negative would rule out his interest in anything further I had to say, which in fairness it may well have done.

"Y'see the worst part about being single is knowing that you're now, like, someone's past."

"Deep." said Adam sarcastically.

"And obvious. What's your point?"

"Well, just that really."

"That's all of it?"

"Well no, there's more."

"If you say you want to get back with Kelly I may just have to drown you out here. For your own good, and ours."

"I don't want to get back with Kelly." I answered honestly.

"I could make it look like an accident."

"I don't want to get back with Kelly."

"They wouldn't find you for, well, ages." He slurred.

"Neil, I don't want to get back with Kelly."

"So what's your point then."

"That was my point. I don't want to get back with her, I just don't want to be one of her stories either."

"Why not?"

"Dunno," I said, I hadn't really thought this through, but sometimes once you've started, you just have to keep going until you reach the cliff. "Like, to the next bloke she's with, I'll be the ex."

"Well duh!" I was getting the distinct impression that further thought was required.

"She might like, sort of trash me."

"A definite possibility. Not without cause either."

"Cheers mate."

"You're welcome."

"If it makes you feel any better, she was very complimentary." said Adam giggling again.

"Shut the fuck up Adam."

126

"Sorry mate, not helpful. Go on." He was still giggling.

"I'm just saying, it's weird knowing that you'll always be a part of their past. A story, or a confession or something. That you'll be compared and contrasted-."

"Like a painting."

"Yes Adam. Like a painting."

"And?" Neil asked.

I sighed. "Doesn't matter, forget it."

"No go on, so you'll be a part of her past. So what? What's the problem?" Neil was about to simplify my angst as he had done many times before. "So look at it this way. Maybe, though I can't personally believe it, but maybe you will be the man to which all others will be judged. There's a very good possibility that to her you'll be the pinnacle of her relationships."

"Fuck off."

"I'm serious."

"So am I!"

"Why's that so bad? You'll be the question that all the other blokes will be thinking about, if not asking."

"What question?" I asked.

"Am I better than Steve." Neil responded dramatically.

"God I hope so," said Adam. Neil laughed and lit a cigarette.

"You think?" I was talking to Neil and ignoring Adam.

"I know, it's the question that all blokes want to know when they get with a new bird. It's instinctual. As natural as fancying their mates and wondering whether they all take showers together at the gym."

"I think that last one's just you Neil." said Adam, matter-of-factly.

"Whatever, you can't help but wonder."

"About the ex or the showering thing?" I asked, my interest in both being equal.

"The ex is the one that matters. Women all have a past mate."

127

"Except Mary." said Adam.

"Eh?"

"Mary, the bird from that play."

"What play?"

"The one from school."

"Mary?" Neil said slowly. "You mean *The Nativity*?"

"Yeah. She didn't have a past." Neil shook his head.

"Okay, all women have a past, except Mary."

"And Mother Teresa."

"Adam, shut the fuck up."

"I'm just saying."

"Shut-the-fuck-up." He shut the fuck up.

"They have a past. It's normally very similar. There's a few casual things after school or college or uni or whatever. Maybe a serious one early on that they remember fondly and do the wistful what-if thing about. There's normally an evil bastard in there somewhere, the one that shagged around or nicked their money or something."

"They all love a bastard." said Adam.

"That they do." Neil agreed, before continuing. "Then there's 'the ex'. The long-standing thought-this-was-the-one bloke."

"Huh." I said, taking it all in.

"You're forgetting one." said Adam.

"Really?" said Neil, never one to be corrected.

"There's the Casanova." Neil clicked his finger at him in agreement.

"Right."

"The what?" I said.

"The Casanova, the amazing lover. The one that makes them wet every time they remember him."

"God I hate that bloke." said Adam knowingly.

"But that's me." I said, genuinely. I believed it to. And, sadly, it wasn't just the drink talking.

"Ha ha ha!" They laughed.

"No, no no," said Neil, "you're the ex."

"But I don't want to be the ex," I said sheepishly. "I'm the Casanova." God I'm pathetic.

"Sorry mate, those are the rules."

"Says who?" I asked defiantly.

"Says life mate, it's not Monopoly, Steve."

"Just as well. I fucking hate Monopoly."

"Exactly. Now I'm not saying that you can never *be* the Casanova. You just can't be Kelly's. The Casanova thing, it's casual. It's what makes the whole experience what it is."

"I don't follow."

"Yes you do. You know what I'm talking about. It's the mystery, the no strings, no commitments, living life in the moment bullshit."

"And women want that?"

"Sometimes." he said, "but not all of the time, and not *for* all of the time. That's the point. That's what makes the times that they do want it so memorable for them. They all feel like they're being spontaneous. Going with the guy their mothers warned them about, blah, blah, blah. They talk about it afterwards like that's the point. To have a story."

"Women have stories." said Adam, philosophically.

"Cos blokes never do that." I said.

"It's bollocks too." Neil said, ignoring me. "When they do it, it's all about empowering the feminine mystique, like they have to reason it off or something. Can't just be about sex, can't just be about enjoying themselves for the sake of it. It's got to mean something, even if its meaning is to mean nothing. They always seem to have to justify it to themselves."

"Women think too much." said Adam.

"Absolutely." said Neil.

"Least they can never accuse us of that." said Adam righteously.

"And that's a good thing?" I felt like a kid again, back at school. Confused all over again. Same urges and none the fucking wiser for the years of experience. Here I had been trying to fit some sort of standard, be the exception to the rule as far as boyfriends were concerned and now I felt like some sort of a tick on Kelly's checklist of experiences.

"The thing, the point that you have to remember, is very basic. It's clear to all. It must be, it's the thing they all keep harping on about and it's the whole bloody point." He sat up on his elbows and looked out over the still waters of the loch, putting it all together. "Men and women, they're different. That's the point."

"That's the point?" Somehow I felt we were talking more specifically than generally.

"That's the point. We're different. We think differently. React differently. Notice things differently and work things out differently. They deliberate, we act, they nest, we procreate. We're not supposed to see things the same way, it goes against nature."

"Against nature?"

"Yep."

"I see." I was far too drunk for this

"Good, cos I've got to go take a piss." And with that he stood up and went down to the waters edge.

"Got it?" said Adam, laughing.

"Oh yeah, it's crystal clear." I lied.

"Thought so." He leaned up on his arms and looked at me. "Piss?"

"No, some of it made sense." Adam laughed and we both hauled ourselves up and joined our friend at the loch, pissing in the wind. It seemed fitting.

Monday

IT'S FUN TO STAY AT THE L.N.C.A.

Ow. Ow, ow, ow, ow, ow, OW! I hated everything. I was in pain. And I was dealing with it with my usual manly decorum. I was in my sleeping bag and somehow my arms were pushed against my sides as if I had been zipped up after getting in by someone else. Which was possible given the state we had been in. My head was throbbing and I was thrashing about trying to roll into the foetal position and hold my head at the same time. I looked like a man wrapped in an oversized condom and I was arching with enough force to insert my head up my own arse. Which at the time seemed to be the obvious and most comfortable place for it.

Alcohol, it seemed, had clearly been discovered by a woman, with the express intention of allowing them to have something irrefutable to both punish and pity us with. It was the ultimate 'I told you so' experiment brought to fruition. Nothing else allowed so many to ridicule so few so completely. We were guinea pigs, laboratory mice exposed to ever-changing test conditions and environments. And we kept on coming back for more. We were the perfect candidates. Living proof that evolution had peaked and was now working backwards. In a lab, the monkey learns not to keep pushing the button the gives him an electric shock and furthermore, he learns to perform the trick that gets him a treat. Men, apparently, can't.

I am willing to bet money on the fact that I have been drunk before. I am positively sure of it. I can't tell you when the last time had been because my brain wasn't working, in fact my brain may never work again. I had precious few brain cells to begin with, now I was left with

132

two and even they were fighting. But I had that sense of nauseous déjà-vu, that familiar sense of inevitable disappointment, as I tasted the bile gurgling at the base of my throat. I have been here before, I thought, this is not my first time. I know what's coming and it's not good. But worse, I know that I am not going to be sick. I remember that I don't do that very often. I may not be able to remember my name, but I'm damn sure I remember something like that. I recall now from past experience that this sense of general unwell will pass, in a day or two. I tell myself the lies in the hope that I may speed up the recovery process. I swear not to drink again, that alcohol will never pass my lips so long as I can *just get through this*. I know that this is the prayer of the wasted. I know I have as much chance of escaping this hangover as I have of escaping this poxy sleeping bag. I look like Houdini's special brother, performing the worlds' least exciting trick.

It's a typical story. Three men have a few beers, exchange wild stories, kick back and relax. They pretend to fish, barbecue some meat, talk about women, camouflage a car. Nobody could be blamed for this. It was bound to happen given the location, the circumstances, the very environment itself was calling out to us to make the most of an opportunity. In the dead of night, three drunk men had attempted to blend a blue Zafira into the background, and given that it actually took us seven minutes to find it, it would appear that we had done a mighty fine job.

In the cold, cold light of day things seemed different. Our protective alcoholic bubble had burst. Reality was slowly crawling across my face like a sunrise. I ate painkillers for breakfast and stretched, urged blood to find the parts of my body not currently responding. I ambled around our campsite surveying the debris. Our fire smouldered and amazingly, given the moisture in the air and the dew on the grass, glowed a deep red beneath a charred stump of tree we had thrown in. I could feel warmth on my ankle as I walked past.

My body began to provide me with a list of requirements, basic things I would need to continue to function for the rest of the day. I needed coffee, I would at some point require greasy food and I would also have to acquire more painkillers. I started with the thing my body needed least of all, a cigarette. Around me was work to do, tents to disassemble, fishing rods to find, maggots to set free. There was also the very real, very obvious need to make some adjustments to the car. I dropped back down in to the doorway of my tent as Neil did the same. I hadn't seen Adam for awhile.

"What the hell did we do to the motor last night?" I asked.

"Adam called it field repairs." said Neil.

"Right, but I wasn't aware that that meant trying to repair the car with things you might find in a field. Dare I ask what the tree poking out of the window is supposed to achieve?"

"Better radio reception."

"But of course." I dragged on my cigarette some more, it helped. "Did we find the bumper yet?" Adam marched into my scope of vision at the bottom of the lane that we had traversed to get down to the plateau. He was dragging something and I had a feeling my question had been answered.

"The bumper?" Neil asked. Adam dropped it in front of the car and continued on towards us, nodding.

"Found it at the top of the lane. Reckon that bloody truck must have shaken it off."

"Jesus Adam, would you let it go, there was no tow-truck." He looked at me questionably.

"No, the logging truck that nearly killed us all must have shaken it off," he said patiently.

"Oh that truck. Sounds likely."

134

"So the day is looking up then," said Neil, laughing at us. "Now then, I need to tell you about this dream I had."

Adam and I looked at him. He must have been joking. Our car had been vandalised by Wombles, we had more tidying up to do than the event manager at Glastonbury and I had a hangover so big I had named it Barry.

"We need to sort this shit out first mate, the dream can wait surely."

"No, no, no. This is more than just a dream, this is a quest." He had that look in his eyes again, the one we had both seen before, the one that was responsible for us all being here.

"Steve, he's got that look again. I'm actually scared."

"Neil, he's right. You've got that look again, and whatever it is, the answer is no. We're already here, in Scotland, miles from home. You, me, Adam and Barry. We're 'living the dream' already." Adam nodded furiously, and pointed. He was counting on me to save him where I had failed so many times before, as if Neil was about to suggest we push on north to Greenland or something.

"Who's Barry?" said Adam suddenly.

"Doesn't matter," I replied swotting the enquiry away and focusing back on Neil. If we were to get out of this I would need to concentrate. "Neil, enough with the dreams." I said decisively. An end to it.

"Lesbians!" Neil proclaimed.

"Where?" said Adam.

"Who? Us?" I said.

"My dream, it was about lesbians." This statement of course changed everything.

"Neil, there is always time for dreams about lesbians." I got comfortable and lit another cigarette. Adam squirted lighter fluid on to the embers of our fire and it roared into life. Any day that starts with lesbians was bound to be both memorable and worth getting up for. I could already feel Barry packing up his stuff. "But you mentioned a quest?"

"Uh-huh. Okay from the beginning, we're camping right?"

"How far back are you going?"

"Shut up. Okay so we're camping, and we turn up at this place, the sun is shining and this grassland is behind these trees, but it kind of opens out on the other side of them. There's a river somewhere nearby which is why we've gone there, but it's really hard to get to. I mean we've practically driven through swamps to get there. We've nearly given up three times already but for some reason we push on, like we know a paradise awaits us. We've travelled miles off any main roads, gone through the mountains on winding trails and tracks. None of us know where we are so we're like 'what the hell – crack on' type thing. And then we get there. We emerge through the trees, and there they are."

"A couple of lesbians?" I asked.

"Oh no, not just a couple lesbians."

"A group of lesbians?" I pushed.

"What is the collective for that?" said Adam.

"A bush?" I ventured. We laughed but Neil hadn't finished.

"Guys, this was more than a group, and these were more than just lesbians."

Adam went to speak, stopped himself, then offered, "So they were hot then? These lesbians."

"A flaming bush of lesbians. Well I'm aroused."

"Shut up Steve, I haven't told you the best bit yet."

"Steady, I'm not sure how much more of this I can take this early, haven't long got rid of the old morning glory mate."

"They were naked."

"Yeah that ought to do it." I said, defeated.

"Excellent," said Adam.

"And it wasn't a group, it was an association." Neil said proudly.

"How could you tell? Did they have badges on?" said Adam laughing.

"Where? How? They were naked. Did you not hear me?"

"So they were giving out pamphlets or something?" I said just to fuck him off.

"No, they were just a very close group, you could tell. They were splashing about in the river-,"

"That explains what happened to our fish then." I said rolling into my tent laughing.

"Towelling each other, strolling around their tents. All naked as god had intended." Neil was daydreaming again. He could have had his foot in the campfire and he wouldn't have noticed. "And we were there, just standing at the clearing, watching these naked angels. Watching them kissing each other and laughing and joking. Watching them going into their tents three at a time. And they saw us too. They saw us and didn't bat an eyelid. They were enjoying the attention. They even, like, beckoned us over to them. They wanted us there. There were so many of them. So many perfect breasts, so much variety." Okay so I too was paying attention at this point, maybe even daydreaming a little. A lot. Completely lost. "They were so fresh, so gorgeous, and they had nothing but smiles for us. No expectations, no harsh words or judgements. They just took each of us over to these rugs and sat us down and kind of washed over us."

"So they weren't practising lesbians then?" said Adam.

"They sound pretty professional to me." I interjected, missing his point entirely.

"Eh?"

"I mean, wouldn't we, as blokes," he waved his arm around indicating the three of us, to avoid any confusion, "kind of go against the grain so to speak."

"Is that a joke about having wood?"

"You know, what with having cocks and all." Adam continued.

137

"It was a dream okay?   So they might have been experimental, or just friendly. Got to be honest Adam, I wouldn't have given a shit if they just wanted me to watch. They were naked, and hot. Hot naked lesbians."

"Hot, naked, syndicated lesbians."   I felt like some semblance of their status as a legitimate organisation might somehow add to Adams ability to enjoy the imagery.

"Thanks mate, now I need a wank." Ah I knew him so well.

"Me three," I agreed, but Neil wasn't finished.

"The thing is, I think they're out there." He said.

"Who?" said Adam.

"The L.N.C.A."

"Come again?" I said.

"The Lesbian Naturist Camping Association." Sometimes you had to hand it to him. As a visionary, Neil was second to none. "They're out there, and we have to find them."

"No, they're not out there. It was a dream." Said Adam.

"No, they are mate, I'm telling you."

"Neil, I think we need to talk about how much time you spend on the internet." He wasn't listening to me.

"What I wouldn't give for Google right now." He stated, proving my point entirely.

"Figures."

"I bet they have a website."

"I don't think you'd be eligible to join Neil, what with having a cock and all!" said Adam impatiently. Hungover and slightly horny was clearly a bad combination.

"I bet they have a website too Neil," I said, trying to draw him back to reality. I knew though, from experience, that this was something we would have to see through to the end.   "But why, of all the glorious and lets be honest warmer places in the world that the L.N.C.A. could be camping, would they be camping in Scotland?"

"Trust me."

"That's not an answer."

138

"During the same week as us too?" added Adam.

"Because we're here for a reason."

"Yeah, I feel like we've covered this."

"Trust me," he said again.

"No."

"You won't be saying that when we find them." Again, he had a point, but why I was even thinking about it I couldn't begin to tell you.

"How would you even know where to start looking?" Said Adam, able to find the sensible in even the ridiculous.

"Man's got a point Neil, I bet they're not listed as an attraction at the tourist information."

"The way to find them," he said, "is to not look be looking for them."

"Mate, if that were true I'd have found them years ago." I finished my cigarette and through the butt into the fire. "Fuck it. I give in, who am I to argue over naked lesbians."

HANS, SHOULDERS KNEES AND NOSE

Icy cold water splashed on my face, one, two, three times.
This would normally have helped, but it wasn't just my face,
the water splashed on my shoulders and arms, my jeans
became soaked within seconds and my feet were splashing
about in an inch of water that was taunting me. It was
getting deeper, and with every splash that came I knew that
it would be crawling higher and higher over my shoes. My
clothes could only absorb so much and after that, it would
just keep coming. I looked around, the others looked the
same, focused, wet, out of it. Were they thinking the same
thing? Had they reached the same conclusion? There was
no way to tell, they wouldn't be able to hear me clearly over
the noise. I just had to hope, hope amongst hope that this
was all just part of the experience.

Our raft crested violently over another rock and my paddle
crunched against stone as I waved frantically in the air trying
to keep my balance. We tried to keep the boat straight, eight
of us and the guide apparently all pushing in different
directions. Commands came flying at me from behind, but
I was at the front of the boat and they may as well have
been in German for all of the sense they were making. I
watched again as the water level inside the boat rose and not
for the first time got the urge to start bailing out. All of a
sudden the boat lurched sideways and Hans yelled at me
again. I looked to the side and pushed away against the
rock, trying to guide the boat straight again.

I looked ahead at the swirling chaos that lay before us,
rocks and ravines and dips and drops. There was a waterfall
ahead so someone was saying, this was the calm bit they
said, where we cut our teeth. Rafting 101, a crash course for

140

beginners before we hit the pro strip. We had paid for this. Someone else had used the word 'rad'.

And then there was Hans.

He looked like me, if I was the rough sketch and he was the finished picture. He was defined and managed to have an all year tan in a country that had a week of sun. I of course was pasty white with a recently developed tinge of green. And Hans was very enthusiastic about his job. He clapped, a lot. And he expected me to clap too. I was still hungover. Hans was clearly a sociopath.

The raft lurched and dropped and dipped deep below the water submerging me up to the waist. I wanted to piss myself, not because I was scared, just because the water was so cold I needed to prove I still had a dick. As we levelled off a wave rose before me and hit me square in the face, taking my breath away. I think I got slapped by a fish but who could tell, either way I fell from my position perched on the front edge of the boat and collapsed head first into Neil's lap, helmet to helmet so to speak.

He looked at me like I had just 'come out' on the boat. I struggled back to my ledge through the water inside the boat and only then realised the gorgeous woman who had been sitting behind me. She was a year or two younger than me, with long blonde hair, and she managed to wear her life jacket like an extra from Baywatch. She smiled at me while I tried not to drown. As first impressions went, mine could have been stronger.

Back in position, I grabbed my paddle with a renewed vigour and tried to laugh like Kirk Douglas in 'The Vikings'. For no reason at all, none whatsoever, I was starting to enjoy myself. I looked quickly at Neil and he gave me a thumbs up, and I managed to look back to Adam who was taking to the whole experience like a duck to, well, water.

I wasn't given long to enjoy the moment though as Hans barked something that may well have been a warning, and then the raft charged on towards the next hurdle. We leapt into the air and I honestly believed the whole boat left the water for a second before we hurtled back to the river, faster and faster or so it seemed. I began to keep a rhythm, tried to ebb and flow with the changing currents and swirling waters so that I wasn't so much rafting as riding the boat like a rodeo.

We appeared to be learning fast as Hans became more and more excited. He was clapping and cheering, the others were laughing and all of a sudden out of nowhere I was having a good time. Our boat caught a rock and we spun round and carried on floating backwards. My teeth were being well and truly cut but I persevered. I even conferred with Neil to successfully correct the boat back around. We were heroes and had automatically earned our right to the front of the raft. Danger lay ahead, but we were ready.

Despite the forward motion and strong current, rafting was surprisingly exhaustive work. Whichever way I paddled, I seemed to be against the flow of the water. My clothes were heavy and my arms burned and my lungs were protesting most severely. We had been on the water for forty minutes, Hans planned to keep us out for four hours. I quite literally didn't have the heart to tell them.

As I pushed on through the pain barrier we tackled a fast and narrow section of the river that bent our rugged boat in half. We rose and fell and bounced and shook and one by one slipped and slid about in the centre, falling over each other and apologising in a terribly British way.

Amidst the carnage of bodies and oars and the ever-increasing water level within the raft I determined that this was going to be a long day. My hands were so cold I could barely form a grip around the handle of my oar. I fought my way back to the front of the boat and we role called our names as Hans tried to ensure we hadn't lost anyone. Fortunately we had all fallen inwards.

The problem as it occurred to me was that no matter how many of us were not in control of the raft at any one time, it continued on its course regardless. Rocks had an almost magnetic quality and were almost always followed by treacherous cross currents and an illogical wash back that would send a wave cascading over the boat to remind us how utterly wet a person can get.

Hans took an opportunity during a momentary lull in action to further heighten my concerns by explaining the perils of the undercurrent on the river. This, Hans informed us, was an entirely natural occurrence whereby a person or other such floating object could be involuntarily sucked under the water level to a faster flowing, less obvious current. This current served no purpose that I could imagine other than to swallow stupid English tourists clearly out of their depths in every sense. I vowed to stay in the boat at all times. Hans had other ideas.

What we needed apparently was an opportunity to bond as a unit. We would be spending the afternoon together and as such it was customary for the group to both introduce and inform each and all about the other. Hans said that it was an integral part of getting us all rowing in the same direction, metaphorically speaking. I suggested to Adam that it was just a way for him to meet girls.

I am not a group hug sort of person. Team building for me is something that football managers do. I am aware that this makes me appear on occasion to be miserable, for the record I've been aiming for mysterious. This however wasn't something I could sit out being that I was on the edge of a raft and sitting any further out meant getting a wet arse.

I was quite prepared to play along until Hans suggested we make things fun by all standing on the rim of the boat and taking it in turns to run around the edge while introducing ourselves. I wanted to have a chat to Hans about what exactly it was that constituted as fun in my life, but I sensed not for the first time that the tide was against me. I watched as each member of our group stood, nervously smiled then proceeded to awkwardly stagger and fall over one another on a perilous journey around the raft. We chuckled as those around us slipped and fell and stared fixated at the unseen undercurrents beyond.

Adam stepped up to the rim with surprising dexterity and grace and proceeded around the boat amusing those onboard with a laugh and a joke. He returned to his space tapping Neil on the shoulder and inviting him to continue on in the new status of the 'funny ones of our group' who would forever be described as such in the 'had to be there' anecdotes people would ultimately tell about this trip. Neil dripped natural charisma in the same way that I sat there and dripped water. While he lacked the light footed folly of Adams jaunt he displayed to those at first concerned that here was a small group of people that would be handy to have aboard. I on the other hand just fell in the water proving that you can always, always get wetter.

I learnt two things in that moment, the first was that he who laughs last is most likely still in the boat. The second was that the attractive girl behind me was called Elizabeth, but I could call her Beth.

We had paid for a day out, spontaneously deciding that white water rafting was something none of us had done before but all had considered. Something that we had each maybe even included on our personal 'things to do before you die' lists. This was what I was thinking about as our now small and insignificant raft bucked its way through water so disturbed that a world class psychiatrist would through the towel in. What we lacked in seatbelts and safety harnesses we made up for in vertical manoeuvres and hang time. This wasn't Scotland, this was the Colorado River roaring in anger.

The sun shone brightly and the day that existed all around the river was serene and in complete contrast to the situation we tackled on the water. I felt like fruit in a

144

blender. Hans with typical sadistic glee deftly guided us to every single hot spot along the way and if nothing else we could all at least say that we had got our moneys worth.

I gasped for breath with every stroke of the paddle and crashing wave of water to the face. We fought to tame a beast of epic proportions in a battle I felt sure we could not win. Our raft had grown tired of our presence on board and was displaying its frustration by attempting to overturn at every opportunity. It succeeded when I least expected to find myself flying through the air backwards momentarily watching in slow motion my eight other shipmates each crashing into the water. Even Hans who had until now appeared to be superglued to the rubber found himself dethroned.

Not being a seasoned rafter I couldn't tell you how or why I landed so far from the boat. Of all the things I was thinking, that one point seemed the least consequential. Our raft was bobbing weightless down the river with only Hans pursuing with any success. I had in my pruned hands the paddle, which together with my life jacket was keeping me afloat. I kicked my way back towards the others and tried to remember the instructions on how best not to drown. I could feel the water beneath me swirling aggressively between my feet and noticed with no satisfaction that there were an equal amount of rocks that I couldn't see just beneath the water at knee level.

Hans was onboard again before I could get in the thick of the others and he had temporarily banked the raft in an effort to allow us all to climb back on board. I exchanged smiles with Beth as I approached the raft and I offered my assistance to those not yet out of the water. My opportunity to embark any further into conversation with Beth however was loudly broken by Adam yelling to me that Neil wasn't with us. I spun around and tried without success to pick out the shape of a man swimming towards us and felt an altogether different kind of fear. Adam must have felt it too and as I leapt into the water he jumped overboard and followed me back towards the middle of the river.

I had been playing up until this point, rolling with the punches, swallowing the hangover, not killing Hans. All of this was part of our day, features of the story we would later tell again over a beer. But all of that changed as I fought my way through the water in search of Neil. We did not speak, daren't suggest the worst or consider the possibilities. How long we had been overturned I couldn't say but I knew the water ran fast and my knees would testify to the sharpness of the rocks. Adam and I communicated through gestures and expressions that would have confused all but the closest of friends - we were as good as family. We swam with renewed vigour and caught the current, eyes darting across the surface in search of any sign of our brother.

We both of us knew that our actions went against instruction. The purpose, we had been lectured of rescuing someone was not to put further people at risk. Ergo, the two of us charging off alone towards further turbulent waters was dumb. This was never more apparent than when against intention or instruction our legs appeared in front of us and we began to carve through the water like unguided torpedoes. We continued to search the banks and rocks but the likelihood of either of us stopping to assist Neil was minimal.

Adam and I locked our arms as we hurtled through the water, frequently having to pull one or other from under the surface and away from an undercurrent. We each crossed our legs as we had been told and tried to relax while we charged towards immovable obstructions at bone shattering velocity. As with all such advice the theory somewhat outweighed the practice, being along the same lines as forcibly punching a fast approaching shark on the nose as a deterrent.

I felt scared and exhilarated in equal measure but my only thought was for that of Neil's safety. Adam and I were aware that our course and journey was beyond our control, the inertia we had gained had removed decision from our minds leaving only instinct and reaction, neither of which helped as we crashed into a boulder. We took the blow and cushioned the impact through a well-timed and extremely fortunate bend of our legs and before the daze could clear we had spun around the rock and were hurtling head first and backwards through the water.

Adam and I unlocked arms and again began to try and swim and steer our way through the carnage. We were bruised and battered and most likely bleeding but we pushed on, knowing that there was every possibility Neil had passed through this alone. I was thankful for our helmets and grateful for the sort of friend that followed without question. Up ahead we saw nothing but white, twisting churning water. We were being flushed through Satan's U-bend, and Hans had pulled the chain.

We tumbled through the water and absorbed each impact through the padding of our life jackets, just trying to keep our feet above the water and out of the reach of the undercurrent. Up ahead, pressed back against a rock so big it was almost an island, was the bedraggled figure we had been searching for. I yelled to Adam and we linked our arms again and fought to aim ourselves towards Neil. Whether he was conscious or not I couldn't tell at this stage, but he was there and almost within reach.

As medical assistance goes, two men crashing into a third is not high on the must-do list of activities but at least the yelling confirmed Neil was alive. He looked genuinely surprised to see us and relieved in equal measure. There would be time enough for questions, at that moment the issue was getting out of the water. We were now a triumvirate, less manoeuvrable and with absolutely no intention of releasing each other. The only way we could go, the only chance we had, was to continue on, down river to calmer water.

At first the waterfall didn't cross our mind. Relief and exhaustion preoccupied our thoughts and any free space available was used wondering if we would get a refund for completing the majority of our journey outside of the raft. As the waterfall approached through the mist of spray however, it was safe to say that it quickly found its way to the forefront of our thoughts. Ominous drops have a way of doing that I've since discovered. Once again, the speed and momentum we had gained prevented us from discussing alternative options so each of us just tried to deal with the inevitability of our fate. Strangely, this involved yelling at the top of our voices.

For the second time that day I found myself flying through the air, only this time I was holding on to Adam and Neil. As circumstances went, I was forced to list this as an improvement to my afternoon. Now fortunately, we were not rafting in Colorado and our drop was only six or seven feet. This was after all a commercial rafting route and we were in Scotland. None of this made the experience any less terrifying or the blood from Neil's nose any less real. He had involuntarily punched himself in the face on impact of the water as we separated mid-air and arse-flopped to the level below. We surfaced and spent a while realising we were no longer moving against our will. I can only describe the sensation as unexpected and as satisfying as being woken up to a blow job.

A wooden bridge crossed the river up ahead and we swam slowly and methodically towards it. Perched on the edge, our feet dangling purposefully above the surface, we pat each other on the back and didn't speak the words of gratification we each felt. Beaten, bruised and bleeding but together and thankful for as much, it was nevertheless a typical day so far.

But as a cure for hangover, I wasn't sure this would catch on.

BETWEEN A COCK AND A HARD PLACE

"It doesn't mean anything." Neil was being as supportive as a training bra and his sincerity wasn't lost through the partitions of the cubicle toilets we were in.

"Yes, it does." I tried to say forcefully, determined not to have this one tiny, pathetic glimmer of cordial contact shat on from a great height.

"Adam?" Neil being in the middle tapped the left side of his cubicle for confirmation. A toilet roll dropped over the top of the siding and hit Neil in the face. I sensed from the swearing that it may have hit him in the nose. "Oi you tit-wank! Ducking 'it be in dnose. What d'you do dat for?"

"Sorry mate! I thought you needed bog roll."

"Actually I think he just wanted you to confirm that my little interactions with Beth meant nothing."

"Uh-huh." Neil stated.

"Oh right. Missed that. I'm kind of dealing with something here."

"Adam, if you're masturbating in there I swear to God I'm gonna kill you."

"Yeah right, like I would be. Actually I think that whole white water experience has left me literally shitting myself."

"Left *you* shitting yourself? I did that alone, how do you think I feel?"

"I wonder what Beth feels like?" I said, apparently out loud.

"Shut up Steve!" They said together. "Adam, are you gonna be long in there or what?" Neil continued impatiently. Like we had somewhere to be. I was grateful to be inside and comfortably above the water for a change.

"Yeah I could be, you boys go on ahead, I'll catch up. Don't go with the bog roll Neil."

"Don't worry, I'll leave three sheets under the door mate." He said.

"Yeah what the fuck ever. You can leave me Beth if you like?"

"Dream on tosser." I called out.

An hour ago we had been hugging each other for dear life.

I had been genuinely concerned for Neil's safety. All manner of thoughts had flooded through my mind while Adam and I were in the water searching for him. I didn't want to picture a life where he wasn't in it but for the briefest of moments it had flashed in there and somehow a silhouette had remained, burned against a wall of my mind. The image was dull and lifeless and that would pretty-much sum up the life that I would have without him.

I tried to imagine having to tell Jane and the kids about what had happened. I wondered whether or not I would step in as a fatherly figure in times to come, ensuring that with any question about him that was asked I would have an anecdote to tell. I would make sure that in every way possible they knew the man their father was. The pivotal influence that he had had on my life, the good times that we had shared, the joy and colour that he had brought. I'd have to comfort Jane too of course, she would be distraught with grief, desperate for a familiar face, a kindred spirit that could share in the baron desolation of the life that once was. We'd grow close, probably end up spending more and more time together, and take showers together-

"Ow! You knobjockey, what did you do that for?" I yelled as the offending wet towel was thrown over a hook on the wall. My arse cheek burned fiercely, as exposed and recently slapped tender skin tends to do.

"Sorry mate, couldn't resist the opportunity. Where were you? You were miles away just then?"

"I was just thinking about shagging your Mrs actually." As brothers, we had no secrets.

"Yeah whatever mate!" Ha ha!

"Well I know who I'd rather be taking a shower with."

"Me too, but leave it out mate I really don't want to see you with a hard on."

"Don't worry, you probably couldn't tell after the day we've had. I mean how cold was that water?"

"Yeah don't I know it." We stepped into the shower room and found our way to separate walls. My arse still tingled and that wasn't a thought I ever hoped to have standing naked next to another man. I pushed the silver button on the wall that would release the cleansing water I so desperately wanted and was forced to scream like a girl as cold water blasted forth from the nozzle. "Leave it a minute mate, it'll warm up in a sec."

"Tell that to my balls, they've taken the high road." I danced around trying to get warm again, or dry, or both. "I can't tell you how sick I am of being cold."

"Mate, stop hopping, you look so gay."

"Cheers mate." I said as steam from Neil's shower started to waft over towards me. It was the warmest experience I'd had since the campfire that morning.

Suddenly Adam appeared in the archway to the shower room and both Neil and I stopped talking. Cold water started pouring down my back but I was momentarily stunned at the sight before me. I couldn't have been more shocked if Adam's cock had been dragging along the floor behind him, which to be honest, it practically was.

"Jesus, it's Nessy." This was Neil, I couldn't speak, my jaw had quite literally dropped, I didn't want to be staring open mouthed at a naked man in the shower but there I was, finishing off the work my hopping had started.

"Alright lads?" Adam said as he approached the spare wall.

151

The freezing water had been spraying me in the back for some time now and I was actually numb from the neck down. Possibly even blue. Neil turned to look at me and I was grateful for the distraction.

"He's a fucking porn star!" He proclaimed incredulously.

"I wondered what had happened to my share, how fortuitous for me to find out." I said. "Adam, if I ever, ever hear you moaning about anything, anything at all, ever again, I'm going to beat you to death with a replica dildo. Alright?" I turned away to face the wall, no longer concerned about the temperature of the water. I could no longer argue that cold water had any noticeable effect on my manhood, in the same way that I could no longer see any reason to bother trying to satisfy a woman sexually ever again. I clearly wasn't up to the job.

Adam however just showered, humbly. He could have ridiculed us, belittled us, in fact he could have slapped me across the forehead from the other side of the room, but he just showered. My battered ego was more grateful than I could ever explain.

"You better pass me the soap before Adam gets it mate." I said to Neil. I felt that in days to come we would be forming a support group. Adam continued oblivious and before long I managed to think of something other than his schlong.

"So how the hell did you end up so far down the river so quickly then?" Adam said to Neil.

"Dunno mate, naturally buoyant I guess. Great fun though."

"Oh yeah, marvellous. Jagged edges, giant bloody boulders and killer undercurrents, top notch entertainment." I said unconvinced.

"But that's what you pay for, the thrill and excitement. It's the most alive I've felt in ages, and that's important. I'm realising that more and more. That's what the experience is all about. It's not supposed to be a day on the river – it's not the bloody 'Wind in the Willows'."

"Yes Neil, but if I'd have wanted a near death experience I could have just let Adam drive us somewhere." Neil was still trying to sell this to me even after everything that had happened.

"In fairness, I suspect it is more fun when you're inside the raft."

"You think?"

"Well you've changed your tune, what about Beth?" Neil added.

"What about her?"

"I thought she had made your day." He performed an exaggerated head-wobble with this sentiment.

"You told me it was nothing?"

"Since when do you ever listen to what I say?"

"Since we ended up white water rafting in Scotland!"

"Fair point." Neil conceded. "But I was only suggesting that perhaps you don't confess your undying love to this one straight away. At least not until she's dried off."

"I only did that once, and I never said I love you."

"No, no, that's right. You told her drunkenly that she was the most beautiful woman you had ever seen." I cringed. "She wasn't even your date."

"Well don't worry, that's not going to happen. Besides, I doubt I'll ever get another woman wet again after today."

"Relax, she seemed like a nice girl. Just don't go building this up in your usual 'all-or-nothing' way. That would kind of be out of the frying pan into the river."

"No, but he could get her number. There's no harm in talking to her again." I had recently developed a newly found respect for everything that Adam said. "Besides, maybe the distance will help. I'm sure it will help her." Neil and Adam burst out laughing at this and I returned to my cold shower. I was only enduring the temperature because it was a good seven degrees less freezing than my previous

153

dousing that day.   I had to bear in mind though that if I
didn't get out of the cold shower soon I might never have
another sexual thought again.

"Why can't you ever just shag them?"

"Eh?"

"The birds in your life, no disrespect, but why can't you
ever just shag them?"

"I have."

"Yeah, but that's never it though is it. You have to roll
them in to some huge meaningful experience. Even the
ones that really are just a shag."

"You make out like that's wrong?"

"Mate, it's me you're talking to not Jane. Yes, sometimes
that's wrong. They're not all keepers Steve." Adam was
laughing while I tried to form an argument.

"I dunno, it just sort of happens to me."

"You're like Mr Commitment, but then you don't
commit."

"I don't cheat."

"You don't have to, you live in your head. You're right
there with them, right up until the point when they're right
there with you, then you stop. It always happens."

"It's happened twice Neil, don't elaborate."

"And how many single birds have you been out with?"

"Two," I coughed. "But what's your point?"

"My point is you have a thing for unsuitable,
overcomplicated and unstable women."

"And you don't call your mother enough," said Adam.
Neil and I stopped to look at him, "sorry, I thought we were
just giving advice." I laughed and finished washing river
scum from my hair.

"This is what happens when you have a near death
experience then is it?" I said to Neil, trying to keep the soap
from my eyes.

154

"Maybe, yes. You're my little brother, it's my job to look out for you. And maybe I owe you after today, both of you."

"If you try and hug me I'll rip out your arms."

"I'm just saying, we've got you back now, or at least we're getting you back, so I don't want to lose you straight away. From now on, for the foreseeable future at least, you don't make a move without me. Deal?"

"Are you gonna hug me if I agree," I said meaning every word. Neil smiled sarcastically. "Fine mate, whatever you think is best."

"Good, so we're agreed, put Beth in the spank bank and move on."

"Already there mate," said Adam.

"She was fucking hot." agreed Neil.

"Can I at least get her number?" I asked, filing her away.

"Dunno bud, you tell me."

The truth it turns out was that I couldn't get Beth's number. I didn't get the chance to and I blame Neil entirely. While Adam and I were risking life and limb in a macho foolhardy way, Hans was turning on the charm. I'm man enough to see that there really was no contest and petty enough to attribute my lack of opportunity on a man that was at risk from drowning, but I could have done without witnessing the gratuitous farewell embrace of the recently acquainted.

Scotland was turning out to be an interesting place, this holiday was turning out to be a literally painful experience and my expectations were growing by the hour. In truth, I wasn't really bothered about the Beth thing. She was gorgeous yes, and had anything of happened between us it would have done wonders for my self-esteem, its true, but I wasn't here for that. A large part of the reason I was here at all was to get over women, well *a* woman to be specific. The absolute last thing I wanted to concern myself with was another one. Besides, Beth had smiled at me first and in my

155

current frame of mind that alone would keep me going for days.

It did get me thinking though. Neil had made some sense before, back in the showers. I did have terrible judgement when it came to women. I lived by the 'if they're right then they're wrong' theory and bore the consequences of my actions at every turn. My problem was thinking. I was a thinker, not a do-er, Hans would have shagged Beth and be finishing his post-coital protein shake before I'd even got around to saying 'hello' again. This was the way things went with me. I'd play out the scenarios while others lived them and before I knew it the opportunity, whatever it may have been, would have passed by. I resembled a chess player, strategizing each and every move, anticipating responses and counter offences and then finally as the hour approached I would make my move. Which is ironic, because I'm fucking shit at chess.

LOGGERS LEAP

"Where we going then?" Adam asked as we crested another hill on a deserted road to nowhere.

"Does it matter?" Neil replied smiling through the tissues sticking out from his nose.

"Well yeah, actually, it matters a little, I'm driving," Adam said weaving through the emptiness of a Scottish B-road.

"All we're looking for is something flat and out of the way."

"Sounds like one of my ex-girlfriends," I said looking out of the windows. They laughed but added no argument.

"I reckon we're close though. Anywhere around here should do, I haven't seen another car or person for ages. And the map says there's a river up ahead."

"Okay, so up ahead it is then." said Adam, cornering on two wheels. I worried about the fact that I no longer worried about that.

"Gonna have to be soon though," added Neil, "Bob's getting curious again."

"Oh cheers mate, thanks for sharing." I said.

"You my friend are welcome. It's a fact, and Adam's driving isn't exactly helping. I'm touching cloth here as it is."

"How can you say that?" He said, taking his eyes off a road that hadn't been straight since the Romans had been around in order to stare at Neil with an incredulous look. I felt he was answering his own question while at the same time drawing me ever closer to the likelihood of shitting myself too.

"Can we stop soon please?" I begged, trying to refocus the group, "I think we left the suspension behind on that

157

last hump." I needed a cigarette but daren't try and light one for fear of losing my eyebrows. I was now past caring whether our chosen spot had a river nearby, or indeed turned out to be a waterlogged bog of treacherous and questionable integrity. I wanted to stop the car and rejoice in the simple pleasure of walking. God wasn't listening.

"Would you two girls calm down please?" Adam always managed to take on a more assertive tone whilst driving, "it's levelling out up ahead, look." He pointed, with both hands.

"Terrific." I said, reaching forward to rest a comforting hand on Neil's shoulder.

The Zafira rattled around us, groaning in protest while maintaining an intention to push on until the very end, ours or its, whichever came first. As the afternoon drew towards early evening I felt once again the chill from the air rushing past the absent rear window creating a vacuum that sucked at the side of my face like a teenage girl at a disco.

I thought about the various sections of our car that were currently held in place with duct tape and then of the many repairs we would no doubt have to complete once we stopped. I tried to distract myself and went to poke my finger through one of the small pellet holes in the door and then the car lurched violently and I stopped myself in time to avoid having to reattach my finger with the aforementioned tape. I found some comfort in that.

I was unable to express my joy when the car finally did stop. I opened the door and fell out. I couldn't have been happier if the L.N.C.A. had been waiting for me. Inertia pushed me onwards and I staggered about the grass like a man fleeing an axe murderer. I rolled over on my back and lit a cigarette, defeated but out in the open. The other two approached me curiously - that is to say, they approached with a look of curiosity on their faces, not that they were walking funny. Neil was walking like a man who had already shit himself but given the circumstances that was an altogether too realistic a possibility for me to entirely rule it out.

As it happened though, they appeared more concerned about the land that we had chosen to stop on. I looked over my shoulder and was confronted by a sea of rabbit holes. The ground, which hadn't been particularly flat to start with, had been ravished to such an extent that I feared the car might subside into an intricate network of burrows that probably ran four feet deep. There were so many holes in fact we would be lucky to find enough solid ground to sleep on. This was the thought that had them both perplexed.

I stood to join them looking out over an expanse of grass desolated by the impact of very small bombs. "Suggestions?" I said.

"Polyfilla?" said Adam, scratching his head. Neil had made some further steps forward, surveying the land with genuine interest.

"There's either fucking hundreds of the little buggers," he said, "or one with OCD."

"Very helpful. But are we staying or what?" I feared someone was going to try and make me get back in the car.

"Damn right we're staying? Why wouldn't we?"

"Oh you know, just because." I waved my hands around, hoping to say everything in that gesture.

"You're always the same Steve, where you see a problem, I see an opportunity."

"Actually I'm with Steve on this one Neil."

"An opportunity?" I said, lost. "You fancy a game of golf or something?"

"If only! But no, grab the stuff and let's get set up, I'll tell you in a bit."

"Set up *where*?" I said, going for the waving gesture again with a little more intensity. "There's not enough solid ground to land a tent peg."

"Don't be such a tart, just get the stuff would you."

"That's your argument then is it? Denial?"

"It's worked well for a lot of years Steve," I looked at Adam, but he just shrugged and made his way to the car.

"One condition Neil," said Adam throwing his bags to the floor, "if the ground starts moving in the night I'm off."

"Yeah whatever Adam, you and I both know you're gonna roll into a rabbit hole and think your lucks in."

We unpacked the tents and I waited for Neil to explain to me where the opportunity lay in our surroundings. From what I could tell, we were in a valley, with a foot wide stream running through it and more rabbits than Ann Summers.

There were mounds and dips and troughs and rocks scattered across the ground in all directions. A bank climbed up to our left and trees valiantly tried to assert their authority over gravity. I struggled to find opportunities. There was an opportunity for me not to be able to cover my ankles in the stream. There was an opportunity for me not to have a good night's sleep, there was even an opportunity for me to get gobbled off by a bunny but none of these things were prospects that I exactly relished.

"Do you plan on enlightening me then or what?" I finally said to Neil.

"How do you mean?" He said as the last of the bags were thrown back into the car. Our campsite had been erected faster than a virgin at a Playboy party and there was a likelihood of food and alcohol in the near future. I needed both, but not necessarily in that order.

"I mean, where is the opportunity you see in the problems Adam and I found." Fuck it, I wasn't going to be the only one looking stupid.

"The rabbit holes," strangely not a question. "Nature's toilet."

"Eh?"

"You can shit down them, like having a u-bend," I just looked at him, this was something he had actually thought

160

about. "A creature comfort so to speak." I fell about laughing.

"That," Adam said, clicking his fingers and pointing excitedly, "is a bloody marvellous idea."

"Hang on lads, I thought we were supposed to be respecting the surroundings, harmonising with our environment and all that, shitting down a rabbit hole doesn't exactly sound like it's in keeping with that ethos."

"There is nothing more natural than taking a shit outside."

"That maybe so, but don't you think they might get a little pissed at finding a giant steaming turd on their doorstep?"

"So chose wisely then young Jedi, it's not like they're all in use is it?"

"What am I supposed to do? Check for a forwarding address? See if there's a pile of newspapers lying unread on the floor?"

"You're the one with the issue Steve, not me. You don't see the rabbits complaining about shitting outside." He had a point of course. I'd stood on more rabbit shit than grass since we had arrived.

"It won't be the same though," Adam said, looking around at the many so-called opportunities. "I need the splash."

"The splash?" I said, lighting a cigarette in sheer exasperation.

"Yeah, you know, the sound you get when you pinch one off."

"Mate! I know what you're on about, but we're talking about shitting down a rabbit hole, if it's in any way the same I am seriously concerned about your house."

"Always deceptive though, don't you think?"

"In what way?" Adam and I asked together in completely different tones.

"Well, the jobby never quite lives up to the noise it makes. You get this enormous splash and think to yourself 'there's one for the books!' and it turns out to be far from the truth."

"Like Wonderbras." Said Adam, nodding to himself.

"Whoah, whoah, whoah, you are not seriously comparing shits to tits are you?" I asked.

"I just meant it's like false advertising. The contents tend to vary from the actual size shown."

"That's inspired, Adam," I said.

"I thank you."

"But," I quickly added, "If you take a shit in that stream I'll make you eat it."

"So, on that note boys," Neil said feeling victorious, "I really need to go and take care of business, so I suggest that if you don't need to, perhaps you can go and get some firewood?"

I walked off not waiting to see which direction either of them went. In my mind the rabbits would not be pleased to find Englishman shitting on their doorstep, we were in Scotland after all and I feared it would only open up historic wounds. But in truth, it made sense, there was a backward logic to it. Neil had once again mastered the outdoors. I stomped off.

Wood evaded me. If I found any, it was invariably wet or soft or soft and wet, sometimes broken, always useless. I don't know why it was wet, it hadn't rained in days, but then everything about this holiday had so far defied normal convention so really I shouldn't have been surprised. The fact was I was going to have to hit the bank, it was unavoidable.

We needed to get a fire going, as sooner or later Scotland's secret of persistently aggressive mosquitoes would be upon us once again. They had appeared on our first night camping and had it not been for the fact that they only stayed around for an hour we would have legged it back to England without stopping to get in the car. I know that there are mosquitoes in England, but in Scotland, they have attitude and bite with the tenderness of a Glaswegian kiss. I hated them and began to itch just thinking about them. I went towards the bank with renewed motivation.

I marched towards the tree line with the sun on my back feeling that in the time that had passed I now had a date with a rabbit hole myself. I began scouring the floor for fallen branches and loose stumps, anything that looked like it could form a casual relationship with lighter fluid. The bank rose up above me and the foliage grew denser. I felt certain I would be able to find dry wood here. I would return victorious, a lumberjack back with the spoils of a hard day's work.

I pushed aside branches and leaves, twigs and bushes, I didn't need to climb the bank, the wood was coming to me. I began picking up suitable pieces and hurling them out in to the clearing. I would collect enough to see us through to the time I passed out from exhaustion, fatigue or post traumatic stress, after that it would be someone else's problem. I continued collecting until I felt sure I had shifted enough to barricade myself in, and then I looked for a deserted rabbit hole.

There are several times in a man's life when he feels at his most vulnerable, when he's exposed without chance of adequate defence. This rule doesn't apply to all men of course but during that moment I discovered that it did apply to me.

I had found a suitable spot, far enough away from the bank to allow me to comfortably squat with absolutely no chance of falling over, or into, my chosen hole, and there I was, hovering. I became convinced that our deserted location would somehow suddenly become flooded with girl guides on a field trip. In my head, for every brown eye there was a Brown Owl, but I remained undetected for long enough to exhale.

I had not at this time contemplated the fact that I was without toilet roll, but such matters, while squatting exposed to the wilderness were of little concern to me. I feared a

163

vicious recrimination on my arse from a disgruntled rabbit or worse still, a mosquito bite on my fella. The wilderness was a hazardous place. It should come with a warning.

Several minutes later I was missing my book and realising that I had actually finished. I looked around for a dock leaf or any such suitable alternative to Andrex but there are some things that you just can't substitute. I reached carefully down to the pocket of my jeans and pulled out my mobile phone, hopeful that either Neil or Adam had taken the quiet opportunity to touch base with their respective others and had the damn things turned on.

I rang Neil but his phone was switched off.

I rang Adam - the tree above me rang back. Of course, I made the mistake of looking up. I couldn't help it, it was a reflex action made in sheer and total surprise at the sudden shocking sound of a ringtone hanging above me. And there it was, suspended over a Y-shaped crook of a tree branch, the best kept secret of the wild, the lesser-spotted One-Eyed Trouser Snake, dangling down at me like a stoned anaconda. I don't know what he was thinking, I don't know why he was up there or even how he had found such a place. I don't know why he hadn't heard me or said something, but most of all I don't know why life is so cruel as to show me a sight that no friend should ever have to see. Husbands don't see as much when they witness the birth of their children. I actually felt sick. And then Adam swore and answered his phone.

"Hello?"

"Ahhhhhhhhhhhhhhhhhhhhhhhhhhhhhhhhhhhhhhhhhhhhh!"

"Steve?"

"Ahhhhhhhhhhhhhhhhhhhhhhhhhhhhhhhhhhhhhhhhhhhhhh!"

"You alright mate?"

"Alright? Al-fucking-right? I'll never be alright again after today. This is too much."

"Where are you?"

"In hell."

164

"Seriously."

"You don't want to know. *I* don't want to know!"

"Hang on, I think there's someone below me-."

"Ahhhhhhhhhhhhhhhhhhhhhhhhhhhhhhhhhhhhhhhhhhhhh!"
I hung up the phone and fell forwards. "You complete tosser!"

"Steve? Is that you? What the hell are you doing down there."

"Collecting logs you fuckwit! What the hell are you doing up there?" I yelled.

"Well I was trying to go for a shit."

"Why couldn't you have used a rabbit hole like everyone else?"

"Well, you got me thinking that it kind of wasn't right to."

"But you're over one now, why do you think I'm here?" I paused for the briefest of moments in the most horrifying episode of my entire life as a thought occurred, "You were trying for a dust splash weren't you Adam?"

"No..."

"Adam?"

"Well -"

"Forget it, I don't even want to know. Just drop me down the bogroll so I can get the fuck out of here. And lets never speak of this again. Ever."

"Um -"

"What's 'um' Adam, I have no time for 'um'." He looked at me sheepishly, it could mean only one thing. "You don't have any do you?"

"No," he paused and I feared he had lost control and was about to squeeze, "But you don't either." As statements went, this one did nothing to make me feel better.

"Great, so you're telling me we need to get Neil over here then, as if this moment wasn't perfect enough as it is?"

"Well I could kind of do with some."

165

"Adam, answer me a question," there was nothing he could say that was going to be right, but I had to know, "have you finished?"

"Um, kind of, well, mid-way through I'd say."

"Call for Neil, Adam, call for him right now." Somewhere very close to me, there was a log with Adams name on it. "And do me one more favour Adam."

"What now?"

"Just clench alright?"

If you've just joined us, this is Mick standing in for Graham on Late Love Live and we're talking about those difficult times in your life when the world is conspiring against you, when it's just coming at you from all angles. I think we've got Steve on the line, Steve?

Mick? Yeah hi Mick, it's Steve

Where you calling us from tonight Steve?

From the car Mick [*muffled laughter*]

Right, excellent. Okay Steve, so you've got a story for us then?

Yeah, sort of, um, its [*quiet prompting from the background*] I mean I don't really think it's suitable but well [*more gestures of encouragement*]

Excellent, great, great, well that's what we're here for apparently...

You see, I've just been shit on from a great height

Uh...

Oh bugger, can I say 'shit' on the radio Mick?

Think you just did Steve, I wouldn't worry too much about it though my producer says no one's listening anyway...

Okay, great, well like I said, I've just been shit on from a great height and I'm not sure how to deal with it.

So who was the woman in question then, sorry I'm presuming it's a woman...?

No it was a bloke actually, what kind of women have you been hanging out with Mick?

My apologies for the assumption, let's just stick to the facts...

I've heard about those girls, who like that, got to say though it just seems a little wrong to me Mick don't you think? I

166

think that's more one for the Sex Confidential show actually-...

I think we're straying from the point here a little Steve, let's just get this story out there and get a little feedback, maybe help you through this...

Right, right, sorry Mick, so anyway, there I was just minding my own business, out of everyone's way, just going along quite happily... I've got wood...

That's... nice for you, this is clearly at the centre of your thoughts Steve

It very nearly was Mick yes,

Okay, I'm with you, so you're just living your life, thinking all is well, getting on with your day...

Um, yeah okay, anyway, out of nowhere, I get shat on, I mean what the hell right?

Absolutely, absolutely, and I think it's interesting that you use that phrase, I mean I think we've all been there, been taken unaware like that, been emotionally covered...

Really? I mean I was thinking this sort of thing was quite uncommon.

God no, honestly? I mean have you never listened to this show? You're not alone Steve, we, all of us have at some point been where you've been....

I seriously doubt that...

You don't have to make allowances for us Steve, tell it like it is... put us there with you, make it so real we can practically smell it

Mick, mate, that's not right...

You sound scarred Steve?

Well I mean I'm gonna have to get rid of the shirt for sure...

A present was it? Don't hold back Steve, let it out, you're not alone, I think we've all felt like the world has shat on us from a great height at some point Steve...

Eh? A present? No, hang on, it was Adam and this is getting out of hand now.

He's your boyfriend? Adam?

Excuse me?

He cheated on you then?

No, he just shat on me! Jesus, no wonder no one's listening – you certainly aren't.

Sorry, sorry, you're saying he literally *shat on you?* [*Uproarious laughter*]

Yes, he was in the tree above where I had sat down. What the hell did you think I meant?

Oh god...

You're fu - [*Click*]

We'll be right back after these messages...

Neil made me do it. The bastard.

Tuesday

G.I.L.F.

We awoke to find that the car had subsided into an intricate network of burrows that probably ran four feet deep. As mornings went, it seemed fairly typical.

"Well, we're screwed." said Adam, summarising our situation succinctly. I think he was going for cheerfully optimistic, he missed by the distance of a country mile.

Neil was about to speak but I cut him off. "If you say one word about seeing an opportunity here," I seethed, but words ultimately failed me. "Just don't alright, don't say a fucking word." Adam laughed and Neil shut up, handing me a conciliatory cigarette by way of a peace offering. I took it and then looked at the car again.

"So, to bring us up to speed then, let's just re-cap," I began. "So far, our motor has been hit head on by a tow truck. The driver's airbag has exploded, the right wing has been shot. We have a small but no-less important window missing; most of our bumpers are taped on – no, no, more specifically, hanging off - the light clusters are now housing dangerously exposed bulbs. We have a tree branch for an aerial and we may or may not still be driving around with mutant sodding maggots crawling all over the place. And now the ground has quite literally opened up and swallowed the fucking thing. Have I missed anything? I mean I think that about sums up where we're at don't you think?"

Adam and Neil looked at me, nodding. I could tell they wanted to say something, something that would put this whole thing into perspective for me, something that would help me get to grips with a set of facts that staggered belief. By rights, the car was a write-off. It seemed to suit us perfectly. "You can be so negative sometimes Steve, Jesus."

"You don't think that this is in some way a problem then?" I asked. On this occasion, I had no issue whatsoever with being proved wrong. Bring it on.

"No, I can see that it's a problem, but it's just one of those things. It's happened and we'll deal with it."

"I think someone's trying to tell us something." I said ignoring his matter-of-fact approach for one of persecution and doom.

"How do you mean?" Adam asked, scratching and stretching.

"This is god, he's punishing me."

"Steve, you're an atheist."

"Exactly, that's why he's so pissed off."

"Right, excellent. Now you have a beef with god. It's not even eight o'clock yet."

"I'm telling you boys, this is a warning."

"Maybe it's not us," Adam said, helpfully. "Or you. Maybe it's just the car."

"Right, of course, god's got an issue with a Zafira. Am I even saying these words?"

"I knew there was something not right about it when you turned up Neil," Adam said, reliving a small nightmare. "This car, it's like Christine, in reverse."

"I'm not even having this conversation." Neil said, walking towards the car.

"He controls the rabbits Neil, nature is rebelling against us." I continued, laughing now.

"The only thing nature is rebelling against this morning Steve is the pile of shit you left in that bush. Now let's figure out how the hell we get out of here."

The Zafira sat unevenly in the middle of a hole that was on closer inspection about two feet deep. It leaned backwards, implying that at any moment it could just disappear through the soil entirely. The way our luck was running, this was a possibility none of us wanted to contemplate.

The situation stood that even if we had wanted to call someone, none of us were covered by anything useful like breakdown assistance, and even if we were, none of us knew quite exactly where we were. We had two choices, embrace our surroundings and try and be resourceful fashioning a crude ramp like structure from lose foliage and branches, or just abandon the car and walk the rest of the way round our holiday. We knew the kind of men we were.

"Look," said Neil, "we packed up the stuff, it'll be fine." He said to Adam as we continued walking down the road.

"That's right, forgive me for not seeing the security of a car with a missing window."

"Well, on the bright side, it's not like anyone can nick the car is it?" I said.

"Well someone's cheered up," Neil said, looking around for signs of life in the hills and valleys around us. The road wound deep through the countryside but as we had seen no one on the way in to our designated camping spot we reasoned that the road had to lead somewhere and we had a better chance just carrying on. "Besides, at least it's not raining."

As the rain fell, we walked on, each of us in our own thoughts and most likely contemplating the blame for our current situation. I don't know how far we walked, being that I tried to avoid it for most of my life I had very little frame of reference. I did know that two hours had passed without so much as a telephone pole coming into view. I wanted to mention this, over and over again, but it didn't quite seem the time. I walked on quietly resolute.

"Do you know we haven't seen as much as a fucking telephone pole?" said Neil, "This road has to go somewhere. I mean they didn't just build it to use up the tarmac surely?"

"Mate, anything is possible, maybe it's just looping round on some scenic extravaganza," Adam said, struggling through the rain.

What we needed was a farmhouse, with a farmer, who owned a tractor. In the scale of wishes, with World Peace or a hand-job from Beyonce being near the top, this stood comfortably near the bottom of actual likelihood. We were surrounded in all directions by wilderness and sheep, occasionally cows and what, according to Adam had been a camel but what I suggested was more credibly going to be a lama. It stood to reason that anyone who chose to live around here was going to be in some way employed in the agricultural sector.

"You know, I didn't get this wet in the river," I said as I considered the choices we had made so far that day. Staying with the car suddenly seemed like the more sensible option. Okay so we may not have been able to drive anywhere, but at least we would have been dry.

"Stop your whining, look, there's a place up ahead, and there's smoke coming from the chimney." I hadn't even noticed it but Neil was right, there it was indeed, like an oasis glistening through the moisture in my eyes.

We approached the property with hope in our hearts. It was white with well-maintained windows and a freshly painted door and a picket fence that separated the garden from, well, more grass. All in all there were very definite signs of life everywhere we looked. And we could see someone though the downstairs window.

I can't imagine how we must have appeared to an unassuming person about to answer their door to three drenched men of varying ages, shapes and sizes. Two of whom were wheezing a little from the exertion of walking up the slight incline of the driveway, another who was tutting quietly and letting us know we only had our selves to blame. Nevertheless, the door was opened, and a small friendly looking lady answered it, young at seventy if she was a day old. The lady smiled politely, as you no-doubt would if mental patients stood on your doorstep. She looked like my gran and I think she was just relieved that we weren't holding bibles.

"Can I help you gentlemen?" she said with a soft and welcoming accent.

"I certainly hope so," Neil began, although where he planned to go from here was anybody's guess. "You see, we've had a spot of car trouble, some way off down the road there, and we were looking for someone who might be able to give us a hand." Neil smiled, while I wanted to clarify that the car itself was fine and that the trouble as Neil had put it lay more with the ground around it, but I felt that the general gist of the situation had been adequately relayed.

"Oh, I see, well that is a bother then. Well, I have some jump leads somewhere, I could drive you back down and we could give that a try?"

"Actually, we may need more of a jump than that," I said, deciding clarity was in fact required. "The car has," I searched for the right word, "Sunk."

"Sunk?" The granny repeated.

"Yeah, funny eh?" I said, patting Neil on the shoulder rather forcefully.

"I wonder, is your husband home at all?" Adam said, in manner that could have come across as a little sinister depending on which side of the door you happened to be standing on. I gave him a look, hoping he might finish by saying 'as I couldn't help but notice the tractor behind the house'. He just smiled while the granny took a small step back towards the door.

"No," she said, slowly, "My William is no longer with us, and I have no need of another man to fill his side of the bed. I take care of myself quite well thank you very much."

"Of course, my idiot friend meant no offence, ma'am." I had never said 'ma'am' before in my entire life, but now seemed as good a time as any to welcome it into my vocabulary.

"None taken," the granny said. "So it's a tow you'll be after then is it?"

"Ideally yes," Neil continued, "unless you're a lot stronger than you look?"

"They'll be less of the cheek if you don't mind young man," was the reply in a tone that made me think she actually was my gran, "let me just get my coat then." And with that she closed the door.

We had set off in search of a farmhouse with a farmer who owned a tractor, what we found was a little old lady with a Morris Minor, a tow rope and a picket fence.

"This should be interesting," said Adam.

"Yep, Beyonce should be along any minute now." I said to myself.

"Eh?"

"Doesn't matter."

I tend not to use the word 'amazing' lightly, but our saviour, a granny in the mountains named Mrs Langdon, put three men to shame that day. Barking orders and instructions like she had been rescuing hapless morons her entire life, which given her location she may well have been, Mrs Langdon had us out of our hole before lunch time.

It is not easy to forget the image of a Morris Minor yanking a custom-blue Zafira from a two-foot deep subsidence. Especially with a white haired old lady yelling out of the driver's window at us 'wheezers' telling us to 'put our back's into it and stop being such a couple of pansies!' But that's the image and without her we would no doubt have still been stuck there. I often look for lessons in life, something to bring reason to a situation not entirely enjoyable or productive from an obvious perspective, being pussy-whipped by a pensioner seemed a lesson enough for one day.

We followed Mrs Langdon back to her property with the simple promise of a few minutes by an open fire and a pot of coffee. I wanted to repay her kindness but could think of nothing constructive any one of us could possibly do to improve her life in any way. It was she after all who had assisted us. Had we the basic resources of ingenuity, inventiveness or wilderness experience we would no doubt have not felt the need to beg favours from the old. Short of pimping Adam and his ample appendage, I felt Mrs Langdon was as close to satisfied with her lot as was possible to be. I was already growing tired of life-lessons.

Mrs Langdon busied herself by providing towels and toilet opportunities, bottomless coffee pots and a kitchen I could smoke in. And just when I felt that there was nothing further this woman could do to prove to us just what a godsend she really was, Mrs Langdon picked up the phone and spoke the words we had all been too ashamed to say. Had I not known better, I would swear she had been channelling us. You have to watch grannies - they know everything.

"No, really, I did not say that I would," Adam was getting more and more agitated in the back of the car, as if we might just turn around and go back to the cottage and spill the beans. He couldn't have been more concerned if he'd have found out Fiona had bugged the vehicle. "Saying I was really grateful for her help and that I want to jump her bones are not the same."

"Yeah okay Adam, we believe you." I wasn't entirely comfortable with the image of Adam and Mrs Langdon taming the beast but the look on his face at the insinuation was truly priceless. "It's just that you keep going on about her. We think you love her. That you might want to kiss her." Neil was doing a little dance and humming the tune.

"All I said is that it was extremely thoughtful of her to make that call and book the rooms for us."

"And that you love her." Foul ball.

"And that she wasn't wrong in thinking that we could all do with a night in a real bed."

"Or a night in her bed." Strike one.

"And that waking up to a cooked breakfast and central heating and a hot shower might indeed be appreciated."

"And a hard on." Strike two.

"I'm not going to bite. You're sick. Both of you." Possibly true.

"What is it with you and old ladies anyway Adam? You're like a slack-fanny magnet." I questioned.

"He really does want to fuck her."

"Aaaaaaaaaaaahhhhhhhhhhhhhh!" he's out. "Tossers!"

PAPA, QU'EST-CE QUE C'EST, UNE 'FANNY STACK'?

It took a couple of hours to reach the Bed and Breakfast following toilet breaks and map checks and the apparent inability of a Scottish council to erect a road sign that might be useful. When we arrived, we all felt that enough time had once again been spent in the Zafira. It was starting to smell so much that Adam had stopped complaining about Neil and I smoking. That may well have been the only sign we had spotted all day.

The bungalow had the same deceptive qualities as the Tardis, being that it stood innocently nestled amongst a row of comparable properties in a street of similar stature to many others we had passed through. And yet once inside it seemed to stretch on more intricately than the rabbit warren that had tried to foil us earlier. This was another trick I felt, played on unsuspecting tourists to give the impression of quiet hospitality in a property with more rooms than the Hilton Corporation. Oddly, we had been booked into a family suite.

The proprietor – a Ms Kincaide - had the kind fortune of being Mrs Langdon's daughter and the misfortune for Adams sake of bearing a striking similarity to the good woman herself. Albeit twenty odd years younger but no less efficient in her efforts to welcome us and see us settled in comfortably, she had the good grace to sound sympathetic when relaying her conversation with her mother and had laid on extra towels for us weary travellers.

We were informed that breakfast would be served at our convenience the next morning and that we shouldn't worry any about sleeping in or the likes. She gave us a key to the room and the front door of the B&B and told us to run along and find her as soon as we were ready to find out about the town. No rush.

We thanked her for her kindness, following her back through the maze and then out to the car to collect our bags for perhaps the first good night's sleep we had had since the previous Thursday. It was three o'clock in the afternoon. Neil and I had trouble sleeping at the best of times, attempting it during the middle of the day was a fool's errand.

"Who's getting the single?" Neil asked, sat on the edge of it. This was another awkward moment, we all remembered the last time any of us had shared a bed. If I thought about it for much longer I'd have to go and take another shower.

We all had to call it, anything else would suggest that we actually didn't mind sharing a bed with the other. I had deep-rooted issues on the subject but my back was forbidding me from suggesting someone sleep on the floor. I'd been that someone for almost the entire time I had been associated with Adam and Neil, I wasn't about to fall for that one again.

"That would be me," said Adam, jumping on the bed and bouncing Neil to the floor.

"Whatever," I tried, matter-of-factly.

"You two love birds deserve each other," he continued, yanking the covers free from the folds.

The room was a good size for the property. It didn't have a window but then I wasn't immediately concerned about someone not seeing the three of us sharing a room together. It did have a toilet and a shower cubicle only marginally larger than the box that holds the soap. There was a picture on the wall of the bedroom of some standard scenery, standard in that it was a truly beautiful landscape, but exactly similar to all of the other truly beautiful scenery we had been enjoying for the past three days. Familiarity really did breed contempt. As for the other fixtures and fittings,

179

tea and coffee facilities were included and we immediately got the kettle on.

"So, the plan. We grab forty here, shit, shower and shave then head on into town for food and a few beers." Said Neil.

"Steve had better start getting ready now if we're going out later, eh?" Adam said from beneath his blankets.

"And no spanking one off in the toilet either." Neil said, apparently just to me.

"What makes you think it would be me? You two are the ones missing out on your conjugals." I replied defensively.

"Two reasons, one being that you're right, we are, which makes you more acquainted with Mistress Palm and her five daughters, and secondly, and perhaps more relevantly, I had the idea first right up until the point I thought about one of you two doing it before me."

"So essentially what you're saying is that you want the bathroom first then?" I asked, "because you can't, and nor can you ever again now."

"Actually," Adam said, "and again let me point out you two spend way too much time together, none of us will be enjoying a shandy in our bog, because you'll notice that there's no door, nor even a curtain. Clearly a space saving thing given the size of the shower, so if either one of you stands in front of that bog for longer than is humanly required to take a piss, I'll flush your head down the toilet."

"Fair comment." we replied.

"But on the subject of conjugal visits, I am now going to go and ring Fiona, so finish making the drinks and for gods sake change the subject." We made the drinks, sufficiently reprimanded.

"Had you not better go and put a call in too then?" I said to Neil, stirring the coffees. Two black, one white with sugar. I was going to get the put on my headstone.

180

"Yeah, probably, later though. I'll ring later. It'll look more like my choice then, not that I'm ringing because Adam has."

"Relationships are so complicated." I laughed. "So what do you think about tonight then?"

"A wild night out in Elgin? On a Tuesday? Should be a riot." He had a point. From what we had seen driving through the town, Elgin could have been twinned with Andover. We would have to check with Ms Kincaide but if the conversation about nightlife lasted longer than thirty-seconds I'd have to move here. "I'll be happy with a decent meal and some place to sit down with a beer."

"Ah the simple luxuries." I agreed.

I walked around the double bed and threw my bag down in the corner of the room. My belongings had a damp quality found only in items that are kept outside for an extended period of time in less than airtight conditions. I probably wasn't harvesting a bacteriological culture just yet, but there was every possibility I was carrying the added wait of a few confused maggots. I relished the thought of liberating them before we left, just hopefully not from my pants.

I sat down on the bed as Neil passed my coffee over and before I knew it we were in a Morecambe and Wise sketch, it was just unfortunate that we were bearing more of a resemblance to Bert and Ernie. We sat legs outstretched on the bed drinking hot coffee in relative comfort and I thought not for the first time that things could have quite easily been worse. Yes I was sharing a bed with a farting, snoring, hairy-arsed father of two, who hadn't seen his wife since the previous Thursday and had missed more special alone time in the last week than I'd had cigarettes. And yes, I too was a little frustrated, still waiting as I was for that hand-job from Beyonce, and yes the chances of a Tuesday tryst in Elgin were slimmer than the local anorexic, but I

181

remained positive. Upbeat. The night was full of possibilities.

"Alright mincers," Adam said crashing through the door and looking at us. "You two got comfy quick."

"Adam, do the words 'go', 'fuck' and 'yourself' mean anything to you?" Neil retorted dryly.

"I'd love to but there's no door on the bog remember?" He replied sitting down on his single bed. Alone.

He downed his coffee and informed us that Fiona was fine, and that Jane and the kids were equally well, and then seemed to feel a little guilty because he then made this big thing about saying that they'd asked after me. Which was great, I suppose. I had surrogate relationships. Marvellous.

"Oh and I spoke to Trisha -" hang on.

"Who the fuck is Trisha?" Ernie and I asked simultaneously. We really did spend too much time together.

"Ms Kincaide," he said in a voice, not his own. "Just about places to go, things to see around here, that sort of thing."

"You don't hang about do you? Straight off the phone to the missus and tapping off with another bird in minutes. Steve here could get lessons from you."

"Yeah because that's what happened." Adam said while somewhat unfairly giving us both the bird.

"No, no mate, she seemed like a nice woman." I was stuck somewhere else, somewhere mundane.

"What's Trisha short for then?" I said eventually.

"Patricia." Adam said, keenly if I had to be specific.

"Patricia," I said rolling the name around, "Pat then?" I said finally.

"I think she prefers Trisha." Adam said quietly.

"Like the big scary lesbian bird from Eastenders?" I continued.

"I can see why." said Neil, laughing. "So did you arrange to meet her later then or what?"

"Meet who?" Adam asked innocently.

"Pat," Neil said. "Your bit on the side."

"No, of course I didn't. Don't be ridiculous."

"She was busy wasn't she?" I asked.

"I just thought she could show us around."

"Nice work my friend." said Neil. "But now we really should try and get some sleep."

"Ah yes, three men, three cups of coffee and an uncomfortable sleeping arrangement. The definition of futility."

"At least the beds are comfortable." said Adam.

"Easy for you to say, you're not sleeping with Neil."

"Oh cheers mate, thanks a lot."

"Please don't try and make out like I should be grateful Neil. This moment is gay enough for me as it is."

"Gay moments are the foundation of a lasting friendship."

"You're choosing now to come out to me?" I said, inching towards the edge of the bed.

"You've always been very special to me Steve."

"Fuck off."

"I think now is as good a time as any to really tell you how I feel." He moved his hand across the bed towards mine.

"Really, fuck off."

"I love you Steve."

"I'm never going to sleep again."

"Neither am I if you two keep on like that." Adam, I felt, as the protagonist in this unfolding nightmare had no right to complain, but anything that was going to shut Neil up would get no objection from me. "Because he's mine you bitch-whore!" He screamed shrilly and jumped on Neil with arms flailing. I fell off the bed trying to get away from them. It was that type of afternoon.

To be honest, sleep was a thousand miles away. The three of us were dry, out of the car for a change and we didn't have to sit on the floor or violate nature to answer its call.

Add to that the chance of a meal that contained more than one food group and this was going to be an all out party. Why we even bothered getting in to bed was beyond me. Stripping down to our boxer shorts, each of us lay trying to face away from the other. Silence lasted all of six seconds.

"Do you know men think about sex every six seconds?" said Adam.

"Has it really been that long since we talked about it?" I asked.

"You two do know I was kidding back then don't you?" Neil piped up from his pillow. "I hear either of you rustling and I'm going to sleep in the car."

"Why do you think that is?" Adam continued, lazily.

"Because I have no desire whatsoever to see your 'O' face." Neil answered truthfully.

"No you twat, I meant why do you think we think about it that often. I mean what's all the fuss about?"

"Beats me, sex just tires you out and makes your dick smell."

"You're the last of the true romantics aren't you?" I said.

"I'm serious. I mean it's ridiculous, sex is sex."

"Yeah," I interrupted, "but good sex is good sex. And great sex is great sex."

"And shit sex is shit sex." Adam postulated.

"But it's still sex." I said, "no-one ever dies wishing they'd had less sex do they?"

"So, that's it then. Sex is sex for the sake of sex?"

"You have a problem with that?"

Adam thought for a second, "Depends on who it's with I guess."

"Go on." Neil prompted lifting his head.

"After a while, it all just gets kind of samey, don't you think?"

"Which one of us has been married forever?" Neil said dropping his head back in to the pillow.

"You ever think about sex with someone else?"

"Um, DUH!" Was the educated response to Adam's question. "The world's most pointless question award goes to Adam." We laughed - Adam probably because he was relieved not to be the only one, me because in or out of a relationship, I seemed to always be thinking of sex with someone else.

"So who's on your list then?" Adam asked trying to pull back some respect.

"People we know, or like celebrities and shit?" said Neil, rolling on to his back. Adam and I followed suit, three of us in very different places all staring at the same ceiling.

"Let's stay safe and stick with the fantasy."

"Okay," said Neil, "top of my list, I dunno, Andrea Corr."

"Your all time fantasy woman is Andrea Corr?" Adam said, pulled from his own speculation.

"What? She's fit. Beautiful, talented and those eyes, and the long hair."

"And the chance of the sisters," I added unhelpfully.

"I know what she looks like, I'm just surprised."

"Why?" He said.

"Because in the scale of things," Adam searched for the phrase, "she's kind of ordinary."

"Oh yeah, she looks like every woman I meet." I said laughing.

"No, but she looks like every woman you *could* meet, or could end up with."

"Like the saying goes, there are women that you shag, and women that you marry, but rarely are there any that are both. Maybe that's what I like about her." Neil said almost philosophically.

"So she's your all time fantasy shag then?" Adam said, stunned, "And you Steve?" he asked.

"Hmmm... Well I've still got a thing for Nicole from the Renault adverts, um, Rachel Stevens, oh and Jet from Gladiators. But I'd do Andrea, sure."

"You can't do Andrea, I'm doing Andrea."

"She might be with you, but she'd be thinking of me." I replied, before adding, "Andrea, you better get off, Neil's getting jealous." Adam laughed.

"Oh really?" Neil said, sort of thrusting his pelvis under the duvet in quite a disturbing fashion, "Well you know who I'm shagging?" He didn't wait for my reply, "Your mum."

"Oh mate, that's just wrong."

"And do you know what? She goes like a train." More vigorous grinding accompanied Adams hysterical laughter.

"I'm not listening, you're sick. And she's so out of your league." Neil responded with a noise like Ivor the Engine.

"Shhtkmp, shhtkmp, shhtkmp." Pelvic thrusts.

"I can't believe you went there." A slow grind.

"Shhtkmp, shhtkmp, shhtkmp." I hit him with a pillow, because I couldn't reach the ashtray. "Actually, we'd better stop talking about mum's, Adam will start dreaming about Mrs Langdon if we're not careful."

"Lads, that's Trisha's mum." Adam said, as if we'd only now crossed the line.

"S'okay Adam, you'll be keeping it in the family. It's fine."

"Alright, alright, go on then Adam." I said. I got out of bed, went to sit in the corner to have a cigarette, somewhere away from Neil. "Whose name are we adding to the fanny stack for you then?"

"The what?" He said.

"Fanny stack. Like the arty photos you see on the internet where they get five or so birds all lying on top of each other face down legs spread, and they take a picture from behind giving this perfectly wonderful-."

"Stack of fanny," Neil finished. "Love those."

"So come on Adam, who's top of your pile, so far we've got Andrea Corr, Nicole, Rachel Stevens-"

"Steve's mum."

"Fuck off."

"Why do you get three? Neil's only got two." Adam asked, leaning up on his elbow.

"Neil has one." I corrected.

"That's right, your mum."

"Enough already!"

"I don't know, I'll think about it." Adam said while I threw a shoe at Neil.

"And you can't have Girls Aloud," Neil said dodging, before hurling a pillow back at me, "That's too easy."

"Trust me," I said, "that's not the reason he can't have Girls Aloud."

"But just to clarify one final time," Adam began, ever the voice of reason, "I really don't have a thing for Mrs Langdon."

"Good, I'm glad to hear it." I said, "Pleased for you."

"I'd shag her daughter though." stated Neil.

"Oh yeah, Pat's totally hot." I agreed.

Adam dropped to the bed defeated. "Six seconds doesn't even come close."

SANDBAGS AND GLADRAGS

It wasn't really a case of getting dressed up, more of trying to find something we could wear that would allow us to eat inside of an establishment that had four walls and wasn't using patio furniture as decor. We found a fish and chip shop that served generous portions with fresh white buttered bread and coffee on tap. Two black, one white with sugar. It was all we could have asked for.

We ate the fish in deference to all the ones that had got away. We were changing, each of us, over the course of the week. I'd like to say we were growing as individuals, embracing each new experience with wonder and joy, taking every lesson learned and using it to become better people. That's crap of course. We were becoming closer as friends, as brothers, and for now at least we were separated from all that we had left behind and not just by the distance.

Neil, I was sure, was using this time to refresh some memories and add some stories to tell at the next gathering of family and friends to which there were always many, and in which we had an exalted status as the ones that did that crazy stuff. That's also crap of course. Most of the things that did happen to us, while unbelievable at times were invariably the result of one or all of us messing around. We weren't any different than anyone else in most respects, except perhaps in our acknowledgement of the importance of our friendship.

This was something that I had been neglecting, something that I was now trying to rectify and something that I had become addicted to all over again. It's shocking to think of the things that you can waste your time doing, when you're most in need of times like these. Work was something I was supposed to do to allow me the money for everything else. It wasn't supposed to be the only thing I did, regardless of the cost. I know that the other man in Kelly's life could have been anyone, the 'who' wasn't exactly important, it was the 'why' I should have been wondering about. If you listen to your friends, or more specifically my friends, the 'why' was because she was a cheating slut of questionable integrity, but then Neil always did have a way with words, but the truth in fact is more likely to be that I was replaced. The boyfriend element of Kelly's life, the part that was supposed to be interested in her, to be planning a future and committing to an idea of us, that was the part that she substituted. Sex was a by-product. Even when I was at home, I was never really there anyway, what was she supposed to do?

"You're thinking about Kelly aren't you?" said Neil, eyeing me suspiciously.

"How can you tell?"

"Well, first because you've got that wistful where-did-it-all-go-wrong look going on, and secondly because you've bent that fork in half and it's not plastic." Shit. "You my friend need to let it go. Kelly, not the fork."

"And?" I said, not trying to be argumentative, I was genuinely asking 'and then what?' What happens after that? It's just me.

"It's not just you, you know?" The man was in my head. There was no other explanation.

"You probably just need to get laid, Steve." said Adam, on the bandwagon. "I went through something similar. You get all tied up in one woman -"

"Actually you got all tied up *by* one woman remember?" Neil said, laughing.

"Whatever, you get some bird in your head and when you finally get rid and clear out the space, you think, 'wow, it's bigger than I remember, what the hell am I gonna fill this up with?' But it passes. Everything passes eventually."

"Exactly, Kelly is just the kidney stone of your life. It's gonna hurt like a bitch but you'll feel better once it's out."

"That's lovely Neil, but Kelly isn't the problem though. It's not her I miss, it's the idea of her, it's the relationship. Mutual understanding and respect, good conversation, common interests. A real connection."

Neil chuckled, "But you never *had* any of that stuff with Kelly."

"I think you're aiming too high personally," Adam interrupted, "why don't you start with conscious and willing and go from there."

"The problem is I never meet the right women anyway." I said, ignoring him.

"Well that's a surprise given that you spend your life at work. Please, give me an easy one to figure out." said Neil, embracing sarcasm.

"So what are you saying? I should quit my job."

"No, just get some perspective. Find that work life balance thing they keep spouting on about all the time."

"And spend more time with us." Said Adam, "it's not right all this single focus. Get a hobby, besides wanking."

"There is no hobby besides wanking, everything else is just stuff you do in between." I said, automatically, no doubt proving his point.

"Get out their, see the world. There's more than just Andover on the map mate. Look at us now, here, in Elgin. A few pubs, a club, who knows what." Adam, the voice of reason.

"You know that would sound so much better if you'd have said Vegas just then."

"Fuck it, we'll do Vegas next year." said Neil enthusiastically.

"I bet this place is just crawling with eligible, fit women that all wouldn't mind having a drink with you." An attractive young waitress came over to collect our plates and clear the table. I hated it when Adam really, really made

190

sense. "Excuse me miss," he said, emboldened, "but where's a good place to get a drink around here?"

"Um, you could try High Spirits over the road." She said, smiling.

"Excellent. And afterwards?"

"Well, Joannas is the only club around here."

"Joannas it is then." Adam thanked her and she smiled again and disappeared into the kitchen. We paid the bill and made our way outside.

"High Spirits," I said, "like that movie from the eighties with Steve Guttenberg? I hope the pub's better."

"Maybe he's working their now," Neil said, crossing the road towards the converted church-come-wine bar. "Would explain a lot. As long as we can get a drink I don't mind if he tries to make us watch it."

We walked through the large wooden doors and through the to the main bar, passed vestibules and a small congregation of excitable pensioners. Approaching the bar we ordered three beers and stood looking around. There was something slightly odd about the idea of a pub in a church, as if there was more than just the landlord watching how much you had to drink.

I pointed over towards the group of pensioners in the corner. "They're playing Bridge aren't they?" I asked.

"How the fuck should I know?" said Neil.

"Language mate, house of god and all that." Adam whispered.

"Really?" I said, "Is he in? I want a word with him about this morning."

"Ha, ha. He's omnipotent." Adam informed me.

"So that's a yes then. It's all you had to say." I said paying the barman as our drinks arrived. "Shall we get a seat?"

We moved over to a pew, for want of a better description. "Do you think they do 'tarts and vicars' in here?" said Neil, sitting down.

"I don't know Neil, but I think you might have just offended the only woman here under sixty-five." Adam responded, trying to wave apologetically at the heavily made-up lady at the table across from ours. I don't want to say she herself was a working girl, because with a face like hers she must have been unemployed for some time.

"She's only just under sixty-five bud, and stop waving or she'll think she's pulled."

"She's about the age Adam's going for at the moment." I said.

"Bollocks to the both of you." We drank in silence for a while after that.

We stayed at High Spirits transfixed by the unfolding drama at the pensioners Bridge table. An accusation of cheating had been made and there were threats of teeth being taken out, or something like that. It was all going on. This was a Tuesday in Elgin.

We drank in comfort and in warmth and abused the privilege of an almost empty bar by loading the jukebox with old rock songs. We hit Creedence Clearwater Revival, Alice Cooper, Lynyrd Skynyrd and The Stones, went back for some Blues music from Hooker, King and Muddy Waters before spitting beer across the bar as Boyzone came on. I don't know when Adam had got to the machine without us but this was not a boating accident. This was enough to start a fight in most of the pubs in Andover, in Scotland I was expecting a riot.

"You tosser, you're actually getting heckled by the pensioners." I said trying to distance myself from Adam by hiding at the bar.

"What? This is an old Cat Stevens track. I think it's a good interpretation."

"Mate, I wouldn't care if it was being sung by Rachel Stevens while she sat on my face, we've told you before about your musical taste and the pain that it brings others. We're probably going to have to leave now."

"There's other pubs around." He said, petulantly.

"I meant leave Scotland Adam."

Neil came out of the toilet and I watched as his brow furrowed. "Who put this on?" He said, taking the stool next to mine.

"You have to ask?" I said, "Reckon it might be time we move on anyway."

"It's happening again?" He asked, shaking his head.

"Every time we go for a drink," I nodded, "Just be grateful the place is almost empty."

We grabbed our jackets and walked towards the exit, I tried to smile pleasantly at a grey haired lady as she eyed me leaving. "Knobheads," she muttered to herself rather surprisingly then stuck her fingers up and went back to the game.

"Every time we go for a drink," I repeated, then joined the others outside.

In the street we discovered the rain had returned while we had been inside drinking and we hurried about looking for the next venue for our evening. Our choices while limited had the added bonus of being obscurely located in relation to each other or in point of fact, anything else in the town. Our next stop became the first place we happened upon, and it was an American theme bar, but at least it wasn't Irish.

Inside again, we rubbed our hands against the warmth and approached what was becoming an all too familiar empty bar. I didn't mind the lack of people so much as my continuing inability to get served, choosing to always take it personally when I got ignored. Now at least my hurt was justified though I felt no better for it.

Three more beers arrived and we joked about there being nowhere to sit then wondered where everyone could be. We hoped of course that the answer would be that they were all at the nightclub waiting for us. I felt that this was optimistic but couldn't argue the point that they certainly weren't here. Neil took this to be a victory and drank his beer smugly.

"I feel that all things considered, we could have planned this a little better you know?" Adam said, looking around. A disco ball spun lonely over a deserted dance floor.

"We didn't actually plan this at all as I recall, that decision was sort of made by your girlfriend." Neil said, tapping the table.

"True," Adam said, ignoring the dig, "but even so, I would have thought that there would be someone out tonight, even if it's just for a quick drink after work. I mean where is everyone?"

"Well, there is someone out. It's just that it's us." I said.

"That's like some existential thing again isn't it?"

"No, it's one of those fact things. It's sad, but true."

"Unless," Neil said, "like I said, they actually are all at Joanna's. In which case, not so bad."

"What time is it?"

"Nine." I said.

"It's still Tuesday right?" Adam said.

"I'm afraid so."

"Rock on," he toasted without conviction, as we clinked our beers.

We moved on to drinking shorts, JD and Cokes' for Neil and Adam, vodka for me. The doubles were on special. I reminded Neil that he had better go and ring Jane before things got too wild. He disappeared from the bar and went outside with his mobile. I looked around the place at the fake 'Route 66' signs and denim jeans hung on the walls. I felt that somehow they had missed the essence of America and it wasn't helped by the accent of the staff, no matter how often they told us to 'have a nice day'. I pictured in my head glamorous Hooters-esque women winking fondly at us with Hollywood smiles, what we got were crooked teeth and

194

breasts that hung like saddlebags after a long cattle drive. And that was just the barman.

"Why don't you want kids then?" I found myself asking Adam out of the blue.

"I do. I've always said that," he said for the first time that I could remember. There wasn't a pause or hesitation of any kind. He was relaxed, it was an honest answer. "I just said I wasn't sure that I wanted them now, or that I'm even ready for them."

"How do you mean."

"I mean that Fiona seems to think that we should have them now because it might be harder to have them later, what with us being that much older, well, her I suppose but you know what I mean."

"And you don't think that's the right reason to have them?"

"Exactly, it's a reason to have them sure, just not necessarily the right one."

"And what is that? The 'right' reason I mean." I had no idea.

"No idea."

"Cool." We finished the drinks and ordered three more, lining Neil's up on the table.

"But I always thought I would know, when the time was right."

"Okay," I thought that too, "but it's nothing to do with Fiona?"

"As a partner?" I nodded. "God no, she's great. Terrific. But she has this now or never thing. Like there are no other options." He looked on the cusp of saying more, but the moment flickered out.

"Maybe there aren't, for her."

"She's not that bloody old."

"No, that's true, but most of her friends have probably already got a kid, or two," I added, thinking of Neil, "and maybe she's feeling like she's missing the boat."

"Why are you sticking up for her side?"

"I'm not, especially. I just think when you know, you know. I think you do know that Fiona will be the mother of your kids. I think that won't change whether you have them now or wait."

"So why can't I wait?" he asked.

"You can wait," I said, "you just can't expect her to, indefinitely." He thought about it for a moment then took a drink and looked at me.

"You're a cheerful fucker aren't you?" he said, "You know, for someone who sucks at relationships, you sure give a lot of advice."

"Hey, I just say what I see," I said, sounding more and more like Maury every minute I sat in the American bar.

"I never said it was good advice." He laughed.

"Point taken. We need to get out of here."

"I think so."

We stood, then downed our drinks as Neil came walking back into the bar looking cold but otherwise well. No bad news was all I could surmise before informing him to drink up as Joannas was calling. I had to get the mood up before we all ended up back at the B&B in tears.

We left the establishment with directions from a barman that started laughing as we left. I took that as a bad sign, but I was getting comfortably drunk enough to have lost the sense of concern that that would normally bring.

Outside, the rain was now drizzling in that invasive way that penetrates your clothing without actually being obvious enough to disturb you. I stepped out on to the pavement and as the cold air hit me I noticed the early signs of inebriation. Fortunately, I wasn't alone and the three of us sort of leaned into each other for support. As is so frequently the case in these situations, I became overcome with the urge to sing all of the verses of American Pie, while in truth only knowing about seven of them. With restraint and the occasional raucous laugh, we shuffled off towards the nightclub.

In Andover, the weekend starts on a Thursday. The bars and clubs are filled with people who are clearly planning to call in sick the following day, or that have the remarkable good fortune to work half days or the constitution to not give a shit either way. Thursday is understandable, it's a pay day for some, close to the weekend for the others and its one of those things that you don't question once you've lived with it.

At the door to the club a bouncer stood just out of the rain and while patting us down informed us that in Elgin, we would discover to our cost that the weekend started on a Wednesday. The law of sod struck again. But as the presence of the bouncer confirmed, that wasn't to say that Joanna's was closed, because it was most definitely open. Tuesday's were generally quiet so Tuesday was ladies night. We entered with trepidation.

Music blared through the entrance room door as we checked our coats and adjusted our damp shirts. The eighties it seemed were alive and well and had just reached Scotland. The music was great and even Adam managed to approve.

We pushed open the doors like cowboys into a saloon and stood surveying our surroundings. The club was jumping, people were laughing and dancing and everyone seemed to be having a fantastic time. "I thought that bloke said Tuesdays were quiet?" Adam shouted as we pushed our way through to the bar.

The next decision would determine the rest of the evening and most likely the following day too. We had started on beers, moved on to shorts, now it was customary to do shots. Shots meant an end to breakfast, a likelihood of lunch too and the possibility that we wouldn't be able to walk home. It was Adam's round so I felt momentarily safe, and then he passed Neil and me the Sambucca.

"Um," I said, staring at the black liquid with curiosity, then up at Adam with some surprise, "What's this?"

"Sambucca," he yelled over the music, grinning. "Thought we might as well crack on."

"Right. You're on a mission then?" I bellowed back.

"Not especially. But while we're here with no real reason to get up tomorrow morning, what the hell eh?"

"I'll remind you of that in the morning." I laughed, "down in one then?" Neil and Adam nodded and on three we took the shots. The liquid burned my throat and brought a startling clarity to the darkness of the room and a momentary sobriety that I knew to be both false, and temporary.

"Well at least we know why there are no men out tonight." I screamed, perhaps a little too loudly, "I mean every woman has the right to be ugly but this lot take the piss."

"I reckon we need something stronger then," Neil piped up. Short of Absinthe, I couldn't think of anything that fit the bill. Other than Diesel.

The name of the drinks that followed merged into one long list of what I presumed were precursors for events to come, Aftershock, Brain Rot, Paraplegia, all now a blur of money exchanged and change not counted. We staggered about fighting off premature blindness and must have given the impression that we had been hired in as some form of cheap entertainment for the gaggle of women around us, like a community help program. I'm not a natural dancer it has to be said but up until that night I always believed I had at least mastered walking.

"Hello again," said a voice that was as clear to me as the one in my head. "You found it then?" The pretty waitress, now in a change of clothes, stood next to me like a vision of perfection in a sea of impurity. She was smiling at me the way sober people often do when conversing with the fantastically drunk. But my word did she look amazing.

I placed her around her mid-twenties, five feet six in heels with long dark hair and hazel eyes that looked like something from a Galaxy chocolate advert, she gazed at me beneath eyelids that seemed heavy from the weight of her long lashes. She was beautiful in an effortless way, unaffected by it, as if it were simply a fact like having a tiny birthmark beneath the waistline. You could see it, if you were lucky, but her life and yours would continue just the same if you didn't. She was slim and yet voluptuous wearing a simple jeans-and-white-top outfit that was flattering enough to show me she was curvaceous in a way that made me want to dribble. There wasn't an angle on her that didn't conform to Natures grand design and I tried valiantly not to notice. And I could say that she looked amazing, because I had seen her sober, when she was just carrying the potential to stun me into submission. It was the truth this time and I even had witnesses. Whatever happened, when the morning came and I said that I had seen her, I would know without question that this one statement was substantiated. It's just that now probably wasn't the best time to spend three minutes in silence thinking about that.

"I'm Louise." She offered, after an embarrassing pause in which simple words escaped me. Her voice poured through the air like honey from a jar. Her accent alone was intoxicating, which given the circumstances was clearly going to be a problem.

"Steve," I fumbled clumsily, "hi, my name's Steve." I tried to stand up straight, then realised I already was so I just ended up sort of thrusting slightly towards her. "Can I buy you a drink?" I asked quickly.

In my mind, all of the lights had faded and I stood alone in a spotlight, probably naked, with the rest of the club patrons staring at me with disdain, the drunken foreigner hitting on the beautiful brunette. Alcohol was supposed to provide confidence, Dutch courage, the amount I had drunk I should have been able to storm the beach at Normandy and yet I felt an empty, acidic whimper in my mouth with every word I tried to form. I needed to splash water over my face and if the facilities provided ingest coffee intravenously. But I couldn't leave Louise here - to turn my back for a second was to succumb to the acceptance of the hallucination. I needed to sober up with the absolute minimum amount of effort, and I needed to do it quickly.

"So are you having a good time in our town then?" Louise asked after I had successfully obtained two drinks in under twenty minutes, a Smirnoff Ice for her, bottled water for me. I looked around before answering, trying to establish the whereabouts of my drinking companions. I spotted them both on the dance floor, moving in a way that suggested a lack of co-ordination at an almost medical level. I don't know how I had become separated from them but it allowed me a moment of professional distance, like a zookeeper looking over his beloved animals through a caged fence.

"Yeah," I replied honestly, "Yeah I really am. It's that obvious I'm not a local then?"

Louise laughed and nodded, "Well apart from the accent, I tend to know everyone under thirty," she said, "all five of them."

"Small-town blues?"

"Something like that," she took my hand with a self-assuredness that startled me and led me towards a quieter more secluded section of the club that I hadn't even noticed. We sat down at a corner table on a cushioned bench and I was grateful for the opportunity to reduce the risk of swaying. "Don't get me wrong, Elgin is fine," she continued, "there are plenty worse places to be I'm sure, but do you ever get that feeling there could be something more out there?"

"It's crossed my mind once or twice," I said trying to convey a nonchalance I wasn't feeling. Louise was making me feel at ease in her company while equally building a nervous anticipation within me that I hadn't been expecting. "Have you lived here long then?"

"Yeah, most of my life, or as long as makes no difference. There's a magnetic quality to this place, makes it hard to pull away. Plus all of my family are here."

"You have a big family?" I slurred.

"Um, you could say that, three sisters and a brother, me somewhere in the middle. Like I said, there's not much to do around here if you get my meaning?"

"Parents needed a TV then?" Louise nodded, smiling.

"I think they had this idea of security in numbers, and my mother was a big Jane Austin fan, hence the sisters." I couldn't tell if she was joking, but the relative closeness of her body made such concerns seem trivial.

"So you work full time at the restaurant then?"

"God no, it's my parents place, we all help out as and when. I'm a nurse at the Infirmary over in Inverness. The pay's lousy, the hours are shite, and that's just the waitressing." I laughed and felt the alcohol slowly dissipate but I was still too drunk not to be at risk from one of my typical errors of judgement.

"Nursing? Must be rewarding," I said, for no possible reason I could think of. I was starting to bore myself to sleep without worrying about what Louise must have been thinking. I needed to calm down, to clear my head and start this again before she realised the mistake she had made in talking to me and left to find the local   man-tart.

Louise looked at me while that very decision must have been considered in her head, "I'll be back in a minute okay?" She said, touching my hand in a 'your sweet but your time is up' fashion I had experienced all too many times before. She got up and walked away before I could even raise an argument.

I sat alone now, in the corner of a strange club in a town I'd never been to before, benevolently scorned by a

201

beautiful woman I'd only just met and suddenly feeling a very long way from home. I wanted the room to start spinning in that unsettling way that tells you that the next few hours are going to be deeply unpleasant but that you'll be too drunk to care and unable to remember them the following day anyway. Oblivion beckoned me in while 'Whitesnake' informed that I was going there on my own, again.

I drank deeply from my overpriced water and laughed to myself at the sharpness of my surroundings, the resolution of which I was now ironically appreciating against my will. I looked at my watch and acknowledged that it was barely past eleven. The club was just warming up. The last stragglers from the pubs in town, wherever they had been hiding, were filing in through the door from the cloakroom, the men of the town arriving to lay claim to their women.

Wondering whether I could get away with ordering a coffee in a nightclub and feeling older than my years I found my head dropping into my hands. What I should have done was find Neil and Adam, I know that now. I was alone and faring about as well as I usually did when in that situation, depressing myself and lacking the inclination to do anything about it. I pulled out my mobile and switched it on, knowing that to be the surest form of validation known to the twenty-first century man - the receipt of a text message when least expected. The likelihood of this was narrowed by the fact that I was on holiday with the two people most likely to get in touch with me. I could still see both of them now, tearing up the dance floor unable to direct their feet let alone their fingers. The logo screen taunted me with its silence.

"Checking in with the Mrs?" Came a voice I was becoming pleasantly familiar with.

"Hmm?" I said with what I hoped was a bewildered charm, "um, no, no just, um, checking my phone. No real reason."

202

"So you're bored of my company already then?" Louise asked questioningly, eyebrows raised expectantly. Looking at her I felt like Dorian Gray's painting. A sheepish protest escaped my mouth as my jaw hung down, I think my bottom lip may have quivered. "Relax," Louise said, "I'm kidding. I just wanted to tell my girlfriends I was heading out, and to inform the two dancing queens not to worry about you. I'm thinking you could probably do with a coffee? Unless, God forbid, you're a tea drinker?" I searched so desperately for something smart to say, something to justify her presence, any-fucking-thing that would let me believe this was happening to me.

"C-c-coffee's 'sgood," was the result of my deliberation. I managed an accompanying smile like a village idiot. I hated myself.

We left the club after collecting our jackets, and I instinctively went to light a cigarette as we stepped outside and then thought better of it. The drizzle had subsided but the clouds were never far away and as we strolled into the dark I was oddly grateful for the damp chill in the air – it seemed to work better than the splash of water I had previously prayed for to sober me up.

I followed Louise like a teenager on his first date, no idea of the protocol, uncertain as to whether it was acceptable to offer a hand or place my arm around her shoulder to huddle from the cold. I didn't want to appear uninterested, but then I didn't want to come across as being too keen. So many doubts, so many concerns all racing through my mind at once it made me wonder where this mental dexterity had been when I had needed it earlier.

Louise led me through the streets of her youth and we strolled without destination, a chance to talk without shouting, to connect without touching. I learned her interests, reading and music and movies, and that her favourite colour was lilac. We talked about her family some more and touched upon relationships. She was currently single, staving off the cliché of advances from the hospital consultants, trying not to be an extra in a poorly written episode of 'Casualty'. A serious relationship had ended some time before, and one or two casual ones had never really started. The serious guy was local and despite a lifetime of proximity, when it came down to it she hadn't really known him at all. It was clear even to my inexperienced ears that we were sharing in a different way to friends. More than just a casual interest, this was like an interview for a job I've always wanted.

In exchange, I spoke about Kelly, out loud, for what seemed like the first time. I struggled as I tried to explain the conflicting feelings I was still wrestling with. I suppose it could have sounded like a line, the magnanimous approach. But I didn't mean it like that. There seemed little point in disguising my shortcomings, the hurt I had ultimately caused by trying to please everyone but myself, and in doing so failing in even that. Being selfish with good intentions is still fundamentally being selfish, especially when you're not even sure what those good intentions were. So I didn't bother lying to Louise, though it crossed my mind to create the image of the perfect man given the relative safety of the distance between us, the truth was, it was just as comforting to be completely honest for exactly the same reason. I had nothing to gain from dishonesty and her fragile trust of the entire male species to lose if I did. Besides, there was something harmonic about a person that hardly knows you knowing more about you than most. As a precursor for future relationships, I considered the possibility of travelling more often.

It failed to occur to me that I had no idea where I was, which direction we had come or even the name of the street my bed and breakfast was in. I was about to raise this point with Louise when she stopped beneath a street light, turned around and kissed me slowly and softly. "I've wanted to do that since the restaurant." She said with a whisper, her face so close I could feel the warmth of her breath on my cheek.

"Wow, how much of a tip did we leave?" I replied before I could stop myself. Louise hit me on the arm then kissed me again as time itself stood still. Rain, pestilence and a plague of locusts could have swarmed around me and I'd have been none the wiser.

I kissed her back, with longing and hunger and desire and the frustration of every failed relationship passed. I kissed knowing there could be no tomorrow, hoping that the feeling could last, realising with an almost tragic inevitability that it was already more than just a fumble in the dark for me.

My hands went to her hair and down her back as she moved into me, her thigh rising to my leg. The tenderness of her touch rose every hair on my body and I shivered as her hand found its way inside my jacket and under my shirt. Louise ran her fingers down the skin of my back drawing lines with her nails, chasing the blood from my head. In that one genuine embrace she awoke in me long forgotten feelings of passion and a clarity of thought and intention that cut through the wasteland of my past like an adrenaline shot straight to the heart. I looked into her captivating eyes and saw possibilities beyond any I had known before.

"Time for that coffee," she said seductively, turning and walking towards the restaurant I hadn't even realised we had arrived at.

Inside, we sat at the back by the counter and lit a wine-bottle candle, staring at each other across the table as the light flickered across the wall. I would have to leave soon, end this before there was no going back for me. Louise was everything that had ever happened to me before magnified by chance and opportunity. I could already feel my heart breaking with every blink of her eyes.

She brushed the hair from her face as she drank her coffee, white, no sugar, staring at me fondly while drawing circles over the back of my hand. I hated the table for keeping us apart, hated the chair for holding her, the clothes she wore for being that close to her. I hated the cup as it reached her lips and the coffee as it rolled over her tongue. And I hated myself for all the same reasons. I felt her foot, shoeless now touch at my ankle, up to my knee rising as the smile on her lips grew. I don't know why I was there, why we had met or what more could ever happen, but in that moment alone I was as close to being alive as I had ever been.

"You can't stay," she said, "but I'll wish that you could have long after you've gone."

"Send me on my way whenever you're ready." I tried to reply calmly. As she looked in my eyes I felt my pulse race, an animal caught in the headlights, transfixed and ignorant of the danger approaching.

"Where have you been all this time?" she asked.

"Living in a town far, far away."

"Happily?"

"Enough to get by," I lied, for the first time that night.

"Enough to need to get away," Louise corrected.

"It's an existence," I agreed. How could I argue any otherwise?

"Is that all?"

"Most days."

"Happy?" she asked again.

"Some of the time."

"Now?"

"More than you could know."

"Good." She leaned over the table, hardly stretching at all, and kissed me again making the room spin in the way I had hoped for some hours before, but for entirely different reasons.

It was then that I noticed how close we were, how that small distance had felt like a mile, how the miles themselves would feel unbearable. I could smell her perfume and the shampoo in her hair, feel the warmth of her lips pressed against mine. All of the sensations were intoxicating in a way that made alcohol seem like water and when she laughed it was infectious and there was no known cure.

Louise stood and walked around the table, I moved my chair out to meet her and she sat in my lap, arms draped behind my neck. She kissed me again as my body responded, her hand sliding over my shoulder and down my chest, fingers popping the top buttons of my shirt. My hand slowly, very slowly moved towards her, finding her knee I inched my way up her thigh to her hip and then up to the luscious curve of her breast. She exhaled passionately as I caressed her, my hand tracing the outline of her bra. Her hair dropped down and we were hidden in the embrace of mutual pleasure, she bit her lip and then my earlobe and neck.

I had to stop, had to, had to, had to stop. And then she stopped, but with a smile that let me know that it was only for the time that was yet to come.

Louise let her hand fall to my lap, my jeans straining against a wanton desire I had no way to fulfil, she let it linger, teasing me before moving to the pocket and reaching in for my mobile. Standing again, letting me feel the cold contradiction of her absence, she went in to the back room and was gone for just a few minutes. I ran my hand through my hair, sobered and yet drunk from the encounter. When she returned looking mischievous I knew that our night had come to an end and I stood to meet her in the aisle. Walking me to the door of the restaurant, I couldn't take my eyes from her.

We kissed as she pushed me to the door, laughing, smiling, pulling me back to her for one final kiss, pushing me back again, a kiss, an embrace, her head against my chest, her hands on my backside, my face in her hair. I stepped through the door, her hand in mine, her fingers lingering like a memory. The cold night air rushed around me again, filling my lungs, shocking me awake. I stepped slowly along the pavement as the door closed behind me, she walked with me behind the window to the wall, waving slowly with affection and I missed her already. Were it not for the journey ahead of me, I would have stayed there pressed against the glass and been happy.

Five more steps around the corner, I searched for an indication of my whereabouts, a landmark to base myself. High Spirits stood opposite me and I gave a nod of appropriateness as I swaggered on towards the High Street with the certainty of dowsing. I didn't care what the time was, didn't notice if it was raining or not. I floated to the music I heard in my mind, drifting down the hill in contentment. Only the music I heard was making me tingle, the pocket of my leg positively shaking for attention. I pulled out my phone to see 'Neil Calling' flashing on the display.

"You done already?" he said through laughter while Adam cheered in the background. Their voices had a quality of sound that Dolby would have been proud of.

"What?"

"Louise, sent us a message to come and find you, said you'd be wandering around the High Street somewhere probably looking for us."

"Eh?"

"Well, actually you sent us the message, but she signed it. Good night then bud?"

"Yeah brilliant," I replied, spinning around. Somewhere in the distance I could hear them rolling up the hill. I carried on down to the sound of their voices until I could wave at them, but they remained oblivious to my efforts. I met them halfway, Neil still talking into the phone while I stood next to them, amazed at how they had failed to see me. I put my phone in my pocket and carried on talking to him for a minute longer.

I tapped him on the shoulder, Neil held up his arm to me without turning around, "Mate, I gotta go, someone wants me." He said and pushed the disconnect button with concentrated effort.

"Bro," I said smiling at him. He looked at me, back to his phone then up at me again.

"Bro!" he yelled and threw his arms around me. Adam was still dancing, or maybe he was just walking and it happened to look that way.

"Alright guys?" I said.

"Blindin', you?" Neil said, one arm still collaring me. I nodded, "My boy!" He said, slapping me on the cheek. He laughed like a Sid James outtake.

"Stevie's gone and pulled, Stevie's gone and pulled, my pal Stevie has only gone and pulled." Adam chanted, dancing La Cucaracha. Neil joined in and they spun arm in arm up the hill with me laughing behind them. "Stevie's gone and pulled, gone and fooled us all, my bro Stevie has only gone and pulled!"

Neil began running on the spot, a little jog forwards, a little jog back, arms waving in the air, fingers pointing to the sky, a celebration of legendary status was occurring while the singing continued. And then he was off, jogging up the hill with Adam and I in close pursuit.

Three steps to go, a long and deliberate approach of some kind, "He shoots!" Neil yelled, leg arcing, sweeping back and with purpose and surprising precision, foot pointed, his leg crested down and with the force of a perfect technique he connected with the immovable sandbag lying on the pavement. His momentum was swallowed and the impact shuddered through his knee as his foot remained lodged beneath the weight of the bag. Neil collapsed backwards, a slow motion crumple as his body folded in on itself. He landed heavily and the scream that surprised me the most came from Adam. Neil had landed on his foot and apparently it was not nearly as funny as Neil and I believed.

Were it not for the copious amounts of alcohol coursing through his body, Neil would have most definitely been more seriously injured. "He scores!" Neil finished, flat on his back in hysterical laughter.

I tried to help, I wanted to help, but the sight was beyond comprehension. Neil lay rolling on the floor, his foot still wedged beneath the offending sandbag, his head resting on Adam's ankle while Adam himself spun about trying to dislodge his foot from the arse of his friend. Adam and I sat down on the floor next to Neil, me by choice, Adam by default, all of us laughing now as the drizzle returned.

"Tuesday night in Elgin," Adam said through the rain, "not so bad after all!"

A moment's pause, a breath, "Altogether now: *A long, long time ago, I can still remember...*"

MY BELLY TO THE JELLY

Untangled and yet no more co-ordinated we moved through the night like shunned pilgrims turned away from the inn. A stagger would have been an improvement, a recognisable form of movement to which we could only aspire.

The drink had come back to us, the second wave as our bodies ingested that which we had continued to swallow long after sense and consequence had been ignored. I was merry, horny, euphoric and destitute with each alternating step. This alone would have been enough to impair my sense of direction without being coupled to ABBA's rejects. But we were in fine voice, of that the local residents were certain.

"I'm fucking telling ya it's not that!" Neil bawled at Adam, "He drove his Chevy to the levee, 'Chevy' 'to' 'the' 'levee', sing it with me." Neil had stopped walking to ensure that Adam finally got this. As songs went, this was our anthem and yet alcohol had robbed Adam of the lyrics in a cruel and unusual punishment.

"You're sure?" Adam slurred, a finger poised in accusative preparation.

"Of course I'm bloody sure-," Neil stated for those in Edinburgh that hadn't been following the conversation.

"He's right," I added before blood was spilt. "He drove his Chevy to the levee."

"Chevy to the levee?" Adam repeated as if the words were foreign to him.

"It's a poignant song about the life, death and influence of the late, great Buddy Holly. Why in the name of all that is honest and good would Don McLean drag his fucking belly to the jelly?"

211

"I thought it was something to do with Elvis." Adam replied.

"Shut up! Just shut up and listen." Neil filled his lungs and began the song from the very beginning. Across the road from us a light had appeared in the front window of a bungalow. I watched to see if anything more interesting would happen and was pleased and equally surprised to then watch a half naked man in slippers appear in the doorway, torch in hand, with his dog.

"Puppy!" I yelled, five years old again.

"Would you keep the fucking noise down!" the man hollered in broad Scots. Like the camel-come-llama of the morning, what at first appeared to be a puppy was now showing itself to be a somewhat more formidable sight, just a little further away than at first registered. This new perspective allowed me to accurately judge the man to be a giant and his puppy to be a hoarse.

"Eh?" Adam answered. Of the three of us that could have, he was fourth on my list to speak. "D'you speak English mate?" He giggled.

"Are you taking the piss?" The man said, stepping out of his doorway and walking the path of his garden, the rottweiler grinning with the blood of foolhardy British tourists dripping from its salivating mouth.

I waited for Adam to respond but he had turned the other way and was conversing with a bush while Neil tried to drag him down the road. The courage I had hoped for earlier found it's way to my legs and against my better judgement carried me across the road towards the man waiting to kill us. I began apologising, trying to placate the man and, if nothing else, allow Neil the time to hide Adam. Words left my mouth without passing through my brain and my hands signed the universal language of arse-kiss. The man shone the torch in my face annoyingly, but he had the dog, and therefore the right.

212

The noise of my friends began to fade in the darkness or was just less audible above the sound of my heart thumping in my ears. "You's need to get yourself to home you hear?" The dog said menacingly. Perhaps that wasn't right but either way it had the effect of making me scuttle off towards my comrades.

"You're such a lightweight," I said to Adam who had started to hiccup. "Unbelievable."

"Are we nearly there yet?" was the drunken response. I had no idea. I was following Neil as we carried Adam between us, six legs moving as awkwardly as sixteen. The pavement seemed to get smaller, the streetlights further apart and the weight of the inebriated more tiring. My brother he may have been but he still weighed a ton.

Suddenly Adam became animated in our arms and I feared a convulsion, blood poisoning brought on by the alcohol or some such state of emergency. His eyes, once glazed, became focused and alert for the briefest of moments and he stared off down the road at headlights too distant for either Neil or I to make out clearly and he watched intently as they pulled out from a turning and headed towards us. Adam began jabbering, pointing wildly and gesticulating like a crazed fool, "it's, it's, look, look at the, the thing, look," he pointed again. Neil and I looked up at the vehicle now indicating left as it turned into the next street ahead but we were blinded by the lights in the darkness and struggling to keep Adam from falling into the gutter.

"Wanker!" Adam yelled again, and this time I turned around, fearful that our new friend and his dog might have heard.

"Would you shut the hell up!" I pleaded through clenched teeth. "What's the matter with you anyway?"

"Bastard!" he shook and bucked in our arms as if he could take flight and pursue the vehicle. I had half a mind to let go and see him try. I looked at Neil but he was as confused as I was. "Come back and face me you cock-sock."

213

Neil stepped in front of Adam, grabbed his collar then slapped him on the cheek. Adam's head lulled over to the side and spit hit me in the face. "Thanks mate." I said, wiping it clean.

"No worries, it's for the best." Neil said to me as Adam lolled his head back up to grin at him. His eyes had glazed over again and the momentary burst of energy had seeped from his limbs.

"Tow-truck!" Adam gurgled by way of an explanation, then burped in Neil's face. We sighed, the man was obsessed.

The excitement over, we pressed on turning corners in the darkness, using the force to guide us, we pushed on through the night, a front door key to hand and the promise of a bed to greet us. These simple pleasures have seen many a man home at night, carrying with them an almost mystical quality that Tolkien would have been proud of.

Our destination, while walking distance from town at the start of the evening now seemed to be a journey of epic proportions and my legs protested with every step we took. Only an hour before I had been enjoying the sensual embrace of a stunningly gorgeous woman who took great pleasure in kissing me, it just wasn't the same when Adam tried to do it.

The bed and breakfast appeared to us through a smoky light like the Hotel California. We moved through the gate in the front garden and shushed each other loudly. Adam, now virtually catatonic rested against my shoulder while Neil struggled with the lock on the door. Coming back for me, the three of us shuffled to the door and into the hallway. Our efforts to remain quiet failed with our usual flare and a blinding light surrounded us as the bulb burst into life. The shock made Neil and I reactively cover our eyes and shield our faces. Adam, unsupported, hit the floor like a sack of shit and groaned unappreciatively. Ms

Kincaide stood in front of us with an expression that left no room for assumption.

"Pat!" Adam yelled from the floor, lifting his hand to give her a 'thumbs up'. His hand and head hit the carpet again with equal force and a slow snore was the only remaining sound. I wasn't entirely sure of the etiquette in such a predicament but when it seemed clear that Ms Kincaide wasn't going to fill the silence, I pushed Neil forwards to speak while I collected the dead weight of Adam from the floor.

"I am so very, very sorry," he began, "we, us, none of us are like this usually."

"Aye, your lightweights I see." She said eyeing us with disdain. "Can you find your way to your room or shall I escort you?"

"I think we'll be fin-," I punched Neil and with a single step he corrected himself before I dropped Adam again. "Actually, if you could just show us that would be grand."

"Follow me," Ms. Kincaide said, turning down the hallway and off through the maze of corridors that I was sure to have died in. "I'm thinking you'll not be wanting breakfast early tomorrow then?"

"I'd say you might be right." Neil said as we finally reached the door to our room. "But please give our apologies to the rest of the guests for any disturbance."

"Fair ye well, it's just the three of you this evening anyway." She said without further explanation and with that she was gone, a 'sleep well' drifted back down the hall towards us. Neil closed the door and we manhandled Adam to the single bed.

We gingerly pulled off Adams' shoes and outer clothing. "Would this be the right time to ask why we're having to share a room then?" I said, eyeing the double bed with unease. Adam groaned again, chased it with a hiccup, a snore and a fart. We hadn't even eaten eggs that day, but life is rarely that cut and dried.

215

Gagging, Neil and I undressed and fell to bed. I could tell that Neil was dying to ask me about my evening with Louise and I was keen to tell him all, but for now I wanted the thoughts to myself, just a few more minutes alone with her.

As my eyelids grew heavy, a sound floated across air that was turning green. A voice, faint in the drowsy slumber of my ears called out, just on the edge of perception. I ignored it as my eyes rolled and sleep drew me in like a lover. "Toilet!" Adam screamed suddenly and Neil and I jerked upright faster than had we been splashed with cold water. With parental aptitude Neil grabbed Adam from the bed as I leapt alongside to assist and we hastily scuttled him across the floor, his feet dragging across the carpet, over to the porcelain haven of Adams needs.

He was asleep again before we got the chance to rest his head against the toilet. He hugged the base, naked but for his pants, his head now resting on the pink splash mat that adorned the fixture. I wasn't going to move him again unless the building was on fire, and then only likely as far as the shower. We looked down at the sight at our feet, Adam, the poster child for sobriety. He chuckled to himself, dreaming something no doubt indescribable and as he exhaled I could have sworn I heard him say goodnight to Fiona.

Returning to the bed, my head thickening to remind me I still had my own dues to pay, we smoked cigarettes to clear the air. I pulled my mobile from the pocket of my jeans on the floor and placed it carefully on the bedside table as if I might be able to will Louise to call me again. Stubbing out the butts, we turned off the bedside lights and as I lay there in the darkness, the strangest thing happened. My phone buzzed across the wood, the shrill tones of a message pulling me once again back from the brink. I reached over to the glowing brick beside me and picked it up to acknowledge receipt. I was amazed to see that Louise had apparently stored her number in my phone, and evidently taken mine in the process. Neil stirred then rolled over and punched me in the arm for disturbing him, but I just read the message, then read it again, and again and again.

All of the warnings, lectures and protestations from Neil were forgotten, drowned in the alcoholic haze of lust and longing, infatuation and fascination. With a single text message, Louise had ruined me, and as I lay there in the glow of my phone, a transcendent smile on my face, I couldn't have been more grateful.

Tuesday night in Elgin, blinding.

Wednesday

TALKING TO GOD

I am a man of few possessions. The combined assets of my life while priceless in sentimental significance bare little in the way of resale prospects. I own a car that doubles in value with a full tank of petrol and my flat is rented and furnished with third hand cast-offs. Some of these worthless items I cherish beyond all other things, my CD collection, books and DVD's, a porn magazine or two I've grown attached to over the years, a coffee mug that my dad used to use when I was a kid. I would have traded every single one of these items for a door to the toilet in our bedroom.

Adam did not have a good night. Neil and I as a consequence did not have a good night.

Our first night in a bed for almost a week and the majority of the time was spent trying to wrap a pillow around our ears. The emanating sound of vomiting can have a reflexive quality that was a risk to which we were not prepared to entertain. Had we been more understanding we may have assisted a fallen man, but both Neil and I felt that manhandling him to the bowl was in itself an act beyond the limits of casual involvement. We couldn't hold his hair back because, well, he didn't have any and besides, as every man knows, the only person you really want when you're being sick is your mum.

Our windowless bedroom was suffering under the strain of three flatulent drunks, two of who were smoking and the third of which was talking to my old friend Barry. Neil and I were on the coffee by four thirty, having enjoyed an hour of dreamless sleep. This was a not a new experience for either of us, practising insomniacs that we were, but tonight should have been a sure fire trip to the land of nod. Food, drink and exercise combined to put most people out for the elusive eight when I would have quite happily settled on four.

Adam would stir periodically, waking only to vomit, wipe, rest and relax. This was the only cure in such circumstances and no amount of brow mopping would have made the experience any less unpleasant. I would have appreciated it though. I replenished Adams water and tried to ensure he drank as much as he lost.

During the lulls, Neil and I sat on the bed whispering anecdotes while taking pictures of Adam with our mobile phones. Of all the beauty we had seen, the places we had camped in, the opportunities we had had to do just that, this night was the first time it had occurred to either of us capture any of it for posterity. Such logic was an indication of our state of mind, the freedom from constraint that we were feeling, the conformity we were ignoring and the trend that we were setting. Or it was simply just a gentle reminder that we didn't have a woman with us to suggest it.

I stared briefly at the digital alarm clock having long ago formed a hateful relationship with the foretellers of time. It flashed to nine minutes past five. Too early for breakfast I cursed. My stomach rumbled for grease and more coffee and would continue to do so until both were satisfied. I thought of Louise as I sat on the bed and wondered what she was dreaming about, hoping that I might feature if only for one night. Something she had said played around my mind, 'you can't stay but I'll wish that you could have long after you've gone'. Seeing me now I suspect would have changed her mind.

I vowed to push her from my mind for the rest of the week and would press on in the spirit that had inspired the trip. Adam had remained quiet and short of being dead that must have been a good sign. At least one of us was sleeping. I pointed at him and Neil nodded, typical that we had been united by a sleepless night even when it wasn't our own. We finished the last of the coffee and Neil suggested we make one last ditch attempt at getting our heads down before all hope was lost. We switched off the lights and each took up position, rolling away from the other. I don't know why the thought didn't occur for one of us to sleep in the now vacant single bed.

For those that know the unbearable oppression of expectant anticipation that is waiting for a state of unconsciousness known as sleep, I feel for you. The quintessential paradox of alertness achieved when the body is supposed to be shutting down is almost enough to make you scream out loud. The phrase 'trying to get out of your own head' was, I'm sure, invented for this very condition. The stimulants of coffee and nicotine were of course contributory factors, and the lateness of the hour past the normal routine, the unfamiliar surroundings, the alcohol to blood level, all could be held accountable. An explanation for being awake however, never made the fact of it any easier to deal with.

My eyelids, no matter how hard I tried would pop open like a broken Tiny Tears doll but I had to allow for the possibility that after having suggested we get some sleep, Neil was actually doing it. I slowly rolled over on to my back and tried to check. He lay almost motionless but for the side of his body rhythmically rising and falling in silent bliss. I sighed, despondent, the answer I got was, "Shhtkmp, shhtkmp, shhtkmp."

"Tosser. You can't sleep either then?"

"Nope. Your mum's relentless."

"I cry for your children mate, really."

"How did we end up suffering the most that's what I want to know? A double bed, a roof over our head and barely a sodding hour of sleep."

"Life is cruel." I sighed again.

"So's your mum, that's why I spank her."

A logistical problem presented itself when we could pretend to sleep no more. Both of us needed to use the facilities that Adam had manifestly occupied without negotiation and though we could argue that he did need them more it was time to take affirmative action. It started softly, the gentle brush of a sock around the nose, moving on to a shake of the arms and body, quickly followed by a light slapping of the face and cold water on his head. The man didn't move.

I looked at Neil expectantly. My glass was half-empty. He shrugged, nodded, and I stepped out of the bathroom. Grabbing a leg each we dragged Adam into the bedroom, hoping that if nothing else would wake him a decent carpet burn might. Still nothing.

I went back to bed and tried to look at anything but the sight of Neil on the toilet. Some things could put you off your breakfast - this could make me anorexic. I searched my bag for the Anadin and swallowed two in preparation for a headache I hoped would never arrive, leaving the packet on the bed for Neil. He showered while I shut my eyes and dreamt of sleep. God only knows where Adam was mentally at, but he was certainly not with us.

Neil finished up, spraying deodorant around without a care for the slumbering invalid beneath our feet and I stepped in to use the toilet myself for the first time in hours. I sat staring into the room both thankful and amazed that I was feeling at least half-human and equally astonished that Neil seemed to be the same. I'd always said that between us we made the perfect man, today we just made a whole one.

Some minutes later I began cleaning my teeth, certain that I had breath like a cancer-ridden cat. A shower followed and I let the heat and steam cocoon me in the glass, easing the fog from my brain and reminding me of the comforts of home. It was only after Neil tapped on the glass that I accepted I had been standing there for as long as it seemed.

I stepped out dripping water across the floor and over Adam and still he did not stir. I sprayed and dressed, picked up the essentials and we headed out to breakfast. It was six forty-five a.m. Breakfast would now be convenient.

Traversing the corridors and hallways we found the dining room and Ms Kincaide sat by the window with a hot drink in hand. "Morning boys," she said without turning to greet us straight away. She was staring at something in the garden and I feared we had brought more than Adam home with us last night. Whatever it was became of no concern as she waved it off and turned to us with a smile, all misdemeanours long forgotten. We sat alone in the room at a table by the window of recent interest as Ms Kincaide scurried off to begin the procession of food.

We ordered without hesitation or preamble, everything on offer for two with coffee. We began with cereal to line the stomach and poured orange juice to accompany the feast about to be received. Toast started to appear at the table in giant racks, fresh butter and condiments followed and then a plate so large it had a health warning engraved on the surface was laid in front of us. The food sizzled gloriously and as I inhaled I felt my arteries waving a white flag. I reasoned in that way people do that my single glass of orange juice would ample compensate for the two eggs, bacon, sausages, black pudding, beans, mushrooms, fried bread and hash browns that were swimming about my plate. I ate with wild abandon and glee.

Outside, the rain had stopped but the clouds remained. The Zafira was visible through the window, parked on the driveway looking for all the good in the world like it had been used to go joyriding, which in a way I suppose that it had. I wanted to say that from afar the damage looked worse than it was, but in truth the distance allowed for an all-encompassing view that verified any damage we had hitherto been praying was superficial to be justifiably worrying.

223

The vehicle glistened with early morning dew and I knew that the damp seats would last well into the day. The issue that was more pressing was the fact that we were most likely still too intoxicated to drive, despite feeling fine and well fed. Ms Kincaide arrived to take our plates and commented on our missing member and we tried to explain that he was just overtired and not that he had spent the night redecorating one of her bathrooms and trying to relocate her toilet. Neil and I made conversation while we sat comfortably in the room admiring the sights of an early morning. Cars appeared more frequently, joggers bobbed along the pavement and an exceptionally large man strolled past walking his dog.

"There goes the town copper regular as clockwork," Ms Kincaide said motioning to the behemoth and his tamed beast. Why this needed clarification I don't know, but it was of more than a passing interest to Ms Kincaide that was clear. I wasn't surprised that I hadn't seen a patrol car parked anywhere nearby, I suspect that in a high-speed pursuit the man just ran after them.

I looked to change the subject that had in my mind peaked the moment the policeman had left my field of vision. I asked Ms Kincaide if there might be anything of interest we could pass a day doing in Elgin, thinking of Louise and saying nothing, and she thought for a second before disappearing into the kitchen again. She re-appeared some time later with a local newspaper and dropped it on the table at a page that was advertising distillery coach tours leaving that morning at eleven. Ms Kincaide left us to deliberate.

"Perfect," Neil exclaimed with amnesiac enthusiasm.

"Distillery tours?" I said, "That's a joke right?"

"Why?"

"I'm thinking Adam won't really be up for it. That's if he's even up by eleven."

"Relax, we'll tell him it's a mystery tour or something, it'll be fine."

"Have you forgotten that he spent the night throwing up?"

"He what?" Ms Kincaide called through.

"Um, throwing up objections to coach trips," I fumbled. I lowered my voice, "I think this stretches the boundaries of acceptable conduct." I said, lighting two cigarettes and handing one over.

"Can I remind you that not only did we carry him home, undress him and put him safely to bed, we also had to carry him across to the toilet and spend the night listening to him chunder. I think we're in credit as far as acceptable behaviour is concerned." Neil had a point.

"I'm not holding it against him," I said trying to defend the absent.

"Neither am I, we had a cracking time last night and it's not like we don't know he has the constitution of an eight year old girl, but A) he bought the shots, and B) he's not here to argue." Again, both valid reasons.

"What happens if he's still asleep?"

"Then he can sleep on the coach, it's probably for the best anyway. In case the driver decides to commentate on our journey."

"Okay," I said, coming around.

"Mate, I had to wrestle my half-naked pal in just my boxer shorts, he should be grateful I'm still able to look him in the eye."

The decision was made.

Ms Kincaide, having finished laughing at our Zafira, informed us we could leave it on the driveway for the day while we were gone and that our belongings would be fine in the room. She wasn't expecting a mid-week rush so all should be well until our return.

The tour would last five hours including a stop for refreshments, leaving plenty of time for us to reach our next destination wherever that turned out to be. We would camp

225

out, back in the luxury of the separate tents and be able to shit contentedly in the privacy of the wilderness. And if things went well we might all get some kip on the coach.

We had two and a half hours to get Adam together and a five minute walk to the bus station. In the words of Mick Jagger, time was on our side. How hard could it honestly be?

A BLEND APART

Eight minutes, a jumper, two shoes and a jacket still to go it could be said that we were cutting things fine. It could also be said that blind people managed to get ready faster than this. Admittedly they had the small benefit of their arms and legs moving with a synchronicity that Adam could only hope to aspire too, but that was still no excuse for him to piss in the sink.

Neil and I had to resort to bullying Adam out of the room. Mean, unsympathetic behaviour it may have been but let's not forget which of the three of us had enjoyed the most sleep that night. Scurrying along the pavement to the bus depot we must have looked like a tribute act to 'Weekend at Bernie's', Adam dragging along between protests of harassment and kidnapping.

Up ahead, further confusion hit as we discovered what the kind folk of Elgin refer to as a bus depot the rest of the British Isles would recognise to be a stop. Fortunately, even The Three Stooges would have been hard pressed to miss the carrot-coloured MOT failure that people kept amusingly stating was our coach, waiting to leave. Leaning Adam against a tyre I purchased three tickets to the tour for the ridiculously reasonable cost of a fiver each, and hustled our way on board.

Inside the coach we walked up the aisle and stopped at the backseats like the cool kids at school. We directed Adam to the corner then positioned ourselves like sentries in the seats directly in front, facing each other over the aisle. Getting comfortable, Adam was asleep again before the doors closed. Neil and I watched as the rest of the seats slowly filled from the front with pensioners. We were the youngest group on board by a hundred years or so, but on the plus side, there was unlikely to be any issues over ID. Neil pulled out the newspaper advert again and laughed uproariously.

"What?" I said, looking out the window.

"It's a SAGA operated tour." He said, after reading it again.

"And?"

"For the over-fifties. That's why it was so cheap."

"So how did we get on then?"

"Have you looked in the mirror today? We'd pass for fifty without a second glance." Ah the many pleasures of alcohol.

"They don't sing on these trips or anything do they?" I asked, suddenly.

"No, they don't sing, I bet they don't talk much either so we better keep the language and conversation in check."

"You mean easy on the fanny stacks?"

"Exactly."

"Got it." The coach pulled away and in a surprisingly short amount of time, we were leaving Elgin and back out in the countryside. "What about sleeping beauty there?" I said, leaning forward to check on Adam as we rolled lazily through the single lane road that led into and out of the town.

"Well I don't think he's about to kick off do you?" I laughed, I didn't think Adam was about to do much of anything for most of the day from the look of him. "We can have a nice, relaxing ride through the countryside, with someone else driving for a change, maybe have a think about which direction we're going to aim for tonight."

"Sounds like a plan." I agreed.

"And maybe we can learn a little something along the way."

"Excuse me?"

"On the tour," he said, "get a little taste of the real Scotland."

228

"You don't think we've had enough culture as it is then?"

"I don't think we've scratched the surface yet."

"Really, so how many near death experiences do you need in a week before you've 'lived the dream'?"

"Mate, easy on the death talk eh? We're in God's waiting room here. All I mean is, we've so far missed out on the taste of Scotland. Let's be fair, our culinary forays haven't exactly been diverse. Sausages, sausage meat burgers, regular burgers, beans, chops, steaks, all great food I'm sure you'll agree, but the taste of Scotland? I think not." Neil was preaching now.

"You don't think Scottish people eat burgers?" I parried.

"Perhaps not as a lifestyle choice."

"I disagree." I didn't, but what the hell.

"Example?"

"Well, how about Ronald McDonald? Purveyor of the burger as we know it."

"Ronald McDonald?" I was grasping at straws, we both knew it.

"Yeah. You know the bloke, his old man had a farm, they wrote a song about it."

"Ronald McDonald, as in 'Golden Arches' Ronald McDonald?"

"As if there could be another."

"First, I don't think the two of them were related-." I stopped him.

"Where did he get that many cows for all of those burgers then?" I said, trying not to laugh.

"And second," Neil pressed on, ignoring me. "He doesn't count."

"How come?"

"Because he was a vegetarian." Bugger. "And I don't think he was Scottish."

"How can you tell?"

229

Neil considered the possibilities, the red hair, the white face, the bright yellow jumpsuit. "The shoes," he said eventually, "Dead giveaway."

"Fair play. Thought you were going to say something stupid for a minute then."

"As if."

"Right." I nodded. Adam snored.

Who said we were still too drunk to drive?

The morning rolled on to early afternoon and yet we had seen no sign of a distillery and I was none the wiser to the lengthy process of Whiskey production. I had thus far paid five pounds to sit in the back of the second most likely vehicle to kill me. If I'd have wanted this much excitement, I could have just stayed at the B&B and watched Ms Kincaide inspect the remains of our bedroom.

The coach spluttered and squealed and rattled and rolled with alarming regularity. I couldn't hear the sound of the engine over the exhaust blowing and to top it all off, the wrinkly passengers had started getting restless. I had heard mention of toilet stops and human rights violations and the SAGA representative was looking most concerned. She herself was flirting with fifty-five and had chosen to fight the ageing process with mascara and hair-dye. She looked like Ozzy Osbourne in drag carrying a clipboard and a nametag that stated to anyone with their reading glasses on that her name was Barbara.

Barbara was losing control of the gang. The appointed spokesman of the mutiny, a lifelong local resident named Geoffrey, was putting forth the suggestion that the coach driver was lost, a notion I found hard to believe given that the road we were on appeared to have no turnings. Geoffrey had apparently boarded the coach with a harem of women who rallied around the end of his every sentence like undead cheerleaders. The sound rolled like a wave up to the back of the coach splashing over the ears of Adam.

230

If there was one thing that was bound to wake him up it was the sound of injustice.

I observed with growing concern as Adam unfolded himself from the corner of the coach and slid along to the centre seat forming a triangle with Neil and I. Up to this point I had no idea whether Adam even knew where he was, it was like watching Robocop 'boot up' when he's first switched on. "Alright knobbers?" were the first comprehensible words he spoke that day.

"Not bad mate, you?"

"I feel like I've got motion sickness. Why?"

"You're on a coach." Neil said. I laughed, people kept trying to call it that. "You feeling alright besides that?"

"Thirsty." Adam said, stretching and scratching. "And starving. Did you say we're on a coach?"

"Yeah, we thought we better leave it a while before heading out on our own."

"Where we going?"

"To a distillery." Neil said, throwing caution to the wind.

"Eh?"

"To watch them make Whiskey." Adam turned a pale green and clamped his hand across his mouth.

"I think I just burped sick."

"I shouldn't worry, I'd say you're all out." I said, flashbacks of last night echoing through my mind's eye.

Up ahead, the cause had gained momentum. The biddies had started chanting and stamping their feet, if you listened closely you could make out the sound of artificial hips popping out of place, it gave the whole event a certain gravitas. Barbara appeared to be consulting her clipboard studiously, as if it might tell her which animal sacrifice might calm the angry mob. The driver, whose appointed union name was Dennis sought some guidance and support from Barbara, what the ensuing situation certainly did not need, was Adam.

231

"What's all that fuss about?" Adam gestured down to the blue rinse brigade who had now broken into a chorus of 'We Shall Overcome'.

"Someone needs a piss."

"Good, me too." He stood up and we watched him traverse the walking sticks strewn across the aisle.

"Should be interesting." I said to Neil.

"I'm not walking back to Elgin, he can fuck right off. He gets us chucked off this coach and I'll never forgive him, not today, not after last night."

"S'okay," I tried to reason, "Look, he's probably just on the pull." Neil laughed and we sidled across our seats and peered down the aisle.

Up ahead, Adam was bonding. Geoffrey had sensed a kindred spirit, an old soul in a younger, more agile form. What a team they would make. I watched as Barbara managed to achieve a whiter shade of pale. Standing to begin a discourse with Adam, she was now practically translucent.

"Okay, Barbara is it? Right, I've had a word with the group here and we need to resolve a few things right now. We need an agenda, a schedule, a planned itinerary, do you have any flipcharts?" Neil and I laughed and nineteen heads turned to face us, it was 'Dawn of the Dead' all over again.

"Sir," Barbara began valiantly, "we're very nearly at our destination, if you could just persuade the others to settle for just a few more minutes we can disembark and stretch our legs for as long as you all desire."

"Well I'm not entirely sure that 'a few more minutes' is acceptable I'm afraid. We've been travelling for," I had sensed he was about to come unstuck when he turned to us and in order to help, Neil and I both gave him the bird, "two hours now. I mean how far exactly are we going?"

"This is Scotland Sir," Barbara tried patiently, "and this tour began in Elgin."

"What's your point?" Geoffrey chimed in angrily.

"My point gentleman," Barbara continued with admirable restraint, "is that Elgin is not exactly in the centre of the map, if you catch my drift?" Wendy tried to raise her eyebrows but the weight of the mascara prohibited impulsive movement.

"Bollocks!" Geoffrey replied maturely. "Your driver is clearly lost, probably drunk or some such thing. Young folk today, no offence there, Adam lad."

"None taken." Adam said bashfully. "My friend makes a good point Barbara."

"Really gentleman, please can we just allow for the fact that we are in a coach, taking it easy, enjoying the scenery and being respectful of the highway laws. The trip is scheduled for five hours and we are well within," Barbara checked her watch and chanced, "and actually a little ahead of time." Dennis chirped and we all looked out of the window. Pacemakers collectively skipped a beat, a distillery had been reached and no one had been killed. Neil and I had breathed a sigh of relief. "So," Barbara tried to beam through colourless cheeks, "if you would all like to follow me, we can begin the tour."

"About fucking time." An old lady grumbled, batting her husband in the arm.

They group shambled off the coach after our guide and with an over inflated sense of self-importance, Barbara popped open a bright blue umbrella and began waving it about in the air. "Stay together group, huddle in and stay together. Buddy up if you like, let's all keep our eyes on the umbrella, follow my blue umbrella." She waved her blue umbrella.

Neil, Adam and I stepped out into the fresh air and surveyed the empty car park. I hoped that the distillery staff were parked somewhere else or we had made a very long, pointless trip. "Is this place even open?" I asked.

"Guess so." Neil said holding Adam back from another run in with Barbara. "Leave it mate, I'm sure it's under control." The blue umbrella bobbed away from us and the group shuffled obediently on after it. The whole scene looked like something from 'March of the Penguins'. Adam was being beckoned into the fold of tweed and knitwear as a now honorary member of SAGA. Neil and I feared we might never again tear him from their icy cold grasp. We hurried to catch up.

As it turned out, the distillery, a large almost mythical looking establishment of towers and turrets and dark wood storage sheds, was open for business as usual. But it dawned on those of us paying attention that we had just about an hour to see the entire place if we were to get back on the road and head for Elgin in the allotted five hour window. Add to that an average walking speed of two miles an hour and a now pressing requirement for a toilet break and that probably narrowed our tour time down to twenty minutes. I wanted to check the advert again, feeling sure it had promised tours in the plural. I suddenly felt like I had been swindled out of my fiver.

"This bit of Scottish culture you're after, it's gonna have to be the abridged version isn't it?" I said to Neil.

"I figured about twenty, twenty-five minutes tops inside. You?" I nodded, smiling.

"If that. And did they promise food or something too?" In answer, the umbrella broke left and the group snaked around the side of the main building to a white burger van parked by the entrance, MacDonalds Burgers. I laughed but more from the look on Neil's face. Life could be so circular.

"Burgers? How Scottish." He said, broken.

Barbara organised away parties with the professional dexterity of Captain Kirk. She had us fed, watered and relieved without so much as a pause in her stride. Neil and I grabbed a quick cigarette while the stragglers finished up and then we proceeded inside to be educated. Barbara handed us over to Robert and for the briefest of moments I feared she was going to tell us to pay attention ready for the test at the end. It all just had that school trip feel to it now. I think it's why we became so excited about getting to the gift shop.

Robert dutifully took us around the lengthy process with anecdotes and facts all long since forgotten by me. The grain, the yeast, the smell, that I can remember, that and the peat and the oak casks and the angels share. The Scots call whiskey the water of life and for many families for many years that has been quite literally true in a number of ways. The tragedy it seems is in the marketing. Any Scot will tell you the difference between a single-malt and a blend, or Whiskey and Bourbon, it's quite easy to distinguish the taste of each as well, even to the amateur. But ask anyone outside of Scotland for a personal preference and a good deal more than half will say Jack Daniel's. With coke. It's not even a Scotch. Water of life is what you're told it is.

Twenty-six minutes later and we were in the gift shop about to finish the tour with a wee dram. A shot glass of the perfectly aged and recently bottled product that the site is famous for. Adam looked terrified, as if his teeth might dissolve upon contact with the alcohol. Our pensioners jostled like teenagers at the door of their parent's liquor cabinet and I hoped I would get the opportunity to find out how many hours on a coach they would travel for something they really liked. I wondered whether retirement was filled with days like these.

We took a leisurely four minutes enjoying the free sample and discussing the many discernible tastes that we could now identify with first-hand knowledge, for Neil and I it was perhaps the hair of the dog, it just wasn't one that had bit us.

Before we could get too relaxed Barbara popped her umbrella signalling it was time to move out. Like the dutiful autonomous beings we had become, we trundled after her and back to a slumbering Dennis in the coach. Adam, who appeared to be going for his Help The Aged Duke of Edinburgh award stood at the side of the coach door offering a hand to those making the first step up. It was a touching sight that seemed to compliment Barbara's herding skill in a way that reminded me of One Man and His Dog.

On the road again, we had two hours to kill. Sleep seemed the obvious choice. Adam was busy getting Werther's so Neil and I crashed out. Sat over the back wheels of the coach I wondered whether Neil was enjoying the benefit as much as I was, then considered whether I really wanted to know the answer to that question. I was about to drift off when Neil spoke. "I miss my kids, and Jane."

"That's only to be expected." I replied through closed eyes, "It's been almost a week since you've seen them. What's wrong with that."

"Nothing. I wasn't expecting it that's all."

"You weren't expecting to miss your wife and kids? I find that hard to believe."

"Sounds awful, doesn't it?"

"I wouldn't worry, I don't believe you anyway."

"I'm serious, a couple of months ago, a week away didn't seem long enough. Now though, I dunno, it's weird. Everything has changed. I'm almost feeling guilty for enjoying myself this much. Because I am bro, I'm having a fucking great time. Hanging out with you and Adam again, I haven't laughed this much or had this much fun just arsing about in ages. Really, ages. But it's like now, we're on this coach and I'm thinking I should be doing this with my kids or something."

"Word to the wise, I'm pretty sure today would have bored them shitless." I said, knowing Neil's kids well enough to state that if it wasn't plugged in somewhere, it wasn't good enough.

"I don't mean the distillery exactly, just something, a day out, anywhere, take 'em to London or something, show them the sights. Ride an open top bus and a take a proper

236

tour. I haven't done anything like that with them yet, and now it's like I really, really want to. And I want to take my boys camping, sit them around a fire and teach them to cook sausages and watch them taste whiskey, maybe whittle or something. Stuff they'll remember when they grow up. Things about me they'll look back on fondly. It always seems like there's something else to do though. I complain all the time about how bloody busy I am, but you know what? I can't think of a single thing I've done recently."

"You've been working." I offered. I didn't want him beating himself up, his heart was always without question in the right place, even if his brain wasn't.

"Great. That's the memory of me I want them to have. The fat bastard sleeping on the sofa."

"Bloody hell mate, you're talking like you've only got a week to live. Okay, so you need to make some changes. Seems only fair you take a dose of your own medicine, you've been on at me to do it all week." His eyebrows furrowed momentarily, the slightest movement that anyone else would have missed. I hoped he was expressing regret for preaching but he could just as easily have been passing wind. I wondered what we were really talking about but believed without question that I would find out eventually, when the time was right.

"I'm not trying to get at you bud," he said, back in the conversation. "We all miss you that's all, I don't like seeing you down, but I like not seeing you at all much less." I let it go. I didn't want this to be about me again. "It's the Jane thing I think I'm most shocked at."

"Why? She's terrific."

"Yeah, I know. But how come I can't see that when I'm there? Why has it taken this to focus my attention?"

"Because you're a dick." I said, with affection while meaning it completely.

"I'm serious."

"So am I, you're a dick. If you can't see what Jane does, even if it's just in the things she does when you're not there, then you really are a dick. She's raising your kids, making your home, working on top of that. You're a team, but it's not the team that needs to change, just maybe the tactics."

"Yeah, because it's that easy."

"No it probably isn't, but it's got to be better than any alternative. You want to be sat on the sub bench while some other star player comes around? Doubtful. And what about this business with your boys? Can't be that hard to make some time in your life for them surely? I'll tell you one thing, this time business is nasty, just ask that lot up there, I bet anyone of them will agree it's gone before you know it." I thought of Kelly, she still did that to me, popped up in there when I least needed her to make my point. "I lost five years, or most of my twenties, if you want to look at it another way but it didn't seem like that at the time. It's only now, afterwards, when it's too late to change it."

"Don't even joke, I remember when Ben was born, now he's the size Tom was then and they're both at school." I remembered it too - I'd been a part of practically everything bar the conception.

"I reckon you make one slight change and it'll ripple through, you go out with the boys, you take Jane, it's a family day out. It's the proverbial quality time, with the whole family together. And let's be honest, you made the time alright for us."

"Jane was fine with it. She didn't even argue when I brought it up. Like I said, she practically pushed me out the door."

"Kind of strange don't you think? Your only week off in ages and you spend it with us and not her and the kids? What does that tell you?"

He thought about the question before answering, "That she understands. That she understands *me*. That she's supportive, and realises how much it means to all of us."

"That all?"

"What more do you want me to say? I get it, she's amazing, I'm a shit." He turned to look out the window, hiding a nerve I had obviously hit.

I wanted him to talk to me, realised only now that all week I hadn't *really* asked him how he was doing? What had been going on with him while I had been squandering six months of my life in a self-obsessed extravagance? He had done all of this, brought us all together, planned and organised and denied doing anything more than making a phone call and yet I had taken it all for granted. Something had pushed him to the edge and yet as his oldest, closest friend, I appeared to be the last to know what that might be. If anyone was a shit, it was in truth most likely me. Small talk didn't really cut it.

"I didn't mean that." I said, somehow still unable to find the words, or the moment.

"So what did you mean then? Jesus you're worse than a bloody woman."

"Well perhaps she just hoped you might *start* to miss her." Neil went to respond, probably in a similar way, but stopped and let the idea run around his head first. He dropped his head in unspoken agreement.

"You tell her any of this and I'll deny it." He said finally.

"I know you will, because you're a dick." I said, smiling. Neil laughed. It's the way it went with us.

"I really do though. I'm missing them like mad right now."

"Good. Then I reckon we don't have to worry." I said closing my eyes again. They stayed that way for seven glorious seconds.

"Weirdest thing just happened," Adam said, startling me. "I was telling this old guy about our trip, and he's nodding and laughing and getting really into it, then as I finish up he gives me this bag." Adam held up a reasonably sized cellophane bag which on this occasion, was most definitely half full. "He said it was his Glaucoma medicine, that I should look after it for him." He leaned in and whispered, "I think it's grass."

Neil and I looked at Adam, deciding which way to go. "I think you're right," I agreed.

"That's way better than a Werther's." said Neil, taking the bag and weighing it up by hand.

Adam sat down with us, a look of sheer bewilderment and gratitude glued to his face. I don't ordinarily condone drugs but very occasionally I got the impression that Adam's parents might have.

The rest of the journey was spent in silence, Neil no doubt dreaming of his better life, Adam gazing out of the window seeing for the first time that which to me was just in reverse. Elgin and the Zafira were fast approaching but sleep still came. I dreamed of Louise, a fleeting thing, much like the time we had spent together. She was around me but not quite with me, always just out of reach. I would go to her only to find she had moved again, but still she would beckon on as if it were me in the wrong place and not her. I felt myself moving closer to her, closing the distance between us, and as she reached me, as my hands touched her again and her lips went to mine, we kissed, and I awoke feeling fantastic.

"You're a selfish bastard aren't you?" Neil said as the bus stop approached, I had opened my eyes.

"Why?"

"I bare my soul, share my innermost thoughts with you, and what do I get in return?"

"The benefit of my life experience and wisdom." I said dryly.

"Excellent," I looked at him, lost. "You're not going to tell me what happened last night with that Louise bird are you?" He said.

"Nope, you're right, I'm not."

"You're such a wanker." I laughed, that's the way it went with us.

A ROAD TO NOWHERE

We were due to camp again that night. The thinking behind this idea was that we would all be refreshed from our night in the bed and breakfast, fed and watered and feeling fine. The truth was that Neil and I were as exhausted as secondary care givers taking charge of their first brood. Nothing had quite prepared us for Adam and the twenty-four hours that had just past. I had watched more fluid pass through one man than the Thames Barrier dealt with in a week. The experience had had a profound effect on Neil and I, we had both managed to sleep in the car.

As it went we felt that Adam owed us. We had near enough carried him from the town the previous night, managed to avoid god knows what from the copper and his dog, negotiated the labyrinth of corridors to deliver the man safely to his bed, only to then watch him spend the next eight hours throwing-up. Looking back, Adam should have owed us for the rest of the week.

The instruction therefore had been simple, check the map and find somewhere we could camp and then drive us there before it got dark. We had been to the shops, we had the food and drinks and all that we needed to do now was set up the tents and bed down for the night. I was quite prepared to sleep on a cliff edge if there was a chance I wouldn't be disturbed for six hours.

In the back of the Zafira, you enjoyed the wind in your face whether you wanted to or not. It was still a little damp but the afternoon sun was doing its best to resolve that, and more importantly keep further rain at bay. I drifted gently between sleep and consciousness in that way that crosses over reality with dreams and merges sounds you hear with

242

things you see in your mind. At the time, I was dreaming of a rollercoaster, something huge, probably American with a name like The Liberator, a ride famous for freeing shit from people. I was enjoying the experience I thought, I felt like I was actually there. Every dip and twist and turn seemed to go right through me. Every drop and fall, every rise and peak were gloriously realised in my minds eye. The sensation was disconcerting, T.S. Eliot was right - human kind cannot bear very much reality.

I opened my eyes. This had been my first mistake so many times before. I frequently forgot to cherish the moment of darkness that exists just before the crack of light illuminates my surroundings. It is forever lost on me, the irony of blissful ignorance. One would think that having thrown caution to the wind as often as we had that week, we would at least have frequent flyer mileage to show for it. But no, once again we found ourselves in a situation that laughed in the face of foreboding sensations and quaffed at the mug of concern. Adam was reading the map, while driving at speed.

The motions of my dream came flooding back to me as I began to realise that I probably hadn't been asleep at all, that my body had just created the pretence to shield me from the horrors of reality. The road such as it was appeared through the windscreen to be both narrow and precarious. Both of these are words that infrequently spring to my mind when I'm asked for a list of preferred qualities that I look for in roads. It was as if at some point in the past, all of the unused corners and bends left over from the Romans had found their way to this location to form a tarmac slalom of death and Adam had found it. I couldn't believe that this road appeared on any map of notary respect. Surely the honcho's at Ordnance Survey would have looked and laughed at such a creation, assuming it to be nothing more than a Friday afternoon prank by bored Scottish cartographers.

I searched for words to relay my concern to Adam and wake Neil from his slumber. I thought it only fair that we should all enjoy this waking nightmare together. I tapped Neil on the shoulder in case a sudden noise might cause Adam to look at the road. He stirred groggily, stretched and then opened his eyes. I can only imagine the horror from the front seat, nothing but a questionable seat belt and an unforgiving windscreen between you and a month in traction.

I leaned forward between the seats, and Adam - ever cheerful - looked across at us both to smile. Now its not that I don't have faith in my fellow man or even that I wouldn't trust Adam with my life, because I would, without question. It's just it's one of those questions you hope are never asked, like when your wife or girlfriend asks you which one of her friends you find the most attractive. We all had our strengths and Adam had clearly made a bargain with the devil that in exchange for his tear-inducing tool he would have to forgo any credible driving ability he ever had. We were now suffering the consequence.

The Zafira rattled and thumped in protest, every moving part whacking out a warning like a Morse code for dummies. The remaining plastic interior as yet undamaged had formed a support group and proposed through an elected member that we stop at our earliest convenience to prevent a thinning of the already small assembly. In no way would our cup holders sustain further impact damage the ashtray said, we shall rebel against this mistreatment via an irritating and unfixable squeak from under the drivers seat. Forever more shall the doors fail to seal properly and the radio only tune to Classic FM. These are our conditions, heed them well.

Adam pressed on and Neil and I could hardly guess our destination, although the A&E department seemed most likely. The road less travelled provided no indication as to the whereabouts of its end. Up ahead in the distance the road continued to snake round the mountainous terrain with alarming persistence, a trail originally carved by the river that ran parallel to us now. From our positions in the car, we watched as the sun flashed in and out of view. We remained diligent to the cause of eventuality and tried not to think of a corner adorned with flowers.

I looked to Adam for answers, he looked back at me for rather longer than I felt comfortable with given the regularity of the bends we were encountering. "Have you got any idea at all where we're going?" I asked.

"How can you say that? Do we ever have any idea where we're going? You can't just go changing the rules just because you let me drive. This, you told me, is what the holiday is about. Taming the open road, going where the flow takes us and all that."

"And where's it taking us Adam?"

"Dunno, but it's stunning scenery don't you think?" He looked out of the window again and I had to agree, wherever we were, it certainly was breathtaking.

"Any chance you could let us do the sightseeing Adam?" Neil said as the Zafira cornered on two of the four available wheels. "Just get us where we're going, alive if at all possible."

"Jesus you two are a couple of ponces aren't you? It's not like there's any traffic."

"Oh yeah, that makes me feel so much better mate, I'm positively placid now," said Neil.

Through the windscreen the visible road amounted to no more than three seconds ahead, meaning we had a second to process the new section, a whole new second to panic and a further second to react. That was it, our road existed in erratic intervals of chaos, quantum theory described in concrete. This was a road of epic construction laid out in understated diversity.

To our right stood a hedge barely three feet high off the road and not strong enough to stop a bad idea, beyond the

245

hedge some eight feet further down were fields and grassland leading all the way to the river. The river as was commonly found was now nothing more than a stream with a good publicist but it echoed that which it once was in the shape of the road we now travelled. To our left, the mountain amused itself with our journey.

From a point of interest, it was worth noting that Adam was pushing the Zafira to the upper end of the national speed limit for a single carriageway road. The ashtray would never let us hear the end of this. I watched with a morbid fascination as the needle on our speedometer bounced between forty and fifty in three-second intervals, I found it soothing to focus on something inside the car that wasn't hurtling towards me with the pure purpose of our demise.

With conviction I lit two cigarettes and handed one to Neil, he took it with a nervous grasp and we each struggled to roll down windows against a centrifugal force that would have turned astronauts green. Adam, with a comic timing that I would never give him credit for, coughed as if our smoking was the most hazardous factor of the day so far.

The road continued to roll beneath us as we ate up the miles on an actual mystery tour. Adam had been right in saying that this was entirely within keeping with the holiday spirit and I was pleased that he had defended himself, but now I just wanted him to stop, soon. I was wide eyed with adrenaline fuelled terror and feeling my energy level sag. I had also begun to experience motion sickness on the rare occasions that the car was level. I didn't realise I would soon look back on the precious three-second-warning period as the golden age of travel.

The Zafira pushed on and we began to climb. Adam had dropped down a gear and gunned the car more for effect than purpose. The vehicle shuddered with exertion and suddenly found a hidden reserve of effort that we had not seen all week, the tyres dug in and we lurched forward unexpectedly. The motion caused Neil and I to momentarily laugh with nervous enjoyment, each of us impressed at our little car and the depths to which we had managed to get it to plunder.

The ascent was gradual at first but at the point when my knees began to lift from the seat I accepted that this was more than just a hill. The car was leaning back at an angle over forty-five degrees but I felt certain that the hill would have to end soon, close as we now were to the summit of the mountain we adjoined. Our view of the road became obscured by its very gradient and we were now forced to enjoy an outlook that stretched no further than the top of the windscreen.

We all watched as the grey tarmac sped through our field of vision with no end in sight until, without a hint of apology, it disappeared entirely and was replaced by a translucent blue sky. The contrast of colour was mesmerising, appearing before us like a rogue cell spliced into a film reel and the impression was almost subliminal. None of us acknowledged the transition, sure as we were that the road would return to fill the windscreen before we could process the change in our situation.

At school, I sustained a perfectly average existence, I was a B grade student with enough A's to balance out my C's. My A's were not in Physics, I won't lie, but were it not for personal experience even I would to this day argue that it is impossible for a Zafira to fly. How little did I know? What it requires is simply a combination of speed and opportunity and Adam at the wheel, how fortunate it was that we achieved all three.

As I have heard is often the case, the moment in question occurred in slow motion. I did not see my life flash before my eyes, I did not feel the prickly sensation of impending doom, nor did I feel myself come alive with the burst of adrenaline I had hoped would precede the extinguishing of my life. All that was noticeable in fact was the change in the

247

surface, from the rough and rugged terrain of our mountain road to the smooth and emancipating joy of air.

I looked out of the side window and felt like a fart in a bubble, travelling with the sole intention of surprise. The scenery floated past us while birds eyed us with suspicion, aware as they were that the bright blue Zafira was a natural predator to the less agile of their species they were nonetheless confused to see us in the air. We swooned with choreographed style tipping and tilting with casual disregard for convention or safety. For perhaps the first time all week, we were truly free, free of the chains of society, free of the restrictions of land, this was living and all at just the point when I felt most likely to die.

It is said that a bullet fired from a gun will fall at the same speed as a bullet dropped - a comparison I had hoped never to have found cause to prove. Our speed and angle of ascent together with the frankly ridiculous decision to place a descending corner at the summit of the hill we had been climbing allowed us to take flight with the ease of a bird. Our momentum alone was enough to launch us into the air as we passed over what should be better indicated as a ramp on the map. The Zafira possessed the aerodynamic attributes of a television and I felt certain that this was as close as the design had ever come to a wind tunnel test.

Barely a second had passed before we had cleared the three foot high hedge at the edge of the road, discovering with inevitable conclusion that its existence was not to keep traffic from careening off into the countryside. By way of reprise, we managed to drag a chunk of it in the undercarriage, which had the same effect at slowing us down as the man that stands waving a red paddle at a landing aeroplane. The ground beneath us dropped away with an alarming indifference to the quality of our suspension and I noticed that gravity had taken hold. We had entered a race to which there could be only one winner and I was already dreading becoming the sore loser. As fast

248

as the ground fell away we chased it, still moving forwards but gaining no ground.

Inside the car social graces had been lost. Panic had taken hold, the ashtray was yelling *I told you so*. A further second had passed by and our situation had not improved. Trapped in the Zafira falling through the air like blue-ice it would be only a matter of moments before the unforgiving ground came up to meet us. The only consolation came in the knowledge that we knew the airbags worked. Had we not had to turn them off, I felt sure we would have been perfectly safe.

The car remained level as we dropped further into the wilderness of our surroundings. The whole makeup of the land had changed since the last time I had tried to take notice. What at one point had seemed like a tranquil picture of idyllic peace now had the ominous status of desolate isolation. There was not a house near here for miles in any direction, not a phone or mailbox, doubtful as much as a passing satellite above. Were it not for the road I would have happily argued that we had found an as yet undiscovered region of Scotland.

And then we hit the ground.

The impact lifted three grown men clear of their seats and into the roof of the car, our seatbelts strained to hold us into position while gravity and inertia contested such a preposterous notion. We bounced and lurched like socks in a tumble dryer, a weeks worth of sandwich containers and coke bottles choosing to slap us in the face as the car hurtled forwards through the grass. Behind me the boot lock exploded and our luggage scattered out through the now open door. Adam fought control of the steering wheel but the muddy surface provided no traction and we span around watching our belongings disperse like the tail end of a Catherine Wheel. I feared we might roll but the car remained stable as the speed dissipated and we came to a halt, shaken, stirred and utterly mortified.

"So," I said as the blood spots cleared from eyes, "how about we camp here tonight then?"

Not for the first time that week, the three of us stood around the remains of our car.

"We should call someone." Adam said. He was probably right.

"We can't." Neil replied, lighting two cigarettes and handing one to me.

"Why not?"

"Who do you want to call?"

"Anyone. Someone. I dunno, but we should call someone. The police?" he offered.

"Can't call the police." Neil said matter of factly.

"Neil's right, can't call the police Adam," I said.

"Why not?"

"Several reasons," Neil said, "To start with, we probably shouldn't have been driving the car in the state that it was in."

"Secondly," I picked up, "we definitely shouldn't have been driving the car in the state that we were in, not for at least another eight hours or so." Neil nodded while Adam stared at us.

"And last but by no means least," Neil concluded, "you my son are carrying around enough grass to push the limits of personal consumption for a regular attendant of Glastonbury."

"Shit."

"Indeed." We agreed.

"A job like this, there's really only one person who could help us anyway." Adam said.

"Who?" we asked.

"Mrs Langdon." He said laughing, "What a woman." For the second time in as many minutes, Adam was probably right.

For the moment though, one fact remained, like it or not we were here for the night. Darkness was a mere couple of hours away and not nearly enough time for us to find a way out. The land immediately around us was flat, the mountain represented the impossible task of getting back to the road and the river signified the continuing passing of time. We scattered to collect our belongings, dragged them to the centre of our base and began to set up camp.

The Zafira stood motionless and yet alive with the energy of recent events. The passenger side window had dropped into the doorframe and the car as a whole seemed a good three inches lower than it had once been. A crack of significant size had snaked its way up the front windscreen and the boot would probably never close again. We had also managed to dislodge the exhaust pipe and it hung forlornly on the ground.

We had as yet to apportion the blame for our predicament, but for once it wasn't that kind of day. I had no doubt that this would be ammunition we would forever use against Adam in days to come, but today it wasn't necessary. We did not feel anger or resentment and there were no accusations thrown. In truth, we were all glad to be alive and amazed to be unharmed.

It could be said that bravado had brought us here to the field, our car crumpling under the strain of our need to be wild and free, that under any normal circumstances we would not have been driving in such a fashion. Yet, under any normal circumstances, we wouldn't have been there at all. Circumstances had conspired in each of our lives to create this moment, call it fate or the mystery of planetary alignment, but we were there, together and the better for it. It is said that a friend will help you get out of jail, but a real friend will be right there with you, sitting in jail next to you. For me, real friends launched you into a field and helped you laugh about it afterwards.

Before long, our tents were assembled and our bags had been recovered, we gathered wood for a campfire and set up the barbecue. Neil and Adam fixed the window in the car while I cooked. By chance or design, this spot had its merit, we were close to water, reasonably protected from the elements, extremely unlikely to disturb anyone and all enjoying a euphoric state of wellbeing brought on by the simple fact of not being dead.

"Should we try and start the car again?" I asked, finishing off a cheeseburger with pork chops.

"Go for it." Adam said handing me the keys and sitting down to eat.

I strolled over towards the vehicle, approaching carefully the way a handler approaches a sedated animal, cautious and respectful in equal measure. The driver's door, as previously warned by the ashtray, hung half an inch lower at the handle end and required the leverage of a foot on the back door in order to open it. Short of welding it shut and entering 'Dukes of Hazard' style through the window, this would have to be something we lived with for the rest of the week. I sat in the driver's seat and it squeaked under my weight.

I looked around at the upholstery, stained with mud and spilt drinks and blood and ash. The car still had the smell of confined men no matter how many ventilation holes we created. It was the fourth member of our holiday, experiencing everything right there with us and asking for more. The seats were browning and water marked, the centre console now aligned as well as the driver side door and the steering wheel remained wrecked from the airbag incident. There was no reason for this car to start.

I reached forward, key in hand. I turned the ignition and the Zafira groggily spluttered into life. It started first time. Unbelievable. I slipped it into first and inched forward trying to bring it round to face the camp. The steering was heavy and almost unresponsive but the car moved. I hadn't bothered closing the door and as I turned I noticed the foliage poking out from underneath the car. I came to a halt, turned off the ignition and got out to pull it free. A long, thin sinewy vine of bush had snagged and refused to come lose.

I walked over to the camp. "I love that car," I said, sitting down by the fire. "Only one problem, we've got ourselves tangled up somewhat. It's going to take some work getting loose from it."

"What is it?"

"If I had to guess, I'd say the top of that hedge we cleared on our way down here."

"No worries," Adam said, standing and walking over to his tent. He disappeared inside and came back out brandishing a knife I had once seen in a 'Rambo' film. "This should do it." He said, flipping it over in his hand and passing it to me handle first.

"The fuck is that?" I said.

"My knife."

"That's not a knife Adam, that's the fourth reason we can't call the police."

"What?"

"It's all about size with you isn't it?" Neil said, missing the point.

"Adam, you could bother a grizzly bear with that thing." He withdrew the advance and looked at the offending weapon, a poster for the benefits of an annual knife amnesty. The blade was close to five inches with a serrated edge that added menace to an already intimidating piece of design. The handle was ergonomic and fit snugly into the palm, no doubt allowing for maximum leverage when plunging deep into the belly of a beast.

"It's just a knife, you two have got them, this is mine." The knives that Neil and I owned, the ones now being comically associated with the Special Forces weapon Adam held, were barely in the same family. We had small useful tools that made the word 'handy' spring to mind, sharp and sturdy but foldable and safe in the same measure. They did not bring to mind words like 'mugging' or 'seven-to-ten years'.

"They don't even compare Adam, the knives we have are useful when camping, they cut string and meat and shit like that, they don't get used for gutting boars." Adam managed to look hurt, as if we had somehow ostracised him from the group. I had to bare in mind the size of the weapon he was holding. "Still," I said, "good job mate, well done." Neil looked at me strangely, I tried to mouth the words 'he's going to kill us' but failed to get the message across.

Neil picked up the thread, "I think it's a great knife, Adam. I don't ever want to know where you got it from, but all that matters is that you have it and it should be just what we need to free the hedge from the car." Adam sat down by the fire and flicked the knife into the soil of the grass. He returned to his food and we sat in silence for the next few minutes.

As it happened, Adam's machete was perfect for the job of freeing the vines from the car. The task was made somewhat harder by our new low-rider styling and the feeling that there was a good chance the hedge was the only thing holding the car together. It was with trepidation that I extended my arms under the car. Having no mechanical knowledge to speak of, I was unable to spot whether anything was out of place, but even I could tell that large dents in otherwise flat panels was unlikely to be a good sign. Unfortunately, my vocabulary was ill-equipped to explain what I saw.

"Car's shagged," was the best I could manage.

"In what way?" Neil said.

"In just about every way mate, I can't be more specific, it would take too long."

"Such a pessimist. You've always been down on this car."

"I love this car."

254

"No you don't, you're just saying that in case it won't start and we end up stuck here." I was so transparent.

"No, really, I love this car."

"Well it wouldn't hurt you to say it once in a while."

"I said it earlier and I'm saying it now, any car that can survive the Amazing Adam is alright with me."

"You just said it was shagged."

"Only metaphysically. Emotionally, she's all good."

"You're sure?"

"Does it matter?"

"Not to me."

"There you go then."

We walked back to the campfire and I threw the hedge cuttings on to the flame. The leaves began to smoke. In just over an hour night would descend upon us. In the back of beyond, the highlands of Scotland manage to achieve a darkness unlike anything created inside. It envelops light, sucking it from a source until it has all but given up hope of illumination. The total blackness is oppressive and weighs on you like a hangover. Sometimes you could feel very alone even in the presence of company, I suggested we go and stock up on firewood. The others agreed, but it didn't mean we were scared.

SUPER FURRY ANIMALS:
GUNS DON'T KILL PEOPLE, RABBITS DO

Sometimes nature reveals itself to be more than just a force, more than the lifeblood of the planet itself. When confronted by beauty that will stop you in your tracks and bring to mind the all-encompassing word that is 'wow', it is easy to forget the other, darker side. The side you watch with fascination and fear on David Attenborough programs. The side that is explained by the circle of life, the bigger picture, the grand design, the place we all fit in.

I have often found myself belittled by the sheer scale of the world, I have seen pictures of the Grand Canyon and Niagara Falls, watched the cliffs of Dover from a ferry and heard stories of the Alps. These creations, these flukes that have occurred over time to become a part of the world that we know do not get questioned, they are just there to be appreciated. Such sights you would consider yourself fortunate to have seen in a lifetime. One alone could justify a journey, a cost or personal expense. These are the ways that nature lets you know your place. That whatever you do or however you may live, in the overall scale of things, you are but a fleck of dust in the history of the world.

I had previously wondered whether the same feeling would be achieved when confronted by a wild animal, a lion or tiger or bear or shark in the water. Something deadly and unforgiving, something beyond reason or compromise that lived to feed and procreate, that killed mercilessly for the purpose of survival alone. Knowing that I was in the wrong place, outside of my designated living space and firmly in the middle of theirs, death would be an expected outcome of such an encounter. A light maiming a certainty beyond

256

reproach. I know now that the answer to this question is 'yes', nature can make us feel very small indeed.

We did not happen upon the creature directly but we stumbled most certainly across a feeding ground, a literal bone yard of fallen prey. We had climbed a hill to higher plane, following a view of trees on our quest for firewood. As we collected the branches to fuel our flame we bent down and it was then that at first we spotted the corpses.

Now I am a grown man and accept that death occurs in all forms to all creatures at some point. I have been responsible for my own fair share of roadkill in my time and have even seen a cat bring in a mouse or two, so I should have been more prepared at least for the sight of a mangled bird lying lifeless in the long grass. But there was a look of terror that made me stop, a frozen moment in the eye of the deceased that hinted at a passing far from natural. Had I been asked, I would have said that this animal had been killed for sport, for fun, for the simple bloodlust of focused carnage.

"You alright mate?" Neil said, stepping beside me.

"No," I said, still staring at the bird, "look, that bird, its still in one piece."

"You still hungry or something? I don't think it's going to taste like chicken if that's what you're after?"

"No, but, look. It's dead right? But why?"

"Is that some philosophical thing, like 'why are we here? What is our purpose?' sort of shit?" Neil moved on without giving the animal a second glance.

"No, I don't mean that, I mean what killed it? Why is it dead? What did it die from?"

"And I'm supposed to know that why exactly? What do you want to do, a post-mortem?" Neil kicked at a stone and stepped on through the grass towards the trees.

Ahead of us, the land was flat and considering our earlier surroundings, empty. We looked on unhindered towards the horizon, the sun setting quickly. There was nothing out here, no sign of life besides us. The mountain was still behind us, the river had been crossed with nothing more than a jump and beyond the hill that we had climbed the landscape was barren. I noticed Adam had also stopped up ahead and was now bending down to examine the grassland himself. Neil walked on up to his side to join him.

"And what have you found?" He said, almost impatiently. The wood that we would need for the night had in the most part been collected at the base of the hill and returned to our camp, our main purpose for being here atop the hill was more for the opportunity to walk off the meal and stretch our legs. I guessed that the interruptions were growing tiresome.

"A skull," Adam said, pointing down at the skull. "Odd shape. And very clean. Clearly a bird or something judging by the size."

"Your point? I'm assuming that you have one."

"It's just not something I was expecting to see," Adam said, moving it with his foot.

"Why not? We're in the wild, this is what happens. Animals live here, and they eat other animals. It's natural, it's instinct."

"Well, where's the rest of it?"

"God what is with you two? Steve's got a whole one if you want to do a swapsy."

"Eh? No, it doesn't matter."

"I know. Now come on, we've got a few minutes before it starts getting too dark to go on." Neil walked on and I caught up with Adam and had a look at the skull for myself.

Adam and I didn't make it three steps before we found more bones, but they didn't match up with the skull and didn't even seem to be from the same species let alone the same animal. I looked at Adam as if to ask whether to call Neil back but Adam shook his head. He was right, what did it matter anyway?

258

Further on though, Neil stopped, looked down and then stepped back. We came up to meet him. On the ground amidst a bloody tangle of guts and intestines were the remains of a large rabbit. It did nothing to settle our stomachs. Next to that, another set of bones were scattered around and then beyond that another animal corpse, this time a shrew or field mouse or something small but equally dead. I felt like we had stumbled upon pet cemetery or the Scottish equivalent.

Now everywhere that we turned we came across a severed head or half of something now unrecognisable. Birds, rats, water voles, rabbits and something larger still, a fox or something, a wolf maybe? Even a newborn lamb lay shredded in the brush. And then the bones, legs and claws, vertebrae and paws, wings that I recognised from Sunday roasts all strewn about like a timeline of death.

Some of the carcasses were eaten, others decayed, others still looked relatively fresh. Whatever was out here, it had the run of the land and a clear ability to hunt. As we turned to go quickly back to our tents, the holes in the ground became visible, distinguishable by the setting sun. And also because Neil fell into one. It dropped him ankle deep into the ground and he screamed in surprise. Birds flew up from the grass all around us like a duck hunt, and this time we all yelled. The grass swayed with the eruption of feathers and the contrast of noise from the silence of the evening became deafening.

We pulled Neil from the hole and hopscotched our way back to the bank and down the hill. We took the river in our stride and ran to the safety of the fire. Out of breath and scared shitless we sat staring back at the bank as the birds disappeared into the blackening sky. Clouds had reformed and the moonlight would struggle to be felt through the coverage. I poured lighter fluid generously over the flame and watched it snake into the sky, waiting for someone to speak.

259

"Where did all of those rabbit holes come from?" Neil said, breaking the silence. "I mean, they weren't there when we walked out, were they?"

"I dunno, I didn't see them, they could have been, well, they must have been really, but it certainly seemed like they just appeared I'll give you that." Adam said, poking the fire. None of us had any intention of letting it drop below a roaring inferno for a good few hours yet.

"And what the hell was with all the dead things?" Neil continued, now joining our collective curiosity. "That's a lot of killing for one animal."

"I don't think it was one animal doing all that," I said, "There was too much variety. What kills birds and rabbits and sheep and whatever that other thing was? Other than people."

"I have no idea, just as long as whatever it is stays way the hell over there, I'm quite happy to never find out."

"My knife doesn't look so bad now does it?" Adam said smiling.

I couldn't let it go though, the butchery, the look on the first animal I found, the expression seemed to come to me in the flames of the fire as I sat staring into it.

"There's only one explanation as far as I can tell," I said, lighting a nervous cigarette.

"If you say aliens I'm going to punch you." Neil said, grabbing the packet off me and lighting one for himself.

Adam stared at us with a furrowed brow, "Why would aliens kill all of those animals?"

"For a laugh? How the hell should I know, I'm just saying if Steve says aliens, I'm going to punch him for being a dick, shut up Adam," Neil said, flicking ash into the flame.

"Not aliens," I said, "something worse."

"Worse than aliens? Did you never see the movie? What's worse than aliens?"

"Killer rabbits," I said.

260

"I think Sigourney Weaver would beg to differ with you there Steve."

"Genetically engineered or something, mutated maybe. Big fuckers, sharp teeth."

"Steve, shut up."

"I'm serious."

"I don't doubt it."

"Killer rabbits?" Adam repeated, trying the idea on for size, "Well, it fits." Neil looked at him like he was the last sane person on a planet of just three.

"Right, killer rabbits. Of course."

"How do you explain it then?"

"Explain what? We're in the wild, things get killed all the time, killed by other bigger things that eat them."

"But not all of them were eaten, some were just dead." I pointed out.

"Maybe they were being saved for later?" Adam added.

"Boys, there's no such thing as giant killer rabbits."

"You just happened to fall down a giant killer rabbit hole." I said.

"Surrounded by the bloody havoc of rabid beasts," Adam pitched in.

"It was just a rabbit hole," Neil replied with more than a hint of scepticism creeping into his voice.

"You're probably right," I said, "besides, why should we worry?"

"Exactly," Neil said, hoping to bring this to an end.

"I mean, you only told us to shit down the holes, why would they hold a grudge?" Neil looked at me and for the first time since we got back to the fire I managed to get him. The idea, however absurd nuzzled at his imagination for just long enough to make him think. You could see the images flash across his face in glorious Technicolor.

"Fuck off." He said eventually.

"Hey, your funeral mate."

"We're all as much to blame. You two did it too."

261

"I'm sure you'll have time to point that out when they come for you Neil."

"Fuck off." He said again. "If I go down, you two are going down with me."

We sat in the doorways of our tents, face down leaning on our elbows, watching the fire dance and listening. We were alert to the sounds of rustling, open to the idea of an ambush and unsettled enough to be holding our knives. But we were men and we couldn't openly admit to being scared, not straight away, not unless the danger was present, visible, poking us with sticks and growling. So what we needed was an excuse and what we came up with was whittling. Neil would no doubt need the practice, in advance for all of those camping trips with his boys.

Foolishly I harboured notions of the three of us carving wooden horses from tree stumps, fashioning a small cattle heard from dry wood and recreating a scene from the dry plains of Wyoming. Of course, I'd never whittled before in my life, but how hard could it be? A small shape made from a bigger lump - a veritable piece of piss task if ever there was one.

We each had picked our starting block and positioned ourselves comfortably for the long haul. We were tired but sleep would not come easily, not with the ominous threat of killer rabbits and the restless spirits of startled field mice keeping us awake all night. And of course the unlikely but still somewhat plausible possibility that it actually was aliens that had killed all of those creatures. We had to keep our minds open and our guards up, in the words of my youth, anything could happen in the next half-hour.

I began slowly at first, feeling confident but respectful of the wood in my hands, a comparison that was strangely familiar to me. I chiselled masterfully, chipping away in places and carving fluidly in others. Beside me, a small pile of discarded remnants lay like a testament to my achievements. My creation was clearly taking shape, a notch here, a line there, a groove and a thread, alone nothing more than marks but together, together they would reveal to the world the gift of imagination.

"How's it coming along boys?" I asked, smugly.

"Yeah, its coming, how about you?" Neil said, rather unconvincingly I thought.

"Can't complain, can't complain at all." I lit a cigarette like a man that's just had a terrific shag and is glowing from the experience. "Adam? All well?"

"Um, kind of," he replied.

"Wassup?"

"Well, what are you two making?"

"I'll tell you in a second," I said, flicking wood shavings into the fire. "What are you making."

"Well it's kind of an either or thing."

"Okay, what's it either, or then?"

"Well, it's either a very small spear, or a pencil."

"Can't be a pencil, I'm making a pencil." Neil said without taking his eyes off of his whittling.

"So it's a spear then." Adam said.

"You've got the biggest knife in Scotland and the best thing you can make is a spear? Isn't that just turning a bigger piece of wood into a smaller piece?"

"It's my first time, and the knife isn't exactly designed for this."

"No, you're right, I can see that." I said sympathetically, "It's more for felling trees."

"Alright chuckle-bollocks what are you making then?" I crawled out of my tent to sit upright and held my creation aloft with pride.

I was most pleased, for a first attempt. In my hands was a simple but recognisable recreation that bore tribute to one of life's most effective designs.

"It's a stick!" Neil yelled. He and Adam had crawled out of their tents to join me while I had been examining the contours of my carving.

"It's not a fucking stick!" I retorted.

"Well what is it then? It's brown, and stick like, it's a stick!" Neil reasoned.

"You wanted the pencil thing, didn't you Steve?" Adam said, mediating. "You can say it, it's okay."

"It's not a stick, or a pencil," I said looking at Adam, "it's a snake. Look," I wiggled it around in the air. Reflected by the light of the campfire I must have look like a confused druid.

"Okay, okay, well if that's a snake, where's its tongue then?"

"In its mouth," I said, knowing I hadn't gone in to such petty details. "Where it should be."

"Fine," Neil said, dropping his knife to the ground, "if that's a snake, then mine's a snake too." He danced his frankly ridiculously looking twig around the air and made 'SSSSSSS' noises. He was fooling no one.

"And mine!" said Adam, joining him. Together they sounded like a speech therapists wet dream.

Not wanting to be outdone, and to prove that my design was far superior, I pushed my snake through the grass. I made the noise too, but with a touch more sinister stealth. I clearly had the better snake, even if no one was going to admit it.

"I think we should keep these outside tonight," I said, "like a deterrent." Neil laughed, but Adam seemed to consider the idea merit worthy.

"Really?" Neil said, "A deterrent? Based upon what we've seen killed so far, you think a collection of the least convincing pencil snakes in history are really going to do the trick do you?"

"Um," I didn't want to back down, to do so meant admitting some flaw in my snake, "Yes. Yes I do."

"Fair enough, away you go then."

"What, that's it? That's all you're going to say is it? 'Away you go then'."

"Yeah. You want to try and scare off killer rabbits with a wooden bloody snake be my guest. I won't try and stop you."

"And what do you propose then? Besides sleeping in the car."

"I have no idea, I'm just not going to try and kid myself." Neil had a cigarette hanging from the corner of his mouth when he spoke again. "If it's my time then it's my time, that's the way it's got to be. That's all I'm saying."

"You sound like you're in a western."

"Sounds to me like you're full of shit," said Adam, "You and I both know if you hear so much as a rustle you'll be out of your tent like a startled school girl."

"Thanks for the support mate, appreciate it." Neil said collecting his knife from the ground.

"You're welcome. But let's be honest chaps, it's a pretty unlikely that we've got anything to worry about, I'm mean, killer rabbits? Come on." He laughed but Neil and I just stared at him.

"Adam, I like the idea of killer rabbits," I said, and not just because I'd thought of them, "killer rabbits suggest that I have an element of superiority. Killer rabbits mean that I don't have to think about anything bigger and worry about that instead. Killer rabbits mean there are no escaped bears, aliens or psychotic highlanders murdering wildlife for sport. So shut up."

"You're serious?" He said, Neil nodded and pointed at me.

"The man makes a good point Adam, I might not think a stick's going to stop 'em, but I'd rather have a stick against a rabbit than wave a pretend snake at a pissed off bear." If ever there was a time to say that phrase, it was now.

"It's a bear now?"

"Could be," said Neil.

"And now you believe this do you?" Adam said sceptically.

"I'm just saying that there's a certain self-preservation theory in envisioning something smaller, rabbits work fine for me."

"And me," I said, flicking my cigarette butt into the fire.

"You two are unbelievable." Adam said, exasperated.

"It has been said." We agreed.

Camping, much like life, means that sometimes you have to endure the rough with the smooth, and that's not just a reference to running short on toilet roll. In the right conditions, camping can be a joyous experience, a chance to hark back to days gone by, sitting around an open fire and staring at the stars. It has a cleansing quality as you cast off the shackles of home comforts, electrical goods and meaningless consumerist wares and return to the basics of existence: food, shelter and warmth. All of this is true, right up until the moment when it starts to rain and then camping becomes a punishment, like community service in Moss Side.

It is only when sitting inside a tent becomes the one option that you accept how small they are, how they resemble the cages you might find a battery hen stuck in. Sure, there are some tents that are bigger than my flat but these are reserved for the types of families that name their children Tarquin and own a little plot in the south of France where they can leave it erected all year round. Our tents - not so generous. In fact it could be said that they are only marginally bigger than an inflated sleeping bag, should you ever happen to see one.

The rain carried with it a sense of melancholy that none of us packed for. We were miles from anywhere and watching the camp fire fight valiantly against the onslaught of water but even such an epic battle has its limits. Sooner or later

266

boredom becomes inevitable and boredom is a killer. People don't realise it, but more injuries and deaths occur each year out of boredom than any other human condition. People don't attempt DIY unless they can't think of a single more constructive use of their time, people don't burn themselves if they are not so bored that their minds wander and carelessness ensues. Arguments, car accidents, suicide, bungee jumping, all activities brought about by someone at some point being bored to sheer distraction. What other possible reason could someone have for throwing themselves off a bridge tied to a rope were it not for being bored one day?

The thing about the rain is that once you're wet, it's very hard to get dry and once you're cold it's very hard to get warm. Become cold and wet and you're very nearly finished. So going outside is immediately ruled out, trips to the car become journeys of absolute necessity only and even toilet trips become a weighty decision.

We couldn't sleep just yet - it wasn't possible. Each of us still had thoughts in our heads, thoughts of isolation, thoughts of nature, thoughts of the L.N.C.A. depending on who you happened to ask. To close our eyes meant to see that which we had not yet entirely come to terms with. Call it petty imagination and cheap trick scare tactics but out in the desolate wilderness, cut off from civilisation, even the most ridiculous and inconceivable notions can suddenly become a harsh and terrifying possibility.

As adults you could safely assume that we had all long ago laid to rest the bogeyman from our youth and the monsters in our closet. But the mind is a curious beast, and far from any friend of yours when the darkness draws in. Everyone has at some point in their life woken to the sound of a creak in the comfort of their own home and managed to convince themselves that it could only be the sound of a burglar. More often than not it's water in the pipes or a cat on a shelf, but for one moment your heart will pound and the hairs on your neck will tingle and the adrenaline will surge as your mind pictures the worst.

How this helps I have no idea. What reason the brain has for providing such images of primeval terror one can only speculate, but it happens none the less. So ask yourself, could you do anything different? Circumstance and opportunity have provided your mind with the basis for a thought that involves you, alone, miles away from help or hope of salvation, to all intents and purposes trapped with a creature of devastating agility and power. At best it wants to eat you and at worst wants to hunt, capture, toy and torture you alive. And all you have to defend yourself is a piece of wood shaped like a stick. Now you try and get some sleep.

When the likelihood of having to play eye-spy in the dark became an increasing possibility, Neil remembered the one thing that could potentially resolve all of our problems. He disappeared from the doorway of his tent and returned some minutes later with an alternative pastime. It was time to embrace the healing organic qualities of weed.

My experience of drugs stretches only as far as the prescription counter at Boots. I am an avid supporter of caffeine and have more than a passing association with nicotine. I am on speaking terms with alcohol most of the time but other than that I know only that Anadin is good for a hangover. I have smoked pot before, and I have inhaled, but that's it. Tony Montana I am not. If I can picture killer rabbits sober, god only knows what LSD would do.

Neil had rolled a joint that even with my limited experience I could tell was substantial and robust. He lit it with confidence and took a drag that made the lit end blaze like the eye of the devil. Through forced breath he mouthed the word 'smooth', coughed and then laughed. He passed it over to Adam who looked at it like someone had just handed him a turd.

"I don't smoke," he said, staring at the joint.

"You'd never guess the way you're holding that," I laughed. "Do you mean to say that you've never, *ever* tried a cigarette?"

"Yeah," Adam said, "never ever. I don't smoke and never wanted to."

"So pass it on to me then." I said, not wanting to pressure him into something against his principles. We weren't like that, on stuff like this. Stupid forfeits or silly dares were one thing but I wasn't quite prepared to be held responsible for a slow and gradual decline of a person's standards. I was still arguing my case for Neil.

"No, I didn't say I didn't want to try, I just said that I don't smoke. I don't know *how* to smoke."

"Are you sure you want to try? It's a slippery slope."

"This is pot right? Not cocaine?"

"Yeah," Neil said, gratefully joining me on the lonely moral high ground. "But there's nicotine in it, and that's an itch you don't want to start scratching, it's not for nothing that smokers say that they wish they'd never started."

"But it's not a cigarette, it's a joint, it's not the same surely?"

"No, not exactly..."

"So as long as I don't actually have an actual cigarette, I should be fine."

"Sorry," I interrupted, "But is that a statement or a question?"

"Either," Adam replied.

"Okay, okay," Neil continued, "But this is your choice, and it matters to me not either way, you want to, you don't want to, I won't look at you less whatever."

"Fine, so what do I do?"

"Well first you hurry up before it burns down completely." I said, still staring at the joint with an unnerving sense of longing.

269

"Don't worry about that, the old fella gave us shedloads and I've gotta be honest I don't much fancy carrying it around for the rest of the week. I say this is a one off party. And Steve, leave him be."

I watched the rain pour and took deep breaths as the smoke drifted between the tents, one part grass to ten parts soggy camp fire. I huddled in my clothes and looked towards the sky for any signs that the weather might break, but the sky remained ominously dark and unrelenting.

"So, nice and slow," Neil said to Adam, "bring it to your lips, and kind of gently suck on it like a straw."

"Or a nipple," I added to Neil's disapproving stare, "what? I thought it might help."

"And inhale, but take it easy, start small because you're likely to throw up."

"Don't make the end all soggy either," I said, sounding impatient and grumpy for it. Adam looked at me apologetically before he'd even moved his hand to his lips.

With the weight of consequence pressing down on him, Adam forced his hand up towards his mouth and opened his lips, greeting the joint with the same enthusiastic embrace children have towards cough medicine. He closed his eyes and drew on the joint, a brief action, starting small as instructed.

"Now hold it in your mouth a second before you exhale," Neil said, "and don't be surprised if the sensation is warming, it burns a little hotter than tobacco." Adam nodded, mouth full of smoke and then spluttered out over the fire coughing and holding the joint at arm's length.

I laughed, he went green.

"Why would you do that?" Adam said, still coughing. "More than once? Why?"

"Don't be hasty, give it a second, try again, we did kind of warn you that might happen."

"But it's foul, it's like swallowing down razorblades, it's what I imagine eating stinging nettles would taste like."

"Yeah, I can see that," Neil said, "but give it a second, let it settle in, let your lungs adjust then try again." Neil had actually rolled a second joint by this point and threw it over at me, clearly he had been right when he said that we had plenty.

I lit up gingerly and inhaled deeply.

"I think you two should quit smoking," Adam said, toking on his joint. Neil and I laughed.

"A tad hypocritical don't you think?" Neil said, pointing at Adam who was quickly growing accustomed to the foreign object in his hand. The second drag had clearly been a little easier to swallow, how easily that could happen.

"I'm serious, this can't be good for you." Adam said, not exactly swaying as yet but certainly building up some kind of motion. "It can't be good for me."

"If only someone had told us sooner." I said. "Perhaps they should put warnings on the packets or something, oh no, wait, yep they do that already." It must have been such a comfort for Neil and Adam to see that weed made me sarcastic.

"Passive smoking, I've read about it, it's a killer."

"I think the statistics are misleading." I said, "it's not the smoke that kills you, it's the moaning about it."

"Ha, ha, ha," Adam said, and then giggled.

Neil and I looked at him wondering whether it was possible to get high that quickly. Given the unfamiliarity of the substance I surmised it was possible, considering that the tobacco alone may well have been enough to get him half way there. Neil and I on the other hand were perfectly fine. Really.

"I'm going to quit," Neil said, "I think we should try. I think we should try and quit. Let's quit. Quit, quit, quit. I'm going to quit. Do you want to quit? I think we should quit. I'm going to."

"Going to what?" I said.

"Quit." Neil said, nodding. "Adam, you should quit too."

"Quit what?" Adam answered defensively.

"Smoking!" I said. Neil nodded emphatically. "It's filthy, a filthy habit. Neil's going to quit. I am to, you definitely should."

"You know what else is filthy?" Neil asked.

"What?" I said.

"Your mum," he giggled. "She nasty."

"Stop it."

"That's what I said, but she just keeps coming."

"I'm scarring, these are deep emotional scars you're making."

"I'd do that Ms Kincaide." Adam said, staring at the fire. "I reckon she'd be filthy."

"We know you would," I said, "You'd do her mum too."

"I wouldn't," Adam said, "Not after I did your mum, she put me right off. She filthy." I threw my stick snake at him and despite what I'd been told all my life, I didn't get close to taking his eye out.

"Can we draw an end to this, right now, mother humping jokes from this point on are banned? Can we do that?"

"I can do that," said Adam, Neil nodded in agreement.

"Good, now let's talk about something important." I said, poking the soaking, rain-stricken fire and taking another drag, I had to admit - it was definitely smooth.

"Such as?"

"I dunno, just something, anything that's not that. Talk about the weather if you like."

"Are you getting touchy?"

"No," I said, somewhat touchy.

"You are, Adam look he's getting touchy." Adam looked while I tried to give my least touchy face.

"Man this rain eh? When's it gonna end?"

"Touchy, touchy, touchy." Adam sang. Apparently I had failed.

"I'm not getting touchy!" I snapped.

"You are so getting touchy, isn't he Adam? Well touchy. Why are you getting touchy?"

"I have no idea."

"It's the weed," said Adam with authority, "makes you paranoid, I've read about that."

"I'm not paranoid!" I yelled.

"How can you say that? An hour ago you thought we were all going to be slaughtered by killer rabbits! Sounds pretty paranoid to me." Neil said.

"What? What are you talking about? That was *before* we got stoned! How can I have been paranoid before we got stoned?"

"You tell us Mulder, maybe it's something in the water?"

"Shut up."

"It's true, Steve," Adam added, "Your behaviour of late, very questionable. Exactly how much weed do you smoke on a regular basis?"

"I don't smoke weed on a regular basis," I said, drawing on the joint. They both looked at me sympathetically, like I'd just admitted falling off the wagon at an AA meeting. "Really."

"I think perhaps it's more serious than we thought Adam, I think maybe we need to get him some professional help. I mean think about it, first there's the business with Kelly, he's making out like she's *always* accusing *him* of cheating..."

"Very paranoid," Adam nodded, starting to count on his fingers.

"And then we've got the business with the Mr Stevens and the hunt, let's be honest, what's the likelihood that they were actually shooting at us?"

"They shot the car!" No one was listening to me.

"And Hans and Beth, clearly they were a couple long before the Monday when we met them. I mean who hooks up on a raft? Other than Huckleberry Finn maybe." Adam added, for whose benefit I couldn't be sure.

273

"That's right, that's right, and he's like convinced that we got thrown from the raft on purpose."

"Yep, and then there's the business with the car sinking the other day, I mean it takes a pretty paranoid person to think that God has got a personal grudge against them eh?"

"I still maintain that's true," I said, "he gave me you two as friends didn't he?"

"And then there's Louise, who he won't talk about because he's paranoid that he'll jinx something."

"That's just crazy talk," Adam said, and giggled.

"And the copper with the dog, the giant." Neil laughed. At me.

"That was Adam! How can you pin that on me?"

"And what's this beef you have with old people at the moment? Got a looming sense of our own mortality all of a sudden have we?"

"I don't have a beef with old people!"

"And this ongoing business with Adam's driving. I mean 'touchy' doesn't come close really. You are seriously, seriously paranoid my friend."

"Neil, he jumped the fucking car into a field! This field!" I screamed, waving my arms around the tiny doorway of my tent. "We're here, because he managed to make a Zafira fly!"

"I'm just saying, perhaps we need to look inside, at the inner Steve, see what's making him tick, find out why he's standing on the paranoia pavement. It must be lonely out there, especially with all of those people watching you."

"Who's watching me?" I said.

"Exactly Steve, who indeed?"

"Fine! Fine! Both of you, forget it, it's fine. Talk about my mum all you want, I give in! You win. Have her."

"Again?" Adam said.

"Been there, done that, boring," Neil said as calmly as he could manage.

274

"Literally." Adam added. He took a final drag of his joint and looked up at us. "This shit's not bad you know. But has anyone got any Hula Hoops?"

"Hula Hoops?" I repeated, confused, lost, disturbed.

"Yeah, got a real craving for Hula Hoops."

"Can't think why," I said, finishing my joint and throwing it through the rain into the fire.

"It's because they're great, I mean, a crisp, with a hole. It's genius, like a feat of engineering or something, an epic design of the twentieth century."

"I admit they are a tasty treat indeed but I think we should not overlook the joy that is the pickled onion flavoured Monster Munch." Neil postulated. "A puff flavoured fandango, a savoury orgasm, the truly serene pleasure of a taste explosion on the tongue." He was salivating, or it could have been the rain.

I scratched my chin, a thought was slowly forming through the smog of my mind, tiredness pulled at me and the remnants of last nights' alcohol gave one last kiss goodbye to my bloodstream. The chances of me lasting much longer without going for a piss narrowed with every raindrop that fell. I would sleep soon and dream, purge my brain of impurities and ridiculous conversations like a spiritual bulimic. But first, first there was something tickling me, scratching away at the bone behind my eye, something that I had to say, something important. "I like Wotsits." I said, which may well have been it.

"What?" said Neil.

"Wotsits."

"Thingymebobs, whaddyamecallums. No idea what you're talking about Steve."

"Wotsits! You're doing this on purpose now aren't you? The cheesy puff, things!"

"Oh Wotsit Wotsits." he said, "Yeah they're good. I'd eat them."

"Tell you what else I like," Adam continued. "Nik-Naks."

"What flavour?" Neil asked accusingly.

"Scampi and lemon."

"NO!" he yelled, "that's the flavour of evil. They're the Devil's food, they smell like cheesy willy!"

"You didn't really just say that did you?" I said, my stomach churning.

"Or Pringles," Adam said, possibly to himself.

"Pringles smell like cheesy willy?" Now they had me at it and the fact that not a single part of that sentence made any sense to me hardly seemed important anymore.

Adam pressed on, "Pringles are good."

I had to stop this, the man had gone too far. "Pringles? I fucking hate Pringles!"

"What have you got against Pringles you fascist?"

"Once you pop you just can't stop? I mean please, fuck off!"

"I suppose you're a Chipstick man then." Adam said defensively.

"I have on occasion been known to succumb to their seductive qualities yes."

"That's so typical of you. I mean you can really tell a lot about a man by the crisps that he eats. Ready salted Chipsticks just about sum you up perfectly."

"Oh do tell, Freud."

"Safe," he said to me, "Middle of the road, just unconventional enough to not be completely boring but otherwise totally and utterly pussy. That is you to a tee. Admit it!"

"You're trashing me over the crisps I eat?"

"Yeah," he said, showing yet another side to his personality. At this rate Adam was in danger of becoming the most complex person I had ever met.

"What about the Wotsits?" I argued, still without a clue as to why I felt the need to rebut.

"You just made that up, you know you'd take the Chipsticks any day of the week." Sadly true.

"This from a man who eats crisps that give him breath like a stale knob?" I scorned. "Fuck off Pringle boy."

"Lads, calm down. It's crisps, lets stay civil at least."

"Why should we listen to you, you eat the crisps of a six year old." Adam said while I mimed the symbol of a dickhead at him.

"That is so childish." He said to us both.

"Bollocks."

We continued on in the same fashion for another two hours. The night ended with the three of us urinating on the campfire from the doorways of our tents. As medicine went, weed beat the hell out of cough syrup.

Thursday

THUNDERBOLTS AND LIGHTNING, VERY, VERY FRIGHTENING

"You know, I'm very quickly growing bored of this camping shit!" I yelled through the Tsunami.

"I think you're over reacting! It's just a little drizzle!" came the reply from Neil's tent.

"Really? Did you know that your tent pegs have started to come loose?" His head appeared in the doorway. I couldn't make out his expression, but I would hazard a guess it was a cross between disbelief and a reluctant acceptance of the fact that we were not going to stay dry this day.

"Bugger."

As yet, we had seen no signs of movement from Adams tent. Sleeping Beauty remained undisturbed. Thunder rolled overhead so close and with such force that I heard the window drop in the door of the Zafira again. Our plight was momentarily illuminated by the startling flash of lightning that blazed behind the mountain, still some way off but growing closer by the minute.

"I do not want to get out of this tent!" Neil bellowed over the howling wind. A peg flew up into the air and we both watched it land in what had quickly become mud a few feet away. The untethered flap of the tent slapped against the force of the wind and tried to convince the other conformist pegs to follow suit.

"I think we're going to have to, I think my tent is coming away too." I tried to peer around the sides and the lashing of rain I received was enough to ensure I kept things brief in the reconnaissance department. "Have you got your torch?"

"Yeah, you?"

"Yeah it's here," I clicked mine on and waved it towards Adam, "shine it at his tent and wake the bastard up."

"That's harsh." Neil shouted to me over raindrops that seemed to have been individually sharpened to sting upon impact. "Actually, fuck it. He's not sleeping again."

"On three,"

"Two, one: ADAM!" We screamed.

Through two now illuminated panels of his tent we watched as the mummy awoke, bolt upright, staggering with the startled grace of Frankenstein's monster. The zip of the door buzzed to the ground and a face appeared, confused at the beams of light directed at him like headlamps.

"Morning Adam." I waved.

"Lads," he said, like any other day. I waited for the realisation to dawn, hopefully before the actual dawn. "Everything alright?"

"Terrific mate, the tents are blowing away, the river is rising, an electrical storm is moments away and the window has dropped in the Zafira again. Oh yeah, and it's raining a bit too!" The man could sleep through anything and it bugged me.

"So what are we doing then?"

"We need to secure the tents." Neil advised.

"With what?"

"With anything."

"Mine seems fine." Adam said.

"Thanks very much pal!"

"I didn't mean it like that."

"Can we discuss it another time please? I didn't get this wet rafting." Neil emerged from his tent and began to scour the ground for the pegs and rocks and anything that would substitute.

"How about the snakes?" I said, standing next to him and yet still struggling to be heard.

"I don't give a fuck about the snakes! I'm sure they're fine!"

280

"Neil, I meant how about we use the wood to stake your tent down." I smiled carefully.

"Brilliant, good, great, do that. Sorry, that's not bad, not bad." The sky burst into brilliant light and we shielded our eyes from the sight.

Adam finally emerged, I tried to hustle him into action and he thankfully picked up the notion of our activities before one of us drowned. He disappeared back into his tent and came back out with his knife. He went into each of our tents and found the other two and started using them to stab the hooks back into the ground. It was a plausible idea, until I considered the dangers of one of the knives being hurled peg-like into the sky. "Make sure you really dig those fuckers in mate." He nodded.

The wind was gusting violently and battering everything around us. The small tress and bushes we had foraged in for wood earlier now seemed bare and defeated. The Zafira with it's missing windows and barn like stature rocked as the air found its way inside the car and tried to break free through the other side. The broken boot that had been until now resting calmly closed but not shut suddenly creaked open as the force of the wind found an outlet. I watched it flip open like a cat flap and ran over to try and secure it before everything that we had brought became drenched.

I tussled through the contents of the car looking for rope or string or dental floss, anything that thought it might be up to the job. I hurled fishing rods out of the car and continued scurrying through the boxes and bags, before the lightning came again flashing above me like the glow of an idea. I turned and began pulling the fishing wire out from the end of the pole and drawing it around my arm. I started to thread it through the remains of the boot latch lock and the wiper mechanism and with the boot door closed started pulling it tight against the towrope. I ran the wire round and round tighter and tighter until I was finally satisfied it would stay shut. Now all I had to do was cut the wire.

All of our knives were otherwise engaged in pegging duties and even my Zippo lighter struggled to spark in the shrieking wind and rain around us. "Fuck it." I yelled, yanking the pole around the side of the car, unwinding the line all the way until I could thread the pole through the open window in the back. It rested on the seat as securely as a fishing pole could be, tied to the back of a car poking out through a window in a rainstorm.

I ran back to the tents and watched with concern as every peg planted replaced another flying lose. The wind was relentless and more aggressive than the elusive killer rabbit. "We're going to have to lie in them, hope for the best." I offered. "We're not going to beat this."

"I was going to suggest we all get in the car?" Neil began, but Adam held up his hand.

"We do that, we lose the tents." Adam said, watching as they buckled and billowed in the gale.

"So we just get back in and hope?"

"I reckon we're going to have to ride this one out."

"That's the best you've got?"

"Afraid so," I said, siding with Adam.

The lightning crossed the summit of the mountain and we dived into our respective tents for cover. The thunder that followed was deafening, like ordnance shells exploding in your garden. I peeked my head out of my zip door and caught the other two doing the same. "Any advice?"

"Stay low, stay warm and hope for the best. Things will look better in the daylight." I looked at my watch. Daylight was three hours away.

"Good luck!" I yelled, and quickly scurried back inside.

I zipped the door up and thought about sandy beaches and sunshine. Imagined the thunder to be the crashing of the waves. I thought of Louise in a bikini, walking across to me smiling as she had done that night, looking for all the world like she lived in paradise and had made up a place for me to. It was nice to be thinking about her, feeling hope when before I would feel sadness or remorse. It didn't seem to matter that I was clearly making all of the same mistakes again, thinking that Louise might well be more than just a night to me. It made me happy to think that way and the very thought of her alone was enough to warm me from the inside.

It never ceases to amaze me the times in life that your cock can get hard. Soaked through to the skin, shivering and concerned for the structural integrity of my sleeping habitat and periodically deafened by the rolling thunder, a momentary thought of a beautiful woman and I'm standing to attention like a lightning rod. It defies belief, I thought, proudly.

I tried to remove my clothes and return to the semi warmth of my sleeping bag but the wind made movements complicated, rolling my tent every time I dared shift my weight to one side. At the very least, the effort was warming. But now I was naked, dreaming of a woman that I really, really wanted to get to know better and nursing a hard-on. It had taken a lot less than that a lot more often in the past. Who'd know?

The explosion that followed was not metaphorical. Barely had I warmed my hand than I was ducking for cover and feeling the tent lift right up from under me. I rolled to the side unable to balance myself after the surprise of the sound, curious as to why the very air around me seemed to crackle. The cold, wet sides of the tent sent shivers through my bare legs and I struggled in the dark chaos to find my trousers again. I scurried half-naked out of the tent, dragging clothing behind me to inspect the cause of the noise. What I saw will stay with me forever.

Neil and Adam were both standing outside looking perplexed in the pouring rain, both undressed, tackle blowing free in the wind like mine, a slowly dampening copy

283

of 'Shaven Ravers' still fluttering in Adams hand, staring as a flame licked the inside window of the Zafira. Smoke poured forth from every opening and none of us could quite get it together enough to move.

"Any of you try and argue that God doesn't have it in for me, I give you this as a testament." I said, pointing at the melted fishing rod contorted and blackened, hanging through the window of the car. As lightning rods go, that pole had thankfully been more successful than my earlier effort.

I pulled on my trousers and I strolled towards the vehicle, urgency gone, panic over, personal safety no longer considered. I forced the back door open against the wind and stood back as the fire leapt at the rush of oxygen. The rain had soaked me to an almost flame retardant consistency and I patted the blaze with the sleeve of my jumper.

A charred hole had appeared in the backseat, the tiny flecks of plastic woven into the fabric had all fused together and the fishing pole had clearly been thrown clear of the seat at the impact of the lightning. All in all, the charge had ultimately been earthed through the tyres of the car and the damage while spectacular in fashion was considerably less than it could have been. Some people would have found comfort in that. By this point, I just found it funny.

Moving back to my tent, Neil and Adam thankfully now dressed but both equally wet and amazed, I pulled it back upright and sat back in the door, wrapping my sleeping bag around me. I lit a cigarette and tried to phrase my next question with care.

"Okay, hands up who here was masturbating when the car blew up?" The three of us raised our hands without protest. "My Gran was right, God is watching." I blew a smoke ring and watched it get destroyed by the elements.

"You know, for an atheist, you sure blame him for a lot of shit."

"Well I'm starting to think he's trying to make a point. He just tried to shove a lightning bolt up my arse. Indulge me."

"Maybe there's another explanation." Adam said hesitantly. "Maybe it was us, you know, we created a sort of static charge." I looked at him but something told me that he hadn't quite finished. "Rubbing," he said.

"A static charge?" Words failed me.

Neil lit a cigarette and stared at Adam huddled in his battered tent, "If you can create that much of a charge mate, you seriously need to trim your pubes."

"Just out of curiosity," I said to Neil, "but what exactly got you going out of everything that's happened tonight? I'm guessing for Adam it was the *articles* in the mag, but you?" Neil took a drag and considered the question and many possible answers.

"Let's see, alone, in the dark, with my cock out. You need something more than that?"

"No, I just wanted to make sure I wasn't the only one."

"You feel any better for knowing?"

"Relieved," I said.

"Lucky fuck," he smiled, "I didn't get that far."

The remainder of the night and early morning was spent trying to fall asleep while the wind attempted to relocate us all around Scotland. I think at some point exhaustion and futility took over, the way a guilty man will fall asleep when imprisoned, eventually my body gave up. I remembered all of the hours that had passed the previous night staring wide-eyed hoping to drift off yet moored to the bed.

In the most tumultuous conditions, sleep found me.

As day broke and the sunlight blazed across the sky the welcome and unfamiliar warmth poured through the sodden tents and roused each of us like a gentle kiss to the forehead. Our tents had survived, we had survived and more importantly, the rain had ceased. All that remained to do now was attempt to get dry, endeavour to get packed and strive to escape from the field, except that everything was wet, our belongings had been scattered and our car had recently been struck by lightning.

Ever hopeful we began the task at hand.

"This is starting to not be fun anymore," Adam said, digging up the knives and hunting around for the remaining loose pegs in the grass near the tents. "I don't mean to sound like a miserable shit but I'm cold, I'm damp all over and my back is killing me. If I go the rest of the week without contracting pneumonia it'll be a fucking miracle."

"Actually, I'm going to agree with you there. I think we need some time to re-group, rest, dry and relax." Neil said, forcing his sopping, unfolded tent into its bag with minimal care and attention. "I vote we get on the road, get the heaters going and find a hotel for tonight. Agreed?"

"No arguments from me mate," I said, trying to wipe mud off of my hands with more mud. "I could stand in a shower for an hour at least."

"Right then, let's get this cleared up and get moving then." Neil finished and marched off towards the car.

I watched him examine the vehicle externally and internally, laughing in a bemused fashion each time he spotted some new defect. I couldn't imagine what it was going to be like riding in the Zafira now, the smell from the burnt seats, the impacted suspension that would now allow us to feel every imperfection on the road, wet seats to add to the stench and broken doors. The maggots.

On the plus side, we could all play car part bingo as we sat waiting for sections to drop off the car on the way to a hotel. My money was on the exhaust, either way I was going to lose.

I didn't bother trying to untie the fishing wire securing the boot, the effort just wouldn't justify the reward. Instead I crawled in to the back seat and man handled bags and tents into the boot. Neil opted to drive and Adam volunteered to sit in the back following a moment of delayed responsibility.

He and I swapped seats and we waited, waited for the car to laugh at us, for the ashtray to taunt our ridiculous notion that we were going to drive somewhere today. Clearly this car was finished, it had no reason to move - the love was lost. Neil knew it too, but try we did.

The key rotated, the engine turned, the spark ignited, the engine revved, the exhaust sputtered, the car shook and the fan belt wailed. As far as we could tell, it was pretty much as it always had been. We pulled off and crawled slowly back towards the road. The route we had used to enter the field wasn't a viable option and so all we could hope to do was follow the road as best we could from below and hope to eventually find an entrance. There must be one somewhere as the land had to belong to someone.

It took ten minutes of off-road driving, ten minutes of bumping over every rabbit hole, branch and dip along the way with teeth rattling and brains aching and arses protesting. The road had begun a slow descent and it became a race to see which would end first, the field or the drop to it. As luck would have it - and luck had had it with us long ago - the entrance to the field was gradual and smooth enough for us not to require a tractor to pull us out. I would have said things were looking up, but I would have been lying.

On the road again, a decision had been chewed over and over until sufficient distance had been made to make the outcome redundant. Someone had suggested we hole up in Edinburgh, a real city with proper things to do and places to stay that were both warm and dry. There were no real objections as such, but it was a decent drive and not one of us wanted to be held accountable for anything else that could possibly go wrong. To say that we had taken an apathetic stance was an understatement. We had become teenagers again, none of us bothered and all hoping to be ignored.

Along the way we hit the CD's, cruising through the greatest hits of Green Day, Nickelback, The Foo Fighters, The Offspring, AC/DC and Iron Maiden. It meant we didn't have to talk and it solved the immediate problem of our radio refusing to pick up any other station than Classic FM. I had a feeling the ashtray was responsible for that – but how could I prove it?

It was good to be out on the road again and I felt safer for having a destination, even one as vague as Edinburgh, to me it meant I was less likely to never be found, buried alive in a Zafira at the bottom of a ravine. There was something about having a cold, wet bum that really brought out the most positive aspects of your personality.

Morning quickly found it's way to lunchtime and that meant food. We drove on looking for a roadside cafe that served coffee and put something hot on the side that we could eat. I can't say that my body needed any more grease or fat or meat but in Scotland coronary heart disease is a national hobby so unless you want your teeth served on a white buttered roll you tended not to bother asking for a healthy option. Besides, what kind of a hypocrite sits smoking cigarettes and then complains about the lack of non-fat alternatives on the menu?

We eventually came across a truck stop that housed an independent restaurant and a tourist information office. We started there. Strolling across the car park I felt like a kitten that had been dragged from a sack at the bottom of a river. I looked like pond scum with a wallet and a less fashionable haircut. My friends barely passed for human themselves. Truck drivers stared at us like roadkill out for a wander. We entered the tourist information office appearing to be the least well informed tourists Scotland had ever had the misfortune of receiving.

"Good afternoon gentleman," Annabel began. She was sporting copper coloured hair and angular glasses that made her look aggressive without the need for her to back it up

288

with actual words. "How can I help?" She chewed gum. Experience had taught me this was not a good sign.

Neil stepped up to the plate, "Hello," he started, "my companions and I have spent the week camping together in the Highlands and are looking for a hotel to spend a night in. Can you help?"

"Do you have a destination in mind?" Annabel had started tapping away at her keyboard, I presumed to close down her game of solitaire.

"Edinburgh." Annabel laughed but offered no immediate information as to why this statement had elicited such a jovial response.

"When for?"

"Well, tonight." Neil said, looking at us to clarify that this point had in fact been obvious. Annabel laughed again, she had to stop typing and rest her hand on her desk for a moment to regain composure. "What?" Neil prompted her.

"Well, I mean, it's just that, you know?" Clearly, we didn't.

"No? What?" Neil continued.

"Well, I mean tonight, this week, well The Rolling Stones are playing in Edinburgh. There are no hotels. We have Americans. Real ones." She said, as if there could be some other kind.

"And?"

"Well, it's full." She said, tapping her pen. I think she assumed this to be the end of the conversation. For a tourist information clerk she was remarkably uninformed.

"Edinburgh is full?" Neil said incredulously.

"Yes sir. Packed. With Americans." Annabel nodded slowly with a 'what-can-you-do?' look on her face.

"Annabel, do you think you could at least check for us? Perhaps see if there have been any cancellations?" Annabel looked confused, as if Neil had just asked her to strip down the engine of the Zafira and rebuild it with paperclips and staples.

"Um," she said.

"Check the computer, one room, one night, no dinner, breakfast optional. Edinburgh, tonight, close to the centre." Annabel appeared momentarily scared. I wondered without checking if Adam had brought in his knife, tucked into his belt or something equally visible and quietly menacing.

Annabel tapped away while I room gazed at the advertised local attractions. Distillery tours were understandably popular, together with a couple of more adventurous trips to John O'Groats and Gretna Green, some boat trips that promised north sea dolphins and other sight seeing escapades to famous battle fields, now sadly just fields. For me though the attraction of Scotland was simply Scotland itself. A huge sprawling expanse of countryside with pockets of unimaginable beauty, aside from the usual dross of the city's and towns the majority of the landscape was picturesque to a quality that inspired artists to paint.

Annabel raised both of her eyebrows and indicated without the exertion of explanation that something had come up. A triple room, close to the town centre, available for tonight, breakfast included. I wanted to kiss her but quickly thought better of it, I sensed many had tried but few succeeded. "Should actually be perfect for you all." She said with a tone I struggled to ascertain straight away, a hint of sarcasm perhaps? Maybe casual indifference or just the unfamiliarity of job satisfaction, who could tell?

"Perfect how?" I asked although why I was expecting an answer I can't tell you.

"Book it Danno," Adam said to Neil, I laughed.

"My name's Annabel," Annabel said, looking confused.

"No, no, I was talking to Neil," Adam tried to explain though I felt this had just complicated matters further.

"So what name shall I book the room under?" Annabel pressed on, apparently choosing to now ignore every third thing that we said.

"The name is Glenn Fiddich." I said, testing it.

"Mr Fiddich, party of three, one triple room for this evening," she hit a button and a printer snapped to attention and chewed out a page of information and directions for us before I had a chance to correct her. Neil punched me in the arm while smiling at Annabel. It was probably time to leave anyway, we were starting to stink out the small, unventilated building and sooner or later we would have to admit that it was us. I figured that was more information than even Annabel would want.

THE MASTER BATES HOTEL

We had left Annabel under a shroud of pretext and an air of body odour that sadly had accompanied us thus far. Our hotel became a mission as dear to our hearts as the search for the L.N.C.A. and nothing along the way could deter us or dampen our spirits.

The Zafira rolled onwards like The Terminator, stripped of all cosmetic aesthetic that might make it recognisable to fellow road users. In fact, such was the demeanour of the vehicle that other drivers voluntarily gave way to our passing without so much as an indicative hand gesture or demonstrative noun. We made a team, us and the car - like the human representatives of earthbound Transformers. We were the proud guardians of Past Optimum Prime.

We ate up the miles and watched as the sparse countryside slowly became more industrialised. Early signs of encroachment even in the most sparsely populated country. I had never been to Edinburgh but felt sure there would be more to see than just festival fringe acts and a castle. The city promised more with its grandiose approach and I hoped not to be disappointed. To be fair, my only comparison from the trip so far would be made against Elgin so the odds were in my favour.

Cities, like Adam, have many sides and most of them take time to discover. You can often see a socio-political template in the rings that emanate out from the centre, zones of wealth and poverty, commerce and industry, renovation and ruin all squeezed together under a skin like an onion. More often than not it is clear to even the most casual open-minded observer the type of area you are in simply by the environment around you. Town houses freshly scrubbed and smog-ridden indicate money and intention while streets with cars on bricks tend to say run, quickly. Of course, these are two very different ends of a scale but it's always clear to see which way the scales are tipping and how much is being done to counterbalance.

As we followed the map, I watched with growing interest the change in our surroundings as opulence gave way to pestilence and draped windows were replaced by boarded ones. The residents stopped strolling along paved streets talking confidently on mobile phones and became huddled hermits scurrying along trying to be invisible in broad daylight. We continued to turn and delve deeper through the arteries of the city like a blood clot searching for a home. When it seemed as if our wrecked and ruined car had become the most valuable vehicle for some miles, Neil pulled over and parked.

"What are you doing?" I asked, locking my door.

"We're here. Apparently this is the place." Neil said, ducking to see out of the window to the row of properties that lined the pavement opposite us.

The street had once been valued. All of the properties stood five storeys tall and had many large windows. The pavement itself had once been paved with fine stone and every indication suggested that big things had been planned for this sector at one point in time. There was even a park next to our car facing the buildings. A patch of green visible to a property in the heart of a city ordinarily meant money was needed to live there, and lots of it.

This street though spoke of a dream now corrupted, as if someone had lost interest after the initial burst of enthusiasm. The once white buildings had faded to a cloudy shade of watery milk that brought to mind images of unspeakable stains. The once fine paving stones were now cracked and uneven, a local council's nightmare of pending law suits and ambulance chasing lawyers. From the window of the car, I could see black bin liners piled and torn,

293

scavenged by animals that had taken a look and thought better of it.

"No, we're not, this is hell." I said, "I think we should have taken a left."

"Sorry, but this is it, The Quality Hotel." I looked at him waiting for the laugh. It didn't come.

"The Quality Hotel? That place?" I pointed and my finger withered. "Satan wouldn't stay there."

"Lucky for us then eh?"

"I don't mean to quibble," Adam said, always growing slightly more British when he was nervous, "but I think Steve might have a point. Given the choice, I think I'd take the car."

"Well you don't have a choice, we have a room. A choice if you'll remember wasn't available. I'm sure it'll be fine."

"Don't say it." I warned. "Say 'how bad could it be?'"

"Well how bad *could* it be?" I punched him.

"Let's go and find out then shall we." I said, unlocking my door and forcing it open. I stepped on to the pavement and a soiled prophylactic squelched underfoot. "That's just nasty." I said, hopping off.

We stood like soldiers at the front line. Across the road was enemy territory and we had been ordered to form an insurgence party by a mad tin-haired tourist clerk with a grudge. We hadn't even made it across the road and I had already trodden on a condom.

"Well that's promising," Adam said, pointing just left of the hotel. Behind the railings a set of stone steps led down to a shop that at first glance appeared to be a twenty-four hour chemist. "It's a fucking VD clinic. Next to our hotel." We laughed, there didn't seem to be anywhere else to go with it.

"Lads, follow me."

Neil led the way and Adam and I followed.

Inside the lobby of The Quality Hotel it immediately became obvious that the establishment had been named as some sort of post-ironic joke. The hallway had wood slat cladding that swallowed light like a vacuum and the reception desk loomed at the far end. We walked through with tentative steps like unarmed Ghostbusters. Pictures of a more prosperous time and clientele adorned the walls with a melancholic grace, a forgotten idea scrawled in haste like the graffiti of an interior designer.

There was a guest book on the counter and a bell that suggested ringing it would be prosperous for the clinic downstairs. An exposed light tried to illuminate a rack of pigeon holes filled with keys and mail and probable test results. A glass door stood open to the right and through it a makeshift bar with stools and tables and chairs. Patrons of the hotel, or of the bar at least, all stopped to observe us as we approached looking for a duty manager or receptionist or even a maid. The men passed no comment at our arrival but the barman walked out and came round behind the counter.

"Gentlemen," the tall, wiry thin man said by way of a greeting, "welcome to The Quality Hotel."

We looked around the place again, waiting for him to apologise.

"We have a room booked," Neil said, "should be under the name 'Glenn Fiddich'." Neil cringed, as did the barman.

"So it's that kind of a party then is it?" The man, whose nametag informed us was called Graham, said. "Well, you'll not be the first and doubtless the last." Graham checked the reservations.

I waited for Neil to clear up the confusion and stamp on any assumption, but he just tapped his fingers on the counter and stared at the blank pages of the guest book. "Quiet at the moment?" Neil asked, pointing to the empty pages.

"Fully booked," Graham replied absently, "Here we go then. Party of three, one night, breakfast. Room 319. Sign here please."

Neil signed the slip and Graham handed him our key. "Do you have luggage?" He asked, rather pointlessly I thought but said nothing. We nodded and Graham suggested perhaps we go and get it before climbing the three floors up to our room. We nodded again and walked back outside.

"You know, I almost wish you hadn't taken that key," I said to Neil as we crossed the road to the car.

"Why? It'll be fine." He said. "Do you want to just get the stuff out by the backseat instead of fighting with the wire on the boot?" I nodded and climbed in.

Adam, who had remained quiet through our encounter so far, looked across at the hotel again and said, "Do you think it's more the type of place that charges by the hour?" We laughed but he made an interesting point.

"Guys, it's fine. It's a room indoors for one night, besides we can hit the town later, we won't be in it much." Ever optimistic, Neil was failing to put our minds at rest.

We grabbed our bags and a few choice loose belongings that needed an opportunity to dry out and began trying to secure the car. This meant slamming the doors to hope they caught the locks while at the same time not so hard that the window would fall into the door again. As for the missing window, Adam suggested we tape a carrier bag over the hole and hope for the best. We guessed that there was nothing much left in the car worth stealing and that failing that the smell alone would be enough to deter would be thieves.

Inside we met up with Graham and began the ascent to our room via the staircase to the left of the reception desk. It occurred to me that The Quality Hotel must have at one point simply just been a residence as the staircase allowed for barely one person and a bag to traverse. Should anyone be coming down the other way an embarrassing tango would have to be negotiated in order to pass. Graham spared no allowance for smokers and charged on ahead.

Each floor we reached spurred off from the stairwell down an equally narrow corridor with plain doors and poor lighting. I looked for the obligatory fire escape routes but found to my utter dismay that the hotel relied on the law of elimination, there is no other exit, ergo this *is* the exit. Onwards and upwards the decor remained equally bleak and the doors equally closed.

Three floors up and we stepped out to the passageway that led down to our room. We had passed a door immediately facing the stairs that had appeared ajar but I ignored it for fear of the sights that would forever keep me awake at night.

Graham pointed to our room at the end of the corridor, or more specifically pointed vaguely away from himself and told us that our room was down the hall, left at the end, right at that end and third on the left from there. Graham then sloped off down the stairs and no doubt back to the bar. The three of us stood bewildered and alone, wondering exactly how far away our room could be that the staff couldn't be bothered to get to it. I only hoped the maids had more diligence.

Fighting our way along the dark and narrow corridor we cursed the poor lighting and drab decor until we came across our room. It had a thick wooden door that implied you could comfortably murder someone on the other side without the risk of disturbing anyone on this side of it. Neil put the key in the lock, turned it carefully and made to open the door, twisting the knob. The door failed to open - an apparent recurring theme through the course of our holiday so far.

With a modicum of effort followed by a shoulder, Neil forced the bowed wood free from the frame and the door swung open to reveal our en-suite room. Directly facing the door was a long narrow bathroom with it's own door, a small but very welcome blessing. Three double beds were arranged in the room two against one wall, one in the middle facing them on the opposing wall. To the left of the furthest bed a large dark wood wardrobe stood stoically, not so much a doorway through to the magical land of Narnia as a portal through to the complaints department of Ikea.

Aside from this one piece of furniture there was a dressing table with stool, a couple of bedside cabinets and a shelf with a kettle and two cups, an odd number considering the genre of the room. Towels lay at the end of each bed and a window bled light into the room from the wall beside the wardrobe. The only other feature of note was the damp in each corner of the ceiling but presumably this was complimentary.

Neil jumped onto a bed jovially and I felt his pain as the mattress absorbed the impact through immovable springs covered by a restorative plank of wood that had been laid beneath the mattress and frame. The beds appeared to adorn the room more for effect than comfort, as if the presence of a bed justified the existence of the room. Adam sat down on his chosen bed and bobbed up and down cautiously, I simply sat on the stool hoping when the time came to enter my bed I could rely on the alcohol induced numbness to see me through the night.

"A room is a room." Neil said philosophically.

"A room by any other name would smell as sweet." added Adam.

"A room with a view," I pointed, knowing that the outside was the best thing about this place.

I walked over to the window and made sure the carrier bag was still deterring thieves. The wardrobe loomed over me and I realised this was because it was actually leaning forwards. I opened the door and stared at the spare blankets that lay gathering dust on the floor inside. Closing the door, I was surprised to be suddenly hit in the face by a

298

rolled up pair of socks. "They came with the room!" Adam said gleefully. I looked down at them and hoped that the brown mark was simply part of the design.

"That's delightful," I said, kicking them into the free corner. "Do you reckon the motor's going to be alright out there tonight? It kind of looks like the most valuable thing in the street, next to the clinic of course."

"I'm a little worried about it." Adam agreed, sitting back on his bed and resting against the wall.

"What are we supposed to do?" Neil asked, "tie a string to the back and thread it through the window? Attach it to our feet while we sleep? Wait and see if we wake up bobbing down the road like bated fish? You two are pathetic - it'll be fine. The room is fine. Everything is fine."

"So you're okay with all of this then?" I asked, indicating the room in general.

"Yes! It's a room, shit, shower and shave then lets head on out and get some food, grab a beer and forget about it all." As always with Neil, simplicity was the most appealing choice.

"Okay, okay." I said, moving towards my bed and my bag and the pile of clothes I had hoped to dry off that night. The presence of damp in the room was not appeasing me.

Adam stood then made his way to the bathroom, closing the door and leaving Neil and I alone to abuse the freedom by smoking. I gave up trying to figure out a way to dry my clothes and opted to leave the bag open and hope for the best. I sat back on the bed and reached over to my pile of hotel towels. Pulling them closer they unfolded to reveal bloodstains that made me choke on my smoke. I was about to speak when Adam came bursting through the bathroom door. "There's pubes on the soap!" He said. I don't know where he had found the marigolds that he was wearing or when he had made the decision put them on but in a strange way they made the statement that much more believable.

299

"Figures," I said dryly, "there's blood on the towels too." I lifted the offending article and waved it at my friends.

I wanted to say more, but where could you go from there?

Adam was standing in the doorway expectantly and Neil, while clearly a little disturbed by such discoveries, was doing his best to remain upbeat.

"We'll be laughing about this tomorrow." He said, clearly not grasping the extent of Adam's distress.

Our friend was borderline obsessive-compulsive, his attire suggesting that a shit, shower and shave could only be achieved if preceded by an anti-bacterial scrubbing of the bathroom and toilet facilities and his very deity, soap, had been defiled by another man's pubes. I feared the worst.

"Laughing? Laughing? Did you not hear me? There are pubes, on the soap!"

"Yes Adam," Neil said trying to placate him, "but it's soap. At the very least we know that the fella that stayed here before us was clean. That's a good thing, surely?"

"Pubes!" He yelled again. I laughed, Adam had gone purple and it clashed with his gloves.

"Yes Adam, pubes. Wash them off, there's a good chap, take control of the situation and wash around a bit if you must." The idea of Adam just 'washing around a bit' was like saying Warren Beatty liked the women a bit.

Adam huffed at us and stomped back in to the bathroom. Inside I imagined him rolling up his sleeves and getting stuck in, teeth clenched and determined. Still, whatever made him happy.

"Blood on the towels is a bit gross though, don't you think?" I pressed.

"The guy probably just had a shave is all."

"But what kind of place doesn't have spare soap and towels?"

"A busy one, during a week of Americans watching The Rolling Stones."

"Mate, not being funny but the clientele downstairs didn't exactly look they'd crossed the pond, most of them just looked like they'd crawled out of one."

"Fair point, but still, busy is busy. The bloke said they were full."

"I don't think I care. Are you seriously telling me that this place isn't making you want to take a shower?"

"Not in here no, there's pubes on the soap!"

"Exactly! I mean where the hell are we anyway? We get out of the car and I tread on a Johnny, we cross the road and there's an all night VD clinic downstairs and inside we're met by Graham the bum-troubler and a bar full of blokes who were eyeing us up."

"That's a little extreme," he said blowing smoke to the ceiling, "they might have been eyeing me up, but you? Doubtful."

"Oh you think this is funny do you?"

"A little, yeah." He said laughing uproariously. "You two are making more of a fuss about this place than you did about camping and shitting down a rabbit hole."

"Mate, everyone's got standards." I said. "Besides, it was cleaner out there."

"Honestly, it's the socks that have worried me the most." Neil said, staring out of the window.

"The socks? How come?"

"Not everyone uses socks to keep their feet warm, I mean there's dirty laundry and there's dirty laundry. Soiled socks? That's just wrong."

"Only you could think of that."

"You asked," he said, "Besides, I thought you'd be grateful for me pointing it out, they hit you in the face after all." He laughed again while I tried not to throw up.

"You know," I said, getting up to stub out my cigarette and check for newly acquired facial warts in the dressing table mirror, "tying you to the Zafira doesn't sound so bad now."

Adam spent an hour in the bathroom and you wouldn't have been far wrong to assume that fifty-seven minutes of that was spent cleaning it. You could take the man away from housework but sometimes you couldn't take the housework away from the man. He emerged through a cloud of steam with a satisfaction on his face that just couldn't be achieved by masturbation alone. Neil and I took turns to use the facilities in the hope of still being able to head out for the night sometime before last orders.

We three left the room clean, while one in particular left the room cleaner than when we had arrived. Heading out into Edinburgh for the night I felt a nervous anticipation the likes of which had not been matched by Elgin. There was something prolific about this evening, as if the week away would be crowned by this event, evidence and proof that despite the driving and all the many hours in the car, we had made it somewhere, we had finally fled the small town. This night we could talk about, this was a place that people knew even if they hadn't been to, somewhere that we wouldn't have to justify as rational.

So much about the week so far had been deeply personal and specific to each of our needs that by simply being in Scotland we were distancing ourselves from those we held most dear in more ways than miles alone. Each of us had needed something from this week, a chance to breath or a change of location. Sometimes it takes more than time to heal, sometimes it needs perspective too. A sense of what you have and what you've left behind, what you can go back to and what you take away. How could you explain that to someone you love without alienation or hurt? It almost made me glad to be single again.

We practically skipped through the hallways and down the stairs to the reception, a giddy delight that needed no explanation. A short bus ride into the centre and our night would begin. There was a sense among us that tonight was a step closer to the end than each of us was ready to admit to or accept. I for one had not nearly begun to fully comprehend the changes in me that I felt, or those that I wanted to make. But together, these things could be ignored, even if just for one more night.

A SLUR ON HIS REPUTATION

Homophobia is not an attractive trait. People don't aspire to be homophobic nor do they admit to it. I'm not homophobic. I don't believe that all homosexual men fancy me, I have not got a complex about being alone with gay men. I am comfortable enough with my own sexuality to be comfortable with theirs. I mention this purely so that you can understand that the only reason I felt uncomfortable was not because two men stared at me, just that that anyone had. I felt the same disbelief when Louise had smiled or kissed me, when any of my girlfriends had before her. I have a low self-esteem - it's why I smoke.

The bus ride was eventful for two reasons, the first because I received affirmation for the second time in a week that I was not as implied by my closest friends, a fugly bastard. The second reason was for the realisation that our less than enthusiastic tourist information clerk had possibly assumed a little more than implied when Neil had mentioned how the three of us had been camping together. It was a common mistake I now believed, given the amount of time we had spent together and the depth of our friendship and familiarity with each other. But I can say with hand on heart that I harbour no latent sexual feelings for either Neil or Adam and they none for me. No matter how close we were sitting on the bus, or how many admiring glances we all received.

Edinburgh, it transpires, has a blatant thriving gay community and our hotel was located on the main parade. Now that we had pieced this all together, things started to become clear. I don't dare to assume that there is any significance in the used condom by our car, in point of fact it probably stands as more of an indication of the opposite given how conscientious gay men tend to be. But the hotel itself now raised questions that led to only one answer. The bar full of men, the looks that we received upon arrival, the intoned utterances of Graham and the odd arrangement of three double beds in one room to name but a few.

On the one hand I immediately became more relaxed about leaving the car unattended but on the other hand I felt that a statement needed to be made. Foolishly I began to drop an octave when I spoke and sit with my legs slightly wider apart. I belched out loud and may have scratched myself obviously too. I cannot tell you why I felt that this would inform the world of my sexuality, but at the very least it might make me a little less appealing to the more discerning patrons on the bus. I am, without question, a twat.

Neil and Adam stared consistently out of the windows of the bus, careful not to make eye contact or recognisable hand gestures. In truth, we are all but a reflection of the friends we keep. The three of us formed a small band of idiots on a bus, expressing all that is wrong with the world. When a stop appeared close to a row of shops and restaurants we stood and coughed and left pathetically. We had become that which is complained about and the L.N.C.A. would never forgive us.

Feeling tight we made our way to a Pizza Hut, the agreement being that none of us could stomach another night of meat with a side of meat. The alternative offering was greatly received and each of us felt better for visiting the salad counter and skipping on desert. Fed, we left the restaurant with an open mind and a taste for a beer and began the search for a suitable venue.

Pub-crawls have always tended to be successful only when in the company of someone that knows the layout of the town. There is nothing worse than sobering up each time a move is made for the aimless wandering of the lost and inebriated. Furthermore the very act of walking often dampens the pleasure of the eventual destination. A pub-crawl therefore should only be undertaken by locals, what we were doing was scouting, and that's entirely different.

The first establishment we came to was filled with yuppie types, the overpowering scent of cologne smacked you in the face as you pulled open the door. Ordering a round of three beers we were shocked to barely receive change from a twenty. Unless we planned to have a dry night, further scouting was indeed required. The second establishment, while certainly cheaper did not appear to have public liability insurance and suggested private medical cover might be required if you planned to sit down, because as we would discover only once 'someone's sitting there'.

Becoming increasingly disheartened with the turnout of our night so far, we strolled aimlessly through narrowing streets that were becoming alleys until all that could be distinguished from the sirens and traffic was a familiar and ultimately welcoming sound of blues music. Neil and I looked at each other with joy and found a second wind for our third beer. Adam remained as always unmoved by our interest or enthusiasm in such things. He spoke only of sitting down and the unpleasant after taste of garlic pizza bread.

Following the sound like bats we turned a final corner and found ourselves at the doorway of a bar called Filthy McNasty's. We were home, and upon discovering that the drinks were a pound a bottle, we were there to stay. Even Adam was prepared to sit through the music for such an offer.

We found an empty table at the front of the area that had been casually assigned to the band and sat down to enjoy live music by a talented guitar player. He was alone on a chair next to a table that housed his amplifier and a pint of Tennent's Lager.

The artist was wearing his sixties on his face and remembering his Sixties with every slide of the strings. His dark hair was stained with grey and nicotine and alcohol coursed through each wrinkle of his skin. He had aged in a way that made him both dignified and interesting and far from frail. He tore through a set that made beers disappear without acknowledgement. An hour into the performance, he looked up at the three of us and smiled appreciatively at our enthusiastic response.

Neil beckoned the man over when it became clear he had stopped for an interval. Gesturing to the barmaid, he ordered the musician a whiskey and we all introduced ourselves. Our table guest was called Jake and tonight had been a booked performance on a national tour. Jake had been touring all of his life, he lived from a suitcase off the strings from his guitar and had at one point or another been in every town in every country worth seeing, or so he claimed. Jake it transpired was something of a drinker.

When the whiskey arrived we raised a toast to a man that had iced the cake of our trip, for Neil and I anyway. Adam refrained from leaving and had begun to appreciate the merits of the music played but more so the man behind it. Jake had not touched his drink for talking and a barman indicated authoritatively that the interval was now over.

The bar had pulsed with people since we had arrived and now stood on the more enjoyable side of full without ever seeming claustrophobic. The place isn't big, it isn't flash or filthy or false, it just has character and plenty of it. The walls have absorbed the atmosphere from a thousand nights of enjoyment and laughter and even when a momentary lull drifted across the room the place still buzzed with energy.

Jake shot his whiskey and staggered back to his chair at the front of the performing area, dropping heavily onto the wooden frame with a movement that had more in common with collapsing than control. His guitar, once an extension of his arm now seemed as awkward in his hands as a third drumstick. He rocked to the rhythm of a tune only he could hear and the barman who had rustled Jake back into action could be heard to sigh loudly over the deafening silence of his act for the night.

A noise began to spill out from the amplifier some moments later, a deep guttural sound that brought to mind images of a tortured life spent lonely and wasted. It was a noise on the cusp of being music, mixed with the jarring resonance of feedback and sprinkled with a drool of bronchial vocals. Neil and I both struggled to embrace the new sound and then he asked me a most accurate question, "Is it me, or is that guitar *slurring?* Is that even possible?"

"It is, it's slurring. Wow." Said Adam, more enthused by the entertainment than he had been all evening.

"How much has he had?" I whispered, pointlessly.

"Clearly more than just the one scotch wouldn't you say?" I laughed and looked towards the barman who was shaking his head, defeated. He moved with the air of a man who had reluctantly agreed to an arrangement on the proviso of a set of conditions that had now evidently been pissed on.

"If anyone asks, you drank that one," I said pointing at the offending empty glass by the chair Jake had recently occupied.

"Yeah, because that's going to be believable."

The music, such as it was, trailed off like a derailed train and crashed into a void of nothingness that was replaced by a wheezing into the microphone standing in front of Jake.

Neil, Adam and I sat embarrassed and quiet, all absently staring at pictures, posters and photos that adorned the walls around us. The barman walked over to Jake and had a word, which may or may not have been 'sacked' but gave up talking any further when it became clear that Jake was wasted beyond reprieve. The old man swayed in the chair mumbling something in Celtic, sloshing his pint for good measure.

308

The barman looked at us accusingly as if he might force us to take to the stage and perform for our lives but again he said nothing. The look on his face asked, nay begged for the hope that such a turn would go unnoticed, that this Thursday night in Edinburgh would pass without incident in the same way it would now pass without a soundtrack.

Walking back to his station the barman left Jake slumbering in the chair cradling the guitar like a child.

A large, dark haired man in an expensive overcoat approached the performance area and at first appeared to be the manager, or perhaps a well-attired bouncer going to clear the straggler. The man wore glasses and a suit that covered thick shoulders and a large frame. He nudged Jake on the shoulder and was met by a snore and a shudder. The man then went to the table housing the amp and began adjusting the controls. Adam suddenly leapt to his feet, startling Neil and I into focusing on a scene we had been observing peripherally so to speak.

"Hang on, hang on. Who the hell are you to be touching that?" Adam questioned. Just as suddenly a smaller man wearing, bizarrely, a loud shell suit stood toe to toe with Adam and poked Adam in the chest. The man was two-foot shorter than his larger more suave companion and a head lower than Adam, brave by association was the phrase that sprung to my mind.

Adam looked down at the poker and furrowed his brow before ignoring him completely and returning his attention to the knob-botherer at the amp. "Mate, stop touching that, it's not yours."

"Why don't you just fuck off?" said the smaller but equally forthright man. Again, Adam just stared him down. The larger man reached for the guitar and removed it from Jake's placid grasp. He rest it against the table before picking Jake up in a fireman's lift that seemed to involve the use of only one hand, and moved him to the corner of the bar to a more robust armchair I hadn't even noticed.

The small man pointed at Adam like a hopped up Ronnie Corbett before Adam grabbed his arms below the shoulders and spun him round away from the performance area and towards the door. The small man staggered and stumbled forwards and I stood to try and calm the situation, not wanting to aggravate a chain of events I felt at least partially responsible for.

The small man upon seeing me stand took a step back and waved his arms and then his larger friend landed a punch that sent me falling and flailing back into my chair with the warmth of blood flowing freely from my walloped nose.

"What'd you fucking hit me for?" I yelled through watering eyes as the crowd behind me parted like the Red Sea before Moses.

Neil stood and held his arms out in a gesture of time-out, simultaneously trying to ensure my wellbeing, restrain Adam and distance the three of us from our new free-fist-flying friend. Little Ronnie Corbett came scuttling up beside me waving a finger annoyingly in my face while I held my head back and swallowed down the blood in my mouth. Adam was yelling and the confusion I felt was more intoxicating than all of the whiskey in Scotland.

The barman rushed over with a towel for me, ignoring all of my pleas for more beer and a cigarette. I wasn't sure whether it was a side effect of the blow to the head or of the frenzied excitement of the minutes before, but I became convinced that I was surrounded by Americans. Real ones. The accents became a blur of dialects from comedy series I had been watching all of my life and before long I was waving my head around to place faces to the voices.

With his typical charismatic flare, I raised my head to see Neil now chatting happily to my assailant while the shorter pit monkey came back to the table with a gaggle of drinks for us all. This was to be a gesture of apology no doubt but my nose was suggesting I hold a grudge for at least another few rounds.

Through the haze of shock and pain I had missed the intertwining events that had gone from me being punched to us all sitting around sharing drinks and jovial conversation. I thought about antagonising Adam again just to get my bearings but the bar seemed to have returned to its former pleasant ambience now that the patrons had established no further violence was forthcoming. Americans could be so fickle, I thought, necking a beer and lighting my cigarette. The barman watched on with relief and returned to serving paying customers before I could gesture thanks for the towel.

I pulled my seat back towards the table and the large bruiser was introduced to me as Tony. He reached a hand across for me to shake with genuine apology and I reluctantly shook it while dramatically and not altogether falsely touching my throbbing nose. Tony explained that he was, many years ago, a session guitarist and had played with bands and artists as varied as Elvis Costello, Van Morrison and The Kinks. Ronnie Corbett was his agent, whose real name was Phil.

Tony then proceeded to take up the chair and guitar and without prompting or permission began to play with the joy and freedom of the annoyingly talented. The barman nearly dropped a tray of drinks at the startling contrast of sounds now pouring forth from the establishment. The Americans began clapping and cheering in accordance with the stereotype and before long beer was flowing and requests were offered and time forgot the misdemeanour and allowed for a night of revelry.

We established that the Americans not there for the concert could more often be found at the University, but that at a pound a drink Filthy's was cheaper than the student union bar. Amazingly, more people flooded in as the hours passed and for such a small and less obvious outfit it stood as a testament to the power of reputation, that and the fiscal existence of student life.

311

The night began to buzz with the energy of creation, becoming a night more than just the hours that filled it. We watched as all parties took it in turns to chair the microphone and slaughter a rendition of a favourite tune or long forgotten song. Tony played with the ease of a man at one with the instrument, barely needing a few bars hummed before he was strumming away with the joy of familiar recognition.

He turned his hand to all and sundry, never taking the microphone himself, just content to accompany others. It didn't matter how bad the singer, how out of tune each note became, Tony played for the enthusiasm of the moment. The music itself became a second to the story behind it, the reason each person had chosen that song, the memory that it evoked, the emotion that it stirred.

The drink flowed with the continuous stream of dollars and pounds, harmoniously achieving the symphony of inebriation. The Americans, even the students, marvelled at the constitution of the Brits and Scots, astonished that we could still sing let alone stand. They cheered and whooped and hollered in that way that only Americans can, talking to each other as if they all grew up in the same street in the same town. The mere fact that most lived whole states apart and those states were exponentially larger than the British Isles combined phased not one of them. Tonight they were brothers in a strange land.

Among all of those present was a large party of Stones fans that had been following the band on tour like a homage to The Grateful Dead. They spoke of hotels in cities in countries I couldn't spell and had a light in their eyes that can only be accomplished by the achievement of a passion realised. They requested early tracks and wallowed in the joyous ironic melancholy of 'Time Is On My Side'. One woman in particular, clad confidently, bravely and perhaps somewhat unwisely in a gold dress began performing eagle squats in front of Tony as he played, a distracting sight when the woman in question is attractive, a positively disturbing sight if the woman is less so.

Adam stood to accompany her to one side and in doing so found that he got heckled into the chair behind the microphone. He sat with hesitation but whispered a track name to Tony and within moments the bar erupted in cheers as our stateside representatives heard the opening bars of Don McLean's American Pie. Neil and I laughed but couldn't fault his timing, if ever there was a unifying tune then that, most fittingly, was it.

In the revelry that ensued not one of us noticed or acknowledged the barman cleaning the bar, sweeping the floor, and lifting the few empty chairs on to the tables. We didn't notice as glasses were collected or bottles refilled and we didn't notice when the doors were locked and the blinds were pulled.

We sat, we sang, we laughed and cheered. We drank and made sweet sounding music, forgetting, remembering, reminiscing and dreaming. We hoped for nights like these and good people to share them with, we remembered those no longer present and all the times that had been shared. But most of all we dreamed, each of us, of that one thing we all felt was missing or that which we still hoped to attain.

For many the goal was short term and within reach - the tickets to the concert already obtained and the pleasure of the night therein. For others there was still time outstanding, committed to an end, a graduation and career with effort rewarded. For us, the three misguided, misunderstood and procrastinating fools, we dreamed of hope, and hoped for salvation. Together we were one but alone we stood vulnerable and open to misinterpretation. We needed the strength to stand unprotected and the courage to face the unknown and we needed to be able to do it without having to take a week off in Scotland afterwards.

313

That was our dream – it's just a shame we happened to be insomniacs.

FEEBLE KNIEVEL

The problem with a lock-in is the disorientation afterwards when you stagger from the bowels of the bar, normally in search of food, only to find that such luxuries finished up hours ago. Taxi's pass you by warily and police officers eye you ominously as you stagger with the pretence of sobriety and try not to get caught pissing in an alleyway next to the local bookies.

Four am, the real witching hour, past club chuck-out time for all but the most hardened ravers and those in London 'only just starting out'. The sky can clear to reveal a view of the cosmos that belittles and fascinates in equal measure and the wildlife of city critters and garbage rustlers are at their most active.

Swaying along a pavement, shushing one another as lights from nearby shop-flats flick on and curtains twitch irritably, you resist the urge to sing only marginally more successfully than you conquer the urge to throw up.

Everyday objects become magnetic in their curiosity, wet benches become the most comfortable furniture invented, bin's become hurdles and the late, late night kebab shop the last word in cosmopolitan status. Sometimes, even abandoned trolleys have a certain exotic appeal.

Some people will say 'you know you're drunk when the room starts spinning' or 'you know you're drunk when the bird at the end of the bar stops looking like the back end of a bus and starts looking like she could stop traffic.' I will always say you know when you're drunk when some idiot suggests you get in to a trolley and you listen to him.

At the top of a pedestrian-only street, where the benches line the brickwork surface four a piece and the bins form a

315

row of Olympic standard track, a lone trolley lay motionless against a phone box, fulfilling not one ounce of it's true potential. Adam saw it first, pointing and giggling like a child accosted by breasts that weren't his mothers. Neil joined in as was the way with these things and I, being the youngest and to quote a phrase 'he with the least amount of dependants', was nominated, volunteered and bullied into sitting inside.

You have to wonder when this would ever ordinarily seem like a good idea. I'm always doing it, looking at extreme sports and saying things like 'moron' or 'psycho' or other constructive and complimentary phrases to those taking part. Where was this voice when I really needed it? Where was the moment of reflection, where was Adam with his goddamned voice of reason? Pushing me, that's where he was!

Atop the hill, looking down into the darkness to oblivion or something equally inevitable and painful I should have hesitated at the moment when Neil said 'at least I wouldn't have to worry about any traffic'. At that point my brain should have asked some questions, like how do I steer? Or more importantly, how do I stop? But no, I was Dumbass the Brave, he who knows no fear, he who should stop drinking beer.

They pushed, I sat on my knees leaning forward hands clasped to the sides of the trolley, knuckles white with anticipation as momentum overtook force and gravity found the gradient. Speed was surprisingly easily achieved for a vehicle that so frequently struggles to move in a straight line, but then even the Zafira could do eighty. The wind parted the hair on my head and the cheeks of my arse as I clenched and farted and tried not to die. Shop-fronts sped by me like 'The Generation Game' for the techno crowd, advertisements became subliminal and even the rats struggled to keep to the agreed six-foot exclusion zone.

As adrenaline mixed with alcohol my body became supercharged by a Redbull mix from hell, the throbbing from my battered nose returning as blood rushed to my feet via the two conveniently placed exit holes of my nostrils. My mouth filled with claret as I hurtled down the hill with as much control over my destiny as I normally had. I dare not move, hardly willing to breathe and struggling to feel my knees pressed against the grill of the steel.

In the distance fast approaching I could see a cylindrical poster display-unit advertising nappies on one side, behind me nothing but the howling shrieks of laughter from my former friends. I tried to exert influence over my direction by leaning without crossing over into tilting territory. I failed. I tried to reduce my speed by sliding to the back of the trolley but only succeeded in increasing the aerodynamic qualities of the cart while proportionally weighting the trolley sufficiently to jump from a small series of steps I had had no time to process.

Onwards I rolled with chaos and abandon, my only hope being to hurl myself from the moving cage of doom towards an unforgiving pavement. It was a stupid plan but stupidity had got me this far and although the odds were most certainly stacked against me, I had up until this point remained nevertheless alive, if not well. I tried to determine which side, left or right, would cause the least damage. I considered which side of my body I could most sufficiently compensate for should the worst happen and amputation be required. I raised my body on to my feet and crouched uncertainly in the shaking carriage, eyes closed.

About to jump, about to leap frog-like into the air, I collided with the nappy advert and flew headfirst into the arms of a smiling mummy. Alcohol in perhaps its only positive attribute caused my body to become numb as I crumpled into the Perspex display case like a rag doll thrown at a window. I bounced and rolled free of the trolley as it crashed loudly on to its side and slid along behind me, grinding to a halt while I continued to roll.

I lay motionless on my back staring at the stars, the cold damp stone on my back making me feel alive while paradoxically giving me an insight into the onset of death. I could hear, still some way off in the distance, the uncoordinated gallop of Neil and Adam hurrying down to meet me. I continued not to move and wondered whether all of the blood I could feel had been there before or was a recent and startling development to what was already a truly memorable night of firsts.

A face appeared in the view of the sky I had been enjoying and Adam nudged me sympathetically with his shoe. I groaned, wanting to be left alone, to be collected up with the morning rubbish run and carried away somewhere to be ignored. Neil grabbed my left arm and draped it over his shoulder, Adam took my right and together they hoisted me into an upright position, a lopsided stance between two men of varying heights.

I didn't pass out, I just don't remember being dragged back to the hotel. I think it's one of those reflex things your mind does, filtering out pointless journeys the same way you can sometimes forget the journey home from work, in a state of auto-pilot control. The brain shuts down none essential functions in order to assimilate other more pressing events, or sometimes just to allow you to think about food, depending on where you are when it happens.

I do know that we got back to the hotel, unaided by taxi or tramp. I know that we made it inside and that I woke up shortly afterwards in a bed. What I didn't know was the name of the man whose bed I was sleeping in.

One of us was in the wrong bedroom, clearly a mistake had been made. I didn't know the three men standing in the open doorway and had no insight into the night that they had had up until the point when I had started screaming like a little girl. They could very well have been as drunk as we were, lost or confused or simply just highly opportunistic. They were relaxed enough to be still laughing and joking at gone four in the morning, but who could tell? The answers to these questions were not immediately obvious from my agitated position.

"Neil!" I yelled again. "Adam!"

Nothing from either of them.

The strangers, quite acceptably startled by my presence, bustled into the room accusingly. I scrambled away from them to the edge of the bed and, grabbing the top sheet, stood by the window. "I don't have much money, but you can take it, take all of it." I proffered.

"Eh?" They replied. My head really, really hurt.

"My wallet, it's on the table."

"What?"

"Turn on the light, take what you want, just go I won't say a word about it."

"Who the hell are you people?" One of the men said aggressively. "Get the fuck out of my room!"

"Neil!"

"Hmm?" came a response. Someone turned on the main light.

Three double beds were revealed, two still occupied.

"Neil!" I snapped. He woke, embraced the moment with grace and consideration then smiled. "Finally," I said, "take your time joining the party why don't you?"

The lead stranger turned panic-stricken to the opposing bed and stared bewildered at his two companions as a hairy, apparently naked, rotund man rose from the covers.

"Tell me what's going on, really quickly." I said.

"Better yet, tell *us* what's go on, right now!" One of the men stated.

"Tell *you* what's going on?" Neil said, "I fell asleep first, how often does that happen?" He yawned and pointed, "Who are they?"

319

"That's not telling me what's going on Neil." I said.

"Where's Adam?"

"Who the hell is Adam?" A man in the doorway sighed.

"How the fuck should I know? Who was carried back again? I leave myself in your care for one night and this is what happens, we get burgled. God knows what would have happened if I hadn't woken up, we could have been involved in an orgy. I told you we shouldn't have stayed here Neil."

"What do you mean *you's* get burgled? You lot are in our room." The taller of the men implored.

"And this isn't an orgy," said the shortest member of the gang rather redundantly. "Not yet anyway."

"This is room 317." Said his friend, but by this point I wasn't listening. I didn't care about the burglary, this was about moral indignation.

"The trolley I could almost forgive, but you wait until my mum finds out about this." I bellowed.

Adam sighed contentedly. The man could sleep through the apocalypse.

"317?" Neil said ignoring me, "no this is 319." He scratched his head. That could not be a good sign. "Adam!"

"Yessum?" Adam said, rolling over. He made a very obvious tent in the bed sheet as he lay prostrate. It was obscuring my view of the doorway.

"Jesus wept," I almost laughed, "*now?*"

"Oh my," One of the gentlemen fluttered, saying so much with so little about more than enough. "Now it's a party."

"Adam!" Neil barked, "What room number are we in?"

"319." He said sleepily.

"Adam, why are these people saying we're in 317?

"You *are* in 317."

"319, 317, it's all much of a muchness anyway." Adam slurred.

The three men burst out laughing, aggression falling foul to the dissipating power of the absurd.

"Works for me honey."

"Much of a muchness?" I repeated through clenched teeth. "Adam, are we, or are we *not* in room 319?"

"Well, technically, we're not." He said slowly.

"Technically?" Neil questioned.

"The door was stuck," Adam answered genuinely. "This one wasn't." Apparently that was sufficient reason for us to be sleeping in the beds of three startled strangers.

"That's it?" I asked, the words just weren't sinking in.

"I don't believe you sometimes Adam really I don't."

I looked apologetically at the men still standing in the bedroom door. They shrugged, possibly dumbfounded. We had been known to have that effect before, or it could have been that my lily-white body identified me as an unnoteworthy threat to which each of the men felt completely at ease with. The tension that had been deflated with the speed of a pierced balloon and suddenly the men were casually among us.

"Well now that you're here, and quite obviously comfortable," one of the men said, "Fag?"

"No I'm not!" Neil yelled.

The calm man sighed and smiled, "Cigarette? Do you want one?" He offered up the packet.

"Oh, yeah, thanks." Neil took two and threw one at me.

Meanwhile my fellow had sat down on what was apparently his bed and had put his feet up.

I pride myself on being a sociable person but this stretched even my talents. I was standing naked but for a bed sheet having stumbled drunkenly into the wrong bedroom and snuggled up in the beds of three very understanding men who as yet hadn't called the police. How do you follow that?

Adam farted.

"So," Neil began, "here for the concert then?"

321

Jason, Gordon and Justin, three men disillusioned with life. Jason, next to Neil, recently dumped and getting over an ex, Gordon, on my side, considering marriage and signing up for same sex adoption, and Justin in with Adam, feeling a little like work was all that mattered now that he'd been settled in a relationship for so long. At first glance startlingly familiar. Maybe we weren't in the wrong room after all.

The hour that followed was filled with conversation, laughter and a remarkable lack of self-consciousness. In normal circumstances such a situation would have been unthinkable, a series of random events too inconceivable to contemplate culminating in the arrival of the three of us in a room with three other men. We had pulled, albeit accidentally.

We didn't change the formation of the seating, for some reason it didn't occur to us to move. Jason, Gordon or Justin made no efforts towards making us leave and the lower inhibitions brought about by the alcohol just aided our relaxation. We were immediately among friends, there was nothing more to it than that. We chased the dawn discussing the beauty of Scotland, recommending sights we had seen and places we had been.

When the weight of my eyelids became too much to bare, Neil, Adam and I made our way back to 319, forcing the door open and collapsing into very separate beds. We had agreed to meet again properly for breakfast in barely three hours time and my throbbing head and borderline concussion ensured I would sleep for all of the one hundred and eighty minutes.

In the space of one eventful evening I had seen a whole world open up around me. I had met Americans, real ones, and renewed a latent passion to travel and meet more of them, I had listened to live music of varying states of quality and been punched for my effort to keep the peace. My nose ached like a bitch and the blood loss while minimal would be prolific in future recitals of the same story.

The point was I had a story to tell again, something to share with new friends and possibly women too. All of these things had happened while I was looking ahead, I had to learn to stop tearing myself up over the past and realise that some things just happened, and some of the best when you had the least control over them. I just hoped I would remember enough the following day to learn a lesson from that.

Friday

BEDFELLAS

This was death personified. Not the peaceful passing-away-in-your-sleep kind of death but a Wes Craven blood-fest. Between leaving 317 and falling into the bed I now lay in I had been hit by a truck and dragged for half a mile. I wondered not incoherently whether Neil and Adam had actually tied me to the Zafira in a moment of it-seemed-like-such-a-good-idea-at-the-time madness and the car *had* been stolen. I could comprehend such things in my diminished capacity - it would all make sense. But this? This creaking, aching, agonising pounding sensation that started in my feet and intensified as it dragged its way up my body to squat in my head for eternity? This was not the work of alcohol alone. I had obviously drunk the piss of the devil and all for the gloriously reasonable price of a pound a pint.

The room was not spinning, there was a tornado in my head. I placed my hands tentatively on the pillows and pushed myself up, the effort gargantuan in comparison to the distance I had moved. I tried to look around, tried to focus on something and aim my essence towards it. The way I felt, nothing else was going to be moving that day. I inched my way across the mattress, its concrete qualities jarring my battered body, the one hotel in the world where it's actually softer to sleep on the floor. At the edge of the bed my arms kept moving, it was inevitable considering that it had taken me so long to get them going in the first place they were probably reluctant to stop for anything. As a consequence, I fell in a slow and deliberate, inescapable way that was more like overzealous tilting. The wooden floor cushioned the landing by way of a tribute to the bed.

This commotion, aside from waking me up, proved that I was alone. I didn't need to check the beds or look in the bathroom to confirm this, I simply had to observe the absence of laughter that was guaranteed to have erupted from Neil and Adam at the sight of me slumped in a heap at the side of the bed. Even with their eyes closed they would have laughed, like a reflex. They were probably laughing now with no idea why. The thought brought me no comfort.

Crawling towards the bedside table I reached and found my cigarettes lit one and heaved myself up the frame of the unit to my feet. I was naked and bathed in sunlight from the window and the sensation resembled a dream where you find yourself standing in a spotlight on a stage with no clothes on. Highlighted I was able to fully appreciate the damage done the previous night. I walked over to the dressing room table and examined myself in the mirror.

My knees were scraped and red, as were my elbows and shoulders. My nose was three times its usual size and glowing like Rudolf with the horn. There was some mild but temporary bruising to my eyes giving me the look of a panda disguised as a clown. I had scratched my forehead and chin a little and the palms of my hands glowed from the burn of the concrete in a way that hadn't happened since I'd discovered masturbation. Overall, an absolute fine figure of a man, enough to either put you off drinking entirely or give you a reason to start in the morning.

I staggered into the bathroom, not caring what time it was or where I was supposed to be. I was so dehydrated I could have a drained a bath by dipping my finger in it and the shower was calling to me like a mirage. I stepped in and let the water pour over me, let the stains of the previous night wash away and the dried blood run to the drain. My body stung and twitched, the pain non-specific and humming in the background of my brain. Pills would suffice to help in the absence of a weeklong refuge in a Swedish spa. I stayed in the shower a few minutes longer. It couldn't hurt.

Drying and dressing I left the room and began the long walk down to the reception desk and then hopefully on to a breakfast room. Amazingly, Graham was still down there though presumably he had at some point left to sleep since the last time I had seen him. Either way, he looked in a remarkably better shape than I did.

I asked him for directions to the dining room and he pointed to a hitherto unseen staircase leading down to a basement. I thanked him and descended down the steps that were steep enough to make me look for a guide rope and welcomed the darkness that greeted me at the bottom. I spun around, not needing much to be confused and finding this situation amply sufficient for the job. Behind me was a corrugated plastic panel framed in black and through the glow from the other side I could make out shapes moving and muffled noises beyond.

I approached the panel like a chess player, sizing up my opponent, running through scenarios so that I had every possible outcome catered for. It was a door, but no reason to get complacent. I tried to open it, nothing happened. I tried again, it didn't move. I pushed it, the door took it. I pulled it, the door rattled. I shook it, lifted it, barged and budged it. The noise was incandescent. I was suddenly aware of a contrasting effect; the more noise I made the less activity could be seen through the door. The shapes slowed, the movements became less frequent. One by one, the patrons in the restaurant were stopping to stare in wonder at the man who couldn't open a door.

I felt my strength ebb from me with my will to live. Barry was taking over. I stopped trying to open the door, it had clearly been locked or more likely welded shut, and instead I rested my head on the uneven panel, defeated. It slid open, expertly propelled by a grand door-opening master and my head bobbed obligingly over the ridges. Adam stared at me,

I managed to raise my head high enough to meet his gaze and he laughed.

Everyone in the breakfast room was looking at me, some with spoons still half-raised to their open mouths, some with toast part-buttered. He gathered me into the room and pointed at a table occupied by my two friends and three men we had recently become rather well acquainted with. I gestured my understanding and he went to sit back down while I headed over to the breakfast counter.

A table was packed with cereal boxes, jugs of orange juice and milk, empty cups and saucers and some larger mugs for coffee. I picked one up with two hands and tried to saunter casually over to the pot of coffee, thankful to see that it was three quarters full. It was hard to act nonchalant when you had recently been outwitted by a door. I was aware that some of the guests were still looking at me quizzically, I glanced down to make sure I was wearing trousers.

Picking up the coffeepot I tipped it and watched as precisely no coffee made it in to my mug. This was a conspiracy, a sketch, a comedy of errors, someone had rigged my breakfast experience to make me look like a prat and I was obliging unanimously. I officially hated everything about The Quality Hotel. I hated the room with its strange unyielding mattresses, I hated the bloody bloody towels and the pube-infested soap. I hated every door in the godforsaken building. I held the coffeepot almost at a right angle and had to resist the urge to shake it. All I wanted was a cup of sodding coffee.

Neil came up behind me and took the pot from my hands. "Mate, sit down for Christ's sake, let me get this. Your breakfast is on the table, not long turned up. Sit down before you fall down."

"Sorry bud, I don't know what's going on."

"You're hungover, and retarded, it's one hell of a combination."

"The door was jammed, that's not my fault."

"The door was fine, it was a slide door is all. Now go and sit down. Jason, Gordon and Justin are over there and they're not holding a grudge. That means they don't want to press charges. So the day is looking up."

"That's what we've got for good news today then is it? The comfort of not being done for breaking and entering."

"It was more likely going to be public indecency, and yes, it is good news. Besides, Adam's made a friend."

"How do you mean?"

"Well let's just say that Justin is hoping to get a little more than *just in.*"

"That's disgusting, and I have no idea what you're talking about."

"Doesn't matter, I'll tell you later, go and sit down." I went and sat down.

"Morning Sleepy," said Jason, smiling kindly. "Good night?" The table laughed and I chuckled and nodded.

"Yeah, terrific. Death-defying experiences aside, cheap booze, a lock-in and live music make for a memorable night."

"What actually happened to your nose? I forgot to ask in all of lasts nights confusion." Gordon said, pointing at me with a lightly buttered triangle of white toast.

"Adam happened, anything more specific than that is largely irrelevant."

"Understood. So what have you lads got planned for today then?" I looked to Adam questioningly as Neil sat down with my coffee.

"Adam?" Adam looked at me, as if I was daring him to speak, as if I had somehow assumed he had signed us up for naked mud wrestling and he knew that I knew.

"Nothing, really. Nothing planned."

"You guys want to hang with us for the morning? See the sights? You all could probably do with at least a few hours of fresh air before getting back in a car again."

"No complaints from me there," I answered, on behalf of my back.

"We wouldn't want to be an imposition." Adam said meekly.

"Honey you couldn't be an imposition if you tried." Justin replied.

I looked at Neil through raised eyebrows and he just smiled at me and shook his head. I could sense Adam pleading for a get out but as far as I was concerned we owed them the courtesy of courtesy and besides that, the last time I had intervened for Adam someone had punched me in the nose, so fuck him.

"Have you gents seen the castle?" asked Jason.

"Nope," said Neil, "but I hear it's something to see."

"Absolutely. Fabulous views of the city, plus there's the Royal Mile which, granted, is more interesting during the festival season but it's still something to cross off the list."

"Well if you guys don't mind, then we'd love to come." Neil said, finishing his breakfast. I had dug halfway into mine but was still going strong. There was something healing about grease and I was milking it for all it was worth.

"So how did you three find yourselves in Edinburgh anyway?" Adam asked.

"Spur of the moment thing really," Gordon answered, "we met at University years ago and had stayed in touch but, I dunno, you ever notice how life gets in the way?" I nodded, "Well, we were sat around chatting the other day for what seemed like the first time in ages and we just said 'you know what? We should go away.' So that's what we did. All of us seemed to have some shit going on which would benefit from a little perspective of distance so we made arrangements to get away and, well, here we are."

"Wow, sounds just like us." I said.

"Why is that a surprise?" Gordon said.

"Well, I mean, it's not, it's just that, well it sounds like the same thing that happened with us, sort of." I was fumbling through a mouthful of beans and sausage and perhaps not paying the right amount of intention to inflexion and tone.

"Sort of?"

"Yeah."

"And?"

"Just makes me laugh, I mean, we've all got problems, but ours are like, mostly chick related. You three don't have those problems and yet you're here, like us. It's funny."

"Funny how?"

I had stopped chewing and swallowed and was starting to pay attention.

"You know, it's funny, like it's a funny story."

"No, no I don't know, you said it, you said it was funny, funny how?" I sensed silence from the rest of the table.

"The three of you, I mean you're guys, and you have like relationship problems, like us, but you're guys. You have 'guy problems'. It's funny." My head was hurting, I wanted to stop talking but the words kept falling out like farts after a tin of beans.

"You think I'm funny? Funny how? Do I amuse you? Like I'm a clown? Like I'm here to fucking amuse you?" I was feeling uncomfortable now, I had somehow crossed a line without even realising I was moving and now I was being called up on it by a more menacing, if somewhat more effeminate, neurotic Joe Pesci fan.

"I, um, no it's, no I mean, *you're* not funny," five sets of eyes were staring at me but I could feel others joining them. The room was turning. All I wanted to do was finish my breakfast, was it so much to ask? "Just the situation, you know, is funny..."

"Funny how?" Gordon hadn't blinked for four minutes now and his stare was bringing sweats back to my forehead.

"I, I...I think I need to go to the toilet." I went to stand and everyone at the table burst out laughing, Gordon was pointing at me nodding and this was clearly the funniest thing that had happened to them all week.

"Sit down you tart," Said Neil through tears. "He was just having you on."

I stared at Gordon, to be sure. He was laughing and wiping his face and the softness had returned to his features and now I couldn't think how I could have possibly been led down such a path. Then again, a short while ago I had lost a battle of wills with a door, was I really in a position to ask?

"You," I searched for the words, "you bitch." I said.

"You have *no* idea."

I followed them all up the stairs, the last to leave the dining room. I wanted to make absolutely sure that the door would be open and no one would be held up behind me. All things considered it was a risky move, had someone of closed it in front of me I could have been stuck there for the rest of the day.

Dragging my tired, abused body up the stairs I heard pleasantries exchanged with Graham ahead of me that were not continued as I staggered past him. The next set of stairs up to our rooms seemed endless and my bladder chose this time to remind of quite how much I'd had to drink the previous night. I wasn't going to make it all the way through the corridors without having to stop first.

At the landing of the second floor I dropped back from the pack and went to find one of the communal toilets that would be servicing the non-en-suite rooms on that level. I hoped not to have to walk too far as I was already finding it necessary to *clench*.

I turned a corner of the hallway and found myself at a T-junction split. Both left and right led to darkness but the door directly in front of me appeared to be the room in question. I tried the handle tentatively, and with just enough relief to not piss myself, found it to be open. The

332

light, such as it was, was already on and what it illuminated was a space smaller than a shoebox. If there was a toilet to be found in here there was every possibility I would have to pee with one leg still in the hallway. I stepped inside gingerly.

As my eyes adjusted to the light inside a second door to my left became apparent but as I had already cracked my knee on the toilet bowl I gave it scant attention and set about my business. The toilet, most oddly, was recessed back only a foot or so into the opposite wall meaning anyone going through to wherever the door to my left went would practically have to step over the bowl in order to pass. But passing was not my intention and therefore not my concern.

I tried, really I tried to close the door behind me. I am seldom referred to as being fat but too much time in that room could quite easily have given me a complex. I breathed in and poked my arse forward and attempted to reach back and pull the door closed but the angles just wouldn't allow it. I tried to lean forwards and suspend myself over the toilet but feared my supercharged stream would splash-back Tsunami-like and crash forth back into the hallway. My bladder ached and stabbed me with pins while my intoxicated brain tried hopelessly to deal with Pythagorean equations. I wavered unsteadily and head butted the exposed white-hot light bulb before giving up on the maths and opting instead to just sit down.

I lowered the toilet seat down, stepped back out into the hallway, turned around and backed myself into the cubicle drawing the door closed on my way. I dropped my jeans and on my downward approach I accidentally kneed the door and it swung open again. My head fell to my hands in agonising despair but I still couldn't bring myself to just piss for all to see. I inched forwards, grabbed the door handle and pulled it shut as I backed in on to the seat, holding firm on to the handle while I shuffled my knees around to the side of the bowl towards the adjoining door. People at festivals enjoyed more accommodating toilet facilities than I currently had to endure.

And then it began, such relief, I just couldn't hold it in anymore. My mouth hung open and I released an "ahhhhhhh" of unadulterated pleasure, my body a conduit, passing more water than all of the aqueducts in Rome. I don't know how long I sat that way but I felt my body deflate, and still I continued. No man alone had peed so much for so long in all the history of the Scottish Highlands Tourists Board. My body was limp, my eyes had closed, my breathing deep. I had released the door handle, the balance of effort for reward tipped largely in the favour of sitting doing as little as possible for as long as I could get away with it.

I'm not sure which of my senses kicked in first, the exposed hairs on my legs registering a slight almost unnoticeable draft of air, perhaps my closed eyes subconsciously picking up on an increase in light. It could have been a scent that wafted by my nose, one that quelled the overwhelming hum of ammonia filling the cubicle, or maybe, perhaps most likely, it was that sixth sense, the one that tells you that you're not alone, that your environment has changed. I opened my eyes and as it happened, they were all right on the money.

Staring at me with a look of horror only achievable by people that have had the opportunity to spend seventy-two years getting it right, was a small old lady in a light blue chequered tabard. She held in her rubber-gloved hands a bottle of Toilet Duck and she appeared to be pointing over my head. Startled and very aware of my vulnerability I smiled as genteelly as I could manage in my situation and only then did I spot the third member of our soirée.

To my right and closer than cousins at a hick wedding was a naked, wet man grinning suggestively at me while apparently trying to flop his todger into my aghast open mouth. I think even the most broadminded would agree that this was taking opportunism to whole new heights.

All things taken into account I felt that the cleaning lady handled things very admirably. She squeezed her Toilet Duck bottle and covered my would-be violator in detergent, tutted her disapproval loudly then slammed the door and ran off as fast as her prosthetic hips could take her. I followed suit and hurled myself out through the door, my white arse flailing about while my ankles struggled against the confinement of my jeans. I fell and fortunately landed on existing cuts and bruises saving me the effort of starting from scratch on new ones.

I wasn't a natural scurrier but scurry I did and most quickly too. Pulling my trousers higher with every step I hop-skipped and jumped my way up the stairs and through the corridors to our room. Crashing through the door I commando rolled dramatically to a halt and lay exhausted on the floor. My two closest friends both eyed me with equal parts suspicion and disregard. I tried to mime the past twenty minutes through wheezes and bloodspots but gave up on the impossible and collapsed back on to the floor.

"You packed yet?" Neil called down to me. I responded in the negative with two fingers and listened as bags were re-packed and belongings were checked.

"Give me five minutes," I managed, clearly needing at least ten.

"You've got three, we need to get out of this room. Out, out!" He echoed, walking over to me and nudging me with his shoe.

"Trust me, I've been 'outed' enough for one day thank you very much." I replied, straining to sit up right.

Adam, with his innate Adamness had kindly packed my bag for me. He couldn't help it but I thanked him anyway. With one final confirmation we were ready to leave the Quality Hotel and not a minute too soon as far as I was concerned. Neil answered a knock at our door, bag in hand, and he smiled to a small seventy-two year old lady in a light blue chequered tabard and rubber gloves. She stepped aside and as the other two left the room she caught sight of me, shot me a look and tutted. I smiled and shrugged but had no words for the moment. Instead I hurried out after the other two and tried to forget ever having been there.

"Man-slag." She yelled as the door closed behind me.

Outside of the hotel, Neil and I stood loading the bags in to the Zafira and smoking while Adam settled up the bill with Graham. It was Friday morning, the sun was shining and for all of my scarring, I was still having a good time. While now barely recognisable to all but my mother I was nevertheless sad that this was the beginning of the end, the start of our last full day in Scotland. I watched as Adam minced down the steps followed by Justin, Gordon and Jason. It was a sight I would not easily forget, the four of them framed by The Quality Hotel with its small queue of men that had formed outside of the VD clinic. I couldn't help but laugh. Adam came up to us both and leaned in conspiratorially.

"You know what?" He whispered with a look of genuine surprise on his face, "I think that might have been a *gay* hotel."

WHAT A DIFFERENCE A GAY MAKES

"Tell me again?" said Jason.

We were walking up the Royal Mile on the way to the castle and the city was strangely serene for a Friday. I don't know on what evidence I was basing that assumption on, as I'd never been to Edinburgh before, but, well, it *felt* serene, for a Friday.

"It's simple, it's a kid's story essentially, but with grown up jokes. Something to keep the adults entertained while they're reading." I answered, keeping pace and taking in the shops and sights around us.

"And it's about a turtle?"

"Bob."

"Oh God," said Adam, close behind us, "here we go."

"And he's curious?" said Jason.

"Like bi-curious?" said Gordon laughing.

"Please, it's a kid's story." I tried to defend our creation, surprised at how deep the cut ran.

"It's inspired by a shit, Steve." said Neil.

"Forget bi then, out and out gay." Gordon said, lighting a cigarette and handing the packet around.

"Hang on a second," I protested, but was quickly interrupted.

"It's a metaphor," Gordon continued, "Bob the Curious Turtle, a shit bobbing around your asshole, the turtle getting curious? Please, it's gayer than I am."

"Well that's just not possible." I said, trying to claw back some points. Gordon punched me on the arm.

"I believe," Jason began again, trying to steer the conversation back to the original madness, "that the idea while certainly entertaining, is fundamentally flawed."

"Go on," I said.

"Well essentially, the problem lies in the character names. I mean c'mon, Fishy Fingers? Really, it's prejudiced."

"*Prejudiced?*" I begged over Neil's uproarious laughter. "Against whom?"

"Us." Justin replied with all seriousness.

"Us?" I needed more.

"Gay people."

"You think our story idea is prejudiced against gay people?"

"Absolutely. It's totally un-PC."

"And therein lies its charm." Adam said.

"You can't pitch the idea in good conscience, knowing that it would potentially influence a whole generation of children in their opinions."

"Their opinions of *what?*" I couldn't believe I was actually getting exasperated. "One minute you're telling me the idea is gayer than Gordon and the next you're telling me its un-PC."

"It is." The three of them said to me in unison.

"How can it be both?"

"Well, even though the protagonist-." Jason began before I cut in.

"Bob," I said.

"That's right, Bob, well even though Bob is basically a metaphor for homosexuality, the fact that his best friend is Fishy Fingers, well, I mean it just says that straight is great."

"It's certainly my direction of choice," said Neil.

"You're repressed." said Gordon. "Your opinion counts for nothing."

"But why," I pressed, "why can't it be gay and straight in harmony, bringing down the barriers of narrow minded homophobia, bridging the distances between the sexuality's in our modern day society?"

"Ha!" Jason pointed at me gleefully. "So you admit it then, it *is* a metaphor for homosexuality." Shit.

338

"Shit. No, I didn't say that."

"You *just* said it."

"Okay I didn't mean it."

"Placating us now then eh?   Tell the queers what they want to hear?"

"AHHHHH!" It was all I could come up with.

"You three love doing that don't you?" said Neil, still laughing and making no efforts to reproach his repressed label.

"Well, it is so easy." said Jason patting me on the shoulder.

"Look, you can't honestly be telling me that we've created a whole multi-layered story – a kids story no-less - with sexual undertones, by accident."

"No, you're right, I'm not saying that." said Jason.

"Good." An end to it.

"I'm saying you did it on purpose." There was more laughter from behind me. I gave Jason a look of   non-committal frustration but it passed un-noticed.

"Well I didn't.   And it's not." I said, sounding like a sulking six-year-old. "Anyway. Blame Neil, he started it."

"Figures." Jason said, and this time it was me laughing.

Edinburgh castle is an incredible sight. Perched atop a hill overlooking the city, watching over proud Scots and marauding English alike, it is steeped in history, beautifully maintained and unequivocally grandiose. That at least is what the brochure said. How much of that is true, I can't tell you. What I can say for sure is that there's a decent cafe nearby serving mugs of coffee and hot food with conveniently located toilet facilities and comfortable chairs to sit on. The thing about a hangover is that even when the head is clear, the gut may still be rotting.

"I'm sorry guys, really I am." I was looking back down the hill we had just climbed, mopping the perspiration from my brow and sweating out alcohol.   One would have thought that after a week of excess my body may have been up to the challenge of a sightseeing tour of wall walks and turret climbing, but the truth was far from it. If nobody was going to let me die quietly in a corner then at the very least I was going to sit down and eat myself well again.

"It's no bother for us." Said Gordon, ordering us all foot-long warm baguettes amply filled with just about everything, from a waitress who wasn't really interested. "We've seen the castle."

"Don't feel bad Steve, I mean, we can *see* the castle from here. And read about it." said Adam shaking the brochure at me.

"Still, not quite the same as actually getting inside is it?" I said.

"Ah the mantra of a lifelong masturbater." Neil said, adding coffees to the lunch order. The waitress laughed but left quickly. We seemed to have that effect.

"So are you three staying in Edinburgh another night then?" asked Adam.

"Why? You feel like joining us again tonight big-boy?" Said Justin, smiling at Adam in what I had to say was a deeply flirtatious way. I looked away, embarrassed and stifling a laugh. Adam went white.

"No," cut in Neil, "we're honouring our last night as we begun the week, three tents, a camp fire and a celebration of a successful holiday."

"Here, here." I said, not wanting to think about the likelihood of ever drinking again. Ever.

"Well we're here tonight and tomorrow, holding back real-life for as long as possible." Gordon said.

"That bad eh?"

"Not bad, just-..."

"Complicated?" I offered.

"Exactly. Complicated. It seems we go years without bother and then everything comes upon you at once. Do you know what I mean?"

"I'd say we've got an idea"

340

"Take Jason for example, he's been in a relationship for a few years, but I guess you won't mind me saying this mate, not settled in it."

"That sounds fair." said Jason.

"And Justin, well he's still in a long term relationship but that's not to say that things are sorted there either, if you catch my drift."

"I'm easily distracted." Justin said. Adam didn't make eye contact.

"I do, but forgive me for not commenting Gordon, I'm feeling a need to confine my words." I said, laughing. He nodded his understanding as the food and drinks arrived. We handed them around the table and I gratefully engorged myself on yet further sustenance.

"And what of you?" said Neil to Gordon.

"Me? Well I'm probably the worst of the three. Universally cautious."

"In what way?" asked Adam, grateful for a potentially safe avenue of conversation.

"Well, I'm thinking of proposing to my fella." Gordon said, sipping at his coffee. "You see, we talked about having kids, adopting obviously," he added for what appeared to be my benefit, "and well I'm kind of old fashioned about that sort of stuff."

"You want to enter into a same sex-marriage so you can adopt a kid and become mutual primary care givers?" I said, "yeah, you sound positively archaic." Gordon laughed.

"Put like that, I get what you're saying. But I don't think of it like that. My parents were married, their parents were married, it just 'fits' better that way in my head."

"You talk to your parents about this stuff?"

"Actually, yeah I do. They're surprisingly down to earth."

"Surprisingly?" Justin said, "disturbingly so is how I'd put it."

341

"You're just jealous because your parents are still waiting for you to meet that special woman who will set you straight."

"She'd have to be a pretty special bloody woman, that's all I'm saying." Justin said.

"Have you ever seen The Crying Game?" Neil asked and the table erupted in laughter.

"That's certainly a thought." said Justin.

"So," I said, back to Gordon, "what's the problem?"

"Well, there isn't one really. It's just I suppose, once you start down that road, you're really doing it. Making a commitment, like there's no going back."

"Well surely that's the point? The creation of a stable family environment?"

"Well yes, it is."

"So...?"

"Well, it's so grown up." Gordon said. I didn't mean to laugh.

"Don't listen to that tosser," said Neil, waving his baguette at me. "He makes shallow, immature and superficial seem like an improvement."

"Thanks mate."

"Don't mention it."

"You're reluctantly ageing too then?" Gordon said to me.

"Aren't we all?"

"I'm not." said Adam.

"Oh really?" Neil said.

"Really. I'm looking forward to it, in a strange sort of way."

"You've changed your tune." Neil countered, chewing.

"That would be the result of a week spent with you two reprobates."

"Seriously, where's this coming from? What's to look forward to? Incontinence, further hair-loss, a lifetime of debt and a slowly shrivelling cock. Granted, you've got a

342

little less to worry about in that department than most, but..."

"I don't know, it's the idea of becoming something, a husband, a father, it carries a certain weight to it. I think it might help to ground me, give me some perspective. At least I'd have something to show for the last thirty five years."

"You've got us." said Neil. I beamed helpfully.

"Exactly." Adam agreed, with a fraction less conviction than I think Neil was hoping for.

"Trust me, it's not all it's cracked up to be," Neil added, "It's a weight certainly. A weight on your mind, on your pocket."

"Yes but people look at you differently, they respect you, your opinion counts for something."

"Not in my house it doesn't."

"Alright, but outside of that. You're a family man. You have a common bond with people, you're not just somebody's kid anymore, you're a father. You're children look up to you."

"Adam, you have met my children haven't you? It's just I think you might be talking about someone else's."

"Yeah whatever, you know it's true." Neil stopped to consider it, I could tell he wasn't convinced, but then Adam was older and seeing things from the outside, I suppose in a way I couldn't blame him for wanting to get his shit together. Isn't that what we all want? One way or another.

"Is there something you're not telling us?" I said, sensing there was something he wasn't telling us.

"It doesn't matter, forget it."

"Well, I agree with Adam." said Gordon, "I think it makes perfect sense."

"Well if that's the case then it sounds like you've made your decision." Adam said.

"Yeah I suppose I have." Gordon nodded.

"You lot don't know you're born." Neil said defiantly.

"Amen!" chorused Justin. "Although, it's a tragedy to see such a splendid tool assigned to just one job." He added, smiling at Adam.

"Okay, enough. What the hell happened in that bed last night?" I said, "Please god tell me before I'm put right off my food."

"Nothing happened!" Adam said, turning white again. I looked at Justin for confirmation and got none.

"Well let's just say that Adam's Mrs is clearly a lucky woman."

"How the hell did you manage to get wood after the amount we drunk last night?" Neil asked, somewhat missing the more obvious questions that were springing to my mind.

"Must just be my charm." Justin said, laughing.

"Look, I'm not always completely in control of certain things okay, let's not make a big deal out of it."

"But it's such a big deal." Justin said, "you practically raised the roof."

"You saw that?"

"Hell yeah."

"Oh my god." Adam said.

"You dark horse. You wait 'til I tell Fiona." I said.

"Don't you fucking dare."

"Mate, this is golden. I'm sorry but how can I not tell people?"

"I will kill you."

"It'll be worth it!"

"Swear now this stays in Scotland."

"I should be so lucky," said Justin.

"Okay, okay. It stays in Scotland." I conceded.

"Swear it."

"I swear. Alright? I promise not to tell anyone outside of Scotland that were ready to bang a bloke, no offence Justin."

"None taken." Justin laughed.

"You're hilarious."

"And you thought Neil was repressed?" I said to Jason. "Always the quiet ones, eh?"

"Can we change the subject? Please?" Adam pleaded. "This weather eh?"

"Yep," Neil said, looking at the beautiful blue sky above us, "it's swinging all ways this week."

"Fuck off."

The day progressed in much the same fashion. We didn't make it out of the cafe. Instead we just caught the sun and watched the locals. Or more specifically, we watched throngs of tourists swarm up and down the streets. Given that we had been sat in the same place for so long, technically that made us the most local people in the city.

I was pleased to be sat down and more so to be feeling better, and I was enjoying the company. It was interesting having a fresh perspective on what seemed to be the same old problems. It was like watching a different team playing your favourite sport, the game was the same, just the players that had changed. None of us were experts, all of us suffering from the same ailments, held back by insecurity or history or a fear of the unknown.

At least a third of our party was claiming to be suffering from the contempt of familiarity and yet another third were trying to get a chance to be so lucky. I found myself watching sometimes, observing the discourse, involved and yet removed from the action somehow like the commentators sitting high up in the stands. My recently elevated position, my alleviated disposition I realised with some degree of concern and more of surprise was almost entirely accountable to a chance encounter with a stranger in a fish and chip shop.

Louise had floated into my life like a cool ocean breeze and refreshed the parts that until now other waitresses had failed to reach. Granted few had actually tried, but her willingness to do so was inspiring in itself. I recognised all of the signs of course, the preoccupation of thought and the way her face wandered into my mind when I put my head down on the pillow, or blinked. Alcohol had only furthered the cause and effect and furthermore the more I drank the fonder my recollection. Rose tinted beer goggles should be illegal.

I was falling for a stranger. It was time to admit that I had learned nothing. One week away, over seven hundred miles covered so far and I had managed to move nowhere. That, I felt, was noteworthy. I wasn't just refusing to learn from my mistakes, I was forgetting that I had ever made any, *ever*. This was failure on a huge scale. I was the Enron of emotional deprivation and impossible relationships. Yes I could make the noises, show the outside world that I was a new man, that I had moved upwards and onwards and seen the light, but the truth was I spent more time in the dark than a tube train driver. It was all just smoke and mirrors, I would be able to lie to everyone but myself. When I got back to Andover, I knew I'd be missing her like crazy. How fucking typical.

A wise man once said 'know thyself', well I knew myself better than anyone, and what I knew was that I was screwed. I was falling for a woman who had shown me some attention and gone someway to restoring my shattered faith in the opposite sex. I knew that she was different, I knew that she was funny and sexy and sensual and gorgeous, that she seemed to get me in a way that no woman had to date, and I knew that in every way on top of those she was absolute hell for me. But essentially, that was all I knew about her. A tad rash of me to discount her entirely based on my superficial knowledge maybe, but then being superficial was apparently one of my talents so perhaps I was better equipped to judge than most. Either way, experience had taught me to fear these feelings. This

346

was going to hurt, and hurt worse than any hangover I'd ever had.

BORED OF THE FLIES

Before long it's easy to see why the Scottish are so hard to impress. We had spent a week in their country and already I was starting not to notice how glorious the landscape was, how spectacular every view from every slightly elevated outcrop appeared to be. The highlands were lowlands to us now, the mountains just hills overcompensating. We had traversed more road in a single week than most Scots would cover in a month and now it was all common place to us. Now we were put out if we weren't impressed by the view, if the gorge wasn't sharp enough or the lochs not picturesque. We had become scenery snobs.

Thankfully then, we currently stood impressed. What we had found at the end of a road that someone's wife must have had to shag to get put on the map was not the most stunning sight, nor the most awe inspiring. What it did do well was be simple, and in that simplicity it was simply beautiful. We had followed water and found the source of perfection. There was however a price to be paid.

"Goddamned mother-fucking flies!" yelled Neil, flagellating himself.

"Ah man they're everywhere, they're inside my clothes, I'm telling you, they are *inside* my clothes." Adam screamed. I think it was the cleanliness issue that was closest to heart.

"Is this place worth it?"

"Yes!" Neil yelled, largely I think because he had been driving for most of the day and the thought of getting back in the car was probably only marginally more appealing than being eaten alive.

"How do you know?" I screamed, rolling about in the grass like a man on fire.

"I just do!"

"The river thing," Adam squirmed.

"Very helpful Adam, yes they're probably here because of the river thing. You want to go and ask them to leave?"

"No, I mean, I'm going to jump in. I can't take this anymore." Adam was scratching at his body, sweeping the flies from his eyes and his ears, blowing them clear from his nostrils and mouth in great clumps. Suddenly he pulled off his shirt and tugged down his jeans and started hopping towards the water.

"Fuck it! I'm with him." I said, tearing off my clothes and following suite.

"Hang on then!" Neil barked, third to catch on. We both skipped dragging denim and cloth behind us as we tried to outrun our own skin. "They're bloody everywhere, I can feel them on my cock."

"Enjoy it, do you have any idea how cold this water is going to be?" I panted, jogging towards the bank watching Adam's white arse bob like a beacon up ahead. "I don't think we're going to be feeling our cocks for about a week after this."

Adam leapt.

In slow motion we watched as his arms and legs flailed through the air, grace and style out of the window in favour of the time honoured bomb-dive. I had no idea how deep the water was, could only hope that Adam had some clue as Neil and I approached at equal pace nevertheless and the time to jump was now upon us. Naked as the day we were born with nowhere to go but in we leapt to the sound of Adam emerging from the water screaming like a choir boy with his nuts in a vice.

I don't know why I flapped my arms, what I hoped to achieve by this abhorrence to gravity was beyond me but flap I did. I flapped as if my bollocks depended on it, and sadly they very much did.

The water engulfed me like a rock dropped from a cliff, a vacuous plummet into a freezing cold darkness, it mattered not that the sun was shining, this water eventually ran to the north sea and would be permanently chilled in spite of all the global warming. The sensation of cold wasn't gradual, the way you slowly inch a foot into a swimming pool when you're feeling particularly feminine. This was like a blanket of ice wrapping itself around your skin. I felt my entire body contract, lungs, stomach, heart, anus, testicles, nothing was impervious. Everything was bitten by the icy fangs pricking at my skin, plucking hairs from me that were straining to react to the sudden shock. What we achieved, I have no doubt, was the worlds' first batch of cryogenically frozen flies.

I eventually surfaced with my eyes and ears stinging, my hands involuntarily shaking and my teeth chattering madly. I could hear similar whimpers from Neil and Adam and knew that they were close by. I forced my legs to turn me in the water to find them, saw them bobbing and shivering only inches away, all of us treading water and begging our blood to forgive us and circulate once again.

"Th-th-th-this is-s-s-s- m-m-m-m-uch bet-t-t-t-t-t-ter." I think I said. Adam nodded and smiled, but it could just as easily have been pulmonary heart failure contorting his face.

"At-t-t-t least th-th-th-the flies hav-v-v-ve f-f-f-ucked off." Neil said, reaching out an arm to me. I took it and in turn reached out to Adam. We formed a circle like survivors of a naturist fishing disaster. "I think, yeah, I can feel my legs now."

"Comes to something when this is an improvement don't you think? How long do you think we have to stay in before the flies go?" I asked, finally catching my breath.

"Dusk probably." Adam replied. I looked at him aggressively, which came surprisingly easy to me.

"Dusk? It's only just gone six, dusk won't be for another four hours."

"You asked."

"Then you should have fucking lied. I'm very fragile at the moment."

"Sorry." He said without apology.

"Well," Neil began, "I say we give it a few more minutes then get the fire going and sit as close to it as possible, or Steve and I could try lighting twenty fags each at once, that might keep the little bastards away?" He paused and looked at us both in turn.

"Sorry, was that an actual suggestion? Are you waiting for me to answer?" I had been momentarily distracted by the strong assumption that I was about to get gobbled off by plankton.

"Yes!"

"Oh, well, okay, great idea, away you go then."

"Why have I got to do it?" Neil protested.

"You have seniority."

"Adam's the oldest." He said defensively.

"Yes but the last suggestion he made cost me the use of my bollocks and all feeling in my legs. So next in line is you."

"Why don't you make a suggestion then?"

"Okay, I suggest that you go and light the fire while I tread water and try and work out whether this blue colour I'm turning is going to be permanent."

"Tosser."

"Not for awhile."

Neil broke free from the circle and swam back to the bank. He crawled up and out ran for the pile of our belongings that marked our progress before the invasion. His figure got smaller and smaller the further he got until it appeared as if Adam and I were watching a puppet show of a man trying to light a fire in the nude. I could make out his figure scurrying around in circles and periodically slapping his skin as all manner of insects took interest in the abundance of exposed flesh jiggling about in an otherwise flesh free

351

environment. To my knowledge we had no firewood collected, but in keeping with the many implied benefits of our location, wood was plentiful and with luck dry enough to ignite.

The show continued slowly for awhile, the circling less frantic and the attention more specific, a moment of kneeling and bending and prodding and poking was followed by a trip to the car and what then appeared to be an ancient Native American fire dance. Whatever it was, it worked and was subsequently followed by a plume of smoke and flame that streaked ten feet into the air. The dancing continued but was now more visibly joyful.

I looked to Adam and he looked at me and we nodded in mutual agreement that it was now safe to go ashore. Moving slowly towards the bank, I noticed in the corner of my eye something recognisable bobbing in the water caught up in some reeds. I swam over to it and with absolute amazement found in my hand a pack of bacon. I can't imagine how it had got there but I felt compelled to collect it and took it with me as I climbed up the bank. I caught up with Adam and showed him my discovery as we approached the inferno that was Neil's creation.

"What's that smell?" I said as my nostrils filled with the scent of burning cloth.

"Ah," said Neil. As I may have mentioned, this had never in the history of our long friendship ever been taken as a good sign, I held little doubt that this fact was miraculously about to change now. "I... needed something dry to start the fire."

"And?"

"I found something in the car."

"What did you find exactly?" I examined the fire more closely while in turn slow baking myself dry.

"A bag full of kindling."

"We don't have a bag full of kindling." I said, because we didn't.

352

"That's true, but on the plus side you also no longer have a bag full of dirty pants."

"You threw my underwear in the fire?" I said, staggered.

"No! I didn't throw it on the fire. I placed your shreddies strategically in order to create, well, that." He pointed at the flaming chaos of wood and underwear before us. I didn't know what to say but 'thank you' didn't seem quite appropriate.

"Why would you do that?"

"Nobody was here to suggest a better plan."

"You total spunk sack."

"Hey, look around, if there was one thing guaran-fucking-teed to rid this place of flies then it was the smell of your burning pants. Some thanks wouldn't go amiss."

"Thank you." Adam said, sincerely. I looked at him and then realised we three were still naked. Adam had a way of bringing things like that to your attention.

"Easy for you to say," I said, "you've still got underwear to go home to."

"Steve, seriously, get over it. It's not the first time your pants have had burning wood in them, just maybe the only time that an ointment won't solve the problem."

"Fuck off."

"Not before you tell me where the hell you got the bacon from."

"What?"

"The bacon, you appear to have stopped at a corner shop on your way back from the river. Fess up." The past few minutes had been so surreal I was caught trying to catch up. I looked at the bacon, forgetting that I'd picked it up. I examined the pack and then chucked it over the fire to Neil.

"Found it in the reeds at the river bank."

"You hungry or something?"

"Ha ha!"

"I'm serious, I can't think of any other reason in the world you would have picked up a pack of Danish bacon that's over a year out of date."

"You're shitting me? A year, wow." Adam said, swinging over to stand by Neil and check out the pack again. For a moment I was overcome by the image of a Swedish butcher's, thankfully it quickly passed.

"Proof of life," I said in my poor defence.

"They have houses for that in Scotland, Steve, we're not that far into the wilderness."

"Look, I dunno okay? It was just there and it caught my attention. I think it's symbolic."

"You think everything is symbolic at the moment."

"It's been that kind of a week."

"Okay symbolic of what exactly?"

"Well, what I said, that other people have been here. That maybe they had a good time."

"Oh yeah, I'm sure it was a blindin' night," Neil said, "'hey darling, fancy playing hide the sausage?' 'Sorry dear, we've only got bacon'!" Adam laughed and managed to fan the fire.

"Look, forget it, it was a crazy idea, I don't know what I was thinking, but can I just say I resent the accusation of strangeness coming from a man who thought that it was a good idea to burn my pants as a deterrent to flies."

"Fair point, and actually while we're on the subject, you know I was just getting you back for making me come and sort the fire out don't you?"

"Yeah," I nodded.

"Good, cause getting rid of the flies was just kind of a bonus."

"I know mate."

"Result!" said Adam helpfully.

"Adam, please, do me a favour and go and put some clothes on for Christ's sake, my image has taken a battering after the river as it is without having insightful comments from fucking Nessy as well. You stand there much longer and I'm gonna have to ring the wildlife commission."

"Um," Neil said, bringing his hands and the bacon down and crossing them over his groin, "can I second that motion?" Adam looked at the both of us and I felt myself, *shorten*, just a little bit more.

"Yeah, as long as you two do as well. I haven't stood this close to a couple of women all week, it's making me horny."

"Hardy fucking ha."

We dressed in self-conscious silence in the warmth of the fire and the gradually setting sun. The evening itself was starting well. The fire, but for the fuel, was burning fantastically and the flies had flown. The bacon, while thankfully unopened, lay safely out of distance away from the food and in the spirit of relaxation Adam had even agreed to listen to an old blues and soul compilation CD that Neil had snuck into the collection. Dobie Gray was singing 'Drift Away' and it seemed to set the mood perfectly.

Sat around the fire, chewing the last burgers we would eat again for months, we cautiously sipped bottled lager at a leisurely pace and stared out at the river disappearing off through a valley in the distance. We were once again cut off, isolated and in every sense of the word alone. Around us hills reached for the sky and the single lane of the road that carried us here appeared once again to be going nowhere. It was if this spot that we had found was a culmination of our collective memories from the week, the tents, burgers and the fire, the flies, the river and mountains. All of it brought to life through one or all of us, a sub-room of the Matrix, a bizarrely unique and personal paradise. Even the music seemed relevant.

I couldn't have wished for more at that point - I needed nothing more than the time afforded me to enjoy the moment. Neil and Adam were laughing and I sat quietly just for a minute, smoking a cigarette, watching the stars chase the sun from the sky. It was serene, the sort of situation that a picture could never truly capture, that I would try and remember in days to come and only just come close to recreating. People would consider themselves lucky to have had a night such as that one - I realised now that I'd had seven of them.

Perhaps it was sentimentality brought about by the foolish consumption of more alcohol or perhaps it was just the melancholy of knowing that real life would start again soon. Whatever it was, it brought a smile to my face that I couldn't shift. That same time tomorrow I would be back in the flat facing the same problems that seemed an entire lifetime ago now, but tonight, even if it would be the last night for a long time, all of that was ahead of me, irrelevant. That's what friends did, one way or another they made things better, even if they didn't know it or did nothing to propagate it, sometimes they just had to be sat around a fire with you, watching your pants burn.

"You know," Neil said, pulling me back into the conversation, away from a daydream and a curious smile, "it occurs to me that what happened earlier, our episode in the river, that was like a baptism."

"I'm an atheist," I said, again.

"Whatever, it's figurative, all of us jumped in, naked and free, together and here we are, re-born."

"How much have you had to drink?"

"Not enough, but I'm being serious. Think about it, tomorrow we're homeward bound, each of us returning to something that pushed us here in the first place, that's relative don't you think? I think it's significant."

I nodded. Adam did too but somewhat more slowly.

"The thing is, I'm not worried about that. About going back home. I want to go back home, I'm ready for it now. I want to see my kids. That's nothing against you two, but I miss my wife, I miss my boys. I miss my sofa."

"Me too." I said.

"You miss his sofa?" Adam asked.

"No, I miss his wife. Cracking tits," Adam laughed and Neil threw his cigarette packet at my head.

"Whatever. I'm serious. I feel re-born. This week has given me the distance I needed to appreciate things a bit more. I have you two to thank for that." I agreed, he did.

"And you think that we've marked the occasion by us all freezing our dicks off in that river then?"

"Yeah. We've been cleansed. We're different people now, closer as friends, stronger as individuals. It is, to quote a phrase, 'symbolic'. I think we've started something."

"Do you need bog roll to finish?" I said.

Neil ignored me. He was looking up to the sky, "Tonight," he said dramatically, "marks the birth of The Brotherhood."

"You've been thinking about that all week haven't you?" I asked, I couldn't help it, cynicism was in my nature, my ex-girlfriends were always telling me that.

"Yeah. But what do you say? Let's make this official."

"You want to get ink?" I said.

"Shall we?" Adam asked. Oh god.

"No!"

"Look, forget that. Let's just agree, while we're here, to do this again and more importantly not leave it so long in between visits." I sensed that despite Adam's geographical distance from our respective residences, Neil was talking to me.

"Agreed," I said.

"Actually, that might be a problem." Neil and I looked at Adam, surprised, and he looked back at us sheepishly. "I think I need to tell you both something."

JUNIOR MEMBER

"Fiona's pregnant." Neil and I spat lager over the fire.

"It wasn't me," Neil said.

"Thank you Neil, I'm aware of that."

"Good, I was just checking, cause, well you know."

"She told me, just before I left, literally, as I was packing after your mysterious phone call she came up to the bedroom and just came out with it."

"What did you say?" I asked, still stunned.

"I think I said 'are you sure?'" I laughed, I guess it's how I would have reacted too. Of course, had it been Kelly saying it I'm fairly sure there would have been an overload of panic and emotion accompanying my question, but that's just me, or her, depending on how you look at it.

"Then what?" Neil continued.

"I sort of dropped down on to the bed like someone had pulled the carpet out from under me. God that's such a typical response, but then I looked at her, smiled and I guess I knew that everything would be okay."

"Then you're a braver man than me," I said, "I would have shit a brick."

"I would have shit a brick if Fiona had said it to you too."

"Fair point, but I mean, like, wow. I mean it's great news isn't it?"

"Is it?"

"Yes, yes it is." I stated, more confidently now, "C'mon Adam, we've been over this already, you're perfect father material. And Fiona is terrific."

"Yes, she is."

"And it's a good time, I think it's the right time for you two."

358

"I can't believe I'm saying this," Neil added, "but I think he's right."

I poked the fire with my empty lager bottle and buried it in the glowing red embers beneath the main bulk of wood and underpants.

"You really think so? I couldn't help thinking it was awful timing."

"That's just nerves. I reckon every bloke thinks that, even the ones that had been planning it. I'm assuming of course that this wasn't planned?"

"Not exactly. I mean we sort of talked about it one night and both said we'd like to have kids and such, and Fiona sort of said that she could come off the pill and I think I sort of said well we could see what happens from there. Talk about non-committal."

I chuckled, I could picture the conversation, imagine Adam looking about his house and worrying about the chaos brought about by a baby. "Sounds like a fairly obvious conclusion that a kid would be the end result, don't you think? I mean I'm no expert, but even I know that if you stop taking the pill and then don't start doing anything *else* the end result is pretty certain."

"Maybe it's me, I just thought that when we did it, we'd have some sort of big grownup discussion, really talk about it, put some things in place before hand."

"It's not a military manoeuvre Adam, you're starting a family."

"Exactly, that's my point, it's more serious than a military manoeuvre, I mean I'm going to be responsible for this kid for the rest of my life. That's huge."

"And?" Neil asked, still not quite getting his point, I guess proving the one defining difference between the man with kids and the two men without them.

"It just seems incredible to me, that's all, I mean this is going to be an actual person, a new life, and the biggest

359

discussion I had about it went something like Fiona saying 'I could come off the pill,' followed by me saying 'okay, cool'."

This seemed to be more my territory so I stepped in with what I hoped were comforting words, "Adam, I *always* think that people are having these huge relationship discussions and I'm always amazed at how I never seem to have any."

"Well that's obvious," Neil said, "you're shit at relationships."

"Shut up Neil, what I mean is, I always think that things are planned and prepared for but most of the time, they do just sort of happen. Life moves on. When Kelly moved in to the flat, we didn't have a huge talk about it, it was just one day she was staying over all the time and the next she had moved in."

"Yeah and we all know how well that turned out." Neil said. "I think Adam is looking for something positive if you have a point to any of this."

"All I'm saying is, take it for what it is. Look around you, all you see is knocked up teenagers and unplanned pregnancy, *they're* the ones that should be killing themselves over it, not you, certainly not Fiona. You guys have good jobs, you've got a house together, a solid relationship, if there was a checklist for this sort of stuff then you'd have the boxes ticked. So what that you didn't agree on an educational standpoint beforehand or talk to your financial advisor first? This is not a bad a thing Adam, really."

"He's right Adam, Jane and I were sort of the same, I'm not saying the timing felt right because I don't think anyone ever thinks they're ready, not really, but I wouldn't change any of it."

"It's not really the same though is it?" Adam said to Neil.

"How do you mean?"

"Well I mean, with you two, it just always seemed like you would, you've been together since school, married and settled, I dunno it just appeared more obvious for you two to have kids."

"Maybe, but that doesn't mean to say I took the news any better when she told me. Doesn't mean to say that for a split second I didn't suddenly find myself thinking 'shit this is it'."

"The question is," I said, looking at the clouds forming over Adam's face, "how do you feel about it?"

"I'm pleased I guess," he said, "I'm excited, nervous. I'm shitting myself if truth be told but that's just bullshit because I wouldn't want to have kids with anyone else but Fi." I began to understand that these words, this insight into his relationship, were entirely genuine. The bravado had slipped away, melted by the fire and the friendship, the bond that we had renewed this week. Fully clothed, Adam was finally naked before us.

And then a penny dropped. I palmed my forehead in belated comprehension. "So that explains everything then!"

"How do you mean?"

"I mean you're odd pre-occupation with babies and responsibility, your crisis of faith so to speak. You've been touchy about this all week, it all makes sense now."

"I wouldn't say he's been touchy all week?" Neil interjected sounding oddly concerned, as if I had passed judgement in actuality on him.

"Alright, not touchy, but sensitive, maybe a little fixated. We've been talking about this a lot this week, Adam and I, in a roundabout sort of way. We have literally been going round the houses. I thought we were talking about decisions still to be made, tensions and arguments and disagreements, pressure from Fiona to stop procrastinating – or masturbating – and get busy getting busy. You implied that there was still an element of choice. This is kind of slipping on the condom after the pregnancy, for want of a better description." I wasn't trying to be crass, I just felt confused. Confused that someone so close had waited so long to tell us something so important. "I mean I get it now. The questions you've been asking, of yourself and

361

your relationship, in context it makes sense to me. I hope we were supportive, I still say that you're the man, Adam. I just don't understand why you didn't tell us sooner?"

He paused before answering, like a man about to leave a message in fridge magnet letters, "I guess I just didn't want this week to be all about me..." he said, his voice trailing off. The implication hit me harder than the punch had the previous evening. I guess I asked for it.

"Oh." I said.

"Sorry, Steve. It wasn't personal, quite the opposite in fact. I mean it was personal, not the 'me not telling you' bit, the bit about why I didn't tell you. That bit."

"Oh, right." I suddenly became aware of the heat from the campfire blazing against my cheeks, but in truth it could just as easily have been coming from the inside. Either way, it was clearly illuminating what a poor excuse for a friend I had evidently been of late.

"I was trying not to rub it in your face." Adam said, meekly. "This week was supposed to be about getting away from all of that, for all of us. And it has been, it's been fantastic. And I can't thank you both enough - even just talking in a round-the-houses way has helped. And I'm sorry about that, but it has literally been the only thing that comes to mind the second we stop mucking about that it's just sort of slipped out." I patted him on the shoulder.

"Mate, you don't have to apologise, it's what we're here for. And also what we're *here* for." I said, by way of an acceptance of his reasoning. Adam smiled with utter relief, as if he honestly thought that our relationship was in jeopardy.

"And now you both know. And you're the first people that do. I haven't even told my parents."

"Well then let me be the first to say congratulation, we're pleased for you." Neil said, because he knew that we both were. He took a sip from his lager and adjusted position, staring back into the fire, "But I think the more important question, the one that really has remained un-answered all week, *the* question of questions is, who would put in your 'fanny stack'?"

Adam burst out laughing and immediately the clouds and concern dissipated, he drank deeply from his lager and contemplated all including most likely his choice in the company that he kept. "It's true Adam, you better tell us now, you'll be grown up and responsible soon, you'll have to take some sort of moral standpoint against 'fanny stacks'."

"How does Neil get away with it then?" Adam asked, questioning the obvious ambiguity.

"I've got a note from Steve's mum." Neil said. "It reads 'shhtkmp shhtkmp shhtkmp!'"

"Thank you Neil," I said, forcing images from my violated mind.

"Okay, the 'fanny stack'. Let's see."

"You still haven't thought of anyone have you?"

"I might have. And I can have anyone yes?"

"Well, hypothetically speaking, I mean I'm not sure your prowess is up to too much, but for the purpose of discussion, yes you can. It was supposed to be just celebrities and such, but we've only got a night left so crack on."

"You wait 'til you've got a kid mate," Neil said, "fanny magnets the lot of them, trust me."

"Really?" Adam said distracted. I couldn't help but think, even if only for a moment, that if Neil had said this at the start of our discussion the last half an hour of inner soul searching could have quickly been avoided.

"Really," Neil nodded, supping at his lager, "I took Ben out shopping with me one day when he was first born, my God I was beating them off. Sensitive caring man with cute kid, it's like a gift mate, a gift. I might has well have been wearing a T-shirt that said 'sleep with me – have good looking babies'."

363

"Oh right." Adam said, smiling, distracted yet again. "Excellent."

"The *stack*?" I prompted.

"Oh yeah, well, okay, don't take the piss, but well, I'd want Fiona."

"Why would we take the piss?" Neil said.

"Well, because..."

"I mean I don't know about you Steve, but Fiona's in my stack."

"Absolutely," I agreed. "Been there from the start." Adam looked at us, stunned.

"And just think, give it about ten months and she's gonna be MILF." That may have been too far but it didn't stop me rolling on the floor laughing.

We left the fire slow burning, the flames having finally subsided to a white hot glowing bowl of embers, a log thrown on top and slowly hollowing out. We walked, strolled, sauntered onwards down the road without destination or purpose. The night was drawing in but it was still mild and the atmosphere relaxed and comfortable. Conversation had become sporadic but not for any reason that any of us had to worry about. We each found ourselves keeping a rhythm to a beat in our heads, a momentum that had reached a crescendo at the end of our week away.

It was easy to feel reluctant to return home, but perhaps that was just me, the one who had seemed the most reluctant to come away in the first place. I didn't fear being alone and as much as I loved the company of my friends I would welcome the first few days of solace and solitude. But after that, life would resume and swarm around me in the way that the ice-cold water had done earlier that evening. It was unavoidable and resistance would be as futile as my efforts to flap my arms and fly.

I knew that work would be there for me, the constant in my life when all other things had spiralled out of control.

And I knew that I would endeavour to keep my promises and cut back the hours, see my friends and my family more, fill up the time between morning and night a little more positively than I had been of late. But somehow even that wasn't enough, I needed something more proactive, I needed more of this week, more of the freedom and the spontaneity that had awakened me, I wanted to take control and not get carried along by the currents of the day-to-day slog. Something had to change, and the only thing I had left was me.

I looked at Neil and Adam, the way that their lives were developing and moving forwards as mine was slowing to a halt. I didn't want these thoughts and furthermore held no jealousy or ill will to either of them. They had made the choices and were reaping the fruits of their labours while I had failed to plant any seeds and was looking forward to a sparse winter. I was the product of my own decisions and blamed nobody but myself for any shortcomings I felt that I had.

In contrast though, I knew without a shadow of a doubt what it was I didn't want in my life, not now, not yet. I didn't want the lives that Adam and Neil had. I loved being a part of them, sharing in their experiences, but what I felt that I was missing, the thing that was ultimately holding me back, was experiences of my own. I still felt that, in spite of everything that had happened to date up to and including that week, I hadn't started living *my* life yet.

What I did fear were my lethargic tendencies, the return to a former state of mind that had ultimately caused me to wind up here, emotionally barren, confused and miserable. Falling back into a rut, so easily done, existing and not living, enduring but not enjoying all that seemed to be out there. Neil had said, right at the start, each of us was missing something, was in need of something to move them on and over the hurdle, but while I felt that Neil and Adam

365

had both managed to find their respective 'thing', mine still eluded me.

"High point of the week boys?" Neil said, pulling me from my thoughts.

"That's a hard one," Adam said, and I was glad that he did. For some reason I had believed that this amount of 'us' time would be hard for him to take, but true to form, Adam had excelled himself all week. "Where to start?"

"You wearing your retro-spectacles again Neil?" I asked, lighting a cigarette.

"Maybe," he said, lighting one for himself, "makes a change from beer-goggles though eh?"

"True. So what's been your high point?"

"Easy." He said, but I thought I could guess.

"Don't tell me, the rafting?"

"Nope."

"No?"

"Nope, don't get me wrong, seeing you and Adam diving in after me and going through that river to rescue me was one of the proudest moments of my life, but that's different. That just left me feeling overwhelmed, lucky to know you both, proud if you like."

"Steady mate, I'm welling up here." Adam said, cutting through the sentimentality with his Rambo-esque knife. "You want us to drop our trousers here or are you going to get us more drunk first?"

"Whatever knobber. I'm serious, that was amazing, but it's not been my high point."

"So what was then?" I said, surprised, "You're not going to say 'the whole week' are you? I may have to punch you."

"Adam? You first."

"Well, lets see. Where do I start, perhaps with getting my nose battered by an airbag? Or watching the tow-truck driver drive off? Oh no, wait, perhaps getting shot at? That was a high point. No, no, not good enough, hmm, maybe half-drowning while hungover saving your arse? Or how about the car sinking into the field and having to be rescued by that old lady?"

"Oh she's that old lady now is she? Couple of days ago she was shaggable. Jesus Adam anyone would think you haven't enjoyed yourself." Neil said, stopping to take in the sight of the river opening up.

"Yeah come on mate, it hasn't been all bad has it?" I said, contemplating a retraction of my earlier opinion.

"All bad? You're joking aren't you, I've had the time of my fucking life. I have not laughed this much in years. This has been hands down the best holiday I have ever had." He *sounded* genuine.

"Really?" I said, warily. It was still too soon to tell if he was joking.

"Mate if that's the case, you need a better travel agent." Neil said laughing but clearly pleased. This had after all been all his idea.

"Straight up. And that's just the start, I mean c'mon, the barbecues, the fires, the live music, the drinking. Laughing when you smashed your nose rafting only for me to end up being the one that gets Steve's nose hammered by that fella at Filthy's. And look at our fucking car! Our beloved Smurf-mobile."

"So you *do* like it!" Neil said, beaming. "Cause it wouldn't hurt for you to say it every now again, either. You're as bad as Steve. That car's been through a lot."

"I love that car, it's part of the family, it's the official mascot of The Brotherhood."

"I think it's safe to say we've lost our security deposit." I agreed.

"I can't thank either of you enough for making this what it has been."

"You don't have to. You don't think we feel the same?" I said. "I'm just glad there are no women around to hear us talking like this. We'd never get laid again."

367

"Speak for yourself," said Neil. "Sensitive caring male, Steve, you should try it. Course it helps to have Jane waiting at home."

"Yeah I bet. A week without wanking has got to be a record."

"Who said it's been a week?"

"You didn't? Adam said, equal parts shock, disappointment and frustration creeping into his voice.

"Yeah. Course."

"That's not your high point is it?" I said, laughing.

"Nope. It's like second or third. But what has yours been?" He said. I thought about it. Like Adam said, where did you begin?

"God, I dunno, getting back to nature I guess. Getting away from it all, spending time with you two, feeling more like myself again. Not coming face to face with a killer-fucking-rabbit is quite high up there. Oh and of course, still being alive after a week of Adam's driving is a bit of a result too." Adam punched me on the arm.

"Don't speak to soon," Neil said, laughing as I rubbed my already bruised arm, "he's driving us home."

I sighed, "Terrific! So what's yours been?"

"Honestly? My high point of the week?"

"Honestly," Adam said, paused for the revelation.

"It was watching you with that Louise bird."

"Seriously?" I said, startled while Adam mocked 'vomiting'.

"My little bro, getting lucky, with someone practically perfect for him. Damn right that's my high point."

"Practically perfect? She's lives over six hundred miles away from me."

"That's just geography. She's practically perfect in that she seemed honest and genuine, was clearly interested in you and not afraid to let you know. She was gorgeous, which is always a bonus, and most importantly she was respectful of

368

us." He grinned. "And she put a look on your face I haven't seen in years. She sounds pretty perfect to me."

"Yeah I guess, but, *that* was your high point?"

"I came away to spend time with my brother, to hang out with my best friends, but most of all, to get you back. I said that at the start of the week and I feel like, maybe, we've done that. Maybe *she's* done that. Hell for all I know she's the only thing that's done that. But either way you'll hear no complaints from me. All I've ever wanted is to see you happy bro." If I were the sort of man that cried, I'd have been balling my eyes out by now.

"You know what?" Adam said, "He's got a point, we've all been saying we've missed you. That smile she put on your face is a serious improvement."

"Jesus you make me sound like a right miserable git."

"Well, we didn't want to just come out and *say* it."

"Okay, well, I'm pleased you're both pleased."

"Like you're not."

"I never said that."

"Like you haven't been thinking about her since you two parted company."

"I can't deny that."

"Like she's not *all* you've been thinking about since that night."

"What can I say? It's ridiculous, we had barely one night together."

"Well, if you say yes, yes you have been thinking about her and would kill to see her again, I guess we know we've got our old Steve back. He always was an insufferable twat over women." I grinned - they knew me so well.

"So what's been your low point?" I said.

"Easy, not finding the L.N.C.A., I'm telling you boys, they're out there and we are *so* close."

Saturday

HOMEWARD BOUND

My feet were heavy, I wasn't drunk or stuck in the mud I was just dragging my mood around with me. The night before had ended with laughter and smiles, jokes and promises. Now though, in the cold light of our last Scottish morning, the day ahead promised to be long and painful. A journey of countless hours made worse by our reluctance to begin. That was the difference between going abroad and staying at home, once you got on the plane, things were out of your control, you were heading home regardless and somebody else was doing the graft. With driving, all you had to look forward to was an aching back and a share of the work.

I rolled my tent up for the last time, having cleared out as best I could a weeks' worth of grass and mud and fag packets and other debris from things I don't even remember having used or seen. The fire still glowed, its heat emanating out from the now hollowed stump of log that had been used to maintain it. I looked in to the ashes to be sure that no pants were visible or identifiable. It had been some years since my mum had last sewn nametags into my skiddies but old habits die hard.

Amongst the pile of burnt wood and cotton I saw the bottle that I had buried in the flames the previous night and I very cautiously pulled it free. The glass had contorted, twisted and buckled under the extreme temperatures of the fire to create something entirely new from that which once was, recognisable as its original yet far from re-usable in the same capacity. In many ways the bottle felt like me, a new object from old material, a different design with the same parts. It was... symbolic.

"Lads," I said, getting Neil and Adam's attention, "come and have a look at this bottle. I think it's symbolic."

"Would you shut the fuck up about everything being symbolic," Neil sighed. "I'll be glad to get home back to where everything is just shit."

"I'm serious, look at this bottle," Adam came up first and examined the glass in my hand. "This bottle," I said, "this bottle is me."

"What?" said Adam, "empty and useless?" Neil laughed.

"Thanks a fucking bunch."

"Well you've lost me," Adam said, walking off.

"And I don't really give a shit, so if we could be getting on, I'd like to get on the road at some point today."

"I'm serious, look, the way this bottle has changed, it's a metaphor for me, after this week, still the same old Steve, but different for the experience. I'm going to keep it."

"Excellent, I'm happy for you, never again will we be able to say that Steve has lost his bottle."

"You're not taking this seriously are you?" I said.

"No, not really. It's eight in the morning, I badly want a coffee and we've got a long and painful journey ahead of us in a car that's missing windows, dragging it's exhaust and somewhat less poky in the acceleration department than a shopping trolley. So no, forgive me if I'm not getting jazzed by your melted bottle."

"I'll show you tomorrow, when you're in a better mood."

"You do that," Neil said, stamping his tent into its bag. "Where's Adam gone now? This is his job."

"I dunno," I looked around and couldn't immediately see him. "Perhaps he's gone for a wash?"

"Adam!" Neil yelled impatiently.

"Guys, come over here a minute," a voice said from behind the car. "You won't believe this."

"Don't you fucking start," Neil said, dropping the handles of the bag in frustration. I walked over to where Adam's voice was coming from, taking I felt, the upper hand in the support stakes that morning.

"Wassup?" I said, trying to follow Adam's gaze into the small two-foot vertical step of bank that marked very successfully the edge of the road.

"Look," he said, pointing I now realised to a log that had been placed bench-like in front of the bank. "Can you believe it?"

"Are you taking the piss?" I asked, still holding my melted bottle. "It's a log, so, yes. Yes I can believe that there is a log in the middle of this foresty woodland expanse of uninhabited land we're in. To be fair, it's not *that* much of a stretch for my imagination."

"No you plank, look what's *on* the log." He pointed, I looked and Neil came up behind me.

What I saw made me drop my bottle.

"You see?" Adam said in amazement.

"See what?" Neil asked. "What are you looking at?"

"That's just weird," I said, taking a step back and collecting my bottle up off the floor. Neil bent down to look for himself.

"HA! I fucking knew it!"

What it was that he fucking knew was that two days prior to our arrival, Natalie, Stacey, Gemma, Sarah and Jo had all camped here, and had had by all accounts quite a good time. They had carved their names and the date into the log with kisses. It didn't mention whether they were lesbians or if indeed they had spent any of their time here collectively naked in each other's company, somehow though, I felt that these details were of scant regard to Neil. In his mind, he had been vindicated. The L.N.C.A., in some shape or form, were indeed out there, even if they didn't know it.

"You're happy now?" I asked.

"I would have been happier two days ago." He said.

"What exactly is it that you think you would have done, exactly?" Adam asked, still staring in disbelief.

373

"Who the fuck cares? I would have been happy just taking pictures."

"You're a dick." Adam said.

"No, I'm honest."

"I can be honest too," Adam said, "honestly, you're a dick."

"Whatever, you just know that I was right. Now we can leave without feeling like failures."

"I didn't feel like a failure," I said.

"Steve, you're holding on to a melted bottle telling people it's symbolic of you. You're a poster child for failure."

"That hurts."

"Adam, go and get your knife." Adam pulled out his knife from the back of his jeans. It appeared given the size of everything that his jeans were so often asked to contain that they were made out of the same material as Mary Poppins' bag. "Oh, you have it. Okay, excellent, well get down there and put our names on the log. Boys, the Brotherhood was 'ere. And they had a fucking good time while they were at it."

We had but one final task to complete before leaving, something meaningful and in many ways relevant to our own situation. We stood at the bank of the river watching the water run by and took a moment in quiet contemplation. When we got in the car, the holiday in many ways would be over. There would be nothing left to look forward to besides the comfort of our own beds, a hot shower and in my case at least some clean underwear. We knew without saying it that these were our last real moments together, that what had happened that week in Scotland would stay in Scotland and forever be a bond between us. These were not words we needed to say allowed. A simple gesture would suffice, and the Danes had just the thing.

"Steve," Neil said in a voice barely above a whisper, "do you have the bacon?"

374

I nodded and held the year old bacon out in front of me. I placed the pack in the water and held it, looking back up at Neil, he crossed his hands and we bowed our heads.

"Spey, the final frontier, this is the voyage of the Streaky Bacon, it's continuing mission to explore new waters and new estuaries, to seek out new lives and new civilisations, to boldly float where no bacon has gone before and to avoid, wherever possible, ever, *ever* being opened."

I released the bacon and the current swept it away from me. I stood and with the others we watched it float away, the three of us following it down the river, each of us wondering how it had come to be in the first place, where it might end up next. It disappeared from sight long before we looked away, the moment holding us. Now we could say that we had left the area as we had found it. The only evidence of us bar the carving on the log would be forensic.

It was time to head home.

"Neil," Adam whined, "the car won't start Neil."

Bugger.

BOLLOCKS TO MONDAY

We managed to cover three miles before smoke and steam billowed forth from the bonnet, just enough distance to get us to what village folk referred to as a main road. Even I could tell that they were taking the piss.

Neil and I had sat down on the bank adding our own smoke to the problem. We had pushed the car off the road, walked to a shop and asked for help, starting with the very reasonable question 'where exactly *are* we?' We bought cigarettes and were given the number for a national recovery company to which we duly called. Upon speaking to the extremely friendly recovery operator it became apparent that the company used the term 'national' to explain that it covered the length and breadth of Scotland, from one office, rather than say a nice recognisable use of the term 'national' incorporating comforting phrases like 'local field agents'. We had no choice but to wait - there were any number of things wrong with the Zafira, in fairness it was quicker to list the parts of the car that were still working rather than those that weren't. I was quietly amazed that we had managed to get the car this far, but given the company I kept, who was I going tell?

Neil had finished the phone call like a needy girl at the end of a first date, constantly begging for reassurances of future contact and promises to call. This was common place, we were informed, apparently Scotland's quite a big country – who knew? – and such insistences were an almost daily occurrence, *not to worry, Sir.* The operator laughed and tried to comfort us by explaining that a vehicle would be along soon enough to pick us up, we were first in line. *Ha ha* I thought. But this seemed to be enough for the woman to stop talking to us and before we could argue we were staring at each other hoping that our opposite had picked up something useful from the exchange, like 'where were they based? How far away *was* the recovery vehicle? How much was all of this going to cost?' The dialling tone failed to give us any answers.

Ordinarily, this would have been exactly the sort of event that would have got me furious. I was impatient, I was insecure about my lack of knowledge about cars and I was seldom keen to spend my Saturday mornings sat on the side of a road. But today, like every other day that week, was different. Today I didn't mind. Today I was happy to sit and watch the occasional cars go by. It passed the time and therefore in its own funny way elongated my holiday. Let them come, I thought. Hell, let them come from Inverness. As it happened, I wasn't far wrong.

Adam was pacing up and down the tiny slice of concrete between the white line and the verge. He seemed to be playing a game of chicken with the approaching vehicles without consideration for speed or weight or the vacuum created by the undercarriage of passing trucks. I hoped not to have to scrape him up off of the road before the day was out, he was about to have a family to consider and there was just no way I could fill his shoes.

"Would you come up here please Adam? Pacing isn't going to get them here any quicker."

"You sound just like a woman." He said to me.

"Then apparently I must be right."

"Whatever, what time did they say they were going to be here?"

"They didn't, as you know, so pull up a tuft and sit down." I gestured to the patchy grass beside me and stared back out at the road.

"I can't believe this," he said, obstinately sitting down beside me. "We said we'd be home today. This is ridiculous. We're miles away."

"Relax," Neil said, "I'm sure we still will be."

"We're going to have to call them and let them know." I assumed the 'them' were their respective others. I felt a slight pang at the mention of the 'them', who was I going to call? Who was worried about me not being home on time? I didn't even own a cat.

"Call and tell them what?" Neil said, "We don't know anything yet. We don't know if this is something simple or complicated, how long they're going to be in getting here, whether whatever it is can be fixed today, whether they can get us home any other way. What would we say?"

"They should know."

"Why? So they can share in our misfortune?"

"It's polite."

"Phone them later then. Let's at least wait for the recovery vehicle. What's your big rush anyway?"

"I just don't like letting people down. We made an arrangement, we should stick to it, I'm a man of my word."

"I wish you were a man of fewer words." I said.

Neil laughed and Adam lay back on the grass sulking. He succeeded in staying there silently for sixty minutes. I was starting to miss the time when he had paced up and down the carriageway, at the very least it had provided a limited form of entertainment, like the wheel of death, only without so many motorbikes and one much bigger helmet.

Neil broke the silence with a casual remark.

"Do you ever think about death?" He said, lighting a cigarette and passing one my way. I guessed this was my cue to respond.

"You're feeling optimistic about when we're being picked up then?" I laughed.

"I'm not talking about now, I just mean generally. Do you ever think about it?"

"Well generally, only when Adam's driving." I replied, honestly. Adam sat up but failed to rebuke, instead he stretched and looked at his watch.

"I'm serious." Neil continued.

"So am I. Do you not remember the field, or more specifically how we came to find ourselves in it?"

"Yeah of course," he chuckled, but he wasn't biting. "But death though, I mean do you ever actually think about it? About what it means?"

"I try not to if I'm honest, mate. Kind of brings down the mood. Why do you ask?"

"I think about it, that's all, I seem to think about it all the time."

"Well that's a positive affirmation for your friends mate, cheers. In what context are we talking about anyway?"

"I don't know, have you ever thought about being killed by something you love?"

"Are we still talking about Adam? Because I don't mind driving home if you two are having some sort of a moment." He seemed to flash frustration, but it was gone before I could mention it.

"It's not about you two, I mean it is, but not the way it sounds, it's about looking at your life, the things you've done, taking stock, making sure the numbers add up." He picked a daisy from the bank and absently plucked at the petals.

"Jesus mate, if you're that bored can't you just go and read the porn mag or something?"

"I have, it didn't help."

"Then you really are sick."

"That might very well be the case actually."

"Alright, you've lost me." I kicked Adam gently for support. "Adam?"

"What's all this about, Neil?"

"Doesn't matter, forget it." I was getting annoyed now, I don't really know why, but when has that ever stopped anyone?

379

"Well it does matter, and I can't forget it, what the hell else are we going to do? Might as well get to the bottom of your maudlin, I suddenly feel like I'm stranded with Eeyore."

"I don't want the holiday to end either Neil, if that's what this is about?" Adam suggested, still the voice of reason.

"It's not that. Don't worry about it, forget I spoke."

"I've been trying that for thirteen years mate, and yet here I am." I flicked ash and watched it fly into the air. "You can't just say, 'do you ever think about death' and then expect everyone to ignore you."

"It's not actually death I keep thinking about, in fairness. Like I said, it's everything else."

"What do you mean 'like you said'? You haven't actually *said* anything!" I stood up and walked down the bank a little way, hoping Adam could make some sense of this. My head was starting to hurt and for the first time all week it had nothing to do with alcohol, which is probably why it was so disappointing.

My impatience was telling, to me at least. I expect Neil and Adam were used to it but to me it signified a desperation, despite whatever the hell Neil was getting at and Adams admission to reluctantly ending this journey, I had the least amount of desire to return home of either of them. Monday to me signified a battle that would either see me falling back into *all* of my old ways, or properly turning over a new leaf. Time would tell, but I know what I'm like, and the one possible motivation I really had for making a fresh start was soon to be over six hundred miles away from me, depending of course on when and if we ever got rescued.

Neil looked up at me, with Adam still staring at him expectantly. "So you boys want to know why we're really here?"

"I don't know, do we?" I said, staring him down.

"The car broke down. It's not my fault." Adam said.

"I don't mean 'here' here, I mean here in Scotland Adam."

"Oh, well yes, then."

"What's going on, Neil? Why are we really here in Scotland?" Neil hung his head low, the words seemed to be gathering at his lips like confused sheep at a cliff edge, one push and they'd all go over. "Talk to us." I urged.

I couldn't see his face clearly, just the outline, the edges, but the short hairs of his beard quivered almost imperceptibly. He was a dam cracking under an immense pressure, we were walking him down a path too narrow to turn back in. In a moment he'd start talking, perhaps for the first time all week and from this point on, we'd get what we get.

"Three weeks ago," he began "I'm lying in bed with Jane waiting for a happy ending to the start of my day when she stops suddenly and jumps up to get her head between my legs. I daren't say anything, but I'm thinking 'fuck me what have *I* done to get so lucky?' when all of a sudden the lights are on and I realise I'm being, *inspected*. She hasn't actually said anything and I'm still hoping that she's just being.... *sanitary?* You know what women are like." He rubbed his chin, bringing it all back, letting it out. "So I'm lying there thinking to myself the ceiling could benefit from an Artex when Jane pops her head up and she's looking at me like something has just dropped off in her hand. She says she can feel something, like a lump but not a lump, like a swelling but not immediately obvious. She says something just feels wrong. I mean, she'd know, right? So she books me an appointment for that morning, starts pushing me out the door immediately and the next thing I know I'm in this god-awful waiting room with the weight of the world in my lap. I remember clear as day sitting there and thinking 'All I wanted was a blow job.'"

"*Cancer?*" My eyebrows furrowed so hard that they actually gave me a cramp in my forehead. Paradoxically, my instinct when the word escaped me was to have another cigarette.

"Are you being serious Neil?" Adam pressed clumsily.

The look on his face suggested to me that he was being deadly serious, although it was a look that I could have happily gone my whole and hopefully long life without ever seeing.

"So what did the doctor say?" Adam inquired, more considerately now.

"That it is what it is. A swelling, a lump, could be cancer, could be a knot, could be a load of old bollocks. I get to go for tests, he'll make some calls, get me in quick, NHS policy for potential cancer, two weeks tops I'll know either way, have a nice day."

"Just like that?"

"Pretty much, I'm of the age apparently." Neil sighed. I couldn't believe how strong he was, the context suddenly smacked me in the face, every smile and laugh and joke made, every day he simply woke up without crying, it was all a testament to his character. The man was a rock.

"So you had the tests?" I said.

"I did."

I looked at him, almost unable to ask the next question. My mind was racing on ahead of me, all of the possible reasons why we were here. The urgency, the 'seizing the moment' bullshit, I felt like I'd been deceived, forced to have a good time under false pretences, I felt like a kid again taken out on a day trip just so that your parents would have an opportunity to tell you they were getting divorced. I didn't want to think about it, I couldn't even believe I was having to.

"And the results?" I whispered, through a sudden dryness in my throat. I had no emotional strength of my own so I just had to take from his.

"I go in on Monday for an orchidectomy." My heart sunk, I actually felt it hit the base of my stomach like someone had dropped a stone through my mouth.

"Monday?" I screeched. I can't believe I actually had the balls to think that *I* had problems – how fucking wrong could I be?

"They look to treat you within two weeks of a diagnosis. I got the results last Wednesday, localised seminoma, early stages, highly treatable. God's way of saying 'I'm watching, sort your shit out'."

"And then? Will it be chemo or something?" Adam asked.

"Fingers crossed, no. Apparently well over half of people just cut and run so to speak."

"And you've been carrying all this around with you the whole week and you never said a word?" I sounded bitter and angry, which is good, because I was. He was a selfish bastard, but it takes one to know one.

"We're in Scotland mate, it's not by accident."

"You couldn't just talk to us?"

"I was, I am. Listen, it's not that easy," he rubbed at his forehead and scratched his head aggressively, "You remember Friday night? When I pulled you both around to mine, sat you down and told you I was bored? Bored of my life? Bored of the rut? All that sanctimonious crap about mortgages and dead-end jobs? Well play it again, but this time change the word 'bored' to 'terrified'. Terrified that I'm going to leave a weight of a mortgage behind, that my shite job organising replacement light bulbs and chasing late contractors is actually something I'm going to have to be grateful doing because I'm going to be lucky to be alive. I've got no excuses for the fact that I don't spend enough time with my kids, I take my wife for granted and I consider a night out in Basingstoke to be 'a real change'. Bottom line, I'm terrified that I've wasted ten years of my life when my own bollocks only planned for eleven."

"You're a good person Neil." Adam uttered. I understood his intention entirely.

383

"But it's got to stop. All of it." Neil continued, almost oblivious to us now, the dam had broken. "This operation, it's got to be the start of something, I'm not going to be the only one that doesn't embrace the cliché. What kind of a selfish prick would I be then? If I get a second chance, I'm not going to waste it. I want to live my life. And I'm not talking about eating veg or going to the fucking gym either. I'm talking about experiences, I'm talking about leaving something behind besides a 'will' and a shit load of unanswered questions. I'm talking about true immortality. Memories that people will cherish. Memories that *I'll* cherish, something other than another ten years of regret."

"You keep saying 'regret', why?" I asked genuinely.

"Look, I love my wife and I adore my kids, but what's the point if I don't show it? It's just words if they don't really know it. I don't want them to think I've only been there out of loyalty, I want them to know I've been there because there's nowhere else on earth I'd rather be. That they are more important to me than anything, hell I've got nothing else to leave behind."

"And you really don't think that they know that?" Adam said.

"I don't know for sure. But I know what I'm like, the way I am, or can be. If I think it, if there's even a possibility of doubt then the chances are they have too. And *that's* just not good enough anymore. I get it now, this is what happens when you tell a guy that waits until tomorrow that maybe there isn't going to be one. You might think your life's going well – but would you bet your nads on it?"

"I get that, but you said that this was early-stages-good-chance-of-recovery cancer." I said. He laughed.

"It is, Steve, but it's not a fucking twenty-four hour thing, it's still cancer. I can't take this lightly, I can't joke this off. People keep using words like 'metastasised' as if the loss of a bollock wasn't bad enough." I don't think he meant to, but he rubbed his crotch fondly. "I don't even care about that though, I care about what I'm being made to think about, I care about the future. This is what I've been thinking about, what I keep thinking about, and I can't waste any more time."

I felt outrage welling up inside of me – for all of the wrong reasons. I wasn't pissed at the injustice of the situation or the fickle nature of fate, although I'm sure that would come later, I was pissed off that once again I had been the last to know. I wanted to scream at the man and shake him, 'what is *wrong* with you?' But I guess I already knew the answer. He had shit taste in friends.

None of us had been concentrating on the road so we were all startled as the articulated lorry rumbled loudly by dragging us all from whatever dreadful thoughts we had each been stuck on. Personally, Neil's confession had sent me reeling in a way that Adams driving could only aspire to. I was confused again, frustrated again, hugely and without question completely fucked off again. I kept struggling with new and frightening terminology, wrestling with words I felt would become unfortunately common to me over the coming weeks - words like 'orchidectomy', 'seminoma' and 'metastasised'- but this language seemed foreign to me. I felt like I'd just banged a med student with truly inappropriate pillow talk. But whatever way I looked at it, someone was still fucked.

An unnatural sound followed shortly after the departing lorry, and I watched as the Zafira finished rocking with a triumphant metallic clank. Something inevitably important had dropped to the ground, the car once again metaphorically and quite succinctly summing up the mood of the group. The bottom had just dropped out of my world, stands to reason that the same should be said for the car.

"That car," Adam said, pointing, "is unbelievable."

"It's something," I said. I didn't even bother going to find out what had happened, given the scale of things, it hardly seemed relevant.

"No, I mean it's incredible, I think it's empathising." I looked at Adam in disbelief.

"It's not fucking Herbie, Adam."

"No, you're right, it's not." He replied, "It's *better*." Deep down I guess we all just wanted to be kids again.

We sat in silence for a while after that, watching the world go by with an entirely different perspective.

"You should have talked to me," was all I managed to verbalise after ten minutes of quiet contemplation. "Or us, we will always be there for you mate."

"And what would you have said, because I don't know what to say? I don't want your pity, don't think you two are getting out of this that easily. This change, this has to be for all of us. You're all a part of this now. You especially Adam, you're just at the beginning of road what with the baby on the way, so start as you mean to go on." Adam nodded respectfully.

"You still should have trusted us." I grumbled.

"Don't do that, I trust you with my life, can't you see that? I had a week to kill before the operation and I'd literally been going crazy. I was driving Jane up the fucking wall, snapping at the kids, I couldn't work, I can't concentrate. I needed an escape, I needed all of this, and I needed you two. You're the only people I know who could provide me with enough of a distraction to get through this, who could make me laugh so much that I would almost forget about everything else. And you have too - this is the first time we've stopped this week when I've had cause to remember. You'll never know how grateful I am for that. "

"I feel used." Adam said and I couldn't help but chuckle.

Neil laughed fondly, "You have been. Well and truly – but for all the right reasons. The question is do you think you could still have done that this week knowing what you now know? Because I couldn't risk it, and why bring you down? Why have it always in the back of your mind every time you looked at me? You two have done the absolute best thing anyone could have done for me this week - you've saved me from myself. And you've made this the start. If nothing else, at least this week we can say we lived."

"We can say that mate, we can certainly say that." I agreed.

Adam sighed. "Jesus, I just can't believe it."

"Yeah well that makes two of us. But what do you do?" I looked around.

"This, I guess." I said, trying to encompass a whole country and a week spent camping in it with a gesture of my hands, "I mean you were right, get away, sort your shit out, recharge and then get on with it. The more I think about it, the more I realise I don't blame you for not saying anything. I spent six months obsessed about a break-up from a woman I only partially liked. Can you imagine what I'm going to be like over this?" Adam laughed in agreement. "But I really think it's going to be alright. You've got to be positive, right?"

"I agree," Adam said, "And you know what? I'm just glad we could help." Adam patted Neil on the back and they leaned in to each other and touched heads.

"Just one thing though," I said, pausing for effect.

"Go on."

"Well, I mean, I don't mean to sound insensitive but, well, you couldn't have waited just another couple of days to tell us? I mean talk about ending on a downer mate – the car's fucked, we didn't even find the L.N.C.A. and now you want to throw this on us?" Neil looked stunned and then threw his head back in laughter.

"Wanker."

"The man's got a point Neil, it's all 'me, me, me' with you isn't it? Talk about unloading on us," Adam said, smiling, "This could be one hell of an uncomfortable drive home now. You've definitely created a socially awkward situation. All you had to do was hold out for just a few more hours, that would have done and then, I dunno, you could have sent us a text or something, 'thanks for the holiday boys, and by the way I've got ball cancer.'"

"Well I'm so fucking sorry," Neil said, warmly, his eyes ever so slightly wet, "excuse me for sharing. Let me apologise for my inconvenient timing and thank you both for being so understanding."

"No, no, mate, honestly," I replied sarcastically, "no thanks required. You're welcome."

"Bite me."

"Actually, do you mind if I don't?" I grinned at Neil, this was after all what he said he needed us for. "You've got cooties."

THE THEORY OF RELATIVITY

"I don't be-fucking-lieve it!" That was a new one on even me.

"What?" I asked, looking to find anything that could have elicited such a graphically diverse expletive from Adam, "S'matter?"

An hour had passed since Neil's disclosure. Time was no longer my friend, my arse was most definitely holding a grudge. I was running low on cigarettes - Neil and I were down to our last twenty - and I had begun to notice a worrying trend of small children pointing and laughing at our car as they drove past sat in the back of their parents fully-functioning German automobiles. I hated them, and I wasn't fussed about their parents' cars either.

None of us had approached the Zafira after it had shat out a vital part of its internal combustion engine, we hadn't actually moved at all, but suddenly though Adam was very animated, alive with the spirit and force of indignation. He had become a man about to be vindicated - he was positively bubbling with repressed rage.

"The God-damned mother sucking cheeky fucking bastard." I had been corrected. Adam pointed off into the distance - years of masturbation having obviously taken no toll whatsoever on his eyesight. I squinted trying to picture a man riding naked with Fiona on the back of his motorbike, or perhaps more likely given the anger, a man riding Fiona naked on the back of a motorbike. "Look!" He pointed again. Perhaps Adam's mother was on the bike too.

"I don't see anything? Give me a clue."

"What's the commotion?" Neil asked, apparently stepping out of a Fantastic Five story.

"Adam, he's hallucinating."

"Hallucinating what?"

"Beelzebub for all I know. He's rabid. I think he might have caught rabies from the grass or something."

"Is that even possible?"

"Are you even asking me that?"

"There!" Adam screamed, "Look!" He pointed. Both Neil and I obliged but nothing, not a single thing on earth could I see that would get a man that excited.

"What?" We yelled.

"That dog wanking quim sniffing rat faced todger flogging bastard of a Tow Truck Driver!" My jaw hit the floor and not from the shock of seeing the very same truck that had tarnished our beloved Zafira but from the sheer creativity of Adam's hatred.

"Dog-wanking? That's just wrong, mate." Neil said.

"No, *that's* just wrong." Adam yelled, pointing the most aggressive finger I have seen pointed at anyone, ever, at the approaching vehicle. "I am not letting that shit-stick anywhere near our car, not after the last time. He probably won't even bother to stop, he'll probably just crash straight through us and fuck off."

"Mate, any chance you can let us do the talking on this one?" I said.

"Yeah, seriously Adam, I really don't fancy spending the night out here." Neil said, stepping down off the bank to stand behind the Zafira and flag down the truck. "Remember your word – we want to get home tonight."

"Whatever, just leave me out of this. That man as good as broke my nose."

"First off, it was your own bloody fist that broke your nose, he just happened to assist the airbag in bringing it into contact with your face, and second, you're a fine one to talk about breaking noses."

"Semantics." He huffed and walked further up the bank.

The elusive truck pulled in to the hard shoulder and slowed to a stop. This was the first time Neil and I had actually seen it since that fateful night. It had Smurf-blue paint imbedded in scratches in the front wing. That was about the only indication of impact visible, on the tow truck at least. I had the sense that Adam was quietly touching his nose not far behind me on the bank. The driver side door opened and a huge giant of a man disembarked. He made the copper in Elgin seem positively average in stature and I began to understand why he needed such a big truck.

"Alright lads? Havin' a spot o'bother are we, ey?" He said, sounding like Billy Connelly's less comprehensible brother.

Neil smiled, the palms of his hands open and outward, the unthreatening gestures similar to those used on a large dog. Neil wasn't a small man but nor was he stupid, the truck driver standing before us looked as though he changed tyres by lifting up the cars himself and sliding new wheels on. Better to be safe than sorry. "Something like that."

"Do I knows you lads?" He said, while I heard the words 'are you staring at me pal?'

"I don't think so, not directly anyway." I said. Adam grunted.

"Are you's sure?" he said, stopping to look at the three of us and then at the Zafira. Recognition crawled across his face. "Wait, no, get away, what are the chances of that?"

"I'm sorry?" I said, sounding more British than the Queen did.

"You's are the boys from the car park, unbelievable." At this, Adam turned and marched down the hill. I didn't want a confrontation, tried not to picture the scene of Adam brandishing his machete at the man who appeared to use something similar to pick his teeth clean.

"Oh, oh so you remember us do you? Part of your tally are we?"

"Remembers you? Are you kidding? I've been looking for you's all over bloody Scotland."

"Eh?" I said, confused.

"Come again?" Adam said, evidently not faring much better.

"Er, how come?" Neil said, self-preservation stepping in.

"To apologise! What do you's take me for? I couldne feel a thing in the rig that night, wasn't 'til I got back to the yard that one of the wee lads mentioned the paint on the wing there, I'd a never known." He pointed at the paint on the wing there and three grown men all leaned in to acknowledge the evidence. "I knay it's not an excuse, but I'd done a sixteen hour day, I stopped in for a break like, a coffee you know, stretch my legs, and then the radio's going and I'm being called off on another job. Couldne even get out for a minute, accident see, police summons and all. Nasty thing, I say, nasty thing."

"Fatalities?" I asked, with genuine interest and concern.

"Ney, I got there alright you know? Ney bother." I looked to Neil for support, but he shook his head quickly and pressed on.

"*Anyway*," Neil said.

"Ay, anyways, I've been all over Scotland this week, keeping an eye's out for you's and hoping to run into you. Didne expect this though, eh?"

"Makes four of us," Adam said, warming, but only mildly. The giant had charm as long as his arm.

"I'm sorry for the delay in gettings to you, come all the way down from Elgin." I looked at Neil and eyed Adam peripherally, enough to see his eyes widen with realisation and joy. We were never going to hear the end of this. "Thought I might be getting a day off."

"Elgin?" Adam questioned. Oh no. "You're based in *Elgin*?"

"Ay, you boys know it?"

"Know it? We love it." Neil said, turning to put a hand on Adam's chest to calm him down.

"I knew I saw you in Elgin, I *knew* it!" Adam said excitedly.

"Get away." The truck driver said, a smile cracking his exaggerated features. "You's been to Elgin this week? What are the chances of that eh?"

"Million to one," I said agreeably, "Got to be."

"My brother owns the fish and chip shop, if only I'd have known. Could've at least got you's a decent meal while in town."

"Your brother owns the fish and chip shop?" Neil said, looking at me now and waiting for the words to sink in.

They didn't.

"Ay. He does. Best fish and chips in Scotland he's says. But he would."

"Your truck has been tormenting me all week. All week I've been saying that I've seen you, all week they've been saying I was mad, that I was obsessed, that I was crazy. All week!"

"Yeah, can't think what gave us that impression eh Neil?" I said.

"Absolutely." He said. Adam was hopping.

"Shall we see what's the bother with your car then?" The giant man said, stepping passed us all with two strides and reaching the bonnet with a third. "I sees you've had some trouble elsewhere eh?" He said, pointing a giant finger towards the extensive remodelling work required to the front of our car.

He lifted the bonnet and began the investigation while Neil and I began the process of calming Adam down. It would take time and could well be more complicated than refitting the entire engine of the Zafira. I suspect Neil hadn't reacted so badly to the news of his diagnosis.

"Mate," I said, "Can we please just let it go? He's apologised, we've acknowledged that you may possibly have seen him *somewhere* before this week, we accept the coincidences. And we are very much aware of the size of him. Do you think there is any chance you could avoid starting a fight with a man that appears to have all of the names of the people he's killed tattooed down his arm? Please?"

"Steve makes a good point Adam, let's think about the bigger picture here, let's think about Fiona and your unborn child. Is this really any way to go? Is this how a soon-to-be-father should behave?"

"You're going there on me already?" Adam said.

"I think I have to, yes." Neil nodded. "It's harsh, but it's fair."

"Fine. Whatever, let him fix the damn car and ignore my nose completely."

"Let's hope he ignores *all* of our noses hmm?" I said.

At the bonnet, something was mumbled in Scottish.

"I tell you what I can't believe," Neil said, lighting cigarettes for us both. "I can't believe we're being rescued by Louise's uncle. I mean that's a fucking coincidence."

"Who is?" I said, the words still not sinking in.

"What?" Neil said, looking at me incredulously. "The fella at the bonnet, Steve. Did you not hear what he said?" I looked at him blankly.

"His brother owns the fish and chip shop in Elgin, with the best fish and chips in Scotland. How many fish and chip restaurants did you see mate? Um duh!" Adam said sarcastically.

They both looked at me, I could hear the words but it just wasn't going in.

"Steve, did you bang your head or something? That bear of a man is Louise's uncle. I'm telling you, ask him."

"You're kidding?" I said, hoping that they were, wondering what the worst thing a man that size could do to a tourist on the side of the road that had not many days ago been romancing his niece. A list formed in my head that I immediately tried to ignore. "Can't you ask him?"

"No!" They said together, rather unfairly and without due consideration for the circumstances, I thought.

"Look, it hardly matters, I just thought that the coincidence might appeal to you." Neil said.

"Why?"

"Well, you know," he said, assuming that I did.

"No?"

"It's symbolic," Adam said, laughing, "You of all people have got to admit that, surely?"

"You think?"

"What?" Neil shrieked. "Of all the shit that you've pointed out to us this week, you're actually arguing this? The man that by chance comes to rescue us on the day that we're leaving Scotland not only happens to be the very same guy that drove into us on the way up here, but also, *also* just happens coincidentally to be the uncle of the woman you have recently become infatuated with. And you *don't* think that that's symbolic?" I looked at him without retort, "You know what? Just fuck off."

"It's certainly random," I said.

"Random?" Adam screamed. "Get out of the way Neil, I'm going to fucking punch him myself."

"What?" I said, taking a step away from a re-enraged Adam.

"You boys alright back there?" The man of debatable lineage asked.

"Actually, you could sort this out for us if you don't mind," Adam said stomping around to the front of the car. "Forgive me for asking, but are you or are you not the brother of the owner of the fish and chip shop in Elgin."

"Ay, I am." The bear said, wiping something greasy and metallic on a cloth.

"And," continued Adam, striking a not dissimilar tone to Columbo at the final 'reveal', "Are you or are you *not* the uncle of a particular waitress of that same fish and chip shop." The giant looked at Adam curiously, as many people have been prone to do over the years.

"Ay, Louise is my niece."

"I thank you." Adam said, bowing.

The words sank in.

"Now that you mention it," I conceded, "That *is* kind of symbolic." Neil punched me on the arm.

"So you know my Louise then eh?" the behemoth said. He had told us that his name was Angus but I didn't believe him. I didn't believe him because he was the most Scottish man I had ever met to start off with, without being called Angus. In fact, he couldn't have been any more Scottish if he'd arrived wearing a quilt on horseback with the Saltire blazing across his face, crying 'Freedom!' The second reason that I didn't believe him was simply because Angus was a name that didn't quite fully convey the size of the man. Angus the Destroyer, maybe.

"Yes, we've had the pleasure of meeting her." I said, aware that his arm was bigger in circumference than my waist. Why I said 'we' when I quite clearly knew that the majority of the pleasure in meeting her was most definitely solely mine, I don't know.

"Fine girl she is. Had her head turned by all accounts though so her dad said, said she's spoke of little else all week."

"Really?" I said perhaps a little too gleefully.

"So he says, but I canney say I'd noticed it. Long as it's not an Englishman that'll be fine by me," he said, "No offence boys, but, you know?"

I have to say, there was some taken.

"Absolutely," Adam said, for reasons I knew we'd be having a very long chat about later. "I wouldn't trust them with my daughter either."

"Your daughter?" Neil said, turning to stare at him. "Your missus has barely turned the stick blue and you're already picking out perspective suitors?"

"And if not an Englishman, who *would* you be comfortable letting her date?" I asked.

"Well, no-one, none of 'em will be good enough for my little girl, but *especially* not an Englishman." Angus smiled, but I sensed it was more out of concern for the mental capacity of his present company than for a sudden united front against the English.

"You're going to be a nightmare with this aren't you?" Neil said, sighing.

"No," Adam lied.

"What happens if you have a boy?" I asked.

"Well, that's different. *He'd* be good enough for Louise definitely."

"Oh right," I rallied, this after all was a matter close to my heart, "So your unborn son is good enough for Louise but I'm not, is that what you're saying?"

"Hang on a wee second their boys, watch your tongues about my niece there alright?" Angus the Destroyer growled. I was indelibly aware of the facts that I had just released.

"Figuratively speaking of course." I stammered.

"You leave her figure out of this you hear?"

"Anyway," Neil interjected, "the engine?"

Angus unclenched his fist and the air-pressure changed, then by grace and good fortune a mobile phone started ringing. Each of us fished in our pockets and to my astonishment I found that it was mine going off. Odd for any number of reasons, not least of all for the fact that everyone I knew that regularly rang me was standing around a broken Zafira. I looked down at the screen - of course it was Louise ringing, why wouldn't it be?

I stepped away from the car, away from the road, away from the slowly building bristling tension that was the mass of Angus. I tried to step out of earshot, there was simply no way that I was rejecting that call, no way that I was going to miss out on an opportunity to talk to the woman that had apparently had her head turned. Even if it meant risking my head being repeatedly turned by Angus. It was a risk I was prepared to take, just as quietly as possible.

I pressed the 'accept call' button on my phone and raised it to my ear.

"Hello." I said.

"Hi Steve, its Louise. From the other night?" Like she needed to clarify.

"Hey," I don't know why but Angus was peering around the bonnet to look at me, which seemed somewhat counterproductive to our situation given that *I* wasn't broken, yet. "It's so good to hear from you. How are you?"

"Yeah I'm good, you know? I was just thinking about you and thought I'd give you a ring. Are you leaving today?"

"Well that was the plan..."

"Oh really? Are you staying?" I was so sure I could hear excitement and anticipation in her voice and it was all I could do to not say 'yes'.

"Sadly, no. Our car has broken down, hopefully only temporarily, but at the moment we're on the side of the road."

"You're kidding, that's a nightmare, is someone there helping you?"

"Yeah..."

"Because, you know, actually my uncle is a recovery driver. I could give him a ring if you like?"

"You know, I think we're good," I don't know why I couldn't tell her outright that her uncle was currently intimidating me with a spanner other than because her uncle was currently intimidating me with a spanner. "I expect we'll be on the road again in no time."

"Shame, I could have come with him to see you." *Shit.*

I looked over at Angus, "Really, you think he wouldn't mind?"

"Uncle Angus?" She said with a gentle laugh, making him sound so cuddly, "He'd do anything for me."

"You know, that is really tempting. I mean *really* tempting, but I don't think I'd know how to explain it to the guy that's here already. I think that might be treading on his toes a little."

"I feel a little stupid saying this," she began, trailing off to a whisper, "But I miss you. Is that ridiculous?"

"I hope not, because I miss you too. Today isn't the first time that you've crossed my mind. In fact if you stay in there much longer I might have to start charging you rent."

"Oh really?" she played, "You sound like you've got a crush."

"And you sound like you don't mind."

"Well, I'm not complaining, no." I could picture her face more clearly than if we'd been video calling. How could I be doing this to myself again? Undoing all of the work, making every mile travelled south just that little bit more painful. "But I hate that you're leaving. I would have called sooner but you said this was a 'boys' week' and I didn't want to intrude. Or sound too keen." She laughed.

"It's fine, and I would have called too but for the fact that a part of me was starting to believe I'd imagined the whole thing. I had this feeling I'd call you up and it would have all been a big mistake."

"Not yet, no. But I think it would be a mistake if we don't see each other again. I think that mistake could be huge."

"Well I hate to make huge mistakes."

"Me too. So I guess it wasn't all in your head then."

"Well, some of it was." I said, lighting a cigarette. "In my head, I didn't leave."

"Funny, in my head you didn't either. You didn't get too much sleep though."

399

"Well at least that explains why I've been feeling so tired." She laughed.

"In fact, you've got quite a lot to live up to. That would be the problem with leaving a girl wanting more."

"No pressure then."

"Hey, none at all. Those kinds of mistakes I'll happily make all day long with you."

"Louise, you're killing me here." She giggled and my heart melted while everything else counteracted. "I've got a long drive home in a car full of men. This kind of talk borders on inhumane."

"You're right, I'm sorry. Forgive me." I exhaled and tried to relax. "I'll send you a picture instead."

"Don't you dare. At least not for about nine hours."

"Is that a request?" She laughed.

"It's a negotiation."

"So what do I get in return, you know, for being a good girl?"

"My undying gratitude."

"Try again."

"What do you want?"

"A promise."

"You've been on a promise since I left you."

"Not that kind of a promise." She giggled, I sensed I might have been affectionately hit at that point too, had I been lucky enough to have been with her. "I want you to promise that you won't do something shit like go back home and forget about me." Louise clearly didn't know me at all. I could provide hours of testimonial to the contradictory likelihood of that happening.

"You know what? That I think I can do. Not forget about you I mean."

"Good, because I don't do this."

"Do what."

"This," she said, probably gesturing generally with her hands wherever she happened to be. "I don't meet guys and chat them up and call them. It's not me."

"Okay," I felt relieved, nervous, fortunate and giddy all at once, "And?"

"I thought you should know that, that's all."

"You thought I should know that you're making an exception, for me?"

"Yes." I laughed. "But in a way that doesn't make me sound too big headed."

"Then consider me informed. And can I just say 'thank you' too, for making the exception. You have no idea how glad I am that you did."

"Well, keep your promise and maybe I'll know."

"No worries," I replied, as coolly as I could manage.

"Maybe you could give me a ring, when you get home?"

"It'll probably be late, are you sure?"

"Yeah, definitely. I mean, only if you want to," she corrected and I laughed again.

"Sure. That would be great." It sounds stupid, but I swear I heard her smile.

"I might be in bed, but I won't be asleep."

"Stop it."

"I'll just be lying there, waiting for you to call me up."

"Please, stop it."

"Wearing a little black teddy."

"Get off the phone." She giggled.

"I'm kidding."

"I don't care, the image is already in my head."

"I sleep naked."

"I hate you."

"Bye gorgeous," she purred, her voice like velvet.

"Bye Louise."

"Speak later." She blew me a kiss.

"Bet on it." I hung up the phone. Angus the Destroyer was standing over me.

401

DESERT ISLAND DICKS

"What did you say to him?" Neil asked me as we sped noisily down a duel carriageway. I assumed the 'him' in question was the six-foot-seven ginger killing machine that I had recently slain, much like George.

"I told him that it was a totally different Louise, and that Adam was in the S.A.S. and that if he wanted to try something he'd have to go through him first."

"You bastard!" Adam said.

"What did you really say?" Neil asked again, hushing him.

"That I meant him no offence, that I respected Louise immensely and hoped that he would trust in her judgement," Neil looked back at me, still coaxing out the words, "And that my great, great, great grandfather had fought at the battle of Harlaw."

"Is that true?" Neil pressed.

"Does it matter?" I said trying to flick ash out of the smokers' crack in the window. There was so much turbulence that it flew forwards and whirled around Adam. He expressed his lack of appreciation emphatically.

"Hang on," Adam said, wiping his eyes and readjusting his position in the driving seat, "that was a clan battle, the English weren't even *in* it."

"Exactly," I replied, proudly, "I couldn't lose, right? Who said I haven't learned anything on this trip?"

"Genius," Neil conceded, "And he was alright with that?"

"Well he didn't break my nose, which puts me one up on one of Adam's negotiations."

"Hey, I resent that remark."

"Good!" I said, touching my nose gently.

"And what about wanting to get in Louise's pants?" Neil asked succinctly.

"Well it may surprise you to hear that I didn't exactly phrase it that way. Besides, for once the distance between us may actually work in my favour. I figure I'll ask Louise to straighten him out. Apparently he's a softy."

Neil laughed, "Yeah, I could tell that about him soon as I saw him."

"More importantly," I said, as Adam crunched the Zafira into fifth gear and settled at the cruising speed of a Tornado jet, "What did he say about the motor?"

"He said mechanically speaking there was not a single reason why this car should be running, period. He said never in the history of his career as a recovery driver had he seen a car less likely to make it to the end of the road than this one." I laughed, but quietly, in case the ashtray was still listening.

"Did he fix it?" Adam asked rather optimistically.

"Well that depends on your definition of 'fixing it', he replaced some minor components that had evidently seized, together with some technical adjustments to the radiator which he claimed had been damaged, and I quote "strangely, in a vertical fashion"." Neil looked accusingly at Adam who rather conveniently and somewhat out of character seemed to be looking straight ahead, "But that, as far as I could tell simply involved hitting bits of it with a hammer and then pouring in some unknown liquid from a plain plastic bottle. Oddly he seemed to take quite a few bits *out* of the engine. But hey, he's the expert."

"I see." I didn't. But, you know.

"Then he checked over some other bits and pieces, whacked this and poked that, and then told me to try and start it. Unbelievably it worked."

"But what did he actually *say*?" Adam insisted, ever one for the details. It didn't seem to be of significance that he was currently driving the car, at speed I might add, so long as a guy in relative authority *said* it was okay.

"Well, he said that it would take him at least a week to make it safe to drive anywhere," I wondered secretly whether that was part of Angus' plan, "And that if we made it to the border he'd be fucking amazed."

We sailed passed the border and I hoped that somewhere, somehow, Angus *was* amazed. I hoped one day to be able to tell him it was symbolic.

"I can honestly say I preferred it when the car was dead." I stammered as Adam pushed cornering to a whole new concept. I had spent much of the last hour travelling sideways and periodically falling into the hole that we had burnt in the back seat of the Zafira. It wasn't anywhere near as enjoyable as it might at first sound. "Do you think we could try driving forwards for awhile?"

"Shut up pussy, we're making good time."

"You drive any faster and we'll be going back in time."

"Tart," he mumbled, "I told you – we need to get home today, I promised."

"Neil, why do we keep letting him drive?" I asked, but Neil didn't answer. He had his eyes closed, a strategy I had tried and was coping with until I had smacked my head on the rear side window for the fifteenth time. I needed to hold on and brace myself in advance for approaching corners, roundabouts, pedestrians and the sound barrier. It was also windy as hell sat in the back, ventilated as the space was by missing glass and bullet holes.

Somehow, Adam managed to catch air. I looked behind us to see if we still had the exhaust attached or whether Adam had jettisoned it for reduced wind resistance, I saw nothing but sparks fly from the back of the car as we made heavy contact with the road. Given our earlier predicament, I had hoped Adam might factor this in to his driving style, but

404

apparently there is any number of times that you can be wrong in a week.

Somewhere in the background I heard the familiar opening bars of Lynyrd Skynyrds' 'Free Bird' drift through the speakers. I felt justifiably relieved - there were few songs in the world I was prepared to die listening to and fortunately that was right up there on the list.

"I love this song!" Adam said, managing to find another fifteen or twenty miles an hour more from the strained engine when the guitar solo kicked in. "Yes!"

We approached a roundabout. At least, the repeated warning signs led me to believe that we were approaching a roundabout, Adam seemed to be in denial. I had to look away, look at anything other than the mound of immovable grass and concrete quickly filling the windscreen. I stared at the foot well. I had to look again.

"I don't believe it," I said, because I didn't.

"What?" Adam asked, calm as a daisy on a summer's day.

"Concentrate on the road!" I yelled.

"What don't you believe Steve?" Neil said, picking up the thread.

"There are maggots still on the carpet." I was conscious of the fact that those could have been the final words I ever spoke. As last words went, they had to be close to 'urgggggh' on the list of forgettable check outs.

"You're shitting me?" Neil said, managing to turn his head against the force.

"I shit you not. I can see them, only a couple, but they're still alive. Is that even possible?"

"Well given the overwhelming evidence Steve I'm going to have to say yes." The voice of reason replied.

"Adam, would you shut up and brake!"

"Sorry, Steve," Adam said, not braking.

"I'm with him," Neil said. "If it looks like a maggot, and moves like a maggot, and it's not *your* cock, chances are it's a maggot."

"That's inspired. I'm going to die with a madman, a philosopher and a car full of pre-pubescent flies." It suddenly occurred to me what I had just said and I feebly attempted to correct myself. "Sorry Neil."

"It's alright, we're all going to die, Steve, but it could be worse."

"How could it possibly be worse?"

"Could be ball cancer."

"Bastard, you're going to do this all the time now aren't you?"

"I believe I've earned the right, yes." He said smugly. Had he realised a week ago that he held in his possession the key to trumping *any* discussion, I believe that there is every possibility our trip would have been superfluous.

We took the roundabout on two wheels and I watched with muted fascination as the contents of the car shifted to the left while I fought to stay out of the hole. My attention stuck on the doors that failed to close properly and seemed to only remain shut out of force of habit. It occurred to me to ask just how much of a kick it might take to break such a habit.

"Adam, you know when I said I needed you as a distraction? Well this isn't what I meant. You killing me is only marginally less appealing than the cancer, just so we're clear. It's just that all of a sudden, Monday doesn't seem so bad."

"I'm with Neil, your driving makes cancer seem like the lesser of two evils," I said, grasping the front seats for support, "I'd swap a bollock to get out of this car."

"I don't know what you mean," Adam said, focused like a racing driver on the traffic ahead, specifically I felt, on a vehicle at least a mile away. "But while we're on the subject. I would like to share something with you boys."

"Seriously mate, I can't take any more revelations, I'm done." I said.

"Oh God, you're not planning a 'Thelma and Louise' thing are?"

"Neil, tell him the cancer is curable please!"

Adam ignored us.

"I think we've spent enough time together this week to not be afraid anymore."

"I don't think there's enough time in the world to not be afraid of this Adam," I said, losing my grip and wincing as the seat belt cut into my chest.

"You know what I'm talking about, cancer, new love, fresh starts, *babies*." he said, "I just feel that given everything that's happened, now would be a good time to share this."

"Share what?" Neil asked, confused and terrified in equal measure.

"I love you. I love both of you." Adam took his eyes off the road in that awful way he insisted on doing when he was behind the wheel. He looked at both of us in turn, me with all colour draining from my face, Neil fighting back the urge to show us all what we ate the previous night. I feared Adam was waiting for one of us to respond, but words failed me.

"What?" Neil yelled. "What do you want me to say?"

"I love you, Neil. It's okay."

"You're kidding me right?"

"Steve," Adam said, catching my dilated pupils in the rear view mirror, "I love you."

"We love you too, Adam, but we'd love you even more if you would just get us home alive!"

Under any other circumstances it could have been quite a touching moment, as it was, the only thing I was touching was cloth.

When we finally hit the motorway the Zafira ate up the miles with a comforting ease. That was the one saving grace about Adam's driving, it was, in the technical sense of the word, efficient. Roads merged into one and junction

407

numbers became a blur. We opted not to stop - all of us perhaps quietly hoping that our sheer momentum and force of will would be enough to get us home. I hated to admit that I was looking forward to my bed, to a shower and clothing that didn't smell like campfire.

The journey home was never going to be a fun one. We may not have been as tired as we had been a week ago but we were certainly not as enthusiastic either. There was an unspoken tension in the car, every bump and dip in the road a potential breakdown, a further four hours lost in a day already too short to be suitable for our needs. We were quiet too, listening to the CD's that had failed to hit the playlist, enjoying the last few moments before the gravity of our lives pulled us out of our orbit together.

A week ago we had all agreed in one way or another that we were in a rut, that our lives were on a course that stretched straight and true into an oblivion of boredom, and yet now we would look back at that time as the glory days. How could any of us have known then what we each knew now? Now we had issues, and no choice but to deal with them. So much had seemed to happen in the confines of the week that it was hard to find perspective. The future was truly unknown.

I had no doubt that Adam would step up to the challenge of fatherhood, he is I have regularly maintained, a stand up guy. Despite a week's worth of evidence to the contrary, Adam will always be a responsible, conscientious man, someone you could look up to, and not just because of his height. I looked forward to seeing him in this new role, he had continuously been the voice of reason since I'd known him and I was keen for it to be put to a more beneficial use. Truth be told, that's just a bullshit way of saying I was eagerly anticipating hearing him nag someone else for a change, after all, if this week had proved anything, it was that I never listened to advice - clearly the key to success is starting early. I wasn't sure how to break it to him but I had a feeling that even after the baby was born, somehow I would still be the most immature person in the room.

As for Neil, I could only imagine what he was really thinking. Each of us had our reasons to be dubious about our arrival home but for Neil it meant something else entirely. While the rest of us had managed to escape our issues and really get away from it all, Neil had quite literally been carrying his around the entire week, returning home just meant facing up to facts. Walking into his house he would immediately be confronted with everything he had to lose and I honestly didn't know how he was going to do it. Neil's problems may have been shared, but they wouldn't be halved until Monday.

I realised now that despite my best intentions, I had been careless with time and careless with my friendships. Neil had been dealing with everything - with *cancer* for fuck sake - without my support, and that was simply unacceptable. I couldn't, no, I *wouldn't*, let him go through this alone. I had to make myself available in any way he needed it, stop him from thinking that everyone else's problems were more important than whatever he may be going through. I had to beat out that instinct he had to just keep making sure everyone else was okay first. It may have been a noble trait, but bollocks to it.

We would make changes together, I would force him to keep his promises of spending real family time with Jane and the boys, I would suggest - albeit reluctantly - that we *both* give up smoking and I would reward him by keeping my promises, to myself and to Louise. I had a feeling I knew which one would be easier, but I accepted that things did have to change and they most likely had to start with me.

This week had shown me that my life had to be better. I didn't want a series of one-offs scattered through a lifetime of same-old-same-old. I wanted more than that. Times like these were few and far between, but considering how easily we had made the week happen, something told me that they didn't have to be. I confidently suspected that Jane would always be ready for a break from Neil – his condition was after all more serious than even man-flu, so I felt her pain as much as his. If we could ever get him to admit it, Adam would surely need the occasional break from Fiona and the baby, or housework, even if only for a night, and I would always need a break from myself.

In the meantime though, my mood was bolstered by the thought of a phone call to Louise. When I got home, got comfortable, took a breath and drew a line under all the shit I had hopefully left in Scotland, I would look to the future – and ask Louise to be a part of it. I didn't plan on proposing or anything, I just wanted to commit to an arrangement, be positive for the right reasons, make a plan or two with her. Something definite, that she could feel confident about. I finally realised that uncertainty is the death of optimism, as far as relationships are concerned. I hadn't worked out the logistics or anything - details were Adams' forte not mine – but whatever happened though, I would make sure that Neil didn't lose a testicle in vein. If Neil's happiness depended on me spending time with a beautiful, funny, intelligent woman, then damn it, that's the friend I would be.

As the colour drained from the sky we searched the radio stations, hoping to catch one last show with Mick, healing the nation apparently morning, noon and night. But no matter how much we needed to hear him, how perfect an ending to our week it may have been, even the hardest working DJ's are allowed one night off.

Signs we passed became increasingly familiar and distances to them smaller. We hadn't spoken about anything other than the occasional recollection as a poignant song from the past week played. It occurred to me that with luck we would all keep remembering those moments, every time that certain song played, and I hoped that we would get a chance to refresh the memories before they changed from joy to melancholy as the months rolled on.

Andover flashed up as being twenty-four miles away, the last leg of the journey somehow always the hardest and the longest. Cigarettes burned faster and eyes grew heavier, time slowed to a virtual halt. We stretched as best we could in the limited space, listening to every creak and groan of the car, listening to the wind howl through the bullet holes and missing windows and doors that no longer fully closed. We sighed more often and lost the thread of conversations too easily, already Neil and Adam had phoned their better halves. Life it seemed was quickly returning.

"I've been thinking," Neil said out of nowhere, pulling my attention away from the repetitive hypnotic quality of the cats eyes in the road. I leaned forward between the seats to listen, "If I had to chose, for whatever reason, like a game show or reality TV program or something, if I had to chose what I'd take with me on to a desert island, do you know what I'd take?" I looked at Adam and he shrugged with mild indifference. Evidently, whatever it was that Neil was planning to take with him was not worthy of his full attention.

"No mate, but can I ask, is this another fanny stack question?" I said, lighting two cigarettes and passing one over. One more day won't hurt.

"No, I'm serious, I've been thinking about this for most of the journey home and I've got an answer." I thought momentarily about Neil's extensive porn collection and my own not insignificant pile, but I sensed that something deeper was about to be revealed.

"Did somebody ask then?" Adam grumbled.

"No, but, it's important. You should ask yourself the question, 'if I was going to be stuck on a desert island what would I want to take with me?'"

"How long for?" Adam said, details, details, details.

"How long for what?"

"How long are we going to be stuck on the island for?"

"Does it matter? It's a desert island."

"Of course it matters, if it's only a week then I'd take a decent book and enjoy the peace and quiet." He said, without a hint of humour. This is what we had become. Three cynical wannabe recluses forced into a car together for an insufferably long journey.

"Well obviously longer than a fucking week, Adam. I dunno, four years."

"Why four?"

"Just answer the question!"

"I don't know the answer." Adam retorted. "Is this another fanny stack question again?"

"No, look, forget it alright. I'm on a desert island for four years, do you know what I'd want to take with me?"

"I think we've established the answer to that question is 'no we don't'," I said.

"I'd take you two." Neil said, looking out of the window, away from us.

"Fag," said Adam.

"Gaylord," I muttered.

"Thanks boys."

"You said it." Adam said, a wry smile creeping on to his lips.

"I *was* being serious."

"So were we."

"If I had to spend four years on a desert island, I think the only way I could cope was if you two were there." This was obviously something important to him, we owed it to our friend to take this seriously.

"You wouldn't rather have a fanny stack?" I said.

"Would you drop it with the fanny stack please?"

"I just wanted to be sure," I said, "because just so we're clear, I am never, *ever* putting out for you."

"Me either." Adam seconded.

412

"I'm not saying that a woman wouldn't be great for like a couple of months, hell Jane would be fine for the entire time but it's not about that. I could live without music, without my sofa, without cigarettes and coffee and all of the other shit that we fill up our days with, but I couldn't live without you guys."

"Hands down the gayest thing you've ever said." I said.

"I'm talking to Jane when we get home, you need a woman, and quickly."

"Would you be serious for one moment, I'm baring my soul here."

"You'll be baring your arse next the way you're going." I said.

"Fuck off."

"What about your kids then? Wouldn't you want to take them?"

"For four years? Could you imagine how bored they would be? They'd drive me crazy, it's bad enough in the summer holidays." I laughed.

"I'd take Jenga," Adam said.

"*Jenga*?" Neil spat, "over me?"

"I'd take Jenga over you *and* a fanny stack." Adam said.

"And you think *I'm* the one that needs a woman."

"Well he's just turned down five." I pointed out.

"It's a great game."

"For four years?"

"I need the practice. Besides, I don't mean to be rude or anything, but I'm not sure we can count on you for four years, if you don't mind me saying, your warranty is somewhat questionable. We'd have better luck with Duracell bunny."

"Thanks mate! Cheer me up why don't you?"

"Is there electricity on the island?" I asked suddenly.

"What?"

"Electricity, I was just thinking, maybe I could take a TV?"

"No, you can't take a TV."

413

"Then what would we talk about?" Adam said.

"Life and shit I guess. I dunno, stuff." Neil was losing his patience, I'd counted five exasperated expressions in as many minutes, I guess we really were nearly home.

"For four years?" I asked.

"How about an iPod, they have their own batteries?" Adam mused.

"Forget it."

"And the new ones supposedly play movies." Adam continued, oblivious.

"Seriously, I've changed my mind. I'd go on my own."

"You miserable git," I said.

"You'd dump us, just like that?" Adam added.

"You're so touchy. Are you due on?"

"Fuck off." He said, making it six.

"Doesn't matter," I said to Adam, "I mean we're all stuck on the desert-island for four years anyway, we could each take whatever we wanted to. You chose us, dumbass, *I'd* let you take an iPod Adam."

"Cheers mate, you can borrow it whenever you want."

"Cheers mate."

"Look it's my island and you two aren't invited."

"Bollocks." I said defiantly.

"Back at you knobhead."

"Doesn't matter anyway," Adam said, "Boys, we're home."

Friday
Two Weeks Later

TO THINE OWN SELF BE TRUE

I chucked my keys on the table by the door and walked through to the living room. The large television dominating the room was muted over credits rolling up the screen. Neil sat there waiting for me impatiently. Waiting for me to drop down on to the sofa, to get comfortable in my arse space I'd spent many years moulding to perfection. Ben and Tom were playing quietly on the carpet and Jane was in the kitchen.

I stood in the doorway, "Jane," I called, "come here darling. There's someone I'd like you all to meet." Jane came walking through the house to the living room smiling and looking as good as ever. "Guys," I said with a smile of my own, "This is Louise." I stood aside to show them Louise, presenting her like a magicians trick with an equal amount of amazement from my audience, "Louise, this is my brother and his family." Neil dropped the television remote.

In the hallway the door crashed open and Adam stepped through excitedly dragging Fiona after him, "Neil, you won't believe this but the Smurf-mobile is *outside*. Outside, right now." They walked into the living room, Fiona smiling and making apologetic eye contact with Louise, the only face that she didn't recognise.

I beamed at Adam, waited for him to realise, waited for the moment to catch up with his arrival. Suddenly he dropped his keys. "That's that Louise bird," he said, pointing, "Neil, that's Louise. Look." Neil just stared in wonderment, finally a detail too much overloading Adam's brain.

Fiona stepped passed Adam and extended her hand to Louise, they greeted each other warmly, "Hi," she said, "I'm guessing you must be Louise, I'm Fiona. This in case you haven't already had the misfortune to meet, is Adam."

"Well fu -" Fiona elbowed Adam in the ribs.

"Hi Adam, Fiona," Louise said happily. I felt proud to be standing next to her, she was more beautiful than I remembered and every time that I looked at her I found something else that I liked. "I've heard a lot about you both."

"Likewise," Fiona said, "although I imagine in a slightly different context." They laughed.

"The Zafira's outside?" Neil said, clinging to the least relevant fact of the last five minutes. "Are you sure?"

"I'm telling you, it's out there," he said, pointing back towards the door. "They aren't going to make you pay for the damages are they?" Adam asked sombrely.

"Boys?" Fiona said sternly.

"Well they never mentioned it before," Neil continued, obliviously, "But then I gave the car to Steve to take back," Neil stood and went to walk outside, past me and more strangely Louise. Louise did not take offence; she just stood back with restrained humour and bemusement.

Jane stared at him in utter disbelief. Ben and Tom watched the whole scene with fascination. "Um, *Neil*, have you forgotten something?" she said, stopping him in his tracks. He turned slowly to face her, and then it happened, a veritable sunrise of awakening blazed across his face.

"Bloody hell," he stammered, "Louise, hi! I am *so* sorry!" He pushed back across the room, literally shoving me aside and reaching out he hugged Louise fondly. "How are you sweetheart? I can't believe you're here! How? When?" he jabbered, "Take a seat, all of you, sit down, sit down." He waved his hands around at the sofas while Jane just stood there shaking her head.

"Thank you, I'm really good thanks, and I just arrived today. I came on the train." I sensed the details were for Adam's benefit, I'd pre-warned her accordingly. She squeezed my hand affectionately and we all sat down, Jane across from Neil, Fiona next to Adam, Louise close to me and the children still on the floor. They had as yet not said a word, evidently all of the commotion was more exciting than a paused DVD.

"Jane," Neil said, trying to make up lost ground, "this is Louise, the girl I was telling you about, the one that Steve's gone stupid over." I gave a sarcastic smile of appreciation to Neil for that. "She's here, look," he said, pointing as if Louise could be some *other* girl in the room.

"Well I'm very pleased to meet you Louise, and what my idiot husband means is we've all been very much hoping we'd get the chance to put a face to the name that we've heard so much about recently." I really didn't know what they could all be going on about. I'd hardly mentioned her.

"I'll say, every bloody day he goes on and on about you. I'm almost bored of you already and you've only just arrived." Even Adam shook his head at that one.

"Yeah thanks for that Neil," I jibed. "I think you'll find it wasn't *every day*, just, *most* days." I sensed I wasn't winning this argument.

"Well I'm sorry to have been the cause of such annoyance for you, Neil." Louise said smoothly, "I'll be sure to try and give him something more interesting to say over the next few days."

"Well if you could, that would be great," he said. Everyone laughed. It was odd, like we'd been doing this for years, all of us.

"If it helps any," Adam added, "he's been both complimentary and gentlemanly throughout." I was sure I'd never met this man before.

"Well I appreciate you saying it," Louise said while biting her lip and stifling a grin.

"Even Neil has been on best behaviour," he finished.

"Now that I *can't* believe!" she laughed.

"Why not?" Neil yelped, "Steve, what have you been saying about me?"

I stared at Louise, panicked, "Nothing mate, I swear." Louise burst out laughing.

"Steve?"

"Honestly, she's making it up," I tickled her in the ribs and was quite aware of exactly how much we were acting like *that* annoying couple. It made a change for me and I liked it, Jane and Fiona seemed to notice it too, once or twice I caught their eyes looking at me fondly, a sort of relief on their faces. I don't know, but I think, I *think* Louise might just have got the seal of approval.

Adam sat back in the sofa and got comfortable, "How did the op go mate?" he said, bold as ever.

"As well as can be expected," Neil answered, with audible relief. He dropped his hand over his lap, but it was probably just a coincidence.

"Well I hope they were careful, I mean you didn't have much to start with."

"Whatever," Neil said. I couldn't stop them now - they were in it. "I'll still be twice the man you are."

"Only in weight bud."

I laughed – and was unbelievably grateful for the opportunity to, for so many, many reasons. Not least of all because the dynamic hadn't changed one bit. All of the women looked at us in bafflement.

"Look, forget that, we'll talk about it later, perhaps in more appropriate company?"

"Oh don't mind us, you boys crack on." Fiona said. Adam hugged her and Neil tried to press on.

"Adam, what were you saying about the Zafira?"

"He was saying," I interrupted, "That it's outside." Neil's brow furrowed.

"Howzat?"

"I bought it off the hire car company."

"You're shitting me?"

"Straight up," I nodded, "It was cheaper than the alternative."

"What was the alternative?"

"Fixing it."

"Yeah you're probably right," he agreed, laughing, "But why are you driving it? Why not just scrap it?"

"Scrap it?" Adam said, "Don't you dare."

"Yeah Neil, you can't scrap it, it's *custom*," I said, echoing words I'd heard somewhere before.

"It's a heap," he retorted.

"But it's our heap," Adam said with affection, "Don't listen to him, Steve."

"Don't listen to me? Listen to you, Mr It's Blue. You didn't even *like* that car."

"Hey, that's not true, I was just slow in appreciating its inner qualities."

"It hasn't got any 'inner qualities', it's got maggots and a hole in the backseat." The girls 'urrrrghd' collectively and each, even Louise, moved ever so slightly away from us.

"On that note, does anyone fancy a drink?" Jane asked. Fiona and Louise nodded.

"Yeah cheers darling," Neil said without breaking stride, "Two black one white with sugar," then he stopped, catching himself. "Oh, and whatever Louise wants." He added, with a grin.

"I couldn't scrap it Neil," I resumed, "and I can't believe you would even suggest such a thing."

"It's not safe." Neil stated. He was probably right.

"You know what, it might *not* be safe Neil," I said, "but it's symbolic, and that's good enough for me."

THE END

The authors and publisher would like to express their thanks to the following people, for pre-ordering this book and supporting its publication.

Charlotte Bironneau
John Bossino
Sue Bossino
Brian Chalkley
Steve Channon
Mike Cook
Ben Dymond
Nick Geaney
Annette Gregory
Chris Griffith
Jade Hyde
Anne-Marie Lant
Sean Lovegrove
Lesley Nash
Jon Newlyn
Paul Pearson
Philip Smith
Mark Smyth
Leslie Taylor
Brian Terry
James Travers
Manuela Wahnon
Steven White
Kara Wilson

Also from www.hirstpublishing.com

A Dinner of Bird Bones
By Robert Hammond

"A Dinner of Bird Bones" is the story of Lloyd Inchley; of heartbreak, new best friends, a girl called Atom, and how the terrible power of sudden new geometry links a mystery now and in the past - and how it is all witnessed by a presence that has silently observed the unspooling events for decades... "A Dinner of Bird Bones" is a story about love.

Also from www.hirstpublishing.com

Vanitas
By Matthew Waterhouse

When you wish upon a star...?

Your dreams come true...? They did, at any rate, for Florinda
Quenby, though not in the way she had planned. When she flew
out to Hollywood to become a movie star, she could not imagine
the terrible struggles ahead of her, from riches back to rags, or
that fame and wealth would finally come from an entirely different
quarter, her fantastical soup factory in Harlem modelled on the
Taj Mahal... Once she was famous, she became one of New
York's grandest hostesses and one of America's most beloved
celebrities. Her parties for the Christmas season in her huge, gold-
lined apartment overlooking Central park were an unmissable part
of Manhattan's social calendar. Those parties grew wilder and
wilder every year, until finally she decided to throw one last party,
designed to top all the others... This is a tale of ambition and
wealth and fame and vanity. This is Florinda's incredible story.

Also from www.hirstpublishing.com

Look Who's Talking
By Colin Baker

To many, Colin Baker is the sixth Doctor Who; to some, he is the villainous Paul Merroney in the classic BBC drama The Brothers. But to the residents of South Buckinghamshire he is a weekly voice of sanity in a world that seems intent on confounding him. Marking the 15th anniversary of his regular feature in the Bucks Free Press, this compilation includes over 100 of his most entertaining columns, from 1995 to 2009, complete with new linking material. With fierce intelligence and a wicked sense of humour, Colin tackles everything from the absurdities of political correctness to the joys of being an actor, slipping in vivid childhood memories, international adventures and current affairs in a relentless rollercoaster of reflections, gripes and anecdotes. Pulling no punches, taking no prisoners and sparing no detail, the ups and downs of Colin life are shared with panache, honesty and clarity, and they are every bit as entertaining and surreal as his trips in that famous police box... for a world that is bewildering, surprising and wondrous, one need look no further than modern Britain, and Colin Baker is here to help you make sense of it all, and to give you a good laugh along the way.

Also from www.hirstpublishing.com

Amusements, Carousels and Candy Floss on Sticks
By Brad Jones

Meet Bernard Stint. A marriage guidance counseller from Hendon, North London. A rather meek and mild man whose idea of a fun day is sitting at the local transport depot collecting bus numbers. Wife, Angela. Son, Sam. Bernard's life is turned upside down one day, when arriving home from work, Angela announces she is leaving him in favour of a muscle-bound fitness instructor. Realising he can't counsel himself when his own marriage breaks up and losing his job shortly afterwards for drunkenly assaulting Angela's new man, Bernard decides a new life beckons. Somewhere new. Somewhere miles away. Closing his eyes and putting a pin in a map of the UK, he moves to the sleepy north-east town of Lympstone-on-Sea. There he meets Melody, newly arrived from Southern Ireland, a music hall style singer who plays to an nearly empty pier theatre most nights. Can Bernard build his new life and revitalise Melody's flagging stage act? Will success and fortune prevail? Will Bernard and Melody fall for each other in this land of amusements, carousels and candy floss on sticks

Also from www.hirstpublishing.com

Tales in Dark Languages
By Cynthia Garland

Geoffrey Midori is a magician and raconteur - a purveyor of ancient tales, lost arts, and dark secrets - and he is having trouble sleeping. His nights are plagued by vivid dreams, bouts of sleepwalking, and a strange sensation that he is not alone in the dark. He takes a break from his travels with a caravan of performers to visit friends, only to find that their daughter is having troubles of her own. She has come of age, and is exhibiting certain specific traits from a vilified race that was exterminated centuries ago - traits that elicit fear and suspicion from those around her. When the authorities come to investigate, Geoffrey takes her on the run. Aided by his companions in the caravan - a soothsayer, dream interpreter, medicine showman, astrologer, and strong man - he must use his fragmented knowledge of ancient mythologies to unlock the secrets of the dead races - all the while battling his own demons and keeping one step ahead of the agents who are pursuing them.

Also from www.hirstpublishing.com

Lemon
By Barnaby Eaton-Jones

Spencer was an insignificant Data Input Operator and this suited him fine. However, when he is mistaken for someone actually significant, due to a mix-up by the Post Office, then his life becomes complicated. By complicated we're talking murder, sex, violence, car chases, beautiful women, and an annoyed fat cat (both of the feline* and big business variety). Spence didn't like complicated things and he was as far removed from being James Bond as Shakespeare was from being a hack plagiarist.

A week in Spence's life usually consisted of nothing more than dull, repetitive, time-wasting tedium. But, not this week. This week was going to be different and Spence wasn't going to like it one little bit.

* Just to add some extra zest to this 'Lemon', you can read all about Spence's love-hate relationship with his feline nemesis in 'Eric's Tale' at the end of the book.

Also from www.hirstpublishing.com

Flight Risks
By Douglas Schofield

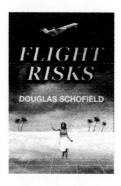

Basel, Switzerland, February 2001 : Fifty-six years after the end of World War Two, Switzerland's bankers finally agree to release 21,000 dormant accounts left behind by Jews who died in the Holocaust. Claims from the victims' heirs pour in from across the world...

New York and Washington, September 2001 : The Twin Towers fall. The Pentagon burns. Western democracies scramble to meet a deadly new threat...

Victoria, Canada, October 2001: For legal secretary Grace Palliser, the post-911 media circus is just background noise. Grace is too busy with the unholy mess she calls her life. But when she stumbles on evidence of a vast international fraud, her life gets a whole lot messier. Framed for murder and desperately searching for the evidence that will clear her, Grace flees across the continent to New Orleans, then to the Florida Panhandle, and finally to a small island in the northwest Caribbean. Hot on her trail is a corrupt former cop with a simple assignment - to Kill Grace Palliser.

From another Andover-based author:

Georgie Jones...
and you thought your family was weird!
By Nicky Gregory

An exciting adventure for 10-13 year-olds

The last thing that Georgie Jones wanted was to have to spend her Christmas Day with Dan Parsons - unknown entity from school. However, when Dan gets sucked into a 'loophole' transporting him to the land of Molitovia, Georgie is quick to follow! How could she possibly have known that her arrival in this strange land was far from coincidence? In fact, if what they said was true, it was not only her birthright to be here - it was her destiny! But should she really believe that she was one of them? They all seemed to have their own reasons for wanting her there and the only person Georgie had to help her try and make sense of it all was Dan, who was not exactly taking the situation very seriously! Georgie had a lot to learn - and most of it about her own family!

www.hirstpublishing.com